FAR FROM NOWHERE

Far From Nowhere

Published by The Conrad Press Ltd. in the United Kingdom 2024

Tel: +44(0)1227 472 874
www.theconradpress.com
info@theconradpress.com

ISBN 978-1-914913-72-3

Printed and bound in Great Britain by Clays Ltd, Elcograf S.p.A

Typesetting and Cover Design by The Book Typesetters
www.thebooktypesetters.com

The Conrad Press logo was designed by Maria Priestley.

FAR FROM NOWHERE

Mark McKay

Chapter One

Detective Inspector Davies was standing inside the entrance to Charing Cross railway station, indulging in his favourite pastime, people-watching. The tidal surge to work had thinned, so he turned his attention to the rain. *Living the dream, another wet Monday...* he mused, while nursing a coffee bought from a vendor on the concourse.

Spotting a familiar face, he called out, 'Frank!'

'Morning, Simon. How are you?'

'I'm good,' they shook hands, 'I see your promotion has been confirmed, it was in Orders on Friday. Detective Sergeant Francis Overton, sounds good, doesn't it?'

'It does, but it's not effective until September, I have to wait a little longer,' Frank grinned, 'I made it! Thank you again for your support, I know it helped to convince the selection board.'

Simon said, 'Don't mention it, I protested in the strongest possible terms when you were passed over last year, but only because I think you would make an excellent D.S.'

Frank said, 'Well your comments clearly swung it this time. Are you off to Crown Court?'

'No.'

'So, what brings you north of the river?'

Simon said, 'I've concluded the enquiry I've been running for the last six months; I was meant to brief my Commander this morning… but I got a message on Friday; I'm summoned to the headmaster's office.'

Frank said, 'That's not necessarily a bad thing.'

'You think?'

Frank shook his head, 'You always did worry too much, don't sweat it. There are many reasons for an invite to the Head-Shed… I'll have to love you and leave you, a day out at the Royal Courts of Justice beckons. I owe you, call me and we'll get together for a pint.'

They shook hands and parted company. Simon watched him walk along the Strand in the direction of the Aldwych. Frank had gone about thirty yards when he turned, and shouted, 'If he offers you anything interesting, rope me in!'

The rain had stopped, so Simon set off, rounding Trafalgar Square he walked into Whitehall, and headed towards his fate.

He entered the building via a large revolving door, only to find his way blocked by an efficient young man in a crisp uniform.

'Good morning, sir. My name is Niall, may I know the nature of your business today?'

The tone of his voice was calm and friendly, but with a slight edge of menace, conveying the importance of the duty he was engaged in, the seriousness of which was emphasised by the holstered semi-automatic pistol attached to his right hip.

'I have a nine thirty appointment…'

'Your name, sir?'

'Simon Davies.'

Niall looked down the list on the clipboard he was holding in his left hand and finding Simon's name ticked a box in the left-hand column.

'You were requested to bring with you the letter, or a copy of the email, sent confirming your appointment, hand it to me.'

Simon took the printed copy of the email he had received from the inside left pocket of his suit jacket, and handed it to Niall, who having examined it, handed it back to Simon.

'Thank you, sir. Please read out the number printed on the top right of your email.'

'3684390.'

Satisfied, Niall said, 'Now all I need is your ID.'

Simon fumbled around, searching pockets for his warrant card, a female officer moved toward him, she had a Heckler and Koch G36 assault rifle slung around her neck, resting across her chest. To his relief the look on her face conveyed curiosity and not concern, but as she moved, she gripped the weapon with both hands, ready to bring it to bear. Simon found his ID and handed it over for inspection.

He was asked to walk slowly toward four large scanners, one of the officers operating the equipment told him to remove all metallic objects from his pockets and place them in a blue tray, he was then told to remove his watch and belt, and place these in the same receptacle, finally he was told to remove his jacket and hand it to another officer, who searched it, then placed it in the same tray, which he put on a conveyer belt. Simon watched as it passed it through an x-ray machine, he worried, *'Does that made things radioactive?'*

On being instructed, he walked through the scanner. Having done so, his jacket was handed back to him, he retrieved the items from the tray, once restored to his former condition, he was told to walk slowly over to the reception desk, which was situated close to the lifts, all the while he was under the constant scrutiny of another two heavily armed officers.

Simon presented his copy of the email to the receptionist and told her his name. The receptionist checked his name and details against her list, and said, 'Thank you, sir. Do you know where to go?'

Simon said, 'No… sorry, this is my first visit since your move here from the old building.'

'I understand. Take the lift to the fifth floor,' she looked down at a building schematic on her desk, 'that office should be the door directly in front of you as you come out of the lift,' she smiled, 'we are all having to get used to our new surroundings.'

Having successfully navigated the security checks on the ground floor of New Scotland Yard, Simon took the lift to the fifth floor. Exiting the lift, he crossed the hall to the door opposite, checked he had the right location, the sign on the wall to the right of the door read, Deputy Assistant Commissioner Brian Cartwright, and printed on the door, D.A.C. Crime, he was in the right place.

Opening the door, he entered a windowless office. Four armchairs were arranged around a small table that was covered in magazines, above this, on the wall, was a large, framed photograph, to the left of the picture, another door, opposite that door a large desk, behind which sat a middle-aged, primly dressed woman, her auburn hair in a bun. Mary Keech was the name on a little sign at the front of the desk. Mary, who was conversing with someone on the phone, raised her right hand to acknowledge Simon's presence, and indicated he should sit in one of the armchairs.

She began writing on a pad, it was obvious to Simon that she would be engaged in dealing with the call for some time. Ignoring her invitation to occupy one of the chairs, he concentrated on the large photograph hanging on the wall. It was a sepia image of six men in Victorian attire, each sporting an alarming display of facial hair, they were standing in a group on the steps at the front of Bow Street police station. A small plaque attached

8

to the base of the frame proclaimed that these worthies were newly promoted detectives, it was dated eighteen-eighty-nine.

Simon registered that Mary had stopped talking, surmising that she had completed her business on the telephone, he turned to face her, 'Davies, I have an appointment.'

'Take a seat. He's just taken a call and will be engaged for a little longer. Would you like tea, or coffee?' Mary smiled, she tried to put him at ease, 'Please take a seat.'

Simon declined the offer of refreshment, and crumpled into one of the chairs, resigned to his fate.

Ten minutes later a buzzer sounded. Mary stood up, straightened her tweed skirt, and walked over to the door opposite her desk, opened it, and said, 'You can go in now.'

With an effort, he rose and slowly walked into the office. It was large, sparsely furnished, devoid of ornamentation, and surprisingly bright.

'Don't dawdle, man. Come in. Sit down,' barked, D.A.C. Cartwright.

'Simon Davies?'

'Yes sir.'

'Sounds Welsh, but you're not, are you?'

'Yes sir, I mean, no sir.'

'Don't babble, can't abide babbling. Now, I suppose you are wondering why you're here?' Simon smiled weakly but made no attempt to reply.

'Do you remember, Detective Sergeant Mackenzie?'

'Mac... Jack?'

'Yes, Jack Mackenzie?'

'Yes sir. Mac's posting to Peckham was around the end of my first year as a probationer, it was Mac who later persuaded me that I had a career in...'

'Well, I'm sure it's a nice trip down memory lane for you, but

I want to know what you thought of him?'

'I held him in high regard; he was honest, hard-working, committed, a natural leader. I was shocked when he resigned.'

'Could not have put it better myself,' Cartwright left his seat and walked round to the front of his desk.

Simon rose to meet him, he was waved dismissively towards a small table and two chairs in a corner of the room, as he moved towards them, Cartwright opened the door and said, 'Pot of tea, Mary.' He looked at Simon, 'You do drink tea don't you? Of course you do, whole bloody Force does. I've a job for you, a difficult one, and it seems you're the only detective inspector awaiting assignment. Don't say anything yet. Not until you have all the facts. I am going to play you a tape. By the way, did I say I was recording this? This tape is of the last conversation I had with Mac. We go back a long way, we were… we are friends. Anyway, at the time I was the detective chief for Southwark, and Mac was a detective sergeant at Peckham… but you know all that… just listen to the tape. I'm starting it at a point six minutes after he entered my office.'

He put a tape player on the table between them, and pressed play. Simon recognised Mac's lilting Highland accent.

'A lie. They say it lets us see the truth. Well today I had my moment on the road to Damascus. Courts? Just self-serving theatre, interested only in the letter of the law, expediently sacrificing both truth and natural justice; ascribing guilt or innocence by discerning which side has lied the least, or worse, has lied the most convincingly, most of the time if truth is present, it's a coincidence, no more than an adjunct, a bloody accident. Justice is an afterthought; legality will always prevail over justice.'

The tape hissed, thinking it was over, Simon began to speak, Cartwright put his right forefinger to his lips, indicating Simon should remain silent.

'All smug and sententious, he says, "Officer, please tell the court why you stopped my client on the night in question?" Right then it hit me, why lie? Why not tell the truth? So, I did; noble cause corruption… that's what they call it, when we lie to make the system work. Why does it require some to sacrifice their conscience so that others may live by theirs? Having to compromise my integrity to prevent society being corrupted is too high a price to pay. If the Government won't pass workable laws to protect the public, then that's their problem. Better to show the law for what it is, and have it held in contempt, rather than trying to make a bad…'

'Mac…'

'I know, we mustn't expose the system's failings. But, waiting for those idiots in Parliament to do something, you may as well watch continental drift… it's just as slow, and as bloody pointless. What… don't give that look, Brian. Confront those idiots with a problem and their default response is to criminalise it, making it a policing matter, and when their pathetic legislation proves to be wholly inadequate, simply because, in truth, it was a social not a criminal issue, hubristic and shameless, they pass the blame onto us, covering their arses and preserving their pensions. When their inadequate legislation fails to protect society, rather than writing workable, and sensible laws, what do they do? They blame us. How often do you hear a politicians say that it's the fault of the police, we have given them the tools, but they are not willing, or are unable to use them? The current crop of non-entities occupying the Dream Factory have produced a staggering fifteen-hundred pieces of newly criminalised behaviour; stuff we did as kids is now a criminal matter? If memory serves it was Tacitus who said that the more corrupt the State, the more numerous the laws. By that measure we're a bloody banana republic!'

Cartwright stopped the tape, 'I was at a loss to understand. Mac was not someone prone to histrionics... anyway,' he pressed play.

'They asked for the truth, they may not have wanted to hear it, but I gave them the truth, the whole truth, and nothing but the unvarnished truth. So, I said, "It was three in the morning when I saw him, slinking down the road, I knew he was up to no good, it was a gut-feeling, nothing more, but I was right. He was a wrong'un, and when I searched him, I found eight stolen credit cards in his pocket." Before his Brief can say anything, the Judge looks at me and says, "Did I hear you correctly, it was a gut-reaction, presumably based upon your extensive experience on the streets?" I just nodded, and he continued, "A detective sergeant with your service and knowledge of the law, knows exactly what he is doing, but I'm not going to allow you to use this court, and this case, to make your point." He then sends the jury out, takes a few submissions from defence council and dismisses the case, explaining that because I failed to apply my powers of stop and search correctly, it followed that my search of the defendant was unlawful, so he gets to walk. I turned to the Judge, and asked him what I was supposed to do with the stolen credit cards I'd found on the defendant, give them back to him? The Judge goes ballistic, and I get both barrels, but no one questioned the idiocy of a system that lets the guilty walk free.'

'Mac, you sound like a precocious probationer, you know we have to have safeguards.'

'Safeguards, Brian? Don't give me that crap about protecting the innocent, it only serves the guilty, and all that highbrow nonsense about it being better that a hundred guilty men go free, than have one innocent man found guilty, it may work in your version of Utopia, but out there on the estates… hell, we're drowning in crime. I don't want to see innocent people sent to prison, no one does, but it would be rather satisfying if a few of the guilty were incarcerated, there must be a better way of administrating justice than this dog's dinner. You know the stats, over a fifth of people murdered in each year die at the hands of nutters, or those already serving time for murder; lunatics freed from happy-farms, apparently cured, and lifers released early, to ensure their rights. What about the rights of their poor bloody victims, whose deaths are wholly avoidable? We have over twelve-hundred murders a year, but the public are only fed the bullshit figures that the Home Office massages. It's only recorded as murder, if there is a conviction for murder, otherwise it's what… administratively undetermined? What the hell do the relatives feel? Their son or daughter is still dead, unlawfully killed by some arsehole, which makes it murder, but not according to government statistics. As far as the Home Office are concerned, they are a non-event, it's as if nothing happened, our version of the disappeared in some fascist state. What can you expect from a criminal justice system, where the whole focus is on the system, and not on justice?'

Cartwright interjected, 'The recording goes quiet for a while; he stood in front of my office window, looking down at the street. I didn't interrupt him, I considered saying something to rebut his erroneous assertions, but I thought he would get whatever it was off his chest, and we could go to the pub and forget it… that bang, that was the sound he made when he smacked his hand on the window, then he turned round to face me; I cannot forget the look of utter contempt in his eyes.'

The tape continued to hiss for further ten seconds, then Mac spoke again, 'Aye, it's a nice view Brian, four floors up, that's a grand distance from the streets, far enough away for political correctness and weasel-words to replace good old-fashioned morality and natural justice. Up here, image may pass for ability, but down there it's getting people killed. Why are we doing this? For the public? They don't give a damn. We put it on the line, and by way of thanks we get accused of perjury or worse, by overfed, overpaid pricks in wigs. We stand our watch, take our turn on the wall, but they fear us, so they pass laws to protect the guilty, then holding us in contempt, mock us for actually having the temerity to do our duty. I never expected gratitude, but bloody ingratitude. I've spent fifteen years shovelling shit against the tide, and for what? We're the three-hundred Spartans holding the pass, but this time no one gives a toss if we win or lose, they just don't see it. They don't get it. If we fail to maintain the peace, everything comes to an end. If there's no law, then there's no order… stuff 'em. You'd better take this; I've got no more use for it.'

Cartwright switched the cassette player off, and said, 'He flipped his warrant card onto my desk, took his resignation letter out of his pocket and handed it to me; he informed me that since he had two months in time-off owed to him, he would leave the next day. I haven't seen or heard from him since.'

There was a knock at the door, Cartwright said, 'That'll be the tea.' He shouted, 'Enter!' A young man wearing a short white jacket came in bearing a tray of tea and biscuits, which he nervously placed on the table in front of them, then left, Mary closed the door behind him.

Cartwright poured the tea, then said, 'Examine this,' he handed Simon a box file, 'I couldn't understand why Mac reacted the way he did, I reviewed that case, even interviewed the defendant, a petty thief from Camberwell, but there was nothing. Two months ago, these case papers surfaced. They were found in a strongbox, hidden in the archives at the old Dulwich police station, a label was tied to a handle,' Cartwright picked up the label, and read it out loud, "This box is to remain locked, do not break the seal, take it straight to the Head of the Criminal Investigation Department, at New Scotland Yard."

Pausing to put the label back into an exhibit-bag, he continued, 'Among the items left to me by my predecessor was a key in an envelope, but no explanation. The key fitted, and the box contained this file, it explains why Mac left, and more. It doesn't leave this office, and nor do you. We will discuss the contents when I return. That cupboard contains pens, pencils, and notebooks, help yourself. The phone in this office will be turned off, there is a bathroom behind that panel, if you require anything just tell Mary. She will order your lunch and organise tea or coffee. I have a meeting with the Commissioner in ten minutes, then I have a lunch appointment at the House of Lords. I should be back about four o'clock, you can ask me any questions then, but I will need your answer before you leave here today. If you don't want to take the case I will understand, it will not reflect on your future career. However, you should know that if you decide to take this investigation it will be... challenging. Read the file, see what you think.'

Simon said, 'If I agree to take undertake this investigation, can I pick my own team? I was thinking of...'

'No! This case, for reasons that will become apparent, requires you to undertake the investigation alone, and in complete secrecy.'

D.A.C Cartwright walked over to his desk, picked up a manila folder, and left.

Chapter Two

'**F**ather John!'
　　'April.'

She jumped up, threw her arms around his neck and embraced him, he held her out at arm's length to look at her, 'How tall you've grown.'

'I'm ten next week,' she said proudly, smiled and continued, 'did you bring me a present?'

'I did, but you will have to wait until your birthday.'

'Oh!'

'Patience child, only another five days to go.'

'John, welcome home. Good trip?' They shook hands.

'Good flight, the train journey took forever. Mac, it's good to be back.'

Jack Mackenzie picked up both suitcases, Father John took April's hand, collected his briefcase, and all three made their way out of the station and into the car park.

Mac turned off the lane onto the track that led to the farm, as they crested the hill above the farmstead, he stopped the Land Rover, Father John alighted, and Mac drove on down to the house.

'Dad, every time Father John visits… how come when we get to the top of the hill you stop, and he gets out and walks slowly down to the house?'

'I'm not sure how explain it. Father John has no family, he was an orphan, and has never had anywhere he can call home. Your mother used to say, that someone without a home or family, is in want of fellowship, and it is the duty of those who have both to welcome them in. Father John is home at last and walking quietly back to the house is his way of reconnecting.'

April gave her father a quizzical look, and said, 'I think I understand.'

Mac laughed, and said, 'Father John has retired. I told him some time ago that when that day arrived, he could come and live with us. We are his family now, and our farm is his home. Walking slowly back to the house is his way of... feeling connected, that he belongs here.'

April looked at her father and smiled.

Later that evening, after April had gone to bed, Mac and Father John sat in the kitchen reminiscing. Father John said, 'Peter has changed. Those last ten years working abroad on the Extradition Squad helped, he led... you could call it a monastic life. His cloister the hotel, silence and solitude enforced on him by language and cultural barriers, and the need to remain detached while he investigated crimes involving our diplomatic staff and property. He survived by retreating into self-education, he has become quite... intellectual.'

Smiling, Mac said, 'Nudged in the right direction by your good self, no doubt?'

'Who else? He's changed,' noticing the disbelieving expression on Mac's face, he said, 'well, not entirely, but he's not the man you knew before, he's quiet, thoughtful... deeper.'

Father John made this last remark with such gravity that Mac felt awkward in seeking any further explanation, to do so seemed discourteous, akin to crossing a boundary uninvited.

Still, the emphasis on deeper intrigued him. He left the table and went to the pantry, but he could not suppress a smirk at the thought of Peter as a monk, he returned, still smiling, with another bottle of 1983 Chianti Classico and a jar of olives.

'Italian wine, Spanish olives, you've come a long way from sausage and chips, Mac.'

'Looks like we both have… the label on your suitcase, Monsignor Roberts, congratulations, John. It's about time.'

'It's nothing, a meaningless gesture, and a redundant title.'

'Isn't it a step towards becoming a bishop.'

'No, it's a title they give you when they are not going to make you a bishop. I could never be one, I firmly believe that the duty of a bishop is not to placate lukewarm Catholics, nor pander to the whims of an atheistic world, it is to save souls, and I am afraid in today's church that places me beyond the pale. I'm not ambitious, I never wanted to be anything other than a parish priest, but I was never granted that privilege, until now.'

Father John paused, drank some wine, and ate a couple of olives, 'I'm sixty-eight this year, I entered the seminary at eighteen. When I turned twenty-three, my bishop summoned me, and told me that I had everything needed to make a good priest, but he felt that I was not worldly enough, and he was right. I was naive in the ways of the world, so I joined the Met, spent four years on the beat at Bethnal Green, three years on the Crime Squad at Limehouse, and three years as a detective constable at Lemon Street. Then I got a letter from my bishop, wanting to know if I still felt called to be a priest. I felt my calling as strong as ever, and three months later I returned to the seminary and completed my studies. Following my ordination, I was sent to Rome, there I became an expert in Canon Law, and an advisor to the Curia on policing, which is how we came to work together.'

Mac smiled, and bowed his head in acknowledgement, and said, 'So you never served a parish, and now you have one?'

'Yes... well sort of...'

'So where is this parish, and how did you get it?'

'As you know I have only ever celebrated Usus Antiquior, the Tridentine or Traditional Latin Mass, happily being in Rome meant I never had to attend the heretical drivel inflicted on the rest of Catholicism. A friend, a fellow priest who organises Traditional Masses, knowing I was due to retire from the Curia, wrote in response to Lord and Lady Whitney, they had contacted him in the hope he could recommend someone.'

'Don't tell me you are going to be the priest at St Oswald's, you're going to be in the next valley?'

'I am. His Lordship wants me to conduct Mass every Sunday, and on Holydays of Obligation. On the last Sunday of each month the church will be open for all to attend, but I have secured permission for you and April to attend every Sunday, which means you can drive over with me.'

'That's great news, when do you start?'

'The end of September, when they return from France. I'm not entirely off the hook, my cardinal made me agree to spend the next year conducting reviews of canon law cases going for appeal before the court. It's not that onerous, I just have to assess the papers, look for any errors, and ensure that the legal advice is correct and appropriate, then attach a short summary of what I see as the salient facts in the case.'

Father John paused, thought for a while, then said, 'Mac, I know you don't want to hear this, but I'm thinking about writing an account of our investigation...'

'John, you can't! We all agreed we would never speak of it again, it's too soon, and too dangerous.'

'I'm not going to publish it. But we need a record of what

happened, and the case papers alone are not enough, without a narrative those papers are largely meaningless, we need a written commentary. I can give it to April, and when she's an old lady, when everyone involved is dead, she can have it published.'

'I admit, I've been thinking about it a lot lately, perhaps it's got something to do with Pete's return… you're right, we need it recorded. Provided it remains unpublished until everyone involved is dead, I'll agree to it, but you're going to have to convince Pete.'

Father John said, 'When does he get here?'

'Next week. Thursday, I think? It's written on the calendar.' Mac pointed to the door that led from the kitchen into the hallway, as Father John went to look at it, Mac stood up, 'Another bottle?'

'Why not… you're right, Thursday; has he said what he's going to do?'

Mac emerged from the pantry clutching two bottles, he back-heeled the door, winced as it closed with a bang, holding the bottles up he said, 'Pinot Noir, one from New Zealand, the other from California, if there is one thing I know about priests, it's that they can out-drink coppers.'

'Pinot Noir, that's truly impressive, I didn't realise you knew how to pronounce it, let alone know what it is.'

'Bloody cheek,' both men laughed. Mac looked at his old friend, and was overwhelmed by affection for him, 'It's good to have you here, John.'

'I'm glad to be here.'

'To answer your question, Pete is setting up shop here. As you know, after Liz died, things got messy. For a while I lost the plot, and came close to losing the place, but Pete stepped in and gave me the money he got from the sale of his flat in London. I couldn't accept his offer, unless he bought a share in the farm, so one third of this place is his.'

Mac paused to drink and pour some more wine. 'I'm sure you already know, Pete trained as a blacksmith before joining the Royal Marines. His father was a smith of some renown, and Pete served his apprenticeship under him. When he turned twenty, he had had enough of the forge and left to join the Marines. That's where we met, we joined together, served seven years, and then left for the bright lights of London and a career in the Met; because of his service in the Marines, he only had to serve twenty-five years for a full police pension, but given his case load they asked him to do an extra year. Rather appropriately, he's occupied what was the farm's old forge, opposite my workshop, we'll each take responsibility for the running of our own business but operate the farm jointly.'

'I had an inkling, a blacksmith. I would never have guessed that after all this time he would go back to it. He wrote and told me he was considering it as an option, but it has been over a year since we last communicated. With my time at the Curia ending, I've been a little distracted, and Peter's been busy, so I wasn't aware he had finalised his plans in that direction. He retired a year ago, where is he?'

'He appeared February last year, and told me of his plans, in anticipation of his arrival I had already decorated and furnished the old cottage, he dumped his few belongings, joined me for lunch, and took off again, returning the following morning with a lorry loaded with all the tools and bits he needed for his forge. It took us the rest of the day to get it all in and sorted, we spent a backbreaking two hours shuffling a giant air-hammer into place. He joined us for the evening meal, during which he informed me he was going to Hereford, then left. It seems that his father's last apprentice, Paul, not only married Pete's sister, but he also inherited the business, nine years ago they relocated from East London to Herefordshire. Pete joined them to reacquaint himself with the mysteries of blacksmithing.'

'A good idea, given his absence from the craft. After all this time, how will you take to having him about the place?'

'I'm fifty-four next birthday and I'm beginning to feel it, so the extra help will be most welcome, and some of his customers may want to buy my furniture, and vice versa, so it should be good for both of us.'

Father John said, 'I knew you apprenticed under your uncle as a cabinetmaker, but was not aware you had returned to it?'

'It's a recent development, I had been dabbling in it, initially making furniture for us here on the farm, but over the years visitors have commented favourably, some even commissioning me to make pieces for them. After Pete arrived, and hearing of his plans, I decided to go into bespoke furniture production, it's not full-time, I work around the demands of farming, but there is time enough to produce at least one item a month, which augments my income, and gives me a break from working outdoors.'

'I will try to help out where I can,' Father John looked down at his soft hands, 'guess I'll have to toughen-up.'

'Your assistance will be most welcome, and appreciated, but we will have to ease you into physical labour.' Mac smiled, drank some wine, and said, 'There are plenty of tasks you could be doing, that don't involve manual labour. How do you feel about bookkeeping, for example?'

Father John said, 'Yes, of course, more than happy to look at your ledgers.'

'Ah… not so much ledgers, more boxes full of paperwork.'

'Sounds like I have a job of work ahead of me,' Father John frowned, then smiled.

Mac said, 'When we first came here, Liz and I had such plans, but at the time what we failed to realise, was that living the good life is hard work, often backbreaking. I'm sure, as April gets older, she will be able to pitch in. But, for now it falls to me, so having the two of you helping about the place will be most welcome. It means I can not only increase the stock, but I can look at growing a variety of crops, and extend the orchard, and maybe get around to planting the fruit bushes, Liz wanted. Drink up, we've still got a bottle to finish.'

Chapter Three

Peter was sitting outside on a bench, to the left of the kitchen door. Mac found him, and holding out another bottle of beer, said, 'You've hardly touched that one, you're not coming down with something are you?'

'No... just thinking... thanks.' He took the second bottle, drank the first in one go and handed it to Mac.

'I'll leave you to your thoughts,' Mac returned to the kitchen.

Peter gulped, then choked loudly on the beer, which brought both his friends out of the kitchen. He looked up at them, 'It's nothing... just wondering.'

Mac said, 'Come back inside, you'll wake April.' He indicated the window above, and to the left of where Peter was sitting, 'You can't even think quietly.'

They sat in silence around the kitchen table. Father John was the first to speak, 'Anna, I suppose?'

Peter glared at him but said nothing.

'Love is, as love does,' said Mac, smiling at Father John. 'What the hell is that supposed to mean?' Peter scraped his chair back across the floor as he stood up.

Father John said, 'It is not what you say that counts. When it comes to love, words have no meaning. What you do matters more than what you say. You kept telling her how you felt, but

24

then acted in ways that suggested otherwise.'

'But...'

Father John raised his hand to silence him, 'Love, real love, is more than mere emotion, or lust. It's a choice, and the choice we make will be evident, not in our words, but in our deeds, in what we do. For whatever reason, you could not commit to Anna. So, when you told her you had applied for a post that would see you working abroad, she said nothing to stop you, because she loved you, and still does. She's carried a torch for you all these years.'

April entered the room walked over to the sink. Mac glared at Peter, then said, 'You're supposed to be in bed, young lady.' She smiled, curtsied, and by way of reply, very slowly filled a glass with water from the tap.

Mac turned to Peter, 'You have a chance to make amends. You have a home here, one third of this place is yours. Anna is coming next week and will be saying for a long weekend, don't waste the opportunity.'

'Katie's coming, Katie's coming,' April sang out, skipping out of the room.

'Katie?'

Mac and Father John looked at each other, then looked at Peter. Mac nodded his assent to Father John, who said, 'Katherine, is Anna's daughter.'

'I didn't know she had a... who is the...?' Peter gulped his beer, 'I mean... how old is she?'

'The same age as April,' Father John spoke rather abruptly, then paused, and softening his tone, continued, 'She is a month younger than April. They're thick as thieves the two of them, more like sisters than friends.'

Looking at Mac, who smiled and nodded, Father John paused, then continued, 'Anna didn't want us to tell you, she knew how you would react. She said that she only wanted you in her life if you wanted to be there, and not because you felt an obligation. How did she put it…?'

'She's mine… I have a child?' Peter turned and rushed out into the yard.

Mac started after him, but Father John pulled him back, 'Leave him. He has to work this out by himself. It's a bit of a shock, still he'll do the right thing, and I'll marry them.'

Father John sent Mac to find April, who had photographs of Katie.

Chapter Four

Entering the forge, he paused inside the door allowing his eyes to adjust to the lesser light. Looking at the fire, and with a degree of frustration, he picked up a small tin, dipped it in the water butt, then dripping the water, gently wheedled the fire back to the centre, adjusting the airflow until the glow was the right colour.

Turning he picked up a wrought-iron bar, this would be the first part of what would be two hinges. Speaking aloud to himself, he said, 'Simple, strong, and efficient; nothing fancy. That's what Mac asked for, and that's what I'll give him.'

He placed a broad cross-peen hammer and a hinge-eye drift next to his huge London pattern anvil, holding the metal in a pair of wolf-jaw tongs he pushed it into the fire, finding the place with the most heat, increasing the air blast, he waited for the fire to react, carefully adjusting the flow to achieve the right temperature.

Seeking the tell-tale yellow and white glow, it showed brightly in the near darkness of the forge. Gripping tightly, he moved quickly to the anvil and worked the metal until it was broad, flat, and just the right thickness. This took several minutes, and he returned thrice more to the fire.

Using a chisel, he cut out three sections, now castellated, it had the appearance of the side wall of a castle. Folding one end over on itself, he inserted the hinge-eye drift into the curve that this formed, and placing it in an offset bottom-swage, hammered each section around the drift, until the hinge was the right shape and size, he then dusted it with borax, before hammering, so it welded shut on the drift. He removed the drift, happy at the result, Peter repeated this process using three other bars of wrought iron, mating the bars in pairs so that two simple hinges were formed, each joined by a long rivet he had made earlier.

Checking that each hinge operated properly, he hot punched holes for screws on the flat plates either side of the hinge. He then spent the next half-hour hand sanding each hinge, cleaned them, then with a soft brush painted on a concoction he had made the day before, his father's secret mix containing Japan dryer.

Then he set them aside to cure. Peter voiced his thoughts aloud, 'When you're ready, I'll apply some wax, then buff each of you, and repeat the process at least three times, to get the finish Mac wants… and some complain that craftsmanship costs too much?' Taking the hinges with him, he left the forge, and sat down on the bench just outside the door, he set them out to dry next to him, and began sketching in a notebook.

Movement in the distance caught Mac's eye, he watched as Peter sat down on the bench outside his forge, and began to concentrate on a notebook, just beyond Peter he spotted Anna and Teresa walking in his direction, they were conducting some sort of survey. Setting aside the old padlock he was cleaning and oiling, he turned to get a better view, the bench under the kitchen window had seen better days and creaked in protest. Mac watched, as they walked slowly past Peter, and continued across the yard.

Observing them closely, he smiled at the differences between them. Anna, short, five-foot on a good day, stocky, but not over-weight, her energy, laughter and general spiritedness made her seem both younger and taller. Her blue eyes and flaxen hair caught out many who took her to be just another brainless-blond.

Teresa was tall, five-foot-ten, and slender, with long coal-black hair, and brown, almond shaped eyes. Mac realised that no matter what she was doing, all her movements were conducted with grace and poise.

He smiled at them both as they walked past, deep in conver-sation they failed to acknowledge his presence. Mac watched as they departed from view, making their way toward the lower byre, he considered the different aspect both presented from behind, causing him to fend off inappropriate thoughts.

Troubled by these thoughts he turned back to the padlock and began again working on the ancient mechanism in the hope it could be restored, it had been a part of the farm for over ninety years, and he hoped it would still be there functioning in another ninety.

Twenty-minutes later he placed it to soak in a bowl of grease-remover, task done he stood up and walked slowly off towards his workshop. Teresa, and the thoughts that her presence encouraged, raised memories of a previous life, and he felt con-flicted.

Mac crossed the yard and headed toward his workshop, Peter was still sitting on the bench outside his forge, concentrating on sketching. At six-foot-four inches, he was two inches taller than Mac, and the last twelve months spent working in his brother-in-law's forge had seen him bulk-up, his body was toned. Not in a gym-bunny, muscle-Mary way, this was work-muscle, strength, power and stamina combined. He had lost his beer-belly, and with his recent crew-cut, Mac thought he looked ten years younger, even though, as with Father John, his hair was white as blackthorn blossom. Peter cut an impressive and imposing figure, yet as Mac considered his old friend, he concluded that it was his lively pale-blue eyes that really grabbed your attention, constantly taking in all around, they animated his countenance.

Peter had just finished drawing a matching lock-plate, when Mac walked over and picked up a hinge, gave it a cursory glance, and put it back, he turned and walked away.

'You miss her, don't you?' Peter's face a mask of concern.

'With every breath I take.'

Peter stood up, placed his right hand on Mac's shoulder, and said, 'So do I.'

Mac smiled, blinking back the tears, and by way of acknowledgement, briefly placed his hand on Peter's arm, turned and walked slowly back to his workshop.

The day after he had finished the hinges, Peter was busy on a new project. Mac stuck his head through the open door of the forge, squinting, he adjusted his eyes to the brightness of the fire, which was accentuated by the darkness of the forge, looking around for Peter, he said, 'Lunch?'

Peter turned, holding a glowing bar of metal, and said, 'Go ahead, I'll finish up, won't take more than a couple of minutes. I'll be there shortly.'

'Okay, but don't be too long,' said Mac.

He walked off towards the table outside the kitchen. Seeing Father John approaching, he asked, 'What we got, John?'

'Camembert, new potatoes, salad, and tomatoes... Peter?'

'He'll be along in a minute; he's just finishing something.'

'Should we wait?'

'Give him five,' said Mac.

Peter joined them a couple of minutes later. 'Have you got plans for Saturday morning?'

Mac looked up from his plate, 'Not really, we're spending our time on the farm this weekend. Why?'

'I've all but finished a new weathervane, I'm going to replace that sorry item on the roof of the stable block.'

Mac said, 'Great, it's never worked since we inherited the place, the tail is missing. What have you made?'

'I'll let that be a surprise, I've got a cherry-picker coming Saturday morning, I can have it for a couple of hours, which should be more than enough time to get the job done. Can you lend a hand?'

'Of course, no problem. Where did you get a cherry-picker from?'

'What is a cherry-picker?' said Father John.

Peter laughed, and said, 'It's a hydraulic platform, it's capable of reaching up to the top of the clock tower on the stable block.'

'Oh, I've seen one, they use them to change the bulbs on streetlights, is that right?'

'Sort of, the one you are thinking of is usually attached to the back of a van or a truck, this is a similar piece of equipment, but it is on a trailer. I did Bob the Builder, down the road...'

'You mean Michael, from Weathertop Farm?' said, Mac.

'Yeah, sorry. I keep forgetting his name, anyway, I did Michael a favour last week. I welded and reinforced the bucket on his mini-digger and negotiated the loan of his cherry-picker as payment.'

'A new weather-vane, that'll smarten things up.'

The days went by, and they settled into a rhythm of work. During the week Father John rose early, and if not required to say Mass for the Whitney's, or for the monks at Bridge Abbey, said Mass in the small chapel attached to the farmhouse, then spent the rest of the morning in the farm office, prepared lunch, and spent the afternoon in the vegetable patch, before cooking an evening meal for all of them.

Mac and Peter, when not working the land, busied themselves in their respective workshops, a lifetime of self-discipline and commitment showed, as examples of craftsmanship flowed to admiring clients, and their individual reputations grew. During term-time, April and her friend Susan, were picked up after school by Susan's mother, and driven to the neighbouring farm. The two girls would set about their homework, then at about five, they would attend to Susan's pony. Around six, Mac would drive over to collect April. Most days, after the evening meal, April joined Mac while he walked the farm, as they walked, Mac voiced his thoughts, which April augmented with her own plans. April retired to bed about eight o'clock, then the drinking and the conversation flowed.

The weekends were different. Father John got to be a parish priest. Peter joined Anna and Katherine in London, or they came up to stay with him on the farm. Slowly he and Anna rebuilt their relationship, he got to know his daughter, and she felt comfortable around him.

Mac and April were joined by Elizabeth's best friend, Teresa. She had been there for both when Elizabeth died and had become a surrogate mother to April. Their friendship had evolved, Teresa and Mac had fallen in love, a move long anticip-ated, and welcomed by all their friends, who now looked forward to a wedding. Of course, Mac and Teresa, being faithful Catholics, could not countenance anything save celibacy prior to marriage, there were times when the strain of abstinence stretched notions of restraint, but not enough to require urgent confession; Mac's Monday-moods were becoming legendary.

Teresa had come over to England from Tolosa, near Bilbao, in

Northern Spain. Teri, as everyone called her, had come to study journalism and stayed. She and Elizabeth started out together on the same regional newspaper; becoming firm friends they moved to London, joining the same broadsheet, going freelance at the same time. They collaborated several times on stories, but mostly helped each other with research and contacts. Teresa was five-years younger than Elizabeth, even so she readily agreed to be April's godmother, and she had accepted the promise that Elizabeth made her take the evening of April's baptism; her Basque heritage demanded that she view it as a debt of honour, but she found it an easy pledge to keep.

Teresa, Mac, and April would alternate their weekends between working on the farm, and walking in the surrounding hills; their ambition, to work their way through the Wainwright series of guides, and they had just completed all the walks in book four, encompassing the neighbouring fells.

Collectively, their lives settled into the gentle rhythm of the seasons. Mac finally felt at peace, he had arrived at a place where he could acknowledge his grief for Elizabeth, and openly express his feelings for Teresa. Before the summer was over, he hoped that they would set a date to marry. He shared his thoughts, April was overjoyed, demanding to be a bridesmaid, Teresa settled for a date the following spring.

Father John had a home and a family, he welcomed the challenge of ministering to a parish, even if that parish was numerically tiny, the Whitney's, their children and grandchildren, the estate workers and their families, Mac, April, Teresa, Peter, Anna, Katie, and of course the monks at Bridge Abbey, no more than fifty-two people. Still, he had souls to nurture, to guide, and protect. He was no longer a bureaucrat, at long last he felt he was the priest he should have been.

Peter felt the isolation of solitude and the weight of duty fall away from him, he had a place and a purpose in the world, and it was a world of peace and fellowship and family, the wearisome days of confronting man's inhumanity to man were behind him; no longer burdensome, his life was tranquil and creative.

Chapter Five

Mac watched April from a distance, it was a couple of hours after school, and he had come to pick her up from Susan's. She and April were busy in front of the stables, grooming a pony. He watched as his daughter carefully brushed the animal's mane and tail and noted the look of concentration in her face. Unbidden, the memory of a conversation he had with Elizabeth, when April was a baby, came to him.

Elizabeth had expressed a desire to buy a pony for April. Something, that due to her parent's straightened circumstances, was never part of her own childhood. She looked forward to teaching her to ride. Emotion burst through, and he turned away, unable to blink back the tears, his composure gone, he started to cry, sank to his knees sobbing, the memory was just too raw, too painful.

If Susan's parents noticed, they said nothing. Susan's mother, urged them to saddle the pony, telling April that if she felt confident, she could ride. Mac stood up and dried his eyes and walked off towards their tractor shed.

Ten minutes later he returned, his composure restored, to find April taking her first ride on a pony. He re-joined Susan's parents, and quietly said, 'Thanks,' Susan's mother smiled, her father nodded.

Her mother said, 'She's a natural.' Mac, though he knew nothing about horse riding, agreed.

On the way home, April said, 'What's wrong, Dad?'

'Nothing.'

April stayed quiet; she knew her father well enough to know he would eventually say what was on his mind.

'I was just thinking… it was about your mother, something she said came back to me, it caught me by surprise.'

They drove together in silence for a couple more minutes.

'Your mother used to say, when it appears that you have been abandoned by life, when doubt leaves you faithless and disconsolate, when you feel spiritually abandoned, then you are far from nowhere. I guess I'm feeling a little far from nowhere right now, that's all.'

April patted her father's arm and said, 'It will be alright, Dad.'

They drove a little further, the silence was becoming awkward, Mac sought to lighten the mood.

'Should we get a pony?'

He was answered by squeals of delight, followed by a rapid, and detailed catalogue of what they would need to buy, and what she would have to do to prepare for its arrival. Her words, filled with pleasure and hope, washed warmly over him, and by the time they reached home any despair had been driven out by her infectious joy.

Mac walked out of the kitchen about half an hour later, and said, 'Pete, you got that barbecue started? John, get the beers sorted. April, get the Dobbin burgers.'

'Dad!'

Chapter Six

Simon visited the farm, he had spent three months reviewing, checking, and reinvestigating the case assigned to him by Cartwright, he could go no further without the help of the team who conducted the original investigation, there were just too many important pieces of evidence missing. He drove down the hill toward the steading and parked by the other vehicles next to a large barn.

As he left his car and began walking toward what he hoped was a gate leading to the house, a large man approached from within the barn, raising his arm in greeting as he did so, 'Simon?'

'Mac?'

'Detective Inspector Davies, so you did take my advice?'

'I did, Mac. All of it… and now I need some more help and guidance.'

'It's all my fault then,' Mac laughed, and shook Simon's hand. He looked him up and down, checking out his attire. Simon was wearing jeans and hill walking boots. 'Good, looks like you listened, you've dressed appropriately, this is a working farm that often sees four seasons in one day. Let's walk, and you can tell me what is so important that it brings you all the way up here from London. I suspect it has Cartwright's podgy fingerprints all over it?'

Simon silently followed, as Mac led the way across the concrete yard and through a gate into the field opposite the barn. He surmised that they were making their way toward an old stone byre squatting on the edge of a wood atop the hill ahead of them. As they progressed through the field, Simon took station slightly behind, and to the right of Mac, both stayed quiet, each seemingly lost in thought.

He observed Mac, it seemed to him that the intervening years had been kind, at six-feet-two-inches tall, Mac remained an imposing figure, his ramrod-spine, shoulders-back military bearing, were still there, he had lost his paunch, his stomach flat, his arms muscular, in the tensile-steel way of those who engage daily in physical work outdoors, the muscles in his back rippled through his t-shirt as he walked. He had kept his fair-haired locks, and even though there was a slight greying at the temples he still managed to look ten-years younger than his age, a look complimented by his tan, undoubtedly the result of exposure to sun and wind.

Although Simon was the same height as Mac, and had a similar frame, he was now conscious of the pale and flabby body occupying it, he was becoming breathless as the slope of the field became steeper, needing a rest, he interrupted the silence between them.

'Cartwright… ordered me to speak to you in person.'

Mac stopped and turned to look at, Simon. 'I guessed as much; we all did. I can't say Pete is particularly disposed to your being here, nor is Father John, he too has concerns. We don't hold you responsible, you're the messenger, but we distrust Cartwright, and hold him in contempt.'

Simon brought Mac up to speed on his investigation. 'I know I am a long way from understanding the whole picture, but…'

Mac interrupted him. 'It's going to rain, and soon. Let's go down to the house and grab a coffee, then we can discuss what to do next, and for that, you will have to have the facts Cartwright left out of the yarn he spun you.'

They walked down to the house in silence, entered the kitchen, Mac made them both a coffee, and said, 'We'll go through to the sitting room, it'll be more comfortable.'

Peter said, 'I've read it, it's a load of nonsense, total guff. How can anyone write this stuff, it should be consigned to the dustbin of history, it deserves to be no more than an obscure footnote, studied only by dusty old academics in drab libraries, and monks in cowled monasteries.'

Father John bridled, rose from his chair, turned his back on Peter, and staring at the bookcase, said, 'It is clear to me that you haven't read it, and that if you have, you failed to understand it. Read it again, and again, until you understand it, then, and only then, can we discuss this book.'

'What do you mean, I don't understand it? How do you know if I've read it or not?'

Father John spun round, and facing Peter, said, 'If I was a lecturer who had assigned a book to a student, and had requested a summation for discussion, then a couple of weeks later the student comes to my study, throws the book down, and says to me "What a load of rubbish", and walks off. I would conclude that my student had not read the book, or had read it and failed to understand it, or worse, had read it, and rejected out of hand the ideas it contained, without any deliberation or argument.'

'If that were the case, where would the fault lie, with the writer, or the reader?' Peter, his face reddening, continued, 'You seem very sure that the fault is mine, that I failed to understand the book, perhaps the author was being deliberately obtuse?'

'You are an intelligent, articulate and…'

Barely suppressing a snigger, Mac said, 'Don't mind us, we're just passing through.' Mac and Simon entered the library from the corridor off the kitchen and walking around the table in the middle of the room, exited through a door into the living room.

Simon looked quizzically at Mac, and said, 'What was that about?'

Mac said, 'For the last five or six years, Pete has been using the spare time he had when abroad to improve himself, and John has been tutoring him. Initially he went down the self-taught route, but like many who try to teach themselves, he got lost, so he wrote to John, explaining what he was trying to do, and that's how John ended up educating Peter. I'm guessing the disputation that we just witnessed was part of that process.'

Mac stuck his head into the library and said, 'John, what book were you... discussing?'

'The Brothers.'

'Oh?' he looked at, Simon, shrugged his shoulders and continued, 'Sorry, none the wiser.'

Teresa, who was sitting in the window seat reading, set her book aside, and turning to Simon, said, 'Dostoevsky's, The Brothers Karamazov, and if you haven't read it, I strongly recommend that you do. That you both read it.' She looked pointedly at Mac and smiled.

Simon said, 'This place is more an asylum than a farm.'

Peter, who had stomped off into the garden, returned to the library, ignoring Father John, he passed through the room and joined them, saying, 'Mac, you've never recommended a book, what would you suggest, preferably something a little lighter than ecclesiastical notions of an entertaining read?' He glared at Father John, who snorted his displeasure, before turning towards Mac and Simon, with a smile on his face.

'That's not an easy question to answer.' Mac walked back into the library turned and said 'I'm never sure how to respond to a question like that; handing you a book and suggesting that you will enjoy it... reading is very subjective... influenced by so many factors, age, maturity, education, politics, belief, the weather, or just your mood at the time. I have been receptive to books, that at another time in my life I would not have on the shelf. Ask me a specific question, such as, I'm studying the English Civil War, or I'm interested in roe deer, and I can recommend a book. Take a book off the shelf and ask me about it, and if I've read it, I will try to provide a brief summary so that you can decide whether to read it... Pete, there are over four thousand books in this room, and another fifteen hundred on shelves in Liz's study, take your pick, each in its own way is interesting.'

Mac walked round the room, and removed two books from the shelf, 'Here. These were sent to me last year by one of John's contacts in the Philippines. Admittedly, the cultural references being foreign, mean that some of the richness and subtlety in the books is lost on me, but both are very entertaining, and informative, and repay close reading, start with these.'

He handed Peter two books, *Noli me Tangere*, and *El Filibusterismo*, written by Jose Rizal. 'Maybe I should just give you a list of authors I think are worth reading, Kipling, Chesterton, Chekhov, PG Wodehouse, Anthony Trollope, Ronald Blythe, Ernest Hemingway, Cormac McCarthy, Evelyn Waugh, George Mackay Brown, Richard Ford...'

'Dostoevsky.' Interrupted, Father John.

Everyone laughed, Mac nodded, then said, 'I could go on, endlessly. Your question is akin to asking how long is a piece of string.'

Peter smiled and said, 'For a difficult question, you've given a Father John answer.' Picking up the two books Mac had offered him, he said, 'I'll try them.'

Simon said, 'What was the first book you bought, Mac? The first that you chose for yourself, rather than being given as a gift?'

'Interesting question. The first book I bought was with pocket money I had saved; it was my entry into the adult world. My father drove me over to Inverness, I was so proud that day, walking alone into the bookshop; in those days a city that size might have four bookshops, now you're lucky if there is one. I was thirteen, but I felt ever so grown-up, I spent an hour browsing, before choosing, *My Family and Other Animals*, by Gerald Durrell, a purchase I've never regretted, I've read the book three times since I bought it. It's there, on the second shelf down, if you want to read it.'

'What do you think of e-books?'

'Not much. Teri has one of those reader things, I get the attraction, you could carry around a whole stack of books, and then some. It is easy to use, and good to read on, I'm not a complete Luddite, and I know many people who swear by them, but I do have an issue with the whole concept. Firstly, I like books, I like the feel, the smell, the weight, the fact that they are tangible objects, in some cases, works of art. In the cupboard over there is a book published over a hundred-and-twenty years ago, printed on handmade paper, with hand-tooled leather binding, and woodcut-prints, it's a testament to craftsmanship and art, a very desirable object, in a way that an e-book can never be. My main concern is that technology is vulnerable, people steal readers and pads, I never went to a burglary where books were nicked. Teri had her reader stolen last year. They're probably vulnerable to cyber-attack, and don't take them anywhere near an electro-magnet, and what happens when the grid goes down? Two winters ago, we lost electricity for eleven days.'

Mac paused, looked at Simon, and wondered if he could trust

him, he decided he could, and said, 'Books contain knowledge, and that makes them important, too important to be left at the mercy of politicians; e-books are accessed via the internet, governments around the world are seeking ways to limit what we can access on the internet, and to monitor our activity whilst on there. They claim to do this in the name of freedom and public safety, citing terrorism, but what they seek is control. Control of information, since to them truth is relative, what they desire is to ensure it is relative to their vision. I can walk into a bookshop anywhere, select a book, pay for it in cash, and walk out with no one any the wiser. That's why so many governments would like to get rid of cash, they want all transactions to be made electronically, they claim it will reduce crime, prevent tax evasion, and decrease costs, since they won't have to keep printing bank notes and minting coins. But what they want is a way of monitoring who is buying, and what they're buying, electronically they can do that, and if the item you buy is a book, then they know what you're reading, and could then decide, based on its contents, whether you are a potential, or actual threat to the system…'

Peter interrupted, 'Can you envisage that? Faceless bureaucrats arbitrarily interpreting what you are reading as a possible threat to the State, or worse, an algorithm doing so.'

Mac said, 'Pete makes a good point. Their argument for control is as fatuous as the one put forward for citizens having biometric ID cards, they claim it will reduce crime and terrorism, but has it made a difference on the Continent? Look at France, almost daily subject to terror inspired incidents. And as for crime, isn't cyber-fraud the fasted rising, and least detected crime these days? Don't forget, the natural default of government is to exert control, it is never for freedom or democracy. The knowledge contained in this library, may one day help to ensure our freedom, no one in authority knows that it exists, and I intend to keep it that way, there will come a day when having your own library will be a lifesaver. Remember, once they start burning books, burning people is never far behind.'

Simon laughed and said, 'Isn't that all a bit conspiracy theory, you sound like one of those nut-jobs who see government spies behind every hedge.'

Mac said, with an edge to his voice, but a smile on his face, 'So you think I'm a nut-job. Books can be a bulwark against dictatorship, they ensure that we can continue to inform and educate ourselves and our children, enabling us to see beyond the lies and propaganda. Books arm us, by providing the concepts and arguments necessary to speak truth to power, our freedom is dependent upon there being books. I fear that over reliance on e-books and the web, may open the road to tyranny. Ever wondered why councils facing financial cutbacks begin by closing libraries?'

Mac paused, searching for the right words, 'Hitler, Stalin, Mao, all burned books, dictators fear books and the truth they contain, more than they fear insurrection. You can shoot opponents, but ideas are bullet proof. Tomorrow belongs to those who can shape today, and that can only happen if they can expurgate yesterday. Control history and you dominate the present, achieve that and you possess the future; having access to facts, to the truth, is as essential to liberty as breathing is to life. Remember, when they start banning books, it won't be long before books are outlawed, then burnt, which history shows, leads to governments murdering their own people.'

Father John stared at Simon, then said, 'All civilisations have a beginning and an end, all follow a familiar cycle. First comes conquest, then freedom, a period, that sadly doesn't last very long, before the culture is overwhelmed by vice and corruption, all driven by greed, and an insatiable desire for money, which sees innovation and adventure stifled by a small-minded bureaucracy wrapped in pointless red tape, and it ends in book burning and barbarism. An intelligently populated library will reveal where in that cycle you currently stand.'

Mac said, 'Nut-job? Only those who do not think carefully about every aspect of the of laws enacted by Parliament, are nut-jobs. Those who do not apply lessons from history in order to anticipate the effect of legislation seven-generations hence, are nut-jobs. For theirs is the lunacy of subservience. So no, I haven't gone down a rabbit hole, there's nothing wrong with being alive to the dangers of politics, which should give rise to caution and scepticism.'

Chapter Seven

It was growing dark when they sat around the table under the wisteria. April and Katie had been put to bed and finally fallen asleep, late as it was, the evening was still warm. Mac and Peter enjoyed a cold beer, Teresa and Anna were drinking a rosé with ice.

Teresa said, 'Who is, Simon?'

Mac said, 'He's a detective inspector from Scotland Yard.'

Anna said, 'No!' Put her hand over her mouth and looked at Peter.

Teresa, sounding frightened, said, 'Is he here because of…?'

Mac said, 'Yes, but Pete and I have told him we are not interested, we will not be getting involved.'

They sat in silence, then Mac said, 'Anna, you called this meeting, you and Teri have something to tell us, so what is it?'

Anna looked at Peter, and then at Mac, but said nothing.

Peter said, 'We are not going to get involved, I promise you. We're both retired, and neither one of us wants to play Sherlock Homes again. So, what is it? What has got you both so fired up? Yes… we've noticed something is afoot, all that whispering, making notes, walking around the fields, sketching. What is it?'

Anna looked from Peter to Mac, 'You promise, no more playing detective?'

'Yes,' said Mac and Peter together, in mock exasperation.

Mac said, 'Simon and John have driven over to the monastery for the weekend, they'll be back tomorrow afternoon. John intends to interrogate, Simon. But he feels the same way we do, we must leave things as they are, what's done is done. Simon asked if he could spend a few more days with us, helping out on the farm, I think he needs a break, so I said he could.'

'Did that terrible man send him?' asked Anna.

'Cartwright… yes,' said Peter.

'I don't like him,' said Anna.

'I've never met him, but if you don't like him, neither do I,' said Teresa, and everyone laughed.

'So?' said Mac.

'Yes,' said Anna, taking a notebook out of her bag, 'we do have some ideas for the farm. Now don't interrupt, don't say a word until we've finished. Teri and I have thought long and hard about this, we have researched, and worked everything out. Okay?'

'Get on with it,' laughed Peter.

'We are both going to give up our jobs, and I'll move here permanently. I will go back to book-keeping. I will take care of the farm accounts, and those of your individual businesses, and I am sure that there are enough small firms around here to give me an income. Teri is going to give up journalism for a while, so no more trips back to London, she's going to write a book she has been fermenting.

We both think that the farm can make money from what it produces, we want to build a farm-shop, we thought that the large shed just along from the stable block could be converted. We'll grow and sell our own produce. When you and, Liz bought this place she had such plans, her idea was to do something similar. She wrote her thoughts down in a journal, I came

47

across it the other day; she was right, this place can be product-ive, it can make money, and if we pool our resources, pool the money we make, we can live a good life.'

Anna paused, took a sip of her wine, and raised her hand to indicate to Mac and Peter, that they should not speak, she then nodded to Teresa, who said, 'We also want to take the farm off-grid, we want to install a small hydro-electric plant in the old byre at the base of the hill by Gimmer Wood, we had a man come over from Kendal and survey the site for us, if we build a collection tank at the top of the woods, next to the stream, then run a pipe underground down to the byre, the fall of water from the head... I think that's the right terminology,' she checked her notes, 'anyway... it's enough to drive a turbine, and provide us with sufficient electricity for all our needs. In fact, he thought that there would be a surplus, and that will turn us into an energy supplier. We could make money. We also want to drill a borehole so that we can have our own fresh-water supply, that way we will not be reliant on services from outside the farm, and our water and electricity will, in time, be free.'

Anna said, 'We want to fence Souterstead Wood, splitting it up into twenty, five-acre plots, and put pigs in on an annual rotation, we've identified a breed, they're called Iron-Age pigs, it seems that they will be the best ones for this location. We also want to raise beef, buy in just-weaned calves and raise them on grass through late spring into early autumn the following year, both the pigs and the cows will be butchered, and the meat sold here on the farm, so we will need a cold-store and a large walk-in freezer. I want to try out a system that uses pasture in rotation, resulting in the soil being organically fertilised; after the calves come off a field we will put free-range chickens on it, then in the autumn plant wheat. Giving us eggs, as well as pork and beef, and eventually organic wheat, which we intend to mill, we will use the fresh flour to make bread, and we will sell all our produce direct to the public through the shop. We also think that by extending the vegetable patch to a couple of acres, the orchard by four acres, and planting two acres of soft fruit, including blueberries, we will be able to supply fresh, healthy seasonal fruit and veg. We will make a slight loss in the first year, given our start-up costs, and very little in years two and three, when we calculate we will break even. We estimate that we will reach optimum production by the fifth year, and be in profit, even without agricultural subsidies, and the money made by both your businesses. I know it will be hard work, but we can make it succeed, what do you think?'

'First off, you are both moving in?' said Peter.

'Why, isn't my moving up here what you and I discussed?' said Anna.

'Yes of course it is, but... I thought you wanted to stay with the company until the end of the year... never mind, it's great news.'

Mac smiled at Anna, and said, 'Fantastic news. April will be over the moon, and with Katie here as well... bloody marvellous.'

Peter sat with tears running down his cheeks, Anna said, 'Pete, this is what we've both dreamed of, but if I am giving up my job and my way of life, then I want something different, both Teri and I want this. We want this place to reach its potential, to fulfil our dreams, but to do that we need your support and your help.'

Peter said, 'You have to ask? Whatever you want, whatever it takes, right?' he looked at Mac, who nodded his assent.

'Whatever it takes, we will make it work,' said Mac, 'The girls are going to be...'

'Loud,' said Teresa, and they all laughed.

They sat silently, lost in thought, then Mac said, 'How is it going to work, the start-up costs for the animals alone... I've been running the figures through my head, buying the animals, housing, feed, fence posts, wire, your farm-shop... It's around thirty-thousand.'

'We made it fifty-thousand, based on one-hundred pigs, fifty calves, a hundred hens, and a cold store and freezer. To save you a question, the borehole, filtration unit and pipes will be another thirty-five-thousand, and the hydro plant has a total cost of eighty-thousand, but that is everything included, even the supply to the house and workshops, and a connection to the grid. Oh, and then if we do decide to grow wheat, we will need another tractor and some additional equipment, which with a new pickup, and a couple of trailers, will be another two-hundred-thousand.'

'A total cost of three-hundred and fifty-thousand?' said Peter.

Anna, turning a page in her notebook, said, 'Actually it's more like four-hundred-and-fifty-thousand, if you add in what we will need to see us through the first five-years, and the plants and equipment for the fruit and veg.'

Peter said, 'Four-hundred-and-fifty-thousand pounds, where in the hell are we going to get that? I don't think the bank...'

Teresa interrupted, 'From the sale of my flat and Anna's house, given the prices in London, we calculate that between us, after paying off mortgages, credit cards and bank loans, we will have a little over six-hundred-thousand.'

'You can't...'

'Why not, if this is to be our home, and the home for our children.' Anna smiled at Teresa, who blushed, 'Then why shouldn't we make the investment. This is where we want to raise our families, where we want to be, with the men we want to spend the rest of our lives with, so you can forget that caveman chauvinist bullshit, Peter Armstrong.'

Peter threw his hands up in mock surrender, 'Fine by me, it's all good.'

Mac was staring at Teri, his mouth open, 'You're not?'

'I am.'

'How long?'

'Eleven-weeks, I'm going for a scan next Wednesday.'

'I'm coming with you.'

'Damn right you are, it's your fault,' Teresa laughed.

The penny dropped with Peter, who said, 'Fuck me, Mac.'

'Rather not, old boy.'

When the laugher, hugs and congratulations subsided, Anna said, 'Well what about our plan for the farm?'

Mac looked at Peter, who nodded his assent, 'Great idea, just tell us what to do and when. The sooner the better if you want to make next year the first year. We can prepare the fields and fence the woods over the winter. Plant trees and fruit bushes in the autumn, and be ready to get going in the spring, but it all depends on the sale of your properties.'

Teresa said, 'I exchange contracts at the end of this month.'

Anna said, 'I have to move out the middle of next month, it's all in motion.'

Peter said, 'Mac, we've been ambushed.'

'Pete, John's going to go ape, you two are going to have to get married.'

'Great idea.'

Anna, trying to look indignant, said, 'Don't I get a say in this?'

'About as much say as I did in you moving in and taking over the farm,' laughed Peter.

Chapter Eight

The following weekend, Father John, Teresa, Anna, and Simon were seated around the table under the wisteria, as light was starting to fade. Simon said, 'I can't believe it, ten o'clock at night and it's still light enough to read by.'

Father John said, 'During the summer months, this far north it's close to midnight before it gets dark, and even then, there is still a glow over the horizon, more gloom than night.'

The evening was warm, but not humid, which, given the heat of the day just gone was a blessing; the table was adorned with beer and wine and food.

Peter joined them, 'Mac?'

'Still working,' said Teresa.

Mac appeared, changing out of a t-shirt into a polo shirt. He leaned over and kissed Teri, then sat down.

Simon said, 'The tattoo on your upper arm, it's the same as Pete's. Is that a Marine thing?'

Mac said, 'Yes.'

Peter said, 'It's history.'

Mac nodded, and said, 'It belongs to another time, it's testament to the recklessness of youth, forget it.' He gulped some beer, then said, 'Pete, with me, it'll only take a minute, I need a hand lifting something.' They both stood up and started toward the workshop.

Rising from his seat, Simon said, 'Can I help?'

'Na, muscles here is enough, it's more awkward than heavy, you carry on, we'll only be a minute.'

Simon sat down, 'I hope I haven't offended them?'

Father John said, 'No I don't think so, they're both too thick-skinned.'

Teresa said, 'Strange, that's the same answer he gave me, he will not talk about it.'

Father John said, 'I do know some of the story, but I'm not sure I should say anything.'

They prevailed upon him to tell them. Father John said, 'Only if you promise to respect their desire for anonymity, and never mention it again, to them, or to each other?'

Having obtained their promises, he continued, 'When I assisted them with their earlier investigation, Mac approached me and asked if I would visit his friend in hospital. He had been in the Marines with them and was dying of cancer. He was Catholic, and Mac felt he would benefit from my visit. I was able to visit him several times before he died, and on the day he died, I was able to hear his confession and give him Extreme Unction.'

Teresa crossed herself, Father John smiled by way of acknowledgement, and continued. 'During our conversations he mentioned that he had served with Peter and Mac, in the same Unit. I asked him about the fish tattoo on the upper part of his left arm. He told me that it was not a fish, it was a dolphin, leaping out of the water at sunset, it signified the joy of freedom. Not long after he died, I attended a dinner party, one of the guests was a historian at the Royal Military Academy Sandhurst. I'm not sure of the context, how it came up in conversation, but at some stage, the significance and role of tattoos in the military was discussed. I mentioned that I had encountered three retired Royal Marines, who each had a dolphin tattooed on their upper left arm. He told me that six Royal Marine Commandos, all part of the same Unit, following a completed mission, had designed a tattoo, a dolphin leaping out of the water at sunset, and all six had it tattooed on their upper left arm, to commemorate their success. It seems that their mission, and I don't know exactly what it was, prevented a near fatal breakdown in détente, remember this was during the Cold War. They were secretly commended by all sides, but nothing was ever said officially, and never will be. There was no official acknowledgement of their actions, hence the tattoo. He did say something slightly enigmatic, "Power corrupts, and corruption is infectious, and those it contaminates it blinds to consequence. The repercussions for one well-armed cabal whose ambition threatened Armageddon, was a brief, but fatal meeting with that team of Royal Marines." I don't know what he meant; I've never asked either of them about it. I've probably said too much, don't mention it to them, we should respect their wish not to speak of it.'

Simon said, 'That could explain why you, and they are still here, the suppression of your investigation should have resulted in all your… accidental deaths. The powers that be, have not shown such restraint before, Mac and Pete must have some high-level patronage.'

'Yes. I think the response was moderated because of the debt owed them, but for obvious reasons I don't think the grounds for such restraint are widely known. All the service records of the marines in that team have been sealed. Knowledge of why they are owed anything will be way above the pay grade of most, the full story of their exploits will be known only to an select few, yet there seems to be a firm acceptance of the present arrangement, which does suggest influential, persistent, and powerful support.'

Teresa looked up, and seeing Mac and Peter returning, said, 'We never speak of this again.'

Mac and Peter resumed their seats, Mac picked up on a slight change in the atmosphere, everyone was a little too deferential, dismissing it, he put it down to an excess of alcohol.

Chapter Nine

The local constable, Tony Maitland, called in the following day. Some time ago he had commissioned Mac to make a Welsh dresser in oak, a present for his wife on their tenth wedding anniversary. The dresser was finished, and now he had to decide on an oil, or a wax finish, and to pick a day for it to be delivered.

Whilst Mac was in the middle of an explanation of the advantages, and disadvantages of the different types of finish, Peter stuck his head round the door to announce that lunch was ready. Dismissing his protestations, Mac invited Tony to join them.

Lunch was taken outside, seated around the broad table, under a pergola twisted by the weight of an ancient wisteria. It was a long leisurely affair, and they idly luxuriated in the heat of the day. Wine was produced and consumed in prodigious quantities, and intelligent conversation gave way to ribald stories, involving a public so dangerously slow-witted, that upon hearing such tales no sentient being could ever give credence to the theory of evolution.

Mac said, 'Pete, do you remember old-man Howorde?'

'Who?'

'Gladstone Howorde.'

Peter frowned, then said, 'The Rabbit Man? You should tell Tony the story, he was asking me about the difference between coppers back in the day, and those in the present. I tried to explain that it comes down to how you perceive your duty, as a problem solver, or just a servant of the court, constrained by legality, but unencumbered by an obligation toward justice. We never shrugged our shoulders and walked away when confronted by the innumerable inadequacies of the law, faced with yet another failure of the legal system to confront injustice, or the complexities of human society, we looked for solutions. Our overriding concern was for the victim and the community, we never gave up just because the law was impotent, we made things happen. Your lot come across as too-grand, over-qualified, and over-paid.'

Peter paused, smiled at Mac, and continued, 'My guess is the politically-correct brigade have brainwashed you into a state of indifference, or worse, blindness.'

Dismissing Tony's protestations, Father John said, 'Tony, it is not about what the law commands, this concerns those areas where the law falls short, or fails to busy itself, your duty is to maintain the peace, and to do so you will have to confront social issues that are not legislated for; solutions are often to be found in the most unexpected places, sometimes circumstances will offer the most unlikely answer.'

Father John paused, drank some wine, then said, 'It's about respect and understanding, not agreement. You can't hate, nor be hated up-close, go back to walking the beat, get out of the cars, talk, communicate, listen, and serve; learn to empathise, be compassionate. I don't mean that airy-fairy fellow-feeling nonsense, I mean develop some sympathy for the lot that life imposes on far too many. It does not require your being soft, nor stepping back from doing your duty, but it will permit you to accord others dignity whilst doing so. Real compassion is not about pity, it's about a robust understanding, coupled with a willingness to forgive when the other person is clearly penitent, it has nothing to do with the pathetic pity that flaccidly passes for compassion today.'

Pausing again to drink, he continued, 'In response to the degradation, squalor, and unremitting violence that marks each day for so many poor souls, the patronising fellow-feeling that is frequently, and insincerely whimpered by our so-called betters, is nothing more than a lack of respect, and humanity.'

Mac stood up, finished his glass of wine, tapped a knife on the side of the glass to indicate that he required silence, and said, 'Gladstone Howorde was a family man, a pillar of society, the manager of a station, an elder of his church, and a homeowner. In the Sixties he left home with a suitcase, and five pounds in his pocket. Driven by raging ambition, he headed for London. From such humble beginnings he progressed, applied himself, and through hard work and diligence achieved much. He had a right to be proud, he had paid his dues, and had earned the respect of those around him. Gladstone was a good man. Except on the third Friday in every month, when he joined his friends for a game of dominoes, the problem was not the competitive way the game was played, nor the almost serious atmosphere it engendered, but with the mango-rum that washed down the goat-curry. Gladstone liked mango-rum, he liked it a little too much, the trouble was that after an evening consuming piratical quantities, he did not mellow into glowing geniality, as did his fellows. No, he turned into a brutish-buccaneer, good man or no, like all of us, he was flawed.'

Mac paused, filled his glass, then drank some wine, and continued, 'Over the years we all attended his monthly demonstrations of respect and affection for his wife. We placed her in an ambulance, took the two children down the street to her sister's, and waited for him to collapse into unconsciousness, which on several occasions was... induced, by busy or impatient constables, unwilling or unable, to remain at the scene until stupefaction rendered him insensible. In those days we could only charge him with assaulting his wife if she substantiated the allegation, which she never did, even if the assault amounted to grievous bodily harm. Obtaining a conviction with a hostile witness, one unwilling to provide the necessary evidence, would have been impossible with the juries back then. It took years for a workable law to be passed, so we were left to find another solution, many were tried, all failed. There was just no way his wife was ever going to press charges, when not under the influence of drink he was a model husband and father, he was kind and loving, and a good provider, so she stoically accepted the situation as her lot in life. The nature of the violence was changing, we feared for her life, his two sons would soon become men, more than capable of confronting their father, we all foresaw the making of a tragedy. Over the years officers intercepted him on his way home, but it wasn't always possible, the dominoes finished at different times, we had emergency calls demanding our attention, but, when possible, he would be arrested for being drunk and refusing to fight, or for drunk and singing badly...'

'Drunk and incapable, drunk and disorderly,' said Peter, in response to a quizzical look from Tony.

'Quite,' continued Mac, 'a couple of days before Halloween, around midnight, Pete and I spotted him rolling his way down the street, tight as a judge. Pete leans in and whispers in his ear, telling him he runs the worst kept station in London, Gladstone goes berserk, we hold him down, and call for the van. Friends and neighbours, concerned by his unprovoked attack on two of London's finest, rush over to help calm him down, and are met by a torrent of abuse, such as would shame a matelot. The van arrives and we haul him off to the nick. That night, the sergeant on duty was one, Anthony Aloysius Higginson.... aye, you couldn't make it up. Now, AAH, as he is known, is as eccentric as his name, his parents were of a nomadic persuasion, and a somewhat unconventional upbringing left its mark. Every year, around Halloween, he joined his large, mostly theatrical family, and helped to put on a show to raise money for a worthy cause, that particular year it was for a local hospital. AAH always played a large white rabbit... why? I don't know. I never attended any of his performances, though those that did, claimed to have been entertained. That evening the performance had overrun, and Sergeant Higginson had come direct from the theatre to work. On our way back to the station we received a gnomic radio message, basically telling us to go with the flow. On arrival at the station, we led the now subdued Gladstone into the charge-room, which was, to our surprise, empty. The other odd thing was the presence of a large armchair atop the charge-room desk, but before we could determine its purpose, the door burst open. A large white rabbit, with elasticated sergeant's stripes on each arm, carrying the huge charge-binder hopped into the room, up onto the bench behind the desk, normally occupied by the custody sergeant, onto the desk, and settled into the armchair. The rabbit preened its ears, crossed its legs, and balancing the charge-binder on its knees, peered down at Gladstone, and said, 'Yuss?'

Mac paused, took a drink, and continued, 'Gladstone staggered back and slumped, we had to hold him up. His eyes were open and unblinking, nostrils flared, he looked wide-eyed from us to the white-rabbit, who was engaging us in conversation, we were looking straight ahead, at the place where the sergeant usually sits, answering all the questions being asked of us by the rabbit, but directing our answers to the invisible sergeant, then the rabbit asked Gladstone a question, there was a smell of fear in the room, and it wasn't me or Pete. Gladstone had the look of a man in a nightmare from which he knows he will not wake. He placidly followed us down to his cell for the night, we tucked him in, and return to the charge room, clearly it had worked.'

Mac drank some more wine, 'AAH was not convinced. Around four in the morning, Gladstone was roused from his slumber, and led into the charge-room, which now had the appearance of a courtroom, there was a jury, the defence council was Pete, and I was the prosecuting council. Following a short trial, the jury found Gladstone guilty of persistent and malicious wife-beating. With great solemnity, and in absolute silence, the judge, the big white rabbit, sat impassively while a black handkerchief was placed between his large ears, he passed sentence, death. Gladstone was to be taken immediately to the yard where he would be executed by firing squad. He was led, unprotesting, head down, into the rear yard of the station, placed in front of the back wall, while six officers armed with empty pistols lined up in front of him. Following the command to fire, another officer, holding two dustbin lids brought them together with a loud bang, Gladstone fainted, and was returned to his cell. In the morning he appeared in front of the magistrate, we made no mention to him of the events of the previous eight hours, and attempted to engage him in light-banter, but Gladstone was having none of it, his usual morning-after contrition and embarrassed jokiness, had given way to solemn introspection, and he wore a look of trepidation. When asked by the clerk of the court how he pleaded to the charge, he replied, "You can't try me, I've been tried and found guilty by a big white rabbit and shot." The magistrate took that as a not guilty plea and decided to hear the matter then and there. I gave my evidence for drunk and disorderly, and the case was proved, Gladstone was given a five pound fine. The magistrate then called us forward and informed us that he was aware of what we were trying to do, he said that he hoped it would work, and made us promise to tell Sergeant Higginson, that there should be no further sightings of the white rabbit. As we always did, we drove Gladstone home from court, but it was clear he was a changed man.'

Peter said, 'I've always wondered if it worked, I know that for the following two years there were no further incidents, then I transferred to the CID, do you think it lasted?'

'Pete, this is what I was trying to tell you the other day. I was in Oxford in February, with April. We had gone to visit Liz's parents for the weekend, and I took the opportunity to visit Blackwell's. I was just leaving the store when I bumped into a young man, I made the usual apologies, and sidestepped, when he asked if I was Constable Mackenzie, I explained that I used to be, and he told me he was Gladstone's youngest. He was in his third year, reading philosophy, politics and economics, he brought me up to date on his family, and then asked if he could shake my hand, explaining that the evening following his arrest, Gladstone apologised to his wife and children for his behaviour, and informed them that he was swearing off drink for the rest of his days, a promise he duly made public in church the following Sunday, when he stood up in front of the entire congregation, and vowed before God to abstain for the rest of his life, he also asked for their forgiveness and support. From that day, Gladstone had not touched a drop, the lad said he did not want to know what we had done to bring about this change, but he and his family were grateful. I cautiously asked him what his father had said about that night, he replied that he would not talk of the events of that evening, but, when pressed, would hold his head in his hands and wail that the angels had sent him a terrible vision of the demon that awaited him if he did not repent and change his ways. I asked him to convey my best wishes to his brother, and his parents, then we parted.'

They sat laughing at the images Mac had conjured.

Mac looked at Tony, and said, 'That was then, but the change in the law has solved little. Politicians, who by treating behaviour which needs to be addressed by intervention from several agencies, place the onus solely on the police, knowing that they can never solve an issue that complex. Why? It's cheap, and deflects any criticism away from the government, they get to dodge the bullet. So, I guess you are still going to have to look for creative ways to maintain social harmony. The idea that simply criminalising behaviour will provide a solution, is laughable…'

Peter rose unsteadily to his feet, and said, 'Way too serious… now talking of rabbits, I'm not sure if you'll be aware of this, but late last year, a seminar was held in Canada, something to do with innovations in policing techniques. Towards the end of the course the instructors took several of the students out to a nearby forest. This field trip was to test the students grasp of the new techniques, and to get them thinking outside of the box. Calling two Norwegian officers forward, the instructor produced a light-brown rabbit with a green stripe on its back, which he released, they watched as it hopped from the clearing into the trees, waiting five minutes, he instructed the Norwegian students to find the rabbit, reminding them to make full use of the new techniques they had learned. With great confidence they entered the forest, emerging ten minutes later with the rabbit, which they returned to the instructor. He turned to the Canadian detectives and repeated the process. Again, he waited for the rabbit to secure the cover of the forest, and after five minutes sent them off to find and retrieve it. The instructor explained to the assembled detectives that they would take longer than the Norwegian pair, as the rabbit, not too dissimilar to criminals, will have learned, and secreted himself with greater effectiveness, but in his opinion, if the Canadian detectives applied their training properly, this should only add five minutes to the test. Sure enough, fifteen minutes later, the gallant duo emerged from the forest with the rabbit. He then indicated that the American officers should join him, two of the LA's finest shambled forwards, hands in pockets, and watched, as the rabbit disappeared once again into the forest. The instructor turned to them after five minutes and began to speak, they waved him away, 'It's already circling the drain.' They shuffled off after the rabbit. Twenty, thirty, forty-minutes went by, no sign of them, after forty-five-minutes the instructors, by now very concerned, discussed their options. The other detectives looked knowingly at each other and sniggered. One hour later, from just within the tree line there came a terrible scream, such a scream as would freeze the blood in your veins. The assembled detectives stood paralysed with fear and watched in horror as a large grizzly bear appeared to leap from the trees into the clearing in front of them, it landed hard, in a crumpled heap, and although breathing, did not move. The two Parker Center detectives slowly walked out from the forest and over to the prostrate body of the bear, adjusting their ties as they did so, upon reaching the bear, one of the detectives grabbed it by the scruff of the neck and hauled it upright, the other walked round and stood in front of the bear, smiled, and kicked it straight in the balls. The bear cried out, 'All right, all right, I'm a fucking rabbit.'

Mac and Father John, laughed.

Tony said, 'I'm not sure I get it.' Peter smiled and clutching a bottle of wine lurched round the table to where Tony was seated and embraced him. 'You have no idea how happy that makes me,' he said, as he filled Tony's glass. 'A toast,' he shouted, 'to the County-Mounties, bless them.'

Mac said, 'Who told you that one, Edward? No... had to be Welsh-Bob?' Peter nodded.

Tony said, 'How am I going to get home?'

Chapter Ten

F our days later Tony reappeared, and sheepishly finalised the decisions he had failed to make about the completion of the Welsh dresser. He had hoped to do so and leave but had come prepared for another bout of afternoon drinking.

As they left the workshop, Tony said, 'Mac, what makes a good detective, I mean, what do I have to learn, is there something, a secret, that separates the great from the mediocre?'

Mac said, 'The great from the mediocre? Attitude, or to put it another way, not allowing yourself to be ground down by life, avoid cynicism, and hang on to hope. The question should be, what is the art of the detective?'

Nodding towards Peter's forge, he said, 'The true art of the blacksmith is not found in the hammer blow, but in the space between the blows. A great poem is wrought by its silences. At Detective Training School we were taught to listen, to hear what was being said, and to recognise how it was being said. Later, under the tutorage of experienced officers, this was widened to include what was not being said. The secret art of the detective, acquired only after years of experience, and then only by a few, is in the silence between words. If you seek the truth, winnow the silence. Couple that with well-honed observation skills; register the things that are there, then note those that should be there, and are not. Finally, identify those that are present, and shouldn't be. Whilst doing so, ensure that you keep objectivity paramount. Never connect a bunch of unrelated facts and weave them into a pre-conceived theory concerning what occurred, for it will prove difficult to unravel, and delay exposing the truth. Acquire, develop, and apply these attributes correctly, and you will be a true detective.'

Tony, looked at Mac, and said, 'I don't understand.'

Mac said, 'No, you don't, but one day you may, and when that day comes, we will talk again.'

Mac brought him over to the table under the pergola, Peter and Father John were already seated, opposite them sat another man, in his late thirties, clearly a police officer, other than his name, Simon, no further introduction was made.

Peter reached over the table and poured Tony a glass of cloudy home-made cider from what appeared to be a bottomless jug. As he sat back down, Peter said, 'You really want to know why? Why areas like Brixton, or Peckham, are the places to work if you want to be a copper?'

Tony said, 'Well I don't get it, the violence, the danger, the futility of it, I read somewhere that the only reason white police officers volunteer for such areas, is because they can live out their racist fantasies.'

Peter started up from his chair, rage flashed in his eyes. Mac said quietly and firmly, 'Explain it to him, tell him why.'

Peter's anger subsided, and he sank back into his seat, he drank slowly and deeply from his glass, leaned back and held Tony's eyes in his gaze for longer than was polite, or comfortable.

When he spoke, it was with a measured tone. 'There is a reason why police officers, real coppers, choose to work in such locations. Serving in that environment is challenging, physically, emotionally, and mentally. In most areas policing consists of long periods of tedium, punctuated by adrenalin-induced rushes of excitement, inner-city areas are wholly devoid of boredom, and fear is an ever-present companion. True, some volunteer because it will look good on their service record and may give them the edge on a promotion board, but those who stay, do so to make a difference. You soon learn and must accept, that most of what happens is beyond your control, the fact that housing is shit, the schools worse than prison, and there are no jobs, may have nothing to do with you, but you will be blamed. It's your fault, not because you have done something, or failed to do something, but because you are an ever-present representative of the state, sometimes the only presence, and therefore the target for every grievance.

Local politicians, black or white, left or liberal, will heap blame on you. The organised criminal gangs will ferment disorder and undermine confidence in you to further their nefarious activities, often aided by the politicians, some for monetary gain, but mostly because politics is a game that can only be played with any relevance among the dissatisfied and the disenfranchised. Look at any stable community and the first thing you notice is an antipathy towards politics, and a healthy distrust of politicians. Life spent serving inner-city communities can seem akin to shovelling shit against the tide, a wholly pointless existence. Change, if it happens at all, is out of step and out of time. Hopelessness, and despair, are ever present companions, or so it seems.'

Peter paused and took a sip from his glass.

Tony said, 'London…'

Peter held up his hand to interrupt, took another sip and said, 'Not just London, but every major city has at least one such district, London has six, but don't think that what I am describing is exclusive to London. I'm guessing that in every inner-city station throughout the country, there will be a moment in the locker room before a shift, when the talking stops, and the officers fall silent, each uttering a silent prayer, a hope that they will be standing there again at the end of the shift. They remind themselves of the twelve-to-six code…'

Tony said, 'Twelve-to-six?'

Mac said, 'It's better to be tried by twelve, than carried by six. Remember that, let it be your guide throughout your service, lay-down your life for the innocent, and for your colleges, but never give it up cheaply.'

Peter nodded, then continued, 'They police an area whose inhabitants are indifferent to them at best, and harbour lethal intent at worst. Their working day will be among the drunks, the junkies, pimps, prostitutes, pornographers, people-traffickers, thieves, burglars, robbers, extortionists, loan-sharks, drug-dealers and their armed-gangs who haunt the estates and surrounding streets, and the many other examples of human-wreckage who ebb in, and flow out of the area. They are expected to carry out their duties, unarmed and subject to daily scrutiny, held to account at higher standard than that applied to any other profession. It's a violent, lonely place, a human-scrapyard, where apathy keeps people sane, and hope is futile, despair is writ large in the faces you meet, lives are ruined forever by the political dance of state and local government indifference… the hunter in you keeps you alive.'

Peter paused, drank, then refilled his glass, 'What you learn after a while, is that politicians have a vested interest in keeping it that way. The white Socialists, Marxists, and Trotskyists who haunt the corridors of the local council, need continued apathy and grinding poverty to stay in power, they make wild promises, but will never deliver. Their failure creates a white left-behind caste, seething with racial resentment, blaming their failure to achieve, on any non-white presence in their community. The black fixers and dealers, who wander the same corridors want the same thing, they encourage the comforting embrace of victimhood, their power is predicated upon a perception of hatred, which they actively promote. Leaving young people trapped in street-culture, confined by a relentless loop that drags them back down whenever they try to escape, reinforcing their need for mutual affirmation. Turning builders into wreckers. The political class feed the fear and ignorance, to ensure their re-election. If you force people to live in shitholes, don't be surprised if some of them turn into raptor-eyed violent criminals…'

Mac interrupted, 'There is a long-standing debate in academic circles concerning the importance of nature and nurture in the development of an individual, those professors should spend a month on one of the sink-estates, that should settle it. Environment dictates the choices available to an individual, if where you live is bounded by social and economic walls, and survival demands quick-witted savagery, the suppression of humanity, and the need to turn feral, then just to survive you will become a violent criminal, in this context, poverty breeds crime…'

Peter interrupted, 'You're as bad as our obdurate cleric… if I may?'

He smiled at Father John, and bowed sarcastically towards Mac, who nodded in response. Peter continued, 'The ensuing mess provides for a political feeding-frenzy and has the added advantage of creating a permanent state of short-termism, politicians have an aversion to commitment. They know something they never share with their electorate, they know that nothing will change because governments do not want, nor can they afford change, and that suits them just fine, because it guarantees their seat in the game. Tree-planters do not number among them, such altruistic behaviour is actively suppressed, for only the present is relevant, the future is immaterial. If that sounds cynical, it's not, it's a fact. Look at what most governments flaunt as change, it's just the same pig with fresh lipstick. No government will ever bring about actual change, think about it; if all the criminals in inner-city areas stopped shooting and stabbing each other, dealing drugs, stealing, committing robbery and burglary, if they just stopped running and hiding from the police, sat down, and demanded better housing, better schools for their children, and real jobs, what could the government do?'

Peter paused, looked at Mac, who said, 'Carry on, I'll jump in later.'

Peter continued, 'All the time they are shooting and stabbing each other, and running away from Plod, they're too busy to demand what is rightfully theirs. The government and local authorities get to save money, and the political class get to play power-games, so everyone is happy, except for the ordinary folk, who through no fault of their own, find themselves living in the nightmare of someone else's plan-B. Never forget, the majority of those who are forced to live in this twilight-world, are decent, hardworking, God-fearing folk, who do not deserve to have this torment imposed upon them. But it's the poor bloody coppers who have to police the resulting shithole, and politicians have the temerity to accuse the police of being institutionally racist. Politicians love grandstanding, and racism is one of those trigger words that shuts down debate, they can speak whatever drivel they like, and no one will challenge them, or question their facts, for fear of being branded racist, which doesn't eliminate racism, it just sends it underground, which of itself begs a big question. Racism is a cancer that eats away at the interior harmony of society undermining freedom, it must be confronted and opposed, not just through legislation, but by education, and by making it so completely unacceptable, as to render the individual engaging in it an outcast. But the State cannot and must not rule over people's thoughts or feelings, that route ends by hiding hate and building resentment, eventually we will face the nineteen-thirties all over again.'

Tony said, 'You should write to the newspapers...'

Peter sneered, 'Yeah, 'cos that's what black people need, another white guy telling them what to do. Most of what needs fixing within the black community, can only be identified and put right by the black community, all we can and should do, is encourage and facilitate that process, then get out the way. Our contribution must be to combat white-racism, by identifying, and correcting its root causes; but racism is a two-way street, it is not only white people who are racist, or who display prejudice, unfortunately it is an all-too-common human trait. I just don't get it, how can you hate, or dismiss another human being because you don't like their skin tone, it's fucking insane. I'm doing a Father John, and wandering off the path...'

Peter drank some more cider, ate some crisps, then continued, 'So, why stay? You stay for the Miracle, you come back each day in the hope of encountering the Miracle; that small wonder, that tiny light in the darkness, it keeps pulling you back, and hope dances in your heart.'

Peter paused, refilled his glass, and Tony noted the smile that passed between Mac and Father John.

'The Miracle? Every now and again you come across something special, something so fantastic, it takes your breath away. It's always the same story, a man and a woman, usually immigrants, married, God-fearing, law-abiding, decent folk, each holding down two or more jobs, working all hours to provide for their family, working hard to put their kids through private schools. Living grimly determined lives, their hope and confidence in the future is powerful enough to influence and inspire their children, who motivated by the belief inculcated into them by their parents, that there are no limits on what they can achieve through hard work and dedication, they go on to become doctors, lawyers, lecturers, teachers... builders not wreckers. Roses in a bed of weeds, refusing to buy into the political lie, to give into the despair, to accept the apathy. It's for them that you come back, for the hope that it brings, and the wretchedness it dispels, that's the Miracle, a true God-given miracle.'

There were tears in Peter's eyes when he stopped speaking, no one broke the silence that followed, until Father John said, 'Does this mean you believe in God?'

'In your dreams.'

They all laughed. Mac stood up and refilled their glasses. Another period of silence followed, Mac looked at Tony and said, 'Nothing is ever straightforward, we all make the mistake of accepting the over-simplification of life, because it quickly leads to generalisation, which is where we find our comfort-zone. It makes life easier, we don't have to think too deeply, which is why politicians and policymakers encourage it, but it always comes with unforeseen consequences. That's why I rejected that life and came here. I grew tired of the bullshit, the lies, the silver-tongued orators who say I care, I feel your pain, I can make a difference, but what they really mean is, once I'm elected, and wallowing in taxpayer emoluments, screw you. The greatest political lie? It's when some politicians claim to have an affinity with the working-class. You look at them and wonder, how that can be? Given most politicians privileged childhoods, how did that come about? Did they spend a wet Thursday afternoon in February talking to daddy's gardener? Because if they did, it's as close as they cared to get to the working-class, who, by the way, are an endangered species. Politicians live in houses we can only dream of, they earn salaries four times the average income, and socialise within an elite coterie. Their background and lives are far removed from the rest of us, yet they persist in peddling this lie, how do we respond? We demonstrate the futility of hope over experience, by hanging our aspirations and our future on that dissimulation. No wonder expectations shrink, and hope fades, cynicism ceases to be a vice, and becomes a redeeming virtue. Welcome to the mendacious world of the social-Marxists, whose principles take on a wraith-like substance.'

Mac drank deeply from his tankard, then said, 'Churchill, thought socialism was, "The philosophy of failure, the creed of ignorance, and the gospel of envy." It seems to me; you could apply that to any of the political parties in Parliament today. These days idealism is nothing more than dignified inertia, for most it's a way to publicly display their moral superiority, they will loudly condemn this or that event, or any adjudged transgression of the zeitgeist, but they won't actually do anything about it. It's a bit like people who put a sticker on their car that reads, no more nukes, that's it, that's all they do, they sit back and feel smug at their own perceived righteousness. They look for the approbation that they believe their virtue-waving deserves. But when Western governments try to prevent rogue states from developing nuclear weapons, they sneer and condemn what they see as Western imperialism. No more nukes? It's hypocrisy writ large, for they do not accuse Western governments of self-interested imperialism when they lecture foreign governments on social justice issues. Condemnation without action is futile, and pointless. Don't protest unless you are also willing to provide a solution and act upon it.'

Mac paused, and clearly addressing his remarks to Simon, said, 'I know that some think that I left the police because of a particular case, I didn't. That wasn't the reason. It dawned on me that I didn't want to be a social-dustman anymore. The futility of trying to keep the lid on the dustbin of society… I saw it as my duty to prevent dignity being bought and sold, and innocence surrendered, to prevent them becoming the commodities of crime… because I dared to hope that I could make a difference. But they took that from me. I couldn't accept a system that consisted of one set of ephemeral rules for the powerful, and laws that were only applied to the rest, why should I be blamed for the failings of the social-Marxists who treat deceit as meritorious? It all seemed so pointless, I stopped caring, and when you do that, you cease being a real police officer and become a uniform-carrier, it was time to step aside. I needed something else, so having protested, I found a solution, and acted. Friends advised against me leaving, mostly because I would lose my pension, but I couldn't face another ten years of despair, nor the futility of it. I had options, I had just inherited this farm, Liz and I knew we could find the life we wanted farming here; and even though Liz was unable to finish the journey with me, it is still worth going to the end of the road, wherever it leads. The life that I have now, is plain, peaceful, and simple, but not simplistic. Nor is it a life that ducks responsibility, I haven't opted out, it's just a different way of living, and it demands of me a quiet fidelity. I live life to the rhythm of the seasons, which calls for art, it requires reverence and empathy, it is a constructive, not a destructive existence. And that, is my answer.'

Peter and Father John nodded in agreement.

Mac continued, 'Tell Cartwright, my answer is no. That part of my life is over, I'm not interested. And as for his clumsy appeal to my sense of duty and honour, tell him it might have worked, if it had come from someone who actually knows the meaning of such words, someone with integrity.'

Tony threw a confused look at Peter, who shook his head to dismiss the obvious question, before pouring another drink. Simon left the table. Tony said, 'Now might be a good time for me to go home.'

Chapter Eleven

They emerged from their workshops at the same time, nodded at each other, and walked off toward the far end of the garden, beyond the yard, to the table under the old, twisted, wisteria.

'You know what? I think being here has been good for, John,' said Peter.

Mac stopped, turned and looked at Peter, saying, 'Good for you as well.'

'True, but remember when John arrived, he was pale, hunched over, he had the posture of a man who spent his entire life leaning over a desk.'

'Which is exactly how he spent his life,' Mac frowned.

'I know. If I may continue? He was overweight; out of breath just walking from the kitchen to the veg-patch. Hell, most took him for being around five-foot-eight, so slovenly did he hold himself, and not the six feet he stands now.'

Mac, wondering if there was a point to this, said, 'Well nothing like fresh air and physical labour to turn a body round. What was it our old PTI used to say? If you want to lose weight, get on the Royal Marine diet...'

Peter and Mac spoke aloud and in unison, 'Eat less. Move more.'

Laughing, they approached the table where Father John was arranging the plates and the food for lunch.

'Something amusing you, want to share, or am I the butt of another joke?'

'Yes, and no,' Mac blurted out, laughing.

'What?'

'Yes, we were discussing you, but no, you were not the butt of a joke. Pete was commenting on how well you look, now you have lost weight and gotten fitter.'

'Really?'

Peter smiled and said, 'Yes, you dozy old prelate. I am proud of the changes in you. You've slimmed down, got fitter, you're standing taller, you look healthy, your appearance no longer displays what we both feared most... a physical manifestation of your impending demise.'

'Well thank you... I think.'

Mac said, 'What culinary delights have you conjured for us today?'

'Beans on toast.'

'Really?'

'No. Do you think after all those years in Rome that would be the extent of my repertoire?'

'I like beans on toast,' said Peter.

Father John threw his hands in the air in mock disgust. It was a fine meal. Father John ensured that various cold dishes kept coming, and they ate, drank, and talked through the afternoon and beyond. Their discussions centred on Simon, the news he brought, and its implications.

Sunset lingered long, night crept in, but the heat remained, the three of them had partaken a little too much of the fruit of the brewer's craft.

'Are you sure about this, Mac? We'll back you, whatever you

decide. I have to say, Simon's offer is tempting. Suspicions have been niggling away at each of us for years, and this is a golden opportunity to get some questions answered,' said Father John.

'John… I'm sure; I'll ring Cartwright in the morning, I won't lumber Simon, you know what Cartwright's like. Seeking answers to our questions will not change what happened, there is no justice to be had, not in the present system, you know my views on that, so what would be the point, merely to satisfy the idle curiosity of three ageing detectives?'

'Ageing? Speak for yourself,' Father John, laughed, 'there is a theory that a truth exposed, a truth spoken aloud, can never be hidden again, it will demand justice, like a festering wound it demands treatment.'

'John, we're being railroaded. If we decide to do something about it, it should be at a time and place of our choosing. Cartwright is trying to fence us in, to leave us little choice, I really hate being manipulated. He wants us to do his dirty work for him. If we succeed, he gets the kudos, this is nothing more than an attempt to further his own ambitions. If we fail, well it's at arm's length, he can deny that it's got anything to do with him. We do the work and take all the risk; it's win-win for him, but for us it can only end one way. You know that if we reopen this investigation, it is quite likely we will have to eliminate a certain individual, and possibly several others. I would like some answers, but not at that price. My life is here on the farm with all of you. I've stood my watch and have earned the right to a quiet existence. I'm on a different road. Cartwright will just have to do his own dirty work. The only thing we need to do is protect Simon, he needs to understand what that bastard is really like. Do you know that Cartwright had the gall to tell him that we were friends?'

Father John said, 'I'm not surprised, the further up he climbs, the more dishonourable he gets. Mac, Peter and I will back you, whatever you decide. Peter agrees with you, he thinks we should stay away from this case... I will not describe the things he suggested doing to Cartwright. The only thing that I care to repeat, and that I could decipher from his slurred utterances, was that we should send Cartwright a short but pithy message, namely, "*Futue te ipsum et caballum tuum.*" I know, education can be a two-edged sword.'

Peter, who until this moment, had been slumped across the table, sat up and said, 'What the fuck you two talking about? You sound like a right pair of... bollocks... I'm going for a piss.'

He staggered to his feet, knocking the chair over, and lurched off in the general direction of the vegetable patch.

Father John looked at Mac, smiled and said, 'That's it for me, I'm off to bed. Now Pete's awake, the conversation's going to get too philosophical.' Taking his leave, he bowed theatrically.

Mac, laughing, called after him, 'Tomorrow, after you've picked them, make sure that you really wash those lettuces.' Father John turned back and looked over at Peter who was trying but failing to stand still while he watered a couple of rows of good-looking vegetables. He walked away with Mac's laughter lightening the weight of a drowsy summer's night.

Chapter Twelve

He remembered spring, when bluebells paraded the woodland floor, and sunlight dappled the ground, its lacy-shadows accentuating their little blue-helmets, a heady scent coloured the dusty path, which was delineated by a two-foot swathe of green and white on either side of its rusty-brown surface, ramsoms made the air thick, pungent and aromatic, blackbird dissidence filled the branches, and the old stone barn, glimpsed through the trees, had looked promising.

Now it was summer, and he was back. The foliage thicker, the woodland floor fuller, and the insects busier; rampant vegetation provided the cover for him to leave the path and investigate. One door had been taken down, and was in the middle of the barn, laid flat on top of two heavy wooden trestles, it was clearly being worked on, the other was still in place, the roof was intact, and the interior of the barn was dry and freshly whitewashed. He walked around to the side that abutted the field overlooking the farmstead.

The bleached bones of a broken wagon leaned against the wall, upright, half-buried in the ground, partially hidden by the long grass beside the barn. Its weathered ribs cadaverously reaching out, he shuddered. He knew that for some this represented a comforting link with the past, a pleasing continuity of human activity, but he saw only moulder and putrefaction. He felt nothing but abhorrence for the past, recoiling he moved away, his face grimaced with loathing, he quickly returned to the path, and continued his investigative tramp through the woods. He hated disorder, and to him the countryside was nothing, but havoc made manifest, a tangle of verdure, insects, birds and animals. *What draff lies within the leaf mould, decomposing and half-eaten? Fuck… if it flies, or walks, it shits here,* his own thoughts unnerved him, he looked down at his shoes in disgust, bile rising, he swallowed. He should never have left the city, and the trees seemed to agree, as they reached down towards him in the wind.

'We shoot trespassers in these parts,' said Mac, stepping onto the path, his shotgun levelled at the man's chest, 'well, if it isn't my old friend, Mason,' his voice dripping with sarcasm and menace, 'what brings you to my woods?'

Mason checked himself, the wind had covered Mac's approach, he felt his initial shock pass, and regained control. 'Put it down, Mac. You won't shoot me.'

'No, but I will,' growled Peter.

Mac smiled as he saw the look of fear pass over Mason's face, and said, 'What are you doing here?'

'I didn't come alone.'

'If you're looking for help from the two Muppets you brought with you, then you're in deep-shit, pal,' snarled Peter, before laughing.

Mac looked at Peter, who said, 'What? He won't tell us anything, and if he does it'll be bullshit, he's broken the deal, let's kill the fucker, and have done with it.'

Mac looked at Mason, then said, 'Perhaps we should.'

'Now you're talking,' said Peter, stepping closer and off to one side, to avoid hitting Mac. 'Fuck you,' replied Mason.

Peter moved quickly; the butt of his gun struck Mason an

angled downward blow on the outside of his right knee. Mason fell to the ground in pain, he gulped in lungsful of air, his face pressed into the damp moist earth, repulsed he shot upright, supported his weight on his outstretched arms, whilst he shifted onto his left side.

He looked up at Mac accusingly, and sobbed as he spoke, 'It's you who broke the agreement. All three of you are here together, which means only one thing, you're reopening the investigation.'

Mac crouched down his face level with Mason's, 'No we're not, John and Peter have both retired, and now live here. You're watching Cartwright; I told him to do his own dirty work… you've bugged my phone, those two aren't muscle, they're technical support.' He looked at Peter, 'That's why they were so easy to take out.'

'And I though we hadn't lost it,' said Peter, laughing.

'I rang Brian, from Anna's mobile this morning, you didn't pick it up… where's the vehicle? You're here to find a relay point. You're in danger of arousing suspicion, so you need to move out of the area. Where is it?'

Mason spat on the ground in front of Mac's boot but did not reply.

'No one knows you're here, do they? Hell, you're so secretive you don't even tell yourself where you're going, maybe I should let Pete have his fun.'

Mason's face twisted into a mask of hatred as he looked up at Mac, 'Fuck you.'

Peter slammed his right foot into Mason's knee and brought the full weight of his body down on it, there was a loud snap. Mason's scream sent the crows at the end of the wood into rampaging dissent above the fields. Mason sobbed; Peter moved to place his foot on the knee again. Mason whimpered, 'Please don't… please… it's parked up by the ruined watermill. By the stream, in the woods opposite.'

Peter stepped back and moved round behind, Mason. He expertly brought the butt of the shotgun down at an angle on Mason's neck. Mason slumped forward. 'Nice one, Pete. He's unconscious, now we'll have to carry him out.'

'I broke his fucking leg, we were going to have to carry him anyway… shit that felt good, made me feel better.' Peter placed his right foot under Mason's left side, and flipped Mason onto his back, he opened Mason's jacket removing a .40 Walther P99 semi-automatic pistol from a shoulder holster, 'He always was old-school.'

Mac said, 'It'll kill you all the same. Found his knife?'

'Hold your horses… here it is… beauty!' Peter held up a Sig Sauer X5, Emperor Scorpion, tactical folding knife. 'Good combat knife, I'll give the fucker his due, he knows his knives, and how to use one,' Peter opened the blade and examined it admiringly, 'I'm keeping both.'

'You're still not right in the head,' laughed Mac. They left the wood and followed the deer path into the scrub at the back of the barn Mason had inspected earlier, entered the field and walked back to the farmhouse, dragging Mason between them.

Father John glared at Mac, 'It's alright, John, he's just uncon-scious.' They dropped him to the ground by Mac's Land Rover.

'One of them has come round, the other is still out cold.' Father John shot an accusing look at Peter, who, grinning like a schoolboy, moved to the other side of the vehicle. He opened the rear door and pulled the unfortunate spy out by his hair, dragged him back round to Mac, and threw him down on top of his supine boss.

'I … I…'

'Was only following orders,' finished Peter, 'don't insult me.'

Mac stepped between them, and said to Peter, 'Take John,

and find the van, bring it back here, extract anything useful, then take it to… Bob the Builder's, we can hide it there. I'll deal with these… gentlemen. Oh, and find Mason's car… is it still that old Mercedes?' Mac looked at the young agent, who nodded. 'Pete, search Mason, find his car keys, and bring it here before you move the van, they'll need it to get back to London.'

'Fine by me, but you're making a mistake, kill him now, or kill him later, but before this is over, we're going to have to kill him.'

Father John, sighed.

'What? You think I'm wrong, that I've reverted… these are evil men, they will murder us all to protect their interests. I'm not a bloody… I know what Mason is, and what he is capable of doing, and I will do anything to protect my family and friends, even if that means cancelling his contract, and I'm no stranger to that.' Peter glowered at the cowering man by his feet.

'We're done here … it's over. Now go and find the Merc.' Mac watched them both leave, he turned and looked down at the spook quaking in fear at his feet. 'When he returns with the car, drive Mason, and your friend, back to London, if Mason regains consciousness, tell him I'm not interested in raking over the past, he has broken the deal we had, but I am willing to reinstate it, the next move is up to him. Tell him his mistake has cost him the van and your secret-squirrel kit.'

Mac paused, lightened his tone, and said, 'You need to understand something, you and your young friend can never speak of this to anyone, just knowing who we are, and Mason's connection to us, will get you both killed. Request a transfer.'

Taking a piece of paper from the dashboard of the Land Rover, Mac wrote down a name, and handed it to the cowering agent. 'Contact this man, tell him I sent you, tell him what little you know, and he will arrange for you to be posted elsewhere, now before you go, you can fill in a few blanks for me.'

Chapter Thirteen

'**W**hy are you up so early?'

'Morning, Pete. Didn't see you there... tea in the pot?'

'Just brewed, help yourself.'

Mac poured himself a cup of tea. 'I'm in a bit of a rush, going to catch the six o'clock to London. What are you doing up so early?'

'Couldn't sleep... this business has me worried. It's not just me anymore, there's, Katie and April...'

'I know, that's why I'm off to London...'

'What for?'

'To find Mason, I need to speak to him, face to face, he must understand that we have no intention of breaking the agreement. He is liable to do something dumb, something which will require us to take a course of action, that John will not approve of...'

'I've been thinking about that. How about we book him an appointment with an industrial-mincer on a pig-farm in, Kent?'

'It may come to that,' laughed Mac. 'You really are...'

'What? Barry owes both of us, he'll do it, you know he will.'

'Well, it hasn't come to that... not yet.'

'Fine, let's go see, Mason.'

'Just me, I need to keep it civilised.'

'Okay, but let me contact, Barry.'

'Not yet.'

'Okay… have it your way. Just one little problem, how are you going to find Mason?'

'I'm going to see the Turk.'

'Bekir Demir?' Mac and Peter turned to see Father John standing the doorway, 'If I remember rightly, he's seriously dangerous.'

'I'll be fine, John. He owes me…'

Peter interrupted, 'He owes Mac large. Mac is quite safe, otherwise I wouldn't let him go.'

'Why are you meeting such a notorious criminal?'

'I'll explain later,' said Peter. 'Mac, we better get going if you want to catch the six o'clock train. Grab that toast, I'll drive you to the station.'

It was after midday when Mac alighted from the number twelve bus at Camberwell Green, he crossed the road, and walked back in the direction of Kennington, then entered a side alley that curved round behind the shops, opening the door at the rear of a mini-cab office, he took the near vertical stairs to the first floor.

He paused to catch his breath, and to allow his eyes to adjust to the dim corridor, which he followed to the front of the building. He opened the last door on the right and entered a small office. Directly in front of him was a desk, behind which sat a pretty, young woman in her early-twenties, to his left, sitting on a worn sofa were two, overweight Turks in their mid-thirties, both wearing identical shell suits, with matching gold chains around their necks, he didn't recognise them.

They rose to meet him, one of them spoke, his accent, Bermondsey meets Ankara, 'You lost?'

Before Mac could reply, the young girl came round the desk,

saying, 'Uncle Mac,' she embraced him.

'Meryem,' he hugged her back, 'You're beautiful, and grown so tall.'

She stepped back laughing, waved the two men away, they sat down. 'How good it is to see you again.'

'I'm surprised you remember me.'

'How can I forget the man who saved my life. Oh, Uncle Mac.' she embraced him again. The door behind her desk opened, and a man around Mac's age and build entered the office.

Mac said, 'Yaman.' The use of Demir's nickname, restricted only to very close friends and family, made the two young men stand in respect. Mac noted their bulges; they were carrying, and from the shape, 9mm Sig Sauer or Glock, he surmised.

'Mac. In the name of the Prophet, peace be upon him. Mac, my brother, welcome.' To Mac's surprise, Demir, embraced him, 'Come in.' He waved him through to the main office, the room he entered took him by surprise, it was an exact copy of a large Edwardian study, 'Tea, coffee? Have you eaten?'

'Tea, please, and no I haven't eaten yet… you've redecorated?'

'I has, you like?'

Mac nodded, as he looked about the room.

'Sits, sits. Meryem, tea, and send them twos down to restaurant, lunch, the special. Mac is good to see you again. What bring you back to London, my friend?'

Mac began to reply when one of the young men came into the office and spoke to Demir in Turkish. Demir, stood up, 'Come, come, is ready, let us to eat.' He led Mac through another door at the back of the office, and down a narrow set of stairs to the restaurant.

Mac said, 'This is well hidden.'

'Yes. Very privates. Only for special friend and familys, and of course for you my good friend.' They sat at a table for four, in a private room off the main dining room, and waited in silence while many courses were served, accompanied by hummus, and a minty dip with cucumber, the name of which, Mac could not recall.

'I'm looking for, Mason.'

Demir visibly paled, drank some water, and said, 'Bad man, very bad, why you wants with him?'

'I need to speak to him; I have to stop him from doing something that could harm me and my family.'

'That bastards, you know what he do to me? He come to me, he say, Yaman… Yaman? He not know me, he call me this? Then he tell me I must help him; I must bring some childrens from Turkey. I say no, I no do this very bad thing. He say, you do this, and he go. Two days, I get a call from my uncle in Turkey, my familys are visit by men, Jihadis, very bad men. So, I do this thing for him, I no want do this, but my familys. He bastards.'

Demir drank some more water. 'Mac, I helps you, he kill my familys, yes?'

'No, I promise you, he will never find out how I found him.'

'This talk you have, he no agree, it go bad, you kill him?'

'Probably… yes, if he doesn't agree to what I ask, I will have no choice but to kill him. Peter wants me to call Mad Barry.'

For a while they ate in silence, enjoying the food, each dish a culinary adventure. Demir thought for quite a while, before saying, 'That Peter, he a good man, you listens to him. I owe you much, my wife, my daughter. Mac, I do this for you. Now, we eats and drinks more.'

Mac enjoyed a fine meal. Demir was as entertaining as ever; a contradiction, a fiercely loyal family man, to whom fidelity and honour was everything, he lived plainly and simply. His wealth was used to help others, there was nothing showy or flash about him. He had been raised in poverty, which gave him an abiding respect for money, and for what it could do, and he did much with it. He paid for a school and a clinic in his village in Turkey, having lost family in a terrible earthquake he donated generously to all and any relief funds. He also paid for the university education of at least six students every year.

Mac could not help but admire him, yet he was a criminal, the head of one of the biggest and wealthiest organised crime families in Europe, which dealt in guns and drugs. The mix of old-fashioned morality, duty, and honour, contrasted with his criminality, in a way that was beguiling, and seemingly virtuous. It always left Mac conflicted.

Their conversation was interrupted by the arrival of a crisp young man, wearing a dark Savile Row suit, he was introduced to Mac, 'This my nephews, Puriz. He my brother son, he good boy. He learning from me, the business, when I not here, he take over. Puriz, this my good friend, Mac.'

'I am honoured to meet you,' Puriz said, and bowed as Mac stood up to shake his hand, 'I have heard so much about you, and the debt we owe you.'

Mac bowed his head in appreciation, noting the accent, neutral, educated, and the voice, confident. Puriz sat down joining them at the table, he declined the offer of food, but ordered a coffee.

'I have been brought in to legitimise the family business, within five years we will be seventy-five-percent legal.'

'And the other twenty-five-percent?'

Puriz smiled, 'If you shrink your business base then you have to aim for the high-end of the market. Complete control and supply, whatever the product; and there may come a day when we need an edge, it pays not to forget, nor to abandon your roots.'

Demir smiled proudly, 'He's clever boy, will do much good for familys.'

Mac said, 'Indeed, but what does Meryem have to say about this?'

'This business not for womans, she agree.'

'Just like that? Knowing Meryem, I am surprised.'

Puriz laughed, 'My uncle has had to agree to her conditions, no arranged marriage, she can marry the man of her choice, and when she leaves to start her own business, it will be funded by the family, but it will be wholly owned and controlled by her.'

'That's more like the Meryem I know,' laughed Mac.

Demir threw his hands up in mock horror, 'Whats can I do, she like her mother.' His face was a picture of pride.

When the laughter died down, Puriz said, 'I'm sorry, but I overheard you talking, what is eight-ball?'

Demir looked at Mac and nodded. Mac said, 'Your uncle will not answer that question while I am present, not because he fears I will break his confidence, but because he does not want to put me in a position where I may feel conflicted. I will tell you what I know about eight-ball, how much is true, and how much is braggadocio I am in no position to judge, having had no first-hand experience. I learned of its existence whilst serving as a police officer in this part of London. I heard of it from several sources, over a number of years, and the stories told were remarkably similar, even allowing for some embellishment.'

Puriz nodded, and Mac continued, 'There's a pig farm in Kent, it is run by Barry Butcher, Mad-B, if ever a man's surname fitted his profession, it's Barry's. He is one evil-bastard. He used to be Tony-the-Greek's minder and problem solver, although Barry's notion of problem solving was remarkably consistent, and never in danger of taxing his grey matter. Anyway, when Tony-the-Greek's life of excess finally caught up with him, the five families held a meeting to discuss what should be done with Barry. The problem being, that although it is useful to employ a well-trained savage psychopath, it's a bit like owning a fire extinguisher, when needed, absolutely indispensable, but most of the time it's a redundant lump, only good for holding the door open, which sums up Barry, he may be a certifiable bovine barbarian, but he's not an inanimate object, and is prone to boredom, and that's a liability when you're trying to stay under the radar of the boys-in-blue. So, what to do? Well, they could murder him, but if they failed in the attempt, he would come after them, and given his background and low cunning, he would probably succeed in killing them all. The next option was for one of the families to employ him, but since that would give his new employers a fearsome edge, that was also ruled out. Which left only one realistic option, they all employ him.'

Mac paused to sip some water, then continued, 'The farm had been used for several years as a place to park... dilemmas. The old farm manager was due to retire, and had been asking for a replacement to train, before he left for a well-earned rest in the Algarve. They decided it was a job for Barry, and he took to it, like polar bear to seal. He surprised everyone by proving to be a fine pig farmer, setting up and running a pedigree breeding program, and the families have between them, been able help him maintain contact with his old way of life, which has prevented boredom from creeping in. Shortly after taking over from the previous manager... who never did make it to the Algarve.'

Mac paused to frown at Demir, 'A bit of a saving there on pension and retirement benefits... let's face it, he literally knew where all the bodies were buried.'

Demir, laughed.

Mac continued, 'Barry came up with the game of eight-ball. A game only to be used on the worst offenders. It was first tried out on a low-life drug dealer, who had raped the seven-year-old granddaughter of the Green family, Solly, the head of the family was none too pleased, and wanted biblical vengeance, and Barry's game fitted the bill. The rapist was naked, tied to a wooden dinning chair by his legs and arms, the seat of the chair had been modified, all but three inches were left, the rest having been cut away in an arc. The chair was attached to chains, and raised off the ground, so that the seat of the chair was at shoulder height. With me so far?'

Puriz nodded, Mac continued, 'On a table, close to the chair, were eight black football-socks, tied into the foot end of each sock was a pool ball. Each of the contestants, which on this occasion included the child's mother and grandmother, placed one-thousand pounds in cash on the table, before selecting a sock. Trousering one-thousand, Barry divided the remaining money between two bowls, into one he placed one-thousand pounds, and into the other the remaining six-thousand pounds. That done, the game could begin, a dice was used to decide the running order, and the contestants lined up in front of the chair, before taking a turn. A little like conkers... have you heard of the game of conkers?'

Puriz nodded, and said, 'Yes, I was sent to a boarding school in Sussex.'

Mac said, 'Okay, well they each had a go at striking the victim's genitals, this continued until he lost consciousness, in his case it took twelve minutes. The player whose blow rendered him unconscious received their one-thousand-pound stake back, then all the contestants untied their, by now, bloodied socks, and the one containing the eight-ball, won the six-grand.'

Puriz said, 'What happened to the low-life?'

'Well, that's why they hold it on a pig-farm, when he came round, Barry dropped him into an industrial-mincer, and the following day he was fed to the pigs. Steam clean the mincer, and hey presto, no evidence.'

Demir laughed, 'Another reason not to eat the flesh of the pig.'

Puriz, nodding his approval, said, "Vengeance and punishment; primitive, it works for me.'

Mac said, 'Primitive, undoubtedly. I call it evil, and I guess the five families thought so too; after, for want of a better expression, that trial-run, they decided that as a punishment it was to be reserved for only the worst cases, and then, only following the unanimous agreement of the heads of all five families.'

Puriz smiled at his uncle, then said, 'That's as it should be,' he shook Mac's hand again, and making his apologies, left to keep an appointment.

Mac and Demir resumed their conversation about Mason. 'I don't know where he live. I try find him once, but he a ghost. There a girl.' Demir wrote down an address and handed it to, Mac, 'She know where, but this a bad place, you takes my men?'

'No, if I do that, he will know how I came by his address,'

Demir shrugged, then nodded his agreement.

'Thanks for this,' Mac put the piece of paper in his pocket, 'I doubt he will do anything; Pete already broke his leg. I'll be fine.'

'That a bad place, Mac. He a bad man, the girl, she a good girl, until he… now is shame. That bastards kill you; I swear I find him and kill him. This is honour.'

They embraced, and Mac took his leave. He wanted to reach the estate before nightfall; he needed to look around, to reacquaint himself with the terrain. From the description Demir gave him, he thought he knew who the girl was, but hoped to hell he was wrong.

Mac spent the rest of the daylight hours on the roof of a tower block in Peckham, it overlooked the low-rise he was interested in, he had seen enough, it was dark, time to start hunting. He recalled the words of the constable who had taught him how to walk the beat, "*Some say this city is infectious, that it will draw you in, enfold, amuse, captivate, and entertain you, for it's a cultural Eden. But you will never see or feel such things. For you work with a view of her underbelly, you'll see her true face, and that will change you forever. This city will steal your innocence, and leave you scarred by suspicion and mistrust, but if it starts to rob you of hope, leave, for that's too high a price to pay. go before it takes your soul.*" He entered the block from the rear, navigated the long dank dark corridor, the lights having been smashed some time ago, he tried not to think about what was underfoot, especially the squishy bits, and forced himself not to gag on the smell of urine, used tampons, condoms, nappies, dog shit, vomit, blood, and other detritus, Mac hoped the puddles were not too deep.

Ahead, in the dimly lit foyer, he could see three youths, one black, and two of mixed-race, all about seventeen or eighteen, part of the feral group he had watched earlier, dealing, squabbling and terrifying the rest of the miserable inhabitants of this hellhole, laughingly called social housing. Mac could think of nothing less neighbourly.

A fourth, a young white man, taller and a couple of years older than the other three, dressed in the unimaginative uniform of the average carnal-hut inhabitant, crossed the foyer, he stopped and spoke quietly to the others, money changed hands, and the white man handed over a small wrap, undoubtedly drugs, most likely crack-cocaine. The white man said something to the others, who laughed, they appeared to be well acquainted, but whatever was said was incomprehensible to Mac, the echo-chamber of the corridor, the accent, South London meets Montego Bay, and the throb of the ghetto-blaster, meant it was impossible for him to make any sense of the little he overheard.

He waited in the shadows, after five minutes the white man left, taking the lift, and the other three settled down. Two of the youths immediately squatted down trying to light a crack pipe, one, who turned out to be the largest of the three, slouched against the wall by the lift, playing with a butterfly knife, keeping time to the rhythm of the bass cacophony emanating from their boombox. Mac guessed that they were there to tax anyone entering the block, he had neither the time, nor the inclination to subject himself to such humiliation. In just over a second, he closed the distance between the darkness of the corridor and the half-light of the foyer, the youth with the knife had barely time to raise it in Mac's direction, the hand holding the knife was turned back and twisted at the wrist, the arm straight-locked, and pulled down and out to the side.

Mac's left knee shattered the elbow, still holding the hand with the knife, he spun the youth, throwing him onto the other two, who were rising to meet his challenge, this movement, jerked, twisted and destroyed the joint. Mac pressed home his attack, an elbow strike to the jaw rendered one unconscious, the other, who was trying to stand up under the weight of the first youth, was pacified by a well-aimed kick to the left side of his ribs, three inches below the armpit.

Mac took the stairs, past experience told him that the lift was nothing more than a mobile urinal, which together with the vomit, blood, and other leavings, turned it into a metal Petri dish, and he wasn't sure his immune system was up to speed, it had been years since he worked in this part of London.

He cautiously stepped onto the balcony of the fourth floor, looked left and right, there was no one there, the barely audible screams from below were probably nothing new, and did not even merit an inquisitive twitch of the curtains, it wasn't that people weren't interested, around here curiosity gets you killed.

He moved quietly along the balcony until he found the front door of the flat, there was no lock, just a hole where a Yale once resided. He pushed the door open with his left foot, waited, listened, then in one movement entered and closed the door behind him. It was a standard single-bedroom flat, a small kitchen to the left, directly opposite a small bathroom, ahead the living room, a doorway to the left into the bedroom, there wasn't an internal door in the flat, he guessed that they had been removed and sold to buy drugs.

He quickly checked all the rooms, they were unoccupied, and devoid of any furniture, he entered the sitting room at the back of the flat. Adjusting to the gloom he began to take in the space, an old sticky blanket was strung across the window blocking the light, he undid one end, it fell to the floor with a slimy thud, a greasy broken sofa was against the wall facing the window. The bare floorboards stained and littered with takeaway cartons and pizza boxes, and in front of the sofa a small table contained two empty vodka bottles, a pub ashtray with a pyramid of butts, and a bong made from an old lemonade bottle, in the corner by the window an old apple crate. Mac surmised that it once supported a television set, which had probably gone the way of the doors.

Slumped on the sofa was a young woman, thirty-going-on-seventy, her drug-addled and emaciated body was weeping blood from the eyes, an existence defined and overwhelmed by addiction and disease.

Mac recognised her, he wondered how a person, once so full of hope and potential, could pass into this world of perdition, how does a life of joy descend into one of hopelessness? He checked, there was a pulse, she was alive, but in a place away from the present, she had gone to a world far from this reality, looking around he could not blame her. He couldn't help but notice how thin she was, a reminder of a time when she was healthier and well-fed.

It was clear to him that Mason did not come here anymore and had not done so for some time. Mac left the flat, closing the door behind him. He walked down to the second floor; on the ground-floor paramedics and police were dealing with the victims of his attitude rectification. Mac turned onto the second-floor balcony and followed the walkway to the next block, before dropping down to ground level, he moved towards a road leading away from the estate, keeping close to the building line.

'You seen her? You seen what that motherfucker did?'

Mac turned, a black man, about his height, but twenty years younger stood ten feet behind him. 'Leroy?'

'Yeah, thought you left the Old Bill?'

'I have.'

'What brings you here, Mac?'

'I'm looking for guy called, Mason. I heard that he had a… your sister… they were… I was hoping she could tell me where to find him. But I guess not. What happened?'

'Not here. I only got out two weeks ago, I'm not in with the new crew. My car's over there, let's get out of here.'

Mac followed Leroy out of the estate, and into a side road, they got into a blue BMW, and drove off towards Camberwell.

Leroy turned down a side road off the high street and parked at the back of a kebab shop. They entered via the back door, passing through the crowded kitchen, Leroy led Mac to a room at the back of the main cafe.

'It's cool, the Greeks, they know me.' Both ordered a coffee and some chips; they had lived too long in this part of London to risk a burger.

Mac said, 'You first.'

Leroy said, 'After you left the cops… sorry, I never thanked you for getting me that job… for years things were good, then Sasha met Mason, he gave her all the pretty things she wanted, but then he started to force her to do him favours, sleep with other men. I tried to warn her off, shit… I tried to get her away from him. Next thing I know, I'm being investigated, for nothing, I did nothing. I tried to get word to you, but the bomboclaat I told, the fat detective inspector at Dulwich, the one who always claimed he was your friend, never contacted you. The day of my trial, I'm taking the bus to court, it stops in traffic, and I look down and I see him in a car with Mason. I see him getting money from Mason.'

Leroy sucked his teeth, 'I got five years for nothing. Then on the day I get released, the raasclaat has me arrested, I stay in custody, and six months later I'm given another five years, for another something I didn't do. I spent six years inside for nothing, for trying to stop Mason abusing my sister. While I'm inside he has her turning tricks for him, he pays her well, then he gets her into drugs… you've seen her. Mac, she's only got weeks left… fucking AIDS.'

'Leroy, I am sorry. I didn't know. I promise you I will deal with Silky, that fat bastard's no friend of mine. But right now, I need to find Mason, can you help?'

Leroy drank his coffee and went off to get a refill. He returned with another cup for Mac, they sat drinking, eventually Leroy said, 'Why?'

'I have some questions that need answering, and I want him to understand what the consequences will be, if he decides to take a particular course of action.'

'That might be difficult…'

'Look don't worry, I'm sure I'll locate him. You take care of your sister.' Mac took out his wallet.

'Thanks Mac, but there's no need, I got cash... that's not it, I know where Mason is, but you're not... it's not going to happen. Not now... not ever.'

'Ah... not entirely bad news.'

'You saw Sasha, I couldn't let it go, he fucked both of us. I got six years, she got life... what's left of it. I learned from some my old crew where he was living, and I've been watching the place since I got out. This morning he turned up in the back of a private ambulance, his leg in plaster, they carried him in; around one in the afternoon a delivery guy dropped off a pizza, that was it, nothing else in or out.'

'Where?'

'The flat above the offices in South Side breaker's yard. A couple of homeboys I'm tight with work there, they got me some casual work. A couple of hours after the pizza was delivered, I got into his place, I went in real silent like, needn't have bothered, he was drugged up to the eyeballs on some morphine pills, off his fucking head. You definitely not a copper?'

'No, I'm well and truly out, and I'm not about to turn you in. Whatever you did, he deserved it. But I have to get into that flat.'

'Now? No way, there's a fifteen-foot high, double-chain-link fence, with razor-wire in between, that runs all the way round, and there's a night-watchman in a cabin by the main gate, with two of the nastiest Rottweilers you've ever seen, you'll never get in.'

'Tell me exactly what you did, and when?'

'This afternoon, around three, he was on his bed drugged-up like, so I put some gloves on, and spent ten minutes feeding him pills, got him to swallow about half the bottle, shit, Mac, all he did was laugh, then he went to sleep, and about twenty minutes later he was dead, no pulse, no breathing. I was real careful, I tipped the bottle of pills over, a few fell on the floor, made it look like he just overdosed, I took nothing, touched nothing, like I was never there.'

'Good, let's go.'

'There's no way at this time of night...'

'Oh yes there is, let's go.'

On the way, Mac explained how he and Peter had managed to surreptitiously search the yard many years ago, by entering through an old Victorian sewer, there was a manhole just under the stairs to the flat, within the area that was fenced and gated off from the rest of the yard. He also explained that the Rottweilers would be trained attack-dogs, and would not bark, and that the chances were that they could enter the flat without alerting the dogs, or the watchman, who undoubtedly relied on the dogs, and probably slept through the night. Both the watchman and the dogs would be conditioned to noises coming from the flat, to the point that such noises would be expected, even anticipated, accepted as normal.

They stopped at a local petrol station, Leroy fuelled his car, and bought a couple of torches. Following Mac's directions, Leroy drove to the disused rail-sidings on the far side of the scrapyard, they parked in one of the old shunting sheds. It took Mac ten minutes to locate the entrance to the sewer, he and Leroy then climbed up an old water tower that overlooked the yard, Mac couldn't see the old Mercedes parked anywhere, but he had a clear view of the offices above which Mason's flat was located. He worked out how far in they had to go, they also noted that the dogs were asleep outside the watchman's cabin, which was in darkness.

The trip through the sewer was not what Leroy had expected, it was a cavernous brick lined tunnel, large enough to drive a lorry through, it was dry underfoot, it had not rained for some weeks, and had not been used for many years, so it did not smell, well not in the way he had feared, in the reflected torchlight he thought it quite beautiful.

Mac climbed the rusting ladder, and with some effort was able to raise the manhole-cover, squeezing out of the hole, he set the cover down quietly, then paused, hearing nothing he climbed out of the hole, then waited for Leroy to join him.

They silently ascended the stairs. Mac produced a picklock kit, selected two and unlocked the door, he drew a Glock 9mm, startling Leroy, who only just suppressed an audible cry of surprise. Mac entered the premises, and Leroy followed, they moved in unison through the kitchen, then the living room, before quietly entering the bedroom. Mason was dead, a bottle of morphine pills lay on its side on the bedside table. Mac left Leroy in the bedroom, and went back through the flat, drawing the curtains and lowering the blinds as he did so, he returned to the bedroom and turned on the light.

Mac told Leroy to search the place for weapons, after ten minutes Leroy returned to the bedroom with three revolvers and two combat-shotguns. 'Fucking wicked, Mac. You seen this shit?'

'We need to find his safe'

They both began by searching the bedroom. Leroy, pulled the chest of drawers back, revealing an old jeweller's safe set into the wall. He rotated the combination tumbler, entering the code Mac gave him, there was an audible click, but when he turned the handle, nothing happened.

Mac said. 'Slide the handle to the left, when it clicks again, pull it down to open it.'

Leroy opened the safe, and stepped back, Mac walked over, he began removing items, a tray of one-ounce gold Krugerrands, a second containing half-ounce Krugerrands, three boxes of 9mm bullets, two of .40 bullets and six boxes of shotgun shells. Mac then found what he was looking for, ten A4 Moleskin journals, notes meticulously kept by Mason, detailing every mission and case he had been involved in, these were accompanied by two boxes of photographs, and an old leather journal. Mac also found a collection of blank and fake passports and birth certificates, and the logbooks for two brand new vehicles, a Nissan pickup, and a Jaguar, he tossed these over to Leroy, 'Take a look, see if they are outside?'

Leroy went into the kitchen, turned out the light, opened the door and quietly stepped out onto the landing at the top of the stairs, he came back a couple of minutes later

'No sign of them, where do think he put them?'

Mac said, 'In one of the arches at Lambeth Walk?' He was reading the deeds to a leasehold on a railway arch, 'He's just taken it out, a twenty-five-year lease, I guess that the cars and the rest of the stuff I want are stored there.' Mac continued to empty the safe, he found two large leather holdalls on top of Mason's wardrobe, he put all the guns and ammunition, all the books and photographs and fake ID into one, into the other he placed half the gold coins, and the certificate of ownership, the car log books, and the deeds to the railway arch at Lambeth Walk.

The safe also contained a very large sum of cash, made up of pounds, dollars, and euros. Mac divided the cash into three equal piles, he put one into the bag containing the deeds, the other two into the bag containing the guns.

A further search of the safe resulted in Mac finding a hidden compartment, this contained four bags of uncut diamonds, and two bags of mixed emeralds and sapphires. These he also placed into the bag containing the guns.

He looked at Leroy, and said, 'I'll give you the address of a solicitor who owes me, she'll make sure that everything is in order, the lockup is yours, as are the cars and the contents of this bag.'

Leroy said, 'Thank you… we need the keys to the arch.'

'Look under the sink, see if you can find a can of wasp spray, undo the bottom of the can, the keys will be in there.'

Mac was searching through Mason's jacket pockets; he produced a small key. 'The lockup has an alarm system, this is the key, the code is written backwards on the fob.'

'How do you know where to look, and what the codes are… and the safe?'

'While you were searching for guns, I looked through his clothes on the chair at the end of the bed, and found this in his trouser pocket,' Mac waved a small black notebook, 'he wrote everything down, mostly it reads like nonsense, but not if you know how his mind works. Time to go. Everything as it should be?'

'Yeah, sweet as, like we've never been here.'

'Good, take the bags downstairs, wait by the manhole, I'll turn the lights off and open the curtains. I left fake ID that matches the name on his hospital bracelet in the drawer by his bed, Mason was so twisted that his employers don't even know where he lives. Local plod, will put this down as an accidental overdose, and the Coroner's Court will record everything in his new identity, and Mason just vanishes.'

Leroy looked into the bedroom, 'Mac, I don't feel better, I don't feel right, I should feel good that the fucker is dead, but I don't. I feel sadness, kind of empty, shameful even…'

'You won't ever feel good about it, revenge is never sweet. Think about your sister, and know this, by killing Mason you've done the world a service, you have ensured he can never ruin anyone else's life. Now get your shit together, and let's get out of here.'

Mac locked the door as they left. Leroy climbed down the manhole first, Mac lowered down the holdalls, then climbed down a few rungs, and replaced the manhole-cover. They drove over to Lambeth Walk, found the railway arch, and opened it up, and turned off the alarm. Leroy drove in, and Mac shut the doors, found the switch and turned on the lights. It was four-thirty in the morning.

They took a walk around the arch, it was about three-hundred feet long and one-hundred feet wide, clean and dry, the far end was bricked up, with three rows of glass bricks at the top, these let in a surprising amount of light, but with the doors closed the internal lights were needed. There was a Portacabin to the left of the doors, which contained a large, well-furnished office, a kitchen and small dining area, a toilet and shower, and a small furnished bedroom. Mac noted that there was no phone and no computer.

The Jaguar and the Nissan were right down the far end, parked next to a new black Ford Transit van, the keys were in it, it was full of fuel, and the logbook was on the dashboard, it was registered to a company in Croydon, as were the other two vehicles. Mac guessed it was a shell-company, nothing more than a letter-drop address, still the van was useful, as was knowing the location of one of Mason's postal drops, and he found the key to the post-box in the glove compartment of the van.

They found another safe, very well hidden, just as described in Mason's notebook. Mac suggested they return to the office.

He said, 'After today, I doubt we will meet again, I know you have questions, but I'm afraid they will have to go unanswered. I don't want to get you involved any more than you are, I'm going to leave you half of the gold, and a third of the cash, both the cars, and the deeds to this place.'

Taking a piece of paper, Mac wrote down a name and address, and then on the other side he penned a short letter, he handed it to Leroy, saying, 'This solicitor owes me, give the letter to her, she will make sure that the arch is registered in your name, with twenty-five years on the lease it has to be worth a few bob, use it, sell it, it's up to you, same with the cars; I'm keeping the other bag, and I'm taking the van, I need it to move the stuff in the safe.'

Mac took a couple of hours to go through and empty out the safe, mostly files, he split the sizeable quantity of cash it contained, placing a third into the bag he was giving to Leroy. They found more guns and ammunition; Mac added them to the load in the van.

'Well, that's it. I'm really sorry about your sister, I will have Silky taken care of,' Mac offered his hand to Leroy, who shook it, 'it's best that we never meet again, speak of this to no one, there are dangerous people behind Mason. More than that, you don't need to know, save, that they will kill you if they ever discover the truth. You must never talk about what you did, nor about what you saw, to anyone, and I mean anyone. I was never here, understand?'

Leroy nodded.

Mac continued, 'Stay away from your old life, start afresh. I will have someone I know erase your criminal record. It won't make up for the injustice done, but it is the best I can do. Don't let any of this get to you, a thing like this can eat away at your soul. You and Sasha have been wronged, hang onto that thought. Have you got plans?'

'No… well not 'til now. I will take care of Sasha until…' he swallowed, and fought back the tears, 'I came out a trained mechanic, only good thing about being locked up. The second time I worked on diesels, lorries and buses, I enjoyed it, I'm good at it.' He looked around the railway arch, 'This will make a great workshop, so I guess... now I can make some plans, and, thanks to Mason, I've got the cash to see them through.'

Mac said, I'm going to speak to The Turk, he's a friend, he'll watch over you.'

Leroy whistled, 'The Turk. That's some mojo, Mac.'

Leroy opened the doors, Mac drove out to meet the day, after the gloom of the arch, the sunlight was painful. Leroy said, 'Thanks for everything, Mac. If you ever need my help, you know where I am.'

Mac called in at the mini-cab office in Camberwell, he had intended to leave a message for Bekir, but was informed that he was already at work.

'Mac, you safe, that bastards no hurt you?'

'No Yaman, he didn't. He won't be hurting anyone... ever...'

'He is?'

'No more.'

'Mac, now I owes you everything. This a great day...'

'You owe me nothing, Yaman. You have my friendship, and I have yours, that is enough.'

'Among mens, this is true,' he embraced, Mac.

Mac said, 'I was helped by the girl's brother, Leroy. He's a good man. He intends to start a business repairing motors, up in the arches by Lambeth Walk. Without him, it would have gone badly, if he gets the business off the ground, could you help him out, send some work his way? I would be grateful.'

'He was there when...'

'Yes.'

'Then this is debt, it honour. I will do as you ask. He will have many customer, and my protections.'

Mac looked at him.

'Of course, free, I owes you, I owes him. Whats can I do?'

107

'Yaman, I have something else to ask of you… and this is not negotiable. Silk, I know that fat-bastard works for you, I need you to burn him, not dead, just put away for corruption.'

'Mac, he very useful man…'

'He's a corrupt copper, lower than whale shit; he gave you to Mason… now hold on, I've seen that look before. I don't want him dead, just locked up.'

'Bastards. I will… I do as you asks. He have long time in prison…and then… I promises… but now we has breakfast.'

Mac enjoyed a hearty, if somewhat cholesterol laden refection. Demir, insisted that Mac sleep, before driving north, he was shown to a well-furnished room on the upper floor, with a sofa-bed, and a promise to wake him for lunch.

Mac left London driving south, to visit an office block in Croydon, to see what the postman had left.

Chapter Fourteen

A couple of days after Mac had returned from London, around three in the afternoon, Simon arrived; unsettling though his visits were, he was, nonetheless, cordially invited to partake in the feast that Anna and Teresa had prepared for the evening meal, he did so gratefully, the food, as ever, was beyond compare.

Mac noticed that he was subdued, reticent, politely laughing at Father John's simple jokes, yet absentmindedly sipping his beer, he was clearly distracted. Later that evening, he shared this observation with Peter, who dismissed Mac's concern, 'He's probably preoccupied, dealing with a complex case, you remember how it was?'

Not long after Elizabeth and Mac had taken ownership of the farm, the old stable block, opposite and to the left of the main house, had been converted into a storeroom on the ground floor, and a studio-come-office for Elizabeth on the first floor; it was one of the first things they had done, securing her income was, at the time, an imperative. A year after her death, Mac had it remodelled, now the ground floor was an open-plan living room and dining room, with a small kitchen occupying the far end, the whole of the back wall was covered in Elizabeth's books, notebooks and files. Upstairs were three large ensuite bedrooms, the largest bedroom doubled as a storeroom for her paintings. This was where Mac housed visitors, invited or not, welcome or not.

Simon could not sleep, the conversation earlier that evening troubled him, and the information contained in the file he had brought from Scotland Yard pricked his conscience. What price disclosure, how would Mac react? He knew that was why, when Mac had walked back with him, he told Mac that it would be better if they discussed things in the morning. Simon left the bed and began pacing, distracted by his thoughts he slowly became aware that he had entered the third bedroom used as a storeroom; behind the door and along the opposite wall, paintings were stacked atop one another, slanted, resting against the walls.

On the wall opposite the window hung a large oil painting; the subject of which was the detailed interior of a workshop, to the left, in the foreground, a wooden workbench with a long plank of wood held firm in a vice, laying on its side was a wooden plane, a broad curly shaving protruding from the top, wood shavings litter the bench and the floor in front of it, some covering the feet of the man, who is standing with his body towards the bench. His arms are wide apart, he is stretching, arching backward, his face turned towards a door located on the right of the wall in the background, which is being opened by a young woman, her right hand holding the door open while she enters, her face hidden, inclined down, she appears to be looking at a mug in her left hand containing, tea, or coffee? Under the painting, on a plaque within the frame, was a short, handwritten verse, the lettering reminiscent of medieval script; its layers of meaning intrigued him, *Plane on wood; shavings and the scent of pine; love is working*. He mused over the inscription, chasing down the various ways of interpreting both it, and the painting. For a while it was a distraction, but the quiet foreboding crept back.

Simon walked over to the window and looked out across the orchard, it waited under a full moon; the trees silvered, genuflecting, crumpled with fruit. An owl meticulously reconnoitred the fields beyond, its melancholy cry articulated the wretchedness overwhelming him; dread crept in, this was going to be harder than he imagined.

In the morning Simon approached Mac, he said, 'I really don't want to do this, but I have something you should see. Cartwright gave me a file. You need to read it. I checked it… checked everything. Last night I went through some of the papers you recovered from Mason's flat, they confirm the contents of this report.'

Intrigued, Mac followed Simon back to the stable block, an hour later, he left, walking off towards the woods, no one saw him until the evening.

Father John said, 'I still don't see why you have to walk up a mountain to think?'

Mac sighed, Father John shuffled in his chair, embarrassed by the silence, concerned he had somehow upset Mac. After an excruciating couple of minutes, Mac replied, 'John, I find it easier to think in the mountains. The geography is humbling, problems become smaller, almost irrelevant. I can put things in context. The solitude… I'm dwarfed by the scenery, it makes it easier to hear my inner voice, to understand what my conscience is telling me… I can feel the sound of silence, I need to carefully consider my actions, and their consequences, and frankly, with all the distractions, I cannot do it here. There's something else… something that I need to do… and before you say anything, I must do it alone.'

Peter said, 'Leave it, John, if he wants to waste a day climbing a bloody mountain, let him, you and Simon can help me with the lower meadow, and Mr, I-want-to-be-alone, can piss off and indulge in introspection.'

Mac raised his glass by way of acknowledgement but did not smile. He spent the rest of the evening deep in thought.

Simon slept fitfully and rose with the sun to walk in the woods, he needed to clear his mind, striding past the old barn at the top of the hill, he turned at the sound of a vehicle starting, and watched as Mac drove off in his Land Rover.

Simon followed the deer trail until it crossed the logging road through the trees, then took this track as it meandered its way along the ridge, leaving on the path that went gently down the slope, curving back into the fields at the front of the house.

Half an hour later he returned to the stable block, shaved, showered, and dressed, before joining Peter and Father John for breakfast.

Father John said, 'Silent is an anagram of listen. I learned from the monks that speaking distracts, listening always informs. Their rule requires that you speak only when you have something worth saying, something that will enlighten, for in silence you find true community, and lasting fellowship. Mac has a point, the world today grants few opportunities to sit quietly, to be silent, and just observe. Everything is in a rush, turmoil and tumult are everywhere, so seeking out the quiet places when you are troubled makes perfect sense. Though I understood what Mac was saying last night, I am troubled. He also alluded to there being something he must do; I have an ominous feeling about that, bad things happen, usually to others, when he has something to do.'

Peter, said to Simon, 'Where's Mac gone?'

Simon said, 'I'm not sure how to answer that?'

'Well, it's simple really. Where the fuck is Mac?'

'I mean, I'm not sure that Mac will want me to tell you.'

'Let me rephrase the question. Tell me where he is, or I will kick the shit out of you.'

Simon, looked at Father John, 'You're okay with him doing that?'

'As you know, I cannot condone violence, it would be a betrayal of my beliefs, but in this case, if you do not answer Pete's question, I will hold you down while he… so delicately put it… knocks the faeces out of you.'

Peter smiled at Father John, turned towards Simon, who put his hands up in mock surrender. 'You know Father, I believe you would.'

Peter, grinned. Simon shook his head and said, 'Fine, I'll tell you what I know, but you will have to tell Mac, that I was forced into revealing…'

'Not forced,' said Peter, 'forced is such an ugly word. A little like coerced, overloaded with nasty implications, and it does not speak well of us.'

Father John laughed, and said, 'No, not forced, perhaps… firmly obliged.'

Simon said, 'There's a file, I'll get it.' He walked off toward the stable block, returning a few minutes later.

Father John, read it first, then handed it without comment to Peter.

Peter, read it, then read it again, glared at Simon, and said, 'You gave him this? How did you think he would react? Are you a total…?'

Father John interrupted the inevitable profanity, 'Enough! Cartwright put you up to this, it has his filth all over it. How did you think Mac would react?' He rose from his seat, waving Peter's question away, 'I'm going to pray, for Mac, for all of us.'

Peter watched Father John walk off towards the house, turned and stared at Simon, 'If anything happens to Mac, I'm holding you, and Cartwright responsible. Where has he gone, what's the address, perhaps we can…?'

'I don't know that page is missing. Pete, I'm sorry…'

'Sorry… maybe John is right? The answer is prayer… you'd better pray that nothing happens to, Mac.' He stormed off towards his forge.

Simon disconsolately picked up the file and walked slowly back to the stable block.

Chapter Fifteen

Dark sullen clouds left the mountain with a scowl. Across the valley, which was still bathed in sunlight, the black doom-ladened curtain descending the slope accentuated the green of the fields and the spinney lower down, mirroring the deep sense of foreboding that had begun to settle on him.

Grimly, he set his mind on what he had to do, reluctantly but resolutely accepting the task ahead. Looking towards the hills at the top of the valley, he could see the storm-head gathering strength, a blue-black anvil shaped cloud writhing into nature-wrought menace. The silence intruded, no birdsong, no lowing, nor bleating, a loud absence of the melody of the fells. *It's going to be a big one*, thought Mac. Standing on the bonnet he scanned the valley, instinct kicked in, storm-light vividly illuminated the whole dale. *Flash flood... I need to... there*. He climbed back into the Land Rover, engaged first gear, swung the vehicle round, accelerating back the way he had come.

By the time he was halfway across the valley floor it hit. The cutthroat-sky intimidated the light, and driving rain bounced off and blurred the track, trepidation gripped him. He accelerated over a small bridge and turned left, taking a narrow track which led up towards a peninsular of woodland. Mac stopped the car on a promontory halfway up the side of the valley, which put him far above the floodplain. It rained heavily, a torrent of water rushed down the mountain sides, pouring into the vale, overspilling the banks of the river, inundating the valley floor, but in mountain country no one built on the floodplain, and years of adapting to both weather and geography ensured that there was no impediment to prevent the floodwater leaving this high valley, so no real harm was done to humans or wildlife. *A spectacular sight*, Mac mused, *but down in the lower valleys there will be flooding and damage.*

After an hour the rain ceased, the clouds parted, and a shaft of sunlight impaled the gloom. The clouds, now lighter, moved on, and within minutes the road along the valley floor was passable, the water no more than four inches deep. Mac leaned forward and started the Land Rover, his fears subsided, his mind focused on the task ahead, whatever happens there is no turning back.

Mac saw the house, set back from the lane, on the edge of a small wood. The lane made a ninety degree turn to the right, the driveway leading up to the property joined at the apex of the bend on the left. He braked, there was no way to approach without being seen, he knew that heavy rain and poor visibility had masked his presence, for now the clouds had passed over, though more were angrily thrashing into another onslaught the other side of the mountain. Mac surmised the next downburst was at least half an hour off. He had halted the Land Rover by a gap in the hedge, he had to take stock, to prepare for what awaited him. Unbidden sound of his father's voice interrupted his thoughts, advice, he had been given as a boy when learning how to stalk deer returned to him, *"Be still, look long, and hold yourself quiet."* He had registered an open gate into another woodland, about one hundred yards back, he reversed along the lane and drove into the wood, manoeuvred the Land Rover so that it was hidden in the trees, facing back toward the lane.

Leaving the car, he moved quickly through the wood and ran across the field into the coppice behind the house. There he waited, partially to get his breath back, but also to get his bearings. Unbidden, he heard his father's voice again, *"Be still, look long, and hold yourself quiet."* Through gritted teeth, Mac muttered to himself, 'That's exactly what I'm doing.'

Although the rain had stopped, the dripping of water from the trees continued, this sound covered his movement through the wood towards the house. He knew from reading Mason's background report that there were two dogs, both trained to attack, he hoped that they had been conditioned to be silent.

He spotted the dogs lying on a veranda at the back of the house. They appeared to be a Ridgeback-Mastiff cross, killers, no doubt about it. Mac screwed a silencer onto the barrel of his .357 Sig Sauer P226. He reached out his left hand shook the branch of a tree next to him. Both dogs stood up, the bigger of the two, the male Mac assumed, silently led the way towards him. About 20 yards from him the dogs split up, the male ran straight at him, Mac fired two shots one into the chest and another into the head as it dropped. He spun to his left and fired instinctively into the fearful gaping maw of the other dog as it leapt at him. The shot was good, it passed through the top of the inside of the mouth, into the brain and exited through the skull. The momentum, of the now dead dog, carried it into Mac knocking him to the ground, unsure whether it was dead or alive he rolled over the top of the dog bringing his weapon to bear. The slightly suppressed sound of the weapon vanished into the natural symphony of water, wind and trees.

Mac adjusted his clothing, he had a baseball cap on under the hood of the jacket he was wearing, and a scarf around his face, now all that could be seen of him, were his eyes. He left the protection of the woods, skirted round the to the left of the garden, keeping a head-high hedge on the right between him and the open lawn. The hedge stopped about ten feet short of the veranda, Mac paused, above the sound of dripping water he could hear the faint sound of music, *Elgar's Nimrod, how appropriate*, Mac smiled to himself.

Listening carefully, he was able to place an occupant in the house, the sound came from a room at the front of the house, on the same side as he was now standing, the faint noises suggested that the individual was reading a newspaper.

Mac waited, most of the windows were open, it was warm, and the humidity was building, he looked up, more rain was on the way, another heavy downpour, he waited.

Five minutes later the clouds opened, the deluge broke around him, the wait satisfied him that the occupant was alone, and that there was not another dog lurking, he moved quickly onto the veranda, and from there through the house to the front room, a study as it turned out. The noise made by the heavy rain outside, and the music inside, masked all sound, Mac entered the room unheard and unseen.

An angular man, with thinning, greasy, light-brown hair, combed back so that it oozed over the collar of the worn and faded Hawaiian-shirt he was wearing, was sitting in a captain's chair, behind a desk which was set into a large bay-window, the window afforded a panoramic view of the front garden and the lane. His back was to Mac, and he was reading a copy of a local newspaper.

Mac, affecting a Northern Irish accent, said, 'Good afternoon, Mr Vale,' and moved into the room, stepping to his left, the silencer on his gun pointed straight at the man's head.

Vale replied, 'Good afternoon.'

He carefully folded the newspaper he was reading, placed it on the desk in front of him, and slowly swivelled round to face his assassin.

Mac levelled the gun at his midriff, walked over towards him, indicating that he should turn round and face the desk, Vale did so, and unbidden placed both his hands on the desk palms up. Mac placed the gun against the base of his skull.

Vale said, 'I've been expecting you, well, not you exactly, but someone like you, an executioner, just… please, tell me why?'

Mac said, 'Because I can.'

'That's no answer?'

'Well, it's the only fucking answer you're getting.'

Mac spent a couple of hours searching the house, starting in the kitchen, he found what he was looking for, a key, it was in an old mug at the back of a kitchen cupboard, he gathered everything he had found, and the rest of the items whose locations had been, after a little persuasion, volunteered by Vale, and placed them in a cardboard box. Carrying the box, he stepped over Vale's body, left the house retracing his original route, another wave of rain hit as he climbed into the Land Rover, it was as torrential as a monsoon he had experienced in India. Mac grimaced and thought, *at least it will cover my tracks, and the tyre marks made by the car, it will wash them clean away, but what of… nothing would ever wash that away.* It was slow driving, eventually, he turned onto the A66, followed the road for about three miles before turning off towards Ullswater, he would take the road over Kirkstone Pass, down into Ambleside, then over both Wrynose and Hardknott Passes, a difficult route at the best of times, downright dangerous in this weather, but it should allow him to travel unobserved. Mac pulled into a lay-by, jumped out, checked he was alone and removed the false, stick-on number plates he had put over the real ones. He screwed them up and put them in the tool compartment in the rear of the vehicle, he would burn them later. He climbed back in and drove home.

Chapter Sixteen

Afternoon became dusk, and still there was no sign of Mac.

Peter said, 'This Vale, I think I remember him.'

Simon, grateful that Peter wanted to engage him in conversation, said, 'You might, but he wasn't a South London officer, he was a detective constable at Tottenham, before transferring to Special Branch.'

He picked up the file and read aloud, 'Robert Vale, detective constable, first S.B. posting, Central London Irish Desk. Second S.B. posting as a detective sergeant to Enniskillen, County Fermanagh, Northern Ireland. Served two years there, then posted to Londonderry, served five years, before being medically discharged.'

Simon paused, read silently for a little while, then said, 'It would appear he lost the plot while in Derry, following a tip off, he made an unauthorised and unaccompanied border crossing into the Republic. He made his way to a farm just outside Buncrana, there he encountered two senior members of the IRA, wanted in Northern Ireland for the bombing of an army barracks, in which soldiers and police officers were killed. The problem was that the IRA lads were there to meet local backers and sympathisers, including two senior members of the Garda Síochána, their supporters proved reluctant to allow this unorthodox extradition of their heroes. In the ensuing gunfight, both Southern Irish police officers and three civilians were wounded, one of the IRA men was killed, the other Vale took back to Northern Ireland. The whole incident was covered up by both governments, it would have been an embarrassing revelation, coming at a sensitive time in the then peace negotiations, it would have proved fatal, in more ways than one, and would have scuppered the negotiations, which were at a delicate stage. Embarrassing, because it showed that police officers on both sides of the border had gone rogue. Vale was sent back to London, given a medal, and after a seemly time on gardening-leave, pensioned off and told to Foxtrot-Oscar.'

'Na… I'm thinking of someone else… I didn't know him,' Peter stood up, 'want a beer?'

'Please.'

Peter returned from the kitchen with two cold beers, he handed one to Simon, saying, 'Don't look so surprised, I know your hand was forced by Cartwright, we were expecting him to do something, but this… it's devastating. I know Mac can be just as persuasive as me, so no hard feelings. I'm… we're worried about what Mac will do.' Simon looked at the file, 'How do you think Mason recruited Vale?'

'Easy, an event like that, it would be all over the intelligence network. For Mason, Vale was a godsend. Totally committed to the state, in love with the idea of serving secretly, a trained and proven killer, with a bonus, he's IG11.

'IG11?'

'Postcode for Barking.'

Simon laughed, 'Not heard that before.'

Tapping the document on the table, Peter said, 'According to this file, on the instructions of Mason, that fucker killed Liz, set it up so it looked like an accident, only the County Mountie who turns up is a Black Rat, a traffic officer, Duncan Vert, an expert in road accidents. He understands that he has to go along with the report Mason has written for him, and he signs it, seemingly accepting Mason's claim about national security, sticks to the script, and everything is cut and dried, post-mortem, Coroner's Court, everything, Mason lines up his ducks, a simple tragic accident. Then our friend, Duncan, goes and writes a full and detailed report, proving that the incident involving Liz's car was not an accident, he even has a lady patho-logist he trusts, examine Liz, take pictures of her injuries, and provide a written description and detailed report. Her findings and judgements, based on twenty years as a medical examiner, are that Mason's helicoptered-in medical examiner was utterly wrong in his conclusions. Liz's neck had been manually and expertly broken before the crash, and to top it all, our dedicated traffic officer photographs Mason outside a local pub, the evening of the inquest, apparently engaged in a conversation with Vale, or at least with someone who matches the photo of Vale in your file.'

Simon said, 'It's definitely Vale, no doubt in my mind.'

'Nor mine. At some point in the intervening years, this very professional County-Mounty, discovers that Liz, was married to Mac, a retired Metropolitan Police detective sergeant, so he has two copies of his file made, one, to be sent by his solicitor to the Head of London's CID, but only upon his death. The other, insurance for him and his wife, in case he should once again have the misfortune to encounter Mason. He died six months ago, I'm guessing that's when Cartwright received the report and started to get interested, but he sat on the evidence until it suited him. He's a low cunning bastard, you watch your back.'

'I will. What do you think Mac is doing?'

'What would you do?'

'Ah, here you are,' Father John joined them. 'I was thinking about, Mac. I guess we all are… no good moping, it'll change nothing. Mac can look after himself, I'm sure he'll be back soon. It is time to change the subject. April has picked up on our concern, time to lighten the atmosphere. I came across one of his letters. Mac, used to write an epistle to me once a month, just to keep me informed about what he and Elizabeth, were up to.'

Father John made the sign of the cross as he mentioned her name, 'He kept me abreast of your doings,' he looked at Peter, and smiled. 'Every now and again his letter would contain a question about faith, or what Mac perceived as a dilemma caused by the tension between belief and the diktats of modern society, but generally it was just news. I always looked forward to receiving them. I was in Assisi when this one arrived. I'll read to you…

"Dear Father John" … there then follows the usual… ah here it is. Peter, it seems you were away on your sergeants' course at Hendon. Mac, was working with John Shoesmith…'

Peter turned to Simon and said, 'John… you remember him?'

Simon looked blank.

Peter shrugged, 'Maybe not, you would have been at Peckham only a few months when he left. He went out to Australia, New South Wales, I think? Never heard from him again, so I guess it went well for him. Good copper, shame to lose him…'

Father John coughed, rustled the letter, and continued. 'Mac described an investigation he was involved in, he never asked me for an explanation, and I never volunteered one. Anyway, after the usual preamble this is what Mac wrote, "It was ten in the morning, and I had just sat down to a full English, the canteen was quiet, there had been an armed robbery earlier, and the troops were out hunting. I saw him approaching, 'Morning Colin, where's your sidekick?'

'Where's yours?'

'Pete's on his sergeants' course. I'm working with JS He's gone down to the locker room to collect his breakfast; it'll be something akin to horse feed.'

'I'll wait. I need to talk to both of you.'

'Sounds serious?'

John returned, and sat down saying, 'Morning Colin, you joining us?'

'Only for a minute John…'

'Where's the wolf?' said John, feigning concern.

'In the van, he's had a busy morning…'

'I just heard. You found the weapons and some of the cash.'

'Yeah, good result, but I had to work him hard, he needs the rest.'

I interrupted them, 'Well now that's got the pleasantries out of the way, my breakfast's getting cold, so can we…'

'Of course… sorry. What are you guys doing this week?'

I said, 'Paperwork, we're grounded. Paperwork and property all week.'

John said, 'Today and tomorrow should see us break the back of it, we've set aside Wednesday to go round and restore all the property we recovered, we've left Thursday free for those unforeseen eventualities, so we will be off the grid until Friday, I'm afraid.'

I said, 'It's a three-line whip, the chief inspector has made it clear we are not to venture out, until we have sorted the backlog of case papers, and disposed of the property we recovered.'

'Okay, what you working Friday?'

'Late,' I looked at John, he nodded in agreement, 'four to midnight.'

Colin consulted his diary, 'Could I meet you in the Beat Managers' office around four thirty on Friday?'

I said, 'No problem, can you give us a reason why?'

'I'd rather leave that to Biggles, it's his gig, and he asked me to get you on board.'

John said, 'Biggles? And he asked for us?'

'Well... he actually asked for, Mac.'

John, looked crestfallen, so I quickly replied, 'No problem, we'll be there.'

'Good, I look forward to seeing you on Friday,' and with that Colin was gone.

John said, 'What do you think that's about?'

'I'm not sure, but if Biggles is behind it, it's got to be interesting.'

Biggles, or Tom Parfitt, was a legend among police officers, awarded the George Medal for bravery, then ten months later had a silver bar with laurel leaves added, which, as you know, is only awarded for acts of bravery that would have merited another George Medal. He had been a dog handler in the same unit as Colin, until his dog was taken from him, and he was kicked out of the dog section.

Biggles crossed the path of a young inspector, a graduate entrant with eight years' service, who had been seconded to the Dog Section in order to broaden his experience of policing. The superintendent sat him down on his first day and told him that he was there purely as an observer, and he was not to interfere with the operational running of the department, further, if he had any issues, he should seek Biggles' advice.

This did not sit well with the young inspector, a petty, self-centred man, devoid of common-sense, given to malcontented envy. He resented the fact that Biggles displayed his medal ribbons on his uniform tunic, and he was especially resentful of having to defer to a man of junior rank whom he considered his inferior. He was two months into his secondment, when all the senior officers in the unit were away on leave, and he was alone, technically in command. That first day, he took his revenge for all the slights he felt he had suffered.

He began by telling Biggles to remove the medal ribbons from his tunic, an instruction that was rightly ignored. Later, at the scene of a bungled armed robbery, now a hostage situation, he instructed Biggles to send his dog in, Biggles refused.

Biggles, and other officers present pointed out the danger in doing so, then recommended that nothing be done until the hostage negotiator, and other senior officers, arrived. Puce with rage the young inspector again ordered Biggles to send his dog in, again Biggles refused. He then told Biggles that he was suspending him from duty for failing to obey him and ordered Biggles from the scene. Unfortunately, Biggles could not resist loudly, and publicly informing the young inspector exactly what he thought of him, and in language that would shame a docker, he then knocked the spiteful pettifogger on his arse and left.

At the disciplinary hearing that followed, rank supported rank, as it always does, as it thinks it must. Biggles was returned to general uniform duty, his dog was taken from him, and fifteen years of loyal, brave, and productive service was flushed away.

Although the senior officers had backed the young inspector, they resented having to do so, they were angry at having to deal with Biggles in such a cavalier fashion, his courage and loyal service deserved better. The young inspector was moved to a backwater gulag, his career at an end, and there he remains to this day, a bitter, pathetic, little man, despised by one and all.

Biggles, to his credit, shrugged his shoulders and accepted a posting as a home-beat officer, with geographical responsibility for quite a chunk of South London. He has proved to be an effective and popular Beat Manager, loved and respected by the public, feared by those intent on crime and mischief, held in high esteem by his colleagues, he's police royalty.

Biggles? The name goes back to his days as a probationer. He was chasing a burglar from the scene of his crime, the thief cut through a building site. Following him, Biggles slipped and fell from the scaffolding, and was seen flapping his arms as he plummeted two floors down into a huge pile of sand, he got up and continued the pursuit, eventually catching his man a couple of streets away. His shift named him Flying Officer Parfitt, but that was soon shortened to Biggles, and the name stuck.

We finished our backlog of paperwork, and by late on Thursday afternoon had restored the outstanding stolen property that we had recovered, following the arrest and subsequent conviction of four burglars. Friday found us waiting in the Beat Managers' office with Colin and his wolf, Buster. Ten minutes after we had arrived the door burst open and Biggles entered, removing his cycle clips, 'Sorry I'm late, had to get the keys.'

'Keys?' asked, John.

'To the gate.'

'Gate, what gate?'

Biggles looked at Colin, tickled Buster's ears, and said, 'You haven't told them?'

'No, it's your case, so I thought...'

'You two up for an adventure, something a little different?'

'Always.'

'Good. Fancy pulling a night shift?'

'When?'

'Tomorrow?'

John complained, 'Night shift on a Saturday?'

I said, 'You never go out on a Saturday, what's the problem?'

'Nothing.'

'Good then that's settled,' Biggles waved away any further discussion, walked over to his desk and unrolled a large map. 'What do you know about Victorian jewellery?'

We both looked blankly at Biggles and shrugged our shoulders.

'That much… impressive. Well, it seems that the Victorians buried most of it with their dead, about ten percent of all Victorian jewellery on sale today is on the market because of grave robbers. Don't buy it unless it comes in the original box.'

Sniggering, John said, 'That's what this is about, grave robbers?'

'John, this is serious, and it's happening on our watch. Are you willing to help?'

'Of course, it's just a bit… cobbled streets, fog-swirled gaslamps, and coppers in capes.'

'I agree, but it is happening right now, and on my patch, and I want it stopped. Every Saturday night for the last three weeks a tomb has been broken into, coffins smashed, and jewellery stolen.'

I said, 'Where?'

'Nunhead Cemetery, that's what the keys are for, to open the north gate.'

As an aside, concerning graveyards, my uncle was a stonemason, and he had this theory that you could tell what people thought about the dead by the amount of granite they piled on top of them. I recall, when I was about twelve, walking with him through a boneyard in Aberdeen, we stopped in front of an imposing monument, a memorial to someone full of his own importance, my uncle looked at me and said, "They really didn't want that bugger getting up again."

Anyway, that is how, on a clear, cold, moonless autumnal night, one Saturday in October, Colin, John, Buster and I, found ourselves sitting inside a roofless, gothic chapel, opposite the main gate on Linden Grove.

About us lay fifty-two acres of overgrown anarchic greenery, punctuated by crumbling marble, and inclining granite. Hidden within this canopy are beautiful and imposing monuments, mainly small crypts and family mausoleums. Leaving the main avenues in daylight was only for the most intrepid. On a dark night it constituted folly of the highest order. Its atmospheric appearance, accompanied by an eerie, ethereal moaning, the result of wind passing through the trees and over marble and granite openings, was enough to discourage most from trespass, especially at night.

Biggles had arranged for two ladders to be placed inside the chapel, to afford us an aerial view of the cemetery, we hoped to spy a light, which would give an indication of the location of the miscreants engaged in this transgression.

The ladders turned out to be of a venerable wooden construction, they leaned inward, creaking alarmingly, bending towards the wall as we climbed them, but they served their purpose, giving us a good view east, south and north.

Colin, and Buster, sat below us on folding chairs Colin had brought with him, they guarded flasks of coffee, and plastic boxes containing bacon and tomato sauce sandwiches, while we balanced precariously high above them. The dark enveloped us, and the cold air punched our lungs, night-mirages plagued us, our vision swam as it fought for something to focus on, time slowed, and the numbing cold threatened our ability to concentrate; worse, hands and fingers had stopped feeling, we were in danger of falling off our trembling perches.

For the second time that night we left our roost and descended in search of hot coffee and a bacon-butty, we indicated to Colin that he should climb up one the ladders to spell us, while we warmed frozen bones by wrapping them around hot cups.

As Colin started his hesitant ascent, Buster uncurled from his chair, padded forward growling low and deep. John and I collected our rucksacks, took out our Maglite torches, but did not switch them on, we stepped out onto the avenue that runs from west to east.

About fifty yards away, to the south, stood a young woman holding a lantern, in which burned a small candle struggling to make enough light to escape the blue glass panes that made up the sides of the lantern.

She appeared to be wearing a full length, rather old-fashioned looking light-green dress, but I soon realised that her dress was in fact yellow. The lantern cast a blue hue, which made the yellow appear green. I looked at John, but the question passed unspoken between us. It was pitch black; how could we see her so clearly? Colin was struggling to get Buster to follow, he had turned from a fearless and ferocious Metropolitan Police landshark, into a fearful, quaking hairball. Feet dug in; he was not going anywhere. Given Buster's strange behaviour, I indicated to Colin that he should follow us as best he could. John and I walked off towards the young woman, who was moving her lantern to and fro, as if signalling.

As fast as we walked, we never managed to close the distance, eventually she turned left, onto an avenue that ran from west to east, and she disappeared from view.

We followed, and as we turned on to the same avenue, I saw her, still fifty yards ahead of us, she continued for another thirty yards then turned right leaving the main avenue. Hurriedly, we reached the same junction. I spotted her standing further along on a narrow path, this track was overgrown and stumbled by tree roots.

Now only eighteen yards from us, I could see she was about

130

twenty, pretty, with long auburn hair. As we floundered towards her, she stepped off the track and disappeared behind a large family crypt. I reached the side of the crypt, and could hear from within, whispered voices and muffled tapping.

As John and I were deciding what to do next, Buster joined us, he appeared to have recovered his composure and was back to his old-self, he sniffed the air, crept forward to a hole smashed in the side wall of the crypt, growled deeply, and produced a magnificent drooling impersonation of the Hound of the Baskerville's, we looked nervously back for Colin; Metropolitan Police land-sharks have previous for not being able to tell the difference between blue serge, and blue jeans! Colin pulled him back, I said, 'Police. Come out now, or I'll slip his lead.'

A frightened voice from within said, 'Okay mister, keep him chained.'

John said, 'First, throw out all your tools and any weapons, then the jewellery you've nicked. Do it right, or by God, I'll throw you back down there and put the dog in with you.'

A bag containing an assortment of hammers, chisels, screwdrivers, and two pry-bars, was hurriedly thrown from within the crypt, this was followed by a small lock knife and a large sheath knife, and then a small leather pouch containing, four rings, a bracelet, and a necklace.

Two men in their early thirties emerged from the hole in the side of the crypt, each was made to lay face down on the ground, handcuffed then searched for weapons, all the while Buster barked and snarled his resolve, dancing around them, as if to make up for his earlier foray into recreancy. Buster stood guard over the two miscreants, salivating his intent should either have the temerity to attempt an escape, while Colin and John tried to secure the side of the crypt as best they could, and I went off in search of the young woman. I had seen her step off the path behind the crypt, yet the long grass had not been disturbed, I walked further along the track, tripping over roots, barged by low branches, until I could go no further, the route was totally impassable, impeded by feral undergrowth.

There being no sign of her, and no response to my repeated calls, I gave up and re-joined Colin and John. 'Better head off back to the gate, before Buster eats these two,' laughed John, 'I've called for the van to meet us there, it's on its way.'

We walked back in silence, until Colin said, 'What was she doing here at this time of night, she wasn't even dressed for the weather, and what about that stupid lamp?' Neither John nor I answered. I was too fearful of my own thoughts to go there, the whole way back to the west gate I never took my eyes off Buster, who, to my relief, showed no signs of fear. I just wanted to be away from there, and out of that claustrophobic green ossuary.

A search of their respective bedsits had turned up another two bags of Victorian jewellery, but, with no victims able to come forward to claim, or identify the property, the dead cannot speak, I was unable to charge them with further offences, even if I could prove that they had been stolen from the dead, I would never be able to show from which dead person. This upset me, since it seemed likely that I would have to return these jewels to them. The two men, one from Liverpool, the other from Manchester were charged, fortunately they had pleaded guilty at the Magistrates court, their solicitor had relatives buried there, and was not about to break sweat providing them with a defence. The Magistrate had decided that his powers were insufficient to dispose of such a despicable crime, so he remanded them in custody for sentencing at the Crown Court.

Two weeks had passed, when Biggles came up to our office, I was alone, writing a summary of the evidence in the case. Biggles was brandishing an envelope containing three albums of photographs, and three statements producing the albums as exhibits for the Crown. The first was of the jewels we had recovered from within the crypt. Biggles explained that he had taken the liberty of having each one photographed, and then appraised and valued by a local jeweller.

The second album was of the damage to the outside of the crypt, taken in daylight it was far more extensive than it appeared in the dark. He had contacted a firm of local stonemasons, coincidentally the same firm which had been responsible for the erection of the crypt back in eighteen-fifty. They had agreed to repair the damage, and before they did so, Biggles had placed the jewels back in the coffin, secured the lid, and then waited while the crypt was made whole once again.

He also suggested that I seek a confiscation order for the other jewels, so that they could be sold at auction to pay the stonemasons for the work they had undertaken, that way the tomb robbers would not profit from their nefarious activities. The cost of restoring the crypt had been over six thousand pounds, which was about the value of the jewels we had recovered, I readily agreed to his suggestion.

The third album was of the inside of the crypt, since none of us that night had entered it, I was keen to see what it looked like. I withdrew two photographs and was looking at them when John came back with Colin, they were carrying mugs of coffee, John set one down on his desk, and reached over to hand me the other.

He said, 'What's wrong?'

I silently handed both pictures to him, he sat down and looked at them, then gave them to Colin. Biggles looked at each of us, 'Enough said.' He then walked off out of the office, Colin, the blood drained from his face, followed Biggles out of the office.

The first picture was of the top of the coffin, the lid had been forced open, and pushed roughly to the side, the body of a woman lay within, long auburn hair, wearing a pale-yellow dress.

The second photograph was of the plinth that the coffin lay on, inscribed on the side was the name of the young woman, the year of her death, eighteen-fifty-six, and her age, nineteen. On the floor at the base of the plinth was an old lantern, it contained the stub of a candle, the wax that had dribbled down one side appeared fresh, one of the panes of glass had fallen from its mounting, the blue glass, still intact, lay on the floor."

Father John folded the letter and said, 'Some things happen that seem contrary to nature, beyond our understanding, beyond interpretation, it is futile to speculate. These are events that surpass rational explanation. The best way of dealing with such things is simply to accept them as they are presented, without looking for an answer, not over thinking... simple acceptance.'

He paused, clearly considering what to say next, 'I need to explain something to you, I know that you both struggle to accept the notion of God, of the value of faith... I guess neither of you believes, that you both reject such ideas...' he held up his hand to deflect Simon's protestation, 'It's alright, Simon. I know, out of politeness, and in order not to cause me offence, you were going to temper your atheism, don't. The world is a mystery, even for believers; one of the most difficult tasks facing a Christian is to try to envisage infinity in eternity. I think you'll agree, not something easy to imagine. How do you visualise something that transcends place and time? It is a concept that stands on the very boundary of thought. Yet it is key to understanding the reality of the universe. What we do is not confined only to the here and now, nor is it enclosed in time, and bounded by geography, whatever we engage in cannot be separated from eternity. What we do today resounds through life, and echoes in the hereafter.'

Anticipating a question, Father John paused, but none came, 'Confronting evil is terrifying, even for those who believe, but believers have an advantage, they have reconciled the fact that we exist not only in the physical world, but also in the spiritual. You do not have that advantage, and this places you in great danger, please accept that there are things in this world, that for you, defy explanation. Whether you like it or not, you have an immortal soul, and I will do my best, despite your lack of belief, to protect you from the malevolent attacks of those who glorify evil.'

An embarrassed silence followed. Peter, his face darkening, scraped his chair back, stood up, and leaned across the table toward Simon.

Fearing the worst, Father John said, 'Place your trust in Divine Providence, you are never alone when you confront evil. We must set our fears aside, and have faith…'

Peter snarled, 'Keep your faith. If anything's happened to Mac, people are going to die, and one of them is going to be that cun…'

April walked over to where they were sitting, saying, 'Uncle Peter, will Dad be back soon, Aunty Teresa and Aunty Anna, want to serve the food?'

Father John, smiled at April and said, 'He should be back later tonight, let's go and help get dinner ready.'

Watching the two of them walk off toward the kitchen, Simon and Peter exchanged glances, Peter said, 'You had better prepare yourself, if Mac doesn't get back soon, we're going hunting,' then he turned and walked quickly off towards his forge.

Simon, called after Father John and April, 'Wait for me, I'll lend a hand.'

Chapter Seventeen

As Mac approached the kitchen table where Peter and Father John were sitting, Peter sarcastically said, 'Enjoy the walk? Not exactly walking weather, and definitely not mountain weather.'

Father John approached him, took him by the left arm and led him silently to a seat. Simon was leaning against the sideboard.

Father John said, barely able to repress his anger, 'What have you done?'

Mac looked at Simon, who shrugged.

Peter said, 'Don't blame him, you should have told us where you were going and why. I should have been with you. I could have...'

Mac interrupted, and said, 'I'm going to take a shower. You want to help? Burn these number plates, there's a cardboard box in the back of the car, put it somewhere safe, then hose out and wash the Land Rover. After my shower I'm going to have a large whisky, and maybe then I'll tell you what happened. Don't get sanctimonious with me... none of you has the right.' He stormed off. Father John, Peter, and Simon exchanged glances.

'I'll fetch the box and burn the plates. You wash down the car,' said Peter, glaring at Simon.

Father John, his face darkening, with fire in his eyes, said, 'I think we just crossed the Rubicon. I'm responsible for your souls, what do I do now?'

Peter smiled, and said gently, 'Pray for us, Father... pray.'

An hour later Mac walked back in, 'Sorry I sounded off earlier. I'll guess I had better tell you what happened.'

They all sat down facing Mac, who said, 'I take it that Simon filled you in on what happened to, Liz?'

'He did, he showed us Vale's file, his background and his role in this terrible affair. Did you kill him? God forgive you.' Father John made the sign of the cross.

Mac said, 'After Simon told me what happened, I was in a white rage, I wanted to tear Vale limb from limb, he had taken my world from me, my wife and April's mother. I wanted him dead so bad I could taste it. I wanted to kill him slowly, get bloody medieval on him, take a week, do it right, let him feel the pain I have lived with, so I paid him a visit, and I questioned him, gratifyingly his answers did require a little... motivation.'

Father John made the sign of the cross.

Mac continued, 'I will not say that it did not feel good to be able to kill the man who murdered, Elizabeth. God forgive me, it did.'

Father John crossed himself again.

'It occurred to me, as I was driving over to visit Vale, that we have a problem. He has worked all these years thinking he was employed by the security services, Mason was his handler, he tasked him, and paid him. He was paid a monthly retainer, handsomely paid, and then given a cash bonus for every successful mission he completed, now that Mason is out of the picture there will be no more money coming in. At first, he would consider it an oversight, then he would try to contact Mason, and having failed to do so, contact MI5 to ask for his salary. That is when it gets tricky for us, they will go digging, snatch him, lock him up somewhere, take their time interrogating him, drugs, not violence. Eventually get the truth out of him, and the location of his papers, his knowledge of their, and Mason's, dirty little secrets. Then they will unearth our story, and that's when it gets dangerous, they may decide that we know too much, that we pose a danger to the state. We will be seen as expendable, and if it is deemed expedient, we will all be terminated, and a great evil will be covered up. Now if Vale was assassinated, and given his background, and the long list of possible suspects, it will be interpreted it as just a rogue Special Branch officer whose past caught up with him. Special Branch and Five's Irish desk will crank up again, and a number of possible IRA operatives will step into the spotlight, then of course there are the new kids on the block, the younger generation out to make a name for themselves, Republicans by another name, the list of possible suspects is endless, and the lads on the Irish desk will enjoy being relevant again. So much so, that the possibility of anyone, other than someone connected to the Boys, being responsible, will be dismissed out of hand. The answer? Make his is death look like an execution, a revenge killing, clean, efficient, emotionless. Under the circumstances, John, killing him is much more than mere revenge, it is self-defence. A case of he dies, or we die.'

No one spoke for some time, then Simon said, 'Mac, what about those papers he will have kept, in the wrong hands they could still expose us?'

'I know, I thought of that, I made a thorough search, a clean search. I found about a dozen desk diaries up in the loft. They're in that cardboard box, there was nothing else. I found and took the paperwork relating to his safe deposit box, and the key that opens it. One day we'll pay it a visit and see what's in there. It's been a long day, I'm bushed, I'll see you all in the morning. We have work to do, gentlemen.'

He started out of the door, turned and said, 'For the record, I didn't kill him, he's still alive.'

He turned to leave; Peter grabbed his arm.

Father John said, 'Not dead?'

'Not dead,' said Mac. He waited for them to calm them down, then continued, 'I wanted to take his life, and I had any number of reasons to do so, he murdered Liz, and his presence could jeopardise our future, but I couldn't do it.'

He waved away the indignant protestations from Peter, and continued, 'Liz would not have wanted me to, and I knew it would be wrong. I have been thinking about this for some time, we must always keep the moral high ground, otherwise we are no better than them. I accept that there might be an occasion when one or other of us has to kill someone, to protect an innocent life, or defend his own life, but it can only be justified by the immediacy of the threat.'

Mac silenced Peter's protestations with a look, 'Vale is no threat. He has the potential to cause mischief, but we have his papers, the key to his safety deposit box, and he... volunteered his security code. Plus, we know who he is, and how to find him, but he doesn't know who we are, and given what we have uncovered so far about his, and Mason's, activities, I'm guessing that we are likely to be a long way down his list of possible suspects; knowing how secretive Mason was, it's more than mere speculation to suggest that Vale never actually knew the names of those he eliminated. Something I suspect, we can establish by examining the diaries I brought back, and that could mean he is not able to implicate us. Added to which, he now knows that what he was engaged in was not only off the books, but also highly illegal, and so potentially damaging to the security services that if they ever found out about his, and Mason's extracurricular activity, they would shoot him on sight. So, he will stay quiet, keep off their radar. I told him Mason was dead, that seemed to flatten him. I am satisfied that he represents no threat to us.'

Mac looked at Peter, then said, 'To save you the question, he's nothing to me, he no longer exists. Liz's memory requires that of me, he's not worth it. I will not hate. I will not seek vengeance. He, like all of us, will one day be judged, he will be held to account for his actions. I look to my own soul; I suggest you do the same.' In silence he walked out of the kitchen, although he felt drained, a sense of peace washed over him.

Chapter Eighteen

The door opened, a large man, about six-foot-four, slim but muscular, stood before them, the silver hair hanging down to his shoulders, complimented by a neatly trimmed white beard, framed his mesmerising azure eyes.

Mac, spoke first, 'Robin Masters?'

'Mac?'

'Yes... we spoke on the phone last week.'

Robin shook hands with Mac, then following introductions, with Father John and Peter.

'Just call me Rob, come in, come in, you're most welcome.' His smiling eyes beaming the sincerity of his welcome.

They were ushered into a large living room, once seated, and following the usual pleasantries, plied with coffee and biscuits, Robin indicated that Mac should begin.

As with all interviews he conducted, Mac began by trying to draw out Robin's history and background, he used this technique on whoever he was questioning. It worked on most people, providing an insight into the character and beliefs of the subject, it also helped to break the ice, and often indicated the direction that an interrogation should take, in order to elicit the information being sought. In this case the response took them all by surprise, and thereafter, a new member was added to the team.

When Mac asked about his background, Robin smiled, and said, 'How do you question someone who is skilled in interrogation?' He laughed, and continued, 'A good technique is to relax the subject, put them at ease, and find sympathetic common ground. You're doing it just as I would; and you want to know my story?'

He stood up and walked over to a sideboard, took out a photograph album, then returned to his seat. Robin left unremarked the look that Peter gave Mac. Placing the album on his lap he said, 'I was born in Africa, in a country called, Nyasaland. A child of the British Empire, I had an interesting upbringing. My parents, though both working class, came from a long line of artisans, both were Edwardian in their manners, in their way of thinking, and in the importance they placed on education. Africa allowed them to occupy a social position unattainable in England. I was raised, schooled, and educated for life in the colonies. I was prepared and groomed for the role of empire-builder, and my future was to be in colonial administration, I harboured the ambition of becoming a District Officer.'

Robin took four pictures from the photograph album and passed them to Mac, as the photographs passed from one to another he continued, 'I was given a classical education; the liberal arts, rhetoric and grammar, it was a full and well-rounded schooling. A deep-rooted sense of duty, and of fair play, the kind that is more than merely an absence of discrimination, together with other tenets considered essential and desirable in a colonial officer, were inculcated into the very fibre of my being. I was educated and prepared for a life of service. It was drummed into me that when we are born, we are each given a gift, and the purpose of life is to discover that gift, and then use it, give it away in the service of others; what it is, and how to employ it, is the purpose of the journey we must all take, and I am certain that the result resonates in the hereafter. Just as I completed my tuition, the world changed, and I left the life of colonial East Africa, for life in England. The only thing that my upbringing appeared to have prepared me for was the life of a police officer, so I joined a county force and rose through the ranks, retiring as a detective chief superintendent.'

Mac said, 'It must have felt strange coming to this country from Africa?'

Robin laughed, 'Strange is not the half of it, I was brought up British, but it was a Britishness that had long vanished from these shores. I'm a paradox. I have spent my life as an outsider, a foreigner within my own culture. The world for which I was prepared is no more, vanished into the mists of time, my life consigned to history before it was lived, a footnote before the page was ever written. I have spent my life lost, feeling abandoned, only at ease with the foreigner so despised by the little-Englander. I live in a society I neither recognise, nor understand; of this age, but out of time, I am an anachronism. Born too late for the world that was, yet too early for the world that is. Does that tell you who I am?'

They sat in silence, Father John smiled and nodded. Peter was the first to speak, 'You just summed up my life, for the first time someone has articulated what I have felt deep-down. Do you think that sense of not belonging, yet somehow attached, is why we became police officers?'

Robin said, 'I suppose so. To draw an analogy, if you see the public as sheep, the criminals as wolves, and the police as sheepdogs, then it makes sense. To the sheep, the sheepdogs will always be strangers, after all, to the sheep, they don't look any different from the wolves, and so we remain outlanders.'

Robin got up and organised more tea and biscuits, whilst doing so he asked them to look at the photographs in the back of the album, once satisfied that his guests had been properly attended to, he asked them to follow him into the dining room, explaining that having a large table would make it easier to pass the case file and photographs around.

Once they were seated, he said, 'I'll save you some time, Mac. You have come here to pick my brains, because I was able to successfully detect, arrest, prosecute, and convict an entire sect for the satanic abuse of children. You want to know about their satanic-ritual, and the extent of its influence in the case I investigated.' Mac nodded, and said, 'In a nutshell.'

Robin gave a thorough, and detailed presentation of his investigation, and of the research he undertook into the beliefs of those involved, in this he was assisted by a Catholic priest, the diocesan exorcist. He then took several photographs from the smaller of three files and placed them on the table in front of him. 'This is a site that was used by a local circle, it is in some woods about a mile from here, after lunch we'll take a walk, and you can see for yourself the different signs to look out for, it's just like looking for animal tracks, after today you will never look at a woodland the same.'

He placed three photographs face up in front of them, 'Satanism is about inversion, it is about replacing good with evil, this other then becomes the object of their veneration. It really does not matter what this other is, so long as it overshadows God in the minds of its adherents. Indications of satanic activity can be hard to discern, especially in open woodland, but if you look long and hard at a potential site, if it is in regular use, you will spot them. You need to detect signs of inversion, symbols that appear to be upside down, or back to front, these can be indicative of their presence. The object of their veneration can be seen by them as real, or figurative... symbolic, so it may not be physically present, sometimes the evidence is slight.'

Robin, paused to pass round some more photographs. Pointing to the first photograph, Robin continued, 'There are other indications, look for something like this,' he pointed at a photograph of a grove of trees, 'a trifurcated tree, instead of one trunk, it has three growing out of common rootstock, or it could be three trees that have grown very close to each other, so they appear to have the same rootstock. Three is a venerated number in satanism. These types of trees are sacred to them and will be incorporated into a stone-circle. This circle will contain rocks, both round and rectangular, although, from experience, it won't be exactly circular, it can be egg-shaped, but the trees will always form a focal point. There will be a pit, not that deep, about six feet in diameter, the other side of which will be touching a large single tree, this is their hallowed ground. The earth in the middle of the stone circle will be burnt, it is there that their portable altar is placed, and a fire lit under it, don't bother looking for the altar, they bring it in for the ritual and take it away afterwards. You will need to take a camera with you, and a set of steps to photograph the site from above, pictures show up details you can miss. Map the area, you will need a notebook and a compass, look to the west and the east, are there streams, or flowing water? They need fire, earth, air, and running water, which they describe as living-water. There will be a larger ring within this area, it may well be camouflaged, often its boundary is a natural bank or fold, there will be a man-made mound in the middle, it is under this that they bury their sacred objects, those imbued with evil during their rituals.'

Father John said, 'You said this was a local coven...'

'Not a coven, Father. These are not witches, but devil-worshipers, the cell I uncovered called themselves Atanx. I never did find out why, nor what it meant. Witches on the other hand are into Wicca, very few pagans will become involved in the type of behaviour I encountered.'

'Please, call me John…'

'Actually, it's Monsignor,' Peter butted in.

'A Monsignor, I am honoured.' Robin bowed slightly towards John, 'I am… you might call me a lapsed Catholic, well maybe not lapsed, just not regular. I still believe, I pray the Little Office, and the Rosary daily, but I don't attend Mass every Sunday, I cannot abide the awful modernistic, insubstantial omnium gatherum, imposed on the Church. Once a month a young priest holds a Traditional Mass in the chapel at the local manor house, which I attend.'

Father John, smiled at Peter and said, 'Excuse him, he's an atheist, but I'm working on it.'

Mac said, 'John has only ever said the Mass in Latin, you two will get on like a house on fire.'

Father John, glaring at Peter, said, 'Returning to the question I was going to ask, this local group of Satanists, has anyone done anything to stop it?'

'It's difficult these days, given the totalitarianism of the thought-police, whose permission is required even if you wish to engage in private rumination, that such a simple and personal pastime is subject to their approval is an affirmation of the tyranny that enslaves us. We are told we must accept all beliefs without question, and the resulting abuse is to be treated as tolerable, it seems that when it comes to religious belief, provided it is not Christian, then anything is bearable. A cultural blindfold slips conveniently over the eyes of those in authority, and innocents suffer, a state of affairs they tell us we must tolerate for the sake of their imposed version of egalitarianism. Do you think they have ever pondered on the paradox of the discriminatory injustice of equality?'

Robin paused, composed himself, and continued, 'A few of

us, a mix of Methodists, old-school C of E, and Catholics, keep an eye on their activities. The local lot are pretty harmless, it serves an excuse for them to get their kit off and fornicate alfresco, no worse than a bunch of wife-swappers, save that there is the added risk of pneumonia.'

Father John said sternly, 'What of the risk to their mortal souls? What does the local Bishop say about this activity?'

Robin said, 'He knows, but is not interested, I'm not convinced he believes in anything, he has never uttered one word of support for the teaching of the Church, and he steers well away from dogma. He's made a career out of ignoring the abuse of children by priests in his diocese, so of course he's going to ignore the abuse of children by Satanists, after all, those priests and the Satanists are one in the same, evil paedophiles. Very few in authority will even acknowledge that satanic abuse is happening, for to do so would court public ridicule, and see them excoriated for breaching the code of political correctness. A local pro-life group approached the bishop because a candidate standing for election as our MP was a vocally committed adherent of the eugenic principles deemed appropriate for public consumption, the rest of that grotesque theory they necessarily keep hidden to avoid the obvious comparison. This wannabe MP was keen to present himself as a faithful Catholic, the area has a large Catholic population, and our vote is essential for anyone hoping to be elected. The bishop told them, that publicly upbraiding him was not charitable, in the bishop's opinion the pragmatic approach was best.'

'I suppose he's now your MP?' said Father John.

'No, we elected a rock-solid Protestant lady, she stands for family life and all the things we value. She despises the bishop, and those like him, whom she sees as weak; his so-called pragmatism failed get him the political influence he craved. He will not be long for the job, he has presided over years of falling attendance at Mass, not a single candidate has come forward for the priesthood under his watch, he has closed innumerable churches and merged several parishes, those who make large donations to the Church have abandoned him, and it is that incompetence which will prove his undoing, you can mess the laity about, but sabotage the income of the Church, and you're toast.'

Father John said, 'I am afraid that for some bishops morality is relative, transgressions are explained by necessity, and since they do not consider sin absolute, anything goes. Years ago, such a Catholic politician, as the one you just described, who brazenly promotes policies that are contrary to Church teaching, yet shamelessly proclaims his faith as a reason to support him, would have been excommunicated, but now? Well, it suits those in the hierarchy who are seeking to realign the Church, to have such heretical examples front and centre. All that really concerns them is that people think well of them, and by people, I mean anyone of influence outside of the Church. They see the red-hat as theirs by right, an award, rather than a call to greater beneficence, notions of duty and service are an anathema to them. Instead of pointing out the path to salvation, they signpost the road to hell. Too many, like your present bishop, are a picture of mediocrity basking on the rocks of fashion, prime examples of appearance over substance. You do have to wonder who they have the dirt on, to get so far up the tree?'

Robin smiled and said, 'Sadly, that's very true. I've often wondered why there is a road to hell, but only a stairway to heaven, perhaps it's an indication of the anticipated traffic flow?'

He paused, looked at Peter, and said, 'I know that the Monsignor is a close friend of yours, and that much of what has passed between you is banter, friendly joshing, but what you are embarking on is both deadly serious and dangerous, and if I am to help you, I need to know that you are committed, and fully understanding of what we are up against.'

Peter, clearly annoyed by the admonishment said rather tersely, 'I am. Have no doubt of that.' Robin continued, 'Good, what we are about to do will be very dangerous. These people crave power above all else and will remove any and all obstacles to achieving that power. And yes, I will be joining you.' He looked at Mac, who smiled, and nodded his assent.

Father John said, 'Peter you must make a stand, commit to the cause. If not, you will be at the mercy of terrible forces. This is no time for prevarication, or lukewarm commitment, this is a war, and we risk more than our lives.'

I know, and I am willing to do anything it takes…'

'I have never doubted your courage, but could you turn the other cheek? Surrender your life to save your soul?' said Father John.

Mac interjected, 'Enough! This has gotten way too deep; we are going beyond the simple investigation I want to conduct. John, I trust Pete completely, and whilst I understand where you and Rob are coming from, let's not lift the painted-veil just yet. This is simply a crime investigation, and these perverts are criminals, sophisticated criminals I'll grant you, but still flawed human beings, and using plain old-fashioned police work is what will catch them. I do not deny that there are some Satanists who are evil enough to wield demonic power, but most are just playing at it, using the whole thing as an excuse to justify and manifest their own perversions.'

Robin said, 'You are right, Mac. Time for lunch, then a field trip to the woods, after which you can talk me through your case.'

Chapter Nineteen

Mac placed a pint of ale on the table in front of Peter, who silently indicated an individual hunched over a table in the far corner of the bar, writing in a notebook. Mac raised his voice, in order to be heard over the throb of conversation, 'Read it out, Tom.'

The bar fell silent, and all eyes turned to the man in the corner of the room. Tom looked sheepishly back, waved Mac away, and took a sip of his whisky. Others in the room took up Mac's request, until the pressure on Tom became irresistible. He stood up, cleared his throat, looked at Mac, and said, 'Why would my scribbling be of interest to you?'

Mac smiled at his childhood friend, 'For as long as we have known each other, and it is longer than I care to admit,' he let the laughter die down before continuing, 'you have always had the ability to articulate the moment, and this is one of those moments.'

Tom said, 'I was just trying to describe the events of this day, and what it means for all of us. There is a decisiveness about today, and it saddens me.'

The room fell silent. Tom picked up his notebook and read aloud.

'We came to mark his passing. To honour the gifts, he gave.

Childhood friends, we stayed in touch with him, but not with each other; embarrassed by the time-wrought faces within which we glimpse the callow days of our youth, we circle slowly, stamping out the cold, mutely conversing. In pairs we fall in behind the coffin, as for the last time he takes the track from the Kirk to the cemetery. Silently we pass the whitewashed byre, its wall still buttressed by an old waggon wheel. Some are able to recall when he converted it into a workshop, now so many years ago. All mark that therein the wisdom of the past was never silenced by the tumult of the present.

The lone piper, bellows his plaid-sack, conjuring an air so mournful my soul weeps. The keenness of the wind and the finality of the open grave conspire to induce a pall of desolation, wordlessly I turn away, seeking redemption in solitude, but betraying thoughts creep in, of hot soup, a consoling dram, and the glowing hearth of the saloon bar.

Duty done, one by one we leave in silence, tramping slowly back toward life, knowing that after today we shall not meet again, he was all that bound us in fellowship. But for now, we have food and drink, and the laughter of shared memories, of a time when we were all closer to heaven.' Tom closed his notebook and sat down.

Mac punctured the silence that followed, 'Once again, Tom, you've captured the moment.'

'Hear, hear,' applause filled the room, followed by demands that Tom send a copy to this or that individual, and then the heartbeat of conversation resumed.

Later, when most had retired for the night, Mac and Peter joined Tom at his table, each bearing drinks. Tom smiled and said, 'About bloody time you two bought me a drink.'

Peter said, 'I want a copy.'

Mac looked at him and frowned, but before the inevitable

exchange, Tom said, 'You want to talk to me about Sandyhills?'

Mac said, 'Yes, you were the lead investigator for customs on that one…'

Tom interrupted, 'Not here, and not now. We'll meet in the morning, about ten.' He looked at Peter, who was clearly the worse for drink, 'Let's make it after lunch, say one o'clock, we can talk as we walk. I was going to suggest the ben, but looking at Pete, the loch might be easier.'

'One o'clock it is,' said Mac.

'One o'clock,' slurred Peter, slumping over the table.

Chapter Twenty

Some had risen early to catch the train, or to take the road south, but most stayed. They stayed to visit friends and family, to walk the old byways, to remember how to forget. A few hung around to justify their voluntary exile from this part of the Highlands, to reinforce their erroneous belief in the uneventfulness of life in this part of Scotland; ignoring the predictable dullness of their comfortable suburban lives. Ahead, a week of contemplative quiet days, punctuated by evenings of frivolity, and conversations about kindly half-remembered bygones, coupled with bouts of epic-drinking. Mac feared some might not survive. All had taken advantage of the discount offered, and the innkeeper revelled in his unseasonable bonanza.

Mac, Peter, and Tom walked in silence through the village, taking the track towards the kirk. Peter fell back, allowing Mac and Tom to walk side by side, it always surprised him to see them together, both the same height and build, Tom had shoulder length ginger hair and a full beard, now flecked with white, but both had the same eyes and nose, it was uncanny, though Tom's lips were thin and Mac's full, they could be brothers. They climbed a stile, and joined the path that rounded the loch, across the water, in the distance, glowered the ben, ruffed with cloud, and the wind brought news of the snow that capped the peak.

Tom said, 'Good morning.'

'Afternoon,' corrected Peter, surprising Tom with his breezi-ness.

'Could we start by revisiting how you originally became involved with Mason?' asked, Mac.

Tom paused and said, 'I'll tell you the whole story, as briefly as I can, and you can ask questions when I'm done.'

Mac said, 'Only if you are comfortable doing so, just being seen with us could be dangerous.'

Tom looked away, watching the waves writhing into foam on the loch, 'Fiona died two years ago, we never got to enjoy the retirement we dreamt of, and I've no one left, if I can't help my oldest friend, what's the point of it all?'

He continued to watch the waves, eventually he said, 'I've known this place all my life,' he turned away from the loch, looked at Mac, and said, 'you and I used to play here as bairns, I always knew I would die here. I'm in the middle of buying the auld manse, I should be in by the spring, when this is over you must both visit, bring your families.'

He fell silent again. They left him to his thoughts, Mac and Peter walked on, stopping by a commemorative bench, stra-tegically placed at the loch-side to exploit the view across the water to the base of the ben, powerfully present on the other side.

Tom caught them up, and said, 'Sorry… where to begin? A customs officer based in New Galloway took his wife and kids to Sandyhills for the day, this would have been mid-June, five years ago.'

Peter looked at Mac, who shrugged.

Tom said, 'Sandyhills is a beach area popular with families and local teenagers, a mixture of wide-open flat sands, rocks, and dunes. The officer noticed a group of about eight men, with four Rigid Raider style boats, they spent a couple of hours going around the point, then coming back into the bay, and running the boats up onto the beach, before repeating the process one boat at a time. To anyone else it might have seemed to be nothing more than a group of pals mucking about in boats, but what piqued his interest was the fact that the boat engines were almost silent, and there was a man up on the point with a clipboard making notes. He thought it odd enough to report, he waited a couple of days, walked around the bay and up onto the point, and worked out that the beach in that bay was the only location from which to launch boats at night and not be noticed. The proximity of a caravan park meant that their arrival and departure would cause little or no interest, and given that Rockcliffe and Kipford, both boating areas, are in the near vicinity, meaning it was highly unlikely that boats being towed along the road would arouse the interest of the local police. His report landed on my desk about ten days after the incident. To me it made sense, one of the Glasgow syndicates had gone dark, and I thought that this might be one of their operations. Talking it through, my team felt that the most credible scenario, was that the ship bringing the drugs in would lay off Pipers Cove on the other side of the point, and the small boats would go out to meet it, bringing the drugs back to shore in the bay at Sandyhills. That called for a high tide around one or two in the morning, and a moonless night. Research quickly gave three possible nights over the rest of the summer. The first of those nights drew a blank, which was fortunate, because we were seriously under-manned. Unlike you boys-in-blue, Customs and Excise are permanently under-resourced, but on the second occasion we scraped a large team together and hit the jackpot. We got everyone, small boats, the shore team, the coaster out in the channel, even the man with the clipboard. Trouble was, that it was not my missing syndicate, nor was it drugs, it was young girls, nine in all. The men we arrested were a mixed bag, two Englishmen, who I had no doubt were ex-military, and judging by their tattoos, members of a Fascist group. The captain of the freighter was Dutch, and his first officer, Danish, the crew were an Algerian, a Turk, and two Somalis. All of them clammed up, and never said a word from the time of their arrest, until their release. We had to wait two days to talk to the girls, the eldest of whom was thirteen, the youngest eight, they had been heavily sedated and the story they told us was beyond belief, but one that is familiar to you. On the third day following the arrests, Mason turned up, he informed us that the smugglers were integral part of an ongoing operation, all top-secret, in the national interest and all that, and we had to let them go. The girls were taken later the same day by so-called social workers from London. I tried, but never found out their fate. I wrote a report, which I copied and distributed, one copy I sent to you for safe-keeping.'

Mac, nodded.

Tom continued. 'Two weeks later I was asked to review my report, I was presented with a new version, written by Mason or one of his flunkies, which I was told to sign. You rang me the day you got the copy of my original report and asked if Mason had requested a meeting with me. He had, and coincidentally it was for the next day in London. I thought it unusual that he had requested that we meet in the East End, at a pub called the Prospect of Whitby, on the banks of the Thames.'

Mac said, 'I rang Pete, who I knew was back in London, and we gate-crashed the meeting.'

'I was glad you did, that bastard can be very intimidating, and the conversation had taken a turn for the worst, I had begun to believe that I would not be leaving London. Mason is of, but not in the security service, he occupies the dark that lays beyond the shadow world. He's a guard-dog patrolling for trespassers, controlling but not controlled, only loosely constrained, and he has only one response to those dumb enough to climb the fence. At any one time there will be only a few like Mason operating in the margins, mostly a force for good, but only if they bide deep in the black. In Mason's case there are holes in his fence, and he has unrestricted access to the twilight-zone.'

'Fortunately for you, we had history with him,' said Peter.

Mac said, 'After you left the pub, we ensured that he understood what would befall him if anything were to happen to you, or Fiona.'

'Which he believed?'

'We can be very persuasive.' laughed Peter.

'Oh, I don't doubt that. But he's still out there, and I fear for you both.'

Peter looked at Mac, who nodded assent and walked off, further along the path.

Tom looked quizzically at Peter, who said, 'You need not trouble yourself about Mason. Mac took care of him six months back.'

'Took care of him, are we talking… with extreme prejudice?'

'We are. He paid us a visit, subsequently it went bad, well… you know, Mac.'

'He did the right thing… heck, this calls for a dram.'

Laughing, he took a hip flask from his coat pocket and offered it to Peter, who drank deep. Tom walked over to Mac, slapped him on the back, and offered him the flask. Mac drank slowly.

Tom said, 'I haven't been this happy since the old king died; thanks to you, our troubles are over. One of us should have done it years ago.'

Mac said, 'I wish that were true, I agree, we should have dealt with Mason years ago, but he was only the monkey, not the organ-grinder. Whoever he or she is, they are still out there, the only good thing is that they have no idea that we exist, that much I did glean, confirmed by the documents and diaries I liberated from Mason's flat. He needed to keep a degree of control to ensure his continued safety and usefulness, so he always kept something important back.'

Peter said, 'That bastard's secretiveness may, in the end, be our only advantage. We need to find out who's really behind this mess and has been from the start.'

Mac looked at Tom, 'Mason killed, Liz.'

'What… it wasn't an accident?'

'No, he thought she was looking into our old case and had her killed.'

'Then there is your answer, whatever Liz was reporting on… she must have inadvertently trespassed in a sensitive area.'

'We looked, but there was nothing. We've all been through her notes and found nothing. The story she was writing was a piece of fluff about city folk moving to the country, and the difficulties that they, and their new communities faced in adjusting. Nothing to connect with Mason, or our original investigation.'

Tom danced a jig, alarming Mac and Peter with his sprightly spontaneity. 'I'm coming back with you. Can you put me up?'

'Yes,' laughed Mac.

'Good, I need something to shake me up, and this is just the challenge, I'll go through Liz is papers and find what we are looking for.'

Peter started to protest, but Tom continued, 'You've been looking for the obvious. I'll examine the links, by mapping the untidy connective-web that individuals and organisations create; sometimes those at the extreme boundaries of the obvious can surprise you, and illuminate what was there all along, but remain just out of sight. Well, a fresh pair of eyes can do no harm, and an extra gun may come in handy.' Tom opened his coat to reveal a 9mm Beretta 92 in a shoulder holster.

Peter smiled, 'I've got a spare MP5 in the car, if you want it?'

Tom said, 'I will, just in case,' they both laughed.

Mac said, 'When you two reivers have quite finished. Welcome aboard, Tom.'

Laughing, they set off to complete their ramble around the loch, their mood lighter, hopeful.

Peter said, 'One thing, it's been bothering me for a while, I know you've been friends since childhood, but are you two related? I mean you look so similar.'

Tom, and Mac spoke in unison, 'Auld-Willie,' then fell about laughing.

Peter said, 'Private joke?'

Mac, still laughing, said, 'No, common knowledge in these parts. When Auld-Willie, was young Willie the men went off to fight in the First World War, his job was classed as an essential occupation, so he stayed home. Seems he spent his spare time going the extra mile in consoling the women left behind, especially the newly widowed.'

Tom said, 'Many families have a grandfather in common, Auld-Willie. So, if we look alike, that might be the answer.'

Peter said, 'Fuck.'

Mac said, 'Exactly.'

All three resumed their stravaiging about the loch in uncontrolled laughter.

Chapter Twenty-One

Tony became a regular, and welcome visitor to the farm, weekends, if he was off duty, he would bring his wife and children along. Father John looked forward to his visits, he had taken to Tony, and was slowly turning him into a project.

Simon was also becoming a regular visitor, though his presence was unsettling. The news and information he brought from Cartwright, was forcing them to make choices they didn't want to take.

Tony said, 'Education? I can't accept what you are saying, there is nothing wrong with the education system.'

'You don't know?' said Father John.

'What's wrong with it?'

Father John said, 'Education in this country is politicised, try suggesting change, the re-introduction of some of the older, time-proven methods of teaching, and the mob will shout you down. You will be branded as a reactionary, make no mistake this political fiefdom has nothing to do with educating, and everything to do with ensuring conformity. Schools are nothing more than a place to park children for eight hours, while their parents work to pay taxes to the state. To keep the children distracted, they feed them Soviet-style propaganda. Most schools have given up trying to resemble institutions of good old-fashioned education, because they no longer can, nor will they ever again, since the teachers themselves are a product of this failing system. It is the very result hoped for by the communists who set this whole debacle in motion. Their project, started in the nineteen-sixties, which they hoped would produce an undereducated, disgruntled, populace, primed for revolution, has come to fruition, the only problem is that the revolutionaries have gone. They all became capitalists, or at least champagne-socialists, and now all that remains is this pointless political football.'

'I'm not listening to this,' Tony stomped out of the back door, and strode off across the yard.

'What's that about?' said Peter, walking over to Mac, who was sitting on the bench outside the kitchen door. Mac set down the shoes he was polishing. 'I'm not sure how it started, but Tony got into one with John about the education system. I think he tried to claim it was near perfect, or something like that, and John has done his usual trick of being deliberately inflammatory, in order to provoke a response.'

'Oops.'

'Yup, and it looks like he's coming back for more.'

'Think I'll stay, budge up, this could be fun.'

Mac moved his shoe cleaning kit and shuffled up the protesting bench.

Peter settled in, and as Tony walked past them, Peter said, 'Don't do it, you'll lose.'

Tony ignored the smirking pair on the bench, and went back into the kitchen, resuming his place at the table. Father John returned from the library holding an art book under his arm.

'Good, you're back.'

'I'm here to defend…'

'The indefensible. Well don't bother. Just listen, and you might actually learn something.' Father John, stood up, asking, 'Coffee?'

'Tea, if you don't mind,' said Tony.

Father John busied himself making tea and coffee, he shouted out, 'What about you two eavesdroppers?'

'Two coffees,' replied Mac.

'One sugar in mine, none in, Mac's,' said Peter.

'I know, I know,' said Father John, 'You two joining us?'

'No fear, we'll stay here,' laughed Peter.

Tea, coffee, and chocolate biscuits sorted, Father John resumed his seat, 'Where to start? What if I just ask you a simple question? Right... this is one is from my Eleven-Plus exam, what is a gerund, and give me an example?'

'A what?'

'A gerund.'

'Never heard of... is it a small furry animal?'

'You maintain that the present education system has not been dumbed down, yet here you are, a fairly recent recipient of the fruits of that system, unable to answer a simple question, one that I was expected to know aged eleven.'

'Go on then, what is it?'

'Peter! Enlighten him.'

'It is a verb that functions as a noun. Swimming is fun. Eating biscuits...'

'Fine, so I didn't know something, that doesn't...'

'Hold your tongue. I knew that you would not understand the question, because it is unlikely that outside of a university course in English you would encounter it. The real problem facing children today, is how to acquire an education? Clearly, not by attending a state school. That system has lost its way, it no longer tries to educate, merely to train pupils like wayward puppies to do tricks, to pass multiple-choice exams; a form of testing that provides the answer, unlike the old system that sought to discover the extent of knowledge retained by the students, and to test their understanding of what they had learned, to see if they could relate this information to other subjects, and use it to provide comprehensive answers. A system that is far superior to the silo-learning inflicted upon the victims of the present abomination. It is not the fault of the schools, they are just as much victims of the same system, it's what happens when politicians are allowed to interfere. No one leaves the present system with anything resembling intellectual independence, everyone regurgitates the propaganda inculcated into them, without exception, and without the means, or the desire to question it. I can see no real way out, since the teachers are also a part of the same flawed system, this social experiment has been running now for nearly sixty-years, and it is getting worse. It has resulted in the wholesale rejection of learning. I set learning against modern education, because learning implies, and requires, that an individual does not accept facts as given, but explores and investigates a subject, so that the truth of it is fully understood and assimilated. Not catalogued in isolation, but set in context, linked to the rest of the knowledge acquired by that person.'

Father John paused, drank some coffee, and ate a biscuit, then continued, 'It is the case for most individuals that this no longer happens, reflecting the paucity of education. Worse, a worrying trend has seen history increasingly bent to the will of social-Marxism, resulting in most believing that history began with their own birth certificate, a very disturbing development. Each of us is born in a specific place, at a specific time, to specific parents. We enter into a specific historical setting, with specific historical qualities, as a specific individual, our uniqueness can only be manifest when we have an unequivocal continuity with history. To be separated from the past is to suffer a dismembered humanity. You cannot live without history. Within the pattern of history is truth, its objective reality is what informs the present. There are those who seek to deny, or to twist the truth, bend it to their will, to enslave history. It will gain them nothing, their today will be a lie, which destroys their chance of a tomorrow. History is timeless, history is today; I fear the direction we are taking as individuals, as a society, as a culture. To survive, human beings need two things, knowledge and language, we must have a sufficient grasp of our language in order to articulate concepts. We need language to acquire the knowledge necessary to recognise, interpret, and fully comprehend the abstract ideas that push the boundaries of knowledge which inform all aspects of our lives as social and enquiring creatures, without an adequate grasp of language we cannot accurately conceptualise.'

Father John took a sip of his coffee, then continued, 'Take evil as an example, relevant to the enquiry that we have embarked upon, people today cannot properly grasp the concept of evil, they cannot clearly define, nor recognise it. Most if asked, struggle to articulate it, at best you get the Hollywood interpretation, the majority reject the notion entirely, just as they reject God. They would rather laugh and mock, than entertain the possibility that either might actually exist. Satan is seen as a fairy story to frighten children, only the simple-minded, superstitious and credulous need concern themselves, as for the rest, the sophisticated, they have no need of such primitive notions. They claim that only the deluded talk about the Devil, and that to do so is a sign that you are unenlightened, and naive, and they will describe you, without a trace of irony on their part, as uneducated. Do they ignore, or fail to see the daily examples of evil and its effects, or is it that are they complicit in its persistence? As for the concept of a soul, only throwbacks like me believe in the existence of a life beyond this one, believe in a personal God who loves us. Not so the educated, or should I say, the conceptually challenged. Primitive it may be, but like it or not, the Devil exists, and there are those who hold him to be the prince of this world, and claim that it is God who is evil, and not the Devil.'

Father John, crossed himself, and continued, 'A society encouraged to ignore the transcendent, begins by banning books, and ends by turning people into fertiliser. History demonstrates that any culture that denies transcendent morality will be governed by unrestrained power, resulting in the loss of freedom, and unrelenting human suffering. The removal of the transcendent corrupts every aspect of the human condition, art, philosophy, politics, economics, and particularly science. Such a society warps human relationships and makes slaves of its people. Which is why education, of the kind that inculcates the love of learning, is so important to our freedom. About the time that the social-experiment in education was being put in place, around the middle of the nineteen-sixties, across the world political, philosophical, and theological changes were being forced on an unthinking populous, who were happy to delight in freedoms that these changes appeared to bring. Now it is clear to the few who can see that those freedoms were in fact, shackles. No Western society escaped, and none of those changes have proved beneficial.'

Father John indicated to Tony that he was going to have another cup of coffee, Tony nodded, and handed up his cup. Father John returned with both cups, and said, 'People turned away from God, rejected all that was good and decent, they tore up the tenets of Western civilisation, which ironically created the freedom for them to do so, in large numbers they flocked to adopt communism, especially that of, Mao. Proudly waving his damnable little Red Book, as if it was the answer to all ills.

Indifferent to the terrible crimes being committed in Russia and China, they closed their minds to the genocide in those countries, some still deny that any wrongdoing took place. This generation hunts down the negativity in historical convention to justify their rejection and failure to observe tradition. But if the old customs are to be discarded, what then? They fail to understand that this is not an end in itself, but a beginning. So, what will they build to replace that which they have unthinkingly rendered asunder? They seem unable to recognise that having torn down the edifice of our culture, they must engage in a process of reconstruction, they must become builders. There is a fundamental principle, which they fail to understand, that solid foundations are required to support a successful civilisation, foundations constructed out of sound principles. What are their new principles? Do they have any? Do they even understand that a positive precept is required? Having rejected the light, and embraced darkness, everything becomes brutish, art, music, drama, even relationships. People give away freedom without realising it, as they walk away from individual responsibility. For society to function, all of us must act responsibly, and if we decline to accept that responsibility, then the state will, but at a cost to our freedom. People do not see that real freedom comes only when we accept responsibility for our own lives, and do not cravenly abdicate such authority to others. Have you noticed that insisting on responsibility is almost a crime? It wasn't his fault, it was the drink, or the drugs, or some other crutch is proffered to excuse the indefensible behaviour of an individual, but never are we to ascribe blame, nor are we to insist that the individual concerned accept liability for their own actions. The minute we accept responsibility, is the moment we begin to take back power from the state, and that will not be tolerated. We have ended up with a society where no one is willing to accept that they are to blame for their misdeeds, they even seek to justify behaviour, which in the past, would have been an occasion for shame and humiliation, yet, today such behaviour is displayed almost as a badge of honour. This has resulted in the shirking-class, wastrels who demand, and take, but never give, they are the fruit of this particular harvest. Generations of feckless individuals passing through life taking all they can, without any sense of responsibility to their fellow citizens, they carry with them a catalogue of entitlements, and a library of rights, but they have no concept of duty towards others. What can be done about it? Nothing, even if we change course today, they will be the lost cohort, under-educated, unemployable, unwelcome, and apparently blameless.'

Father John sipped some coffee, added half a teaspoon of sugar, stirred, and finished the cup. He then said, 'Education, education, education, that was the mantra proclaimed from the rooftops, a new world beckoned, apparently a new direction was required, so the Progressive Way was ushered in, and it was to be implemented through education, but they really meant, propaganda. Language is the root of all, it is the means by which we access the world around us. As Wittgenstein claimed, there is no thought outside of language, without the ability to conceptualise, we are little more than…'

Tony interrupted, 'I get it, so what's to be done, what's the answer?'

'It is because the world is wonderful, that we wonder about the world, which is, in itself, an act of wonder. The unintelligent examination of the world by politicised science has banished wonder, claiming that reality is found only in material things, and as a result many are driven to believe that only physical force can act on substance, which leads to the conclusion that the only answer to the human condition is force, that only power shapes reality, and history shows that leads to barbarism. We need to help children discover that sense of wonder, we must give children an education that results in intellectual independence, better and comprehensive teaching of English and Philosophy would be a good start. But that is a discussion for another time… I didn't mean to start a conversation about…'

Mac and Peter's, laughter interrupted him. Father John opened the art book he had earlier placed on the kitchen table, searched for a particular painting, and finding it, turned it round for Tony to see. 'Ignore them. Describe that painting, and tell me what you think it means?'

'An old man, a carpenter, drilling a hole in a piece of wood, while a boy, possibly his apprentice, looks on, the boy is holding a candle.'

'Good, good, what else?'

'What can I say? It's a nice painting, well executed, skilful, I like the way the light has been painted…'

'Yes, yes, but the painting contains a message, the clues are all there, you've already pointed most of them out. There are clues and hints left by the artist for you to interpret. Now look again.'

'Nothing… sorry.'

'You do know the answer. Okay… the painting is called St. Joseph the Carpenter. It was painted in sixteen-forty by, Georges de la Tour. It contains both open and hidden Christian iconography, messages for the educated viewer. Another example of just such a painting is…' Father John turned over a couple more pages, 'the Mérode Altarpiece, painted by Robert Campin, around fourteen-twenty-six. Standing in front of it… well… it's a triptych, it's in three parts, hinged together, if we just take one of the panels, it depicts Saint Joseph, he has made a mousetrap, symbolising Christ's trapping the Devil, in another Saint Joseph is making equipment used in winemaking, symbolising Eucharistic wine, and Christ's Passion, and so on, these are the hidden messages of Christian iconography.'

He flipped the pages back, finding the previous painting, 'Now keeping that in mind, look at this painting again, and interpret the Christian imagery for me. See if you can decipher the two most obvious ones?'

Tony spent a minute or two examining the picture, then said, 'This is taking me back to my Sunday School days.'

Peter said, 'Give up, John, he's Church of England, they believe everything and nothing, how's he going to know what's in the picture?' Peter, and Mac laughed aloud.

Tony joined in the laughter, then said, 'You're all being a little too smug… the child is Jesus. He is holding a candle, the Light of the World. The way the wooden beam is aligned with the auger… makes it look like a cross, or is it… an anticipation of the crucifixion?'

'Well done, you got it. Clearly you paid attention at Sunday School,' Father John continued, 'There is actually a point to this… shut up, Mac.'

'I didn't say anything?'

'Not out loud, but I know what you were thinking.'

Mac, and Peter laughed, and Tony suppressed a snigger.

'This investigation calls for the ability to be able to find and interpret signs and symbols, understand their meaning, and place that information in the right context; right now, you don't have that level of understanding. I'm sorry Tony, I do not want to sound cruel, you were trained not taught. The problem is your passivity. Since joining the police, you have successfully attended various training courses, and you have clearly responded well, you have the makings of a fine police officer. But, a burglary, is a burglary, theft, is theft, and an assault, is an assault, you have been trained to deal with and respond to about eighty percent of what you will encounter in your service. Experience will help you to refine and build upon this knowledge, and with application you will undoubtedly become a competent investigator. You are clearly intelligent...'

'What is the problem?'

'Your acquiescence. If I tell you something, because you trust and respect me, you will accept it unquestionably, and assimilate it wholeheartedly. If I try to impart the same information to those two... yeomen. They'll claim it's interesting, then go off and find out as much as they can about it, partly to challenge my assertion, and partly to further their knowledge, which is what their education, and experience has taught them to do. In your case the onus is entirely on me, I have to ensure that you have been thoroughly briefed, and that's the problem, if I fail to cover an issue, or omit to place a particular fact before you, I could put this entire investigation in jeopardy. You're inclined towards pedagogical passivity... such is the paucity of your education. If you miss a sign, or fail to spot a symbol, or to pick up on the behaviour of an individual, or group, it could prove dangerous... we cannot afford to overlook a single clue, doing so places us all at risk. Now do you understand why a lifetime spent learning something new every day, is better than one that submissively waits for knowledge to be imparted? You have some way to go to achieve intellectual independence. I don't mean for this be insulting... this conversation is not going the way I intended'

Tony put his hands in the air in an act of submission, and said, 'Okay, educate me. These young girls and boys who are being transported around the globe, where do they come from? Doesn't anyone care, or make a fuss? They are missing, where are their families? What are their governments doing?'

Mac, and Peter upon hearing his question came into the

kitchen, joined by Simon, who had just walked over from the stable block, they all sat around the kitchen table.

Mac said, 'We have outlawed slavery, but not eliminated it. For some countries it is an active and essential part of their economy, and it is a way of life for many.'

'So why don't we do something to stop it?' said Simon.

Mac said, 'Because those countries in which slavery is practiced are on our side, critically linked to the functioning of our economy, and our national security. So long as there are countries where there is the legal right to male ownership and control of women, then slavery will never be eliminated. Basically, it comes down to the attitude that prevails in the West, one that states, who cares if a few peasants get dragged out of their mud huts to work as slaves for a rich potentate? At least they will be clothed and fed. Unfortunately, so long as the rich continue to indulge in luxury, and you and I have a job, and a roof over our heads, we collectively turn a blind eye...'

Peter interrupted, saying, 'The general attitude, spoken or unspoken, is, why should we care if someone we don't know, and will never meet, has their life destroyed? As long as we get to live a good life, fuck'em. It's a subject never spoken of in polite society, justified by wrong thinking that claims that the new life of the slave will be better than their old way of living.'

The degree of emotion with which Peter spoke, took all by surprise, he continued, 'The trouble is, they're not better off. They're fucking slaves, daily subject to beatings and starvation, they are raped and sodomised, any resulting children they have, face the same lifetime of abuse. Western governments will denounce the few instances of slavery exposed by the media, but ensure that the impression left, is one that presents such incidents as isolated, one-off events, and definitely not part of a global trading network worth billions of pounds a year. Having managed to pass off such instances as no more than the random villainy of a few criminals, the same governments will then do nothing to interfere with the network.'

Mac said, 'Like you, I couldn't understand it at first. All these children go missing and there isn't an outcry? We discovered that they volunteered or were volunteered by their parents. They believed they were destined for a better life in the West, a life of hard, but well-paid work. The families wanted them to go, so they could send money back home, and eventually, having settled in a Western country, bring the rest of the family over. It's simple economics.'

Peter said, 'Yeah, simple economics, but it doesn't have to be this way, if we just change the way the world organises its affairs, if a better system could be found to share out the wealth, there would be no need for these poor people to send their children into a nightmare world of slavery. I saw it when I worked overseas, it sickened me, and the worst of it is, that we here in the West just acquiesce. To fix it, we must improve their economies, their education system, their healthcare facilities, and ensure that they live in a just and free society; given the way capitalism is presently organised, and the fact this can only be achieved at a cost to our own economy, it ain't going to happen anytime soon.'

They all sat silently, waiting for Peter, who was obviously disturbed by what he had said, to calm down.

Father John said, 'It is an unfortunate truth, that when a need arises, someone will come along to feed it. Today we have a situation where those fulfilling the desires of others, are also the ones manufacturing that desire. The best example I can give is pornography, it has always been around, you can find it on the walls of buildings in Pompeii, until recently it was not that easy to come by, both expensive and rare, it was confined to the wealthy classes, which explains much. Now we have the internet, a truly great resource, a boon to mankind, but it has a dark side, and lurking there we find pornography. From what I have read, there are very few young men and women, or even teenagers, who have not viewed pornography, most are exposed daily to this tide of septic filth. It is already altering the relationships between men and women, and it will eventually infect the whole of society, as this generation grows older, we will arrive at a point when sex replaces emotion in human relationships, when lust, not love, drives society. Many of those children who are being trafficked will end their short lives, casualties of this sordid trade, but none of the slavering sweaty onanists who buy this filth, will stop to think about their victims. It is telling that those who oppose restricting access to this corrupting obscenity, are mostly social-Marxists. Paedophilia has always been with us, some among the Ancient Greeks tried to turn it into a virtue, but it was frowned upon, even then. Opportunities for these reptiles to ply their trade were limited, but with the arrival of the internet, and the anonymity of access that it grants them, there has been an explosion in this vile and sordid activity. Those who would feed that desire, use the internet as a platform to ply their filth, they both create, and feed the demand. I guess what I am trying to say is, that even apparently benign actions can have unforeseen consequences, usually because we have not taken the time to think things through, and that applies to new technologies, now more than ever. Yet, even when we can anticipate the result, we don't avoid the outcome. We choose not to do the right thing, because it is too difficult, because the present arrangement of our economic system will not allow us to do the right thing. Mahatma Gandhi said, "As long as the superstition that people should obey unjust laws exists, so long will slavery exist."

Father John paused to compose himself, then said, 'So the

slave trade continues unabated, because to stop it would require not only the political will, but also a collective desire to do so, and that will never happen, no one in this society is going to surrender their right to a new kitchen, just because some peasant in a faraway place they've never heard of, and can't pronounce, is having a tough time.'

Father John stood up and busied himself making some more tea and coffee.

Mac said, 'Tony, we live in a society that is, nominally at least, tolerant of difference, particularly of race. It's not perfect, but generally we are seen as a tolerant people. On the surface we do not appear to be a racist society, racist words and deeds are against the law, and those who behave that way are generally shunned by polite society. This is both a good, and a bad thing. One consequence of this general tolerance is that sexual relations have crossed the racial divide, a good thing, especially if you are a slaver. It was getting hard to find uneducated, gullible, economically straightened communities in Western Europe, from whom to take children, but now that inter-racial sexual relations are acceptable, well there is a whole world of girls and boys to trade. I am not saying that the creation of better racial relations, or the breaking down of barriers to assimilation were a bad thing. They were not. It was necessary for the founding of a just and free society, and for the establishment of lasting social stability. The problem has arisen because when thinking about how to achieve this, those in authority should have considered the consequences, one of which was to create new opportunities for slavers, they should have anticipated it, and put in place an effective means of dealing with it, but they didn't even ask the question, they never do, it is a consequence of the short-termism engendered by headline driven party politics, and of the paucity of informed public debate in this country. The only way to stop this vile trade is, as Pete pointed out, to improve health, education, employment, justice, and the distribution of wealth in those countries from where these children are taken. It would also require changes in those counties in which slavery is a way of life, and neither of these things can, or will happen within the present arrangement of global economic affairs. So, we hold huge charity concerts and events to assuage our collective and individual conscience. We send enormous sums of money, which inevitably ends up making the rich richer, while a tiny amount dribbles through the cracks in the system and eventually drips down to the poor. Again, we are told that this cannot be helped, it is realpolitik, nothing can be done about it, and we turn away. Slavery as a subject for polite conversation is always in the historic context, never the present reality, for it conflicts with our comfortable view of the world, which is far from the sordid reality of so many, to think on it would be to shatter the illusions of the metropolitan elite. Those who run the system consider it acceptable to feed the poor, but never have the courage to ask why the poor need feeding, asking that will see you branded an anarchist. What is it the poor really need? Simple, to stop being poor.'

Peter said, 'For now, the wealthy in the First World bask by their swimming pools, while the poor in the Third World walk miles to their waterholes, and their children are enslaved, raped and sodomised. It's a great system. The slaver has a wealth of customers, and an abundance of victims, he creates and controls both the market and the commodity, the very model of present-day capitalism!'

Simon said, 'So that's it, nothing is done to stop it?'

Father John, who had had finished fussing, sat down and said, 'If it could be done without harming the economy, it would be, our politicians are not total philistines; the truth is, that in order to achieve the complete eradication of poverty and slavery in the Third World, there would have to be a radical lowering of living standards in the West, and no political party will take that step, it would be electoral suicide. Our economic system, and the way of life it has produced, is the issue, influenced by the false desires created by the commercialisation of our dreams, our lives are occupied by the acquisition of stuff, we are obsessed with stuff. The real problem is that our sense of value, of right and wrong, has been twisted by our idiotic notion that things are a necessity. The answer is modesty, truth is found within modesty, so blinkered are we by the acquiring of things that we do not need, that we are becoming blind to the simplicity of life, and there-fore, to truth.'

Peter said, 'So we continue to be the cause, we permit the market that drives slavery to exist, and our management of the world's financial system ensures that the poor will stay that way. You had better get used to putting your hand in your pocket to assuage the conscience of the nation and get used to the idea that your new car has been bought on the bodies of sodomised chil-dren.'

'That's a bit harsh.' said Simon.

Mac said, 'Is it? The rest of the world does just that, there is a collective pretence perpetrated on society, that ensures that the few cases of slavery that make it into the media are seen as isol-ated aberrations, certainly not part of some multi-billion-pound global business. This case presents us with a chance to make a stand, to draw a line and say this far and no further, to do any-thing other is to condone it.'

'But is it worth it? Even if we succeed, no one will know about it, no one will care?' said Tony.

Mac said, 'We will, and that should be enough.'

'But is it?' said Simon.

Peter said, 'What if the children they had taken were April or Katie, or one of yours, if you get round to having any?'

Tony groaned, 'How can I ever buy a new kitchen again, in all conscience I can't?'

Mac said, 'It's not about kitchens, and in any case I suspect, Mrs Maitland, may have something to say about it, and you will quickly set your newly acquired scruples to one side. The driving force for our investigation is about doing the right thing, we are all a part of this world, we have not abdicated our social responsibility, we remain autonomous beings. We must act according to conscience, and if our representatives in Parliament, those elected to serve us, fail to do so, then it is incumbent on us to act. Nothing prevents us from doing so, truth is not relative, it is not something decided by Parliament and justified by decisions handed down by the courts, nor is it the beneficent pronouncement of an anonymous coterie of the elite. If something is wrong, then it is wrong, everywhere, and for all time. Truth is absolute, and we have an absolute duty to stand up to evil, and that is all we can do, so it will have to be enough.'

Father John said, 'I am sure you have heard it said that all it takes for evil to thrive, is that good men do nothing, we must always speak truth to power, for if we do not, we ensure that same fate for ourselves. The power of evil is consolidated by the cowardice of the good, silence in the face of evil, is itself evil. Let me read you something, it might help you to see the bigger picture.'

Father John, left the room, returning a few moments later with a book on European political history. He said, 'A piece of advice, beware when a noun disguises itself behind an adjective, it's always followed by the curtailment of freedom and a rampant period of oppression.'

Tony and Simon, looked blankly at Father John.

'National Socialism, Social Democrat, or similar.' He began

flicking through the pages of the book. 'Here it is,' Father John read the article out loud: *"The Green Party in Germany in nineteen-eighty, set up a national working group, Bag SchwuP, an eclectic mix, they had links to other similar groups across the globe, including the Man-Boy Love Association, whose motto is: 'Sex before eight, before it's too late.' The Greens lobbied for the law banning sexual relations with children to be abolished. The Greens convention in North Rhine-Westphalia in 1985, backed the legalisation of paedophilia. That same year, Baden-Württemberg's Green Party committee called for the abolition of all protective-ages for mutually consensual sexual relations."* Father John put the book down.

Simon said, 'That was the Sixties revolution playing itself out, most of those people are dead or retired, you can't use that to justify your argument for events today, that kind of thinking is dead and gone, along with the social experiments that spawned it.'

'You think?' said Mac, as he produced a copy of a newspaper published the previous week. He read aloud from an article: *"Laws banning incest between brothers and sisters could be scrapped, after a German government ethics committee concluded that they were an unacceptable intrusion into the right to sexual self-determination. The German Ethics Council report stated, 'Criminal law is not the appropriate means to preserve a social taboo... the fundamental right of adult siblings to sexual self-determination is to be weighed more heavily than the abstract idea of protection of the family.' Whilst it is generally accepted that incest carries a higher risk of children being born with genetic abnormalities, the Ethics Council dismissed that argument, on the basis that other genetically affected couples are not banned from having children."* Setting the article aside, Mac continued, 'Thinking that oozed out of Left-wing circles in the nineteen-sixties has certainly not gone the way of the dodo, it is still present, still informing the mindset of opinion-makers. Western governments, so obsessed with talk of rights, have ironically tossed natural-law, and the actual rights that flow from it, out the window, what we will end up with is not a right, but a sanctioned wrong. In that piece I just read, did you note that sexual self-determination is accorded primacy over the protection of the family, which they describe as, abstract?'

Father John said, 'It was no different here, influential individuals in today's Parliament, supported this position, they try, as you just did, to defend the indefensible by claiming that it was a product of its time. Freedom is a much-misunderstood word, they shook off what they perceived as dogmatic shackles, only to find themselves enslaved by their unfettered passions. Many of the individuals, responsible at that time for the position taken by the Greens and others on the Left, are now in prominent, and influential positions within the mechanism of government, and judging by the piece that Mac read out, still corrupted by that agenda, it is clearly a deep-rooted perversion. We have entered a period of government without values, a totalitarian tyranny of liberalism, which attacks any who hold views which do not have their stamp of approval. An odd freedom, free to say and do whatever you want, so long as it conforms to their sanctioned position, silencing all opponents, through fear, or imprisonment, it has a worryingly familiar ring to it. The real problem is that the West has politicised politics. Rights driven social engineering is bearing fruit, across the West we are seeing the normalisation of every conceivable perversion, the unnatural as natural, evil as virtuous, embedding these corruptions into a new normal. Those who seek to advocate traditional values and integrity will be branded subversive. In the EU, anti-Europe laws have already been passed to prevent

179

such dissent, no questioning of their policy decisions is to be permitted. Laws are being passed here, and around the world, to corral thought, to restrict what you can say or write, to ensure that only the approved and sanctioned version of the message the Left wants presented as truth, is granted public access. The fact that it is patently false, if not an obvious lie, is irrelevant, for them all that matters is that their truth, their voice, their words, are the only one you will see or hear. Challenge or confront them and you will suffer public banishment and censorship, later, once their lie is generally accepted by a compliant citizenship, harsher punishments will follow, gulags, death camps, and assassinations. What we thought we had rid the world of, has returned; the idiots who espouse social-Marxism, in most cases solely to appear Woke, will see their virtue-waving destroy them and all those they enlisted and supported along the way, as communism re-establishes itself. For the first thing that will happen will be the immediate execution of the anarchists, and the useful idiots who supported them, well, who wants counter-revolutionaries hanging around to challenge the new order. I guess it is true, if you don't study and understand the message of history, you will end up repeating it.'

Mac said, 'These new rights are nought but a series of wrongs, this bending of the truth to the service of fashionable concepts will result in chaos and death. Chaos, as each new right is replaced by an even newer one, as trends ebb and flow. Death will arrive through the courts, as legalism rejects the truth, and mere occurrences become the measure of right, so parliament will move from supporting a right to die, to a position where the state decides when you die; inevitable, if you elevate wrongs to the status of rights, and dismiss rights as wrongs. Consider, if a law states that you may do something as a matter of personal choice how it inevitably morphs into a position that claims you ought to do it, then it becomes okay for others to insist you that do it, and if you won't, then the state will force you; all laws that start out providing a right of individual choice, eventually become universal. The question that none who advocate such innovative values care to answer, is who decides what is right and what is wrong, and by what authority is this brave new world being built? It is upon these mendacious foundations that this great new liberal project is being erected, it will be a monument to barbarism, that will make the savagery of the past seem nothing more than a Sunday School picnic. The root cause of this problem is, as Father John so frequently points out, the fact that too many cannot tell the difference between philosophy and ideology…'

Simon interrupted, 'You just lost me?'

Father John looked at Mac, who nodded and said, 'Go ahead John.'

Father John said, 'Philosophy is the love of knowledge, the search for truth, an enterprise that utilises reason. Philosophy is universal, excluding none, embracing all, it seeks to understand the depth and breadth of reality. Ideology is a set of limited ideas, restricted to a select few, who are only interested in an isol-ated and tiny fragment of human endeavour; they cast aside reason, and predicate their argument on what they claim to be an incontestable assertion, though usually it is nothing more than an emotive rant. If philosophy dies, then so does reason, and with it, freedom and culture. However, I continue to have faith in the innate goodness of my fellow man, even though some test my faith.'

He looked over at Peter, who laughed nervously, before every-one joined in. Father John continued, 'Society today is no better, or worse, than it has ever been, it is still a mix of saints and sinners. There are however, two distinct breaks with the past, the first is technology, which has sped up our ability to ensure that man's inhumanity to man can be brought about with great accuracy, on a much wider scale, and with a rapidity that is unnerving; the second, is the rise of relativism, which has resulted in too many these days thinking that plummeting is flying. Whilst it is the default position of those conditioned by political correctness to ignore the obvious, and dispute with commonsense, there still remains an inevitability about gravity, and those driven to denying the truth, face a future that points toward a sudden and fatal meeting with reality. For all that, I still believe in the inherent goodness of man. I firmly believe that good will ultimately triumph over evil. The meek will inherit the earth. You can see that in the young, there is a growing collective consciousness that the road we are on is the wrong one. They recognise that there must be a better way to run our affairs, that the economic system enslaves all of us. We should be, but are not, masters of our fate. The young believe that their economic safety cannot be at the price of another's peril. Peter articulated this view, and one day soon, we will just stop. We will collectively reject the lies, and the excuses, we will refuse to acquiesce in the face of power, we will break its hold over us, and change the way things are done. The real irony is that it is we, who grant the powerful their dominion, gift them the right to exercise control over us. William Marshall, the first great knight, over eight-hundred years ago recognised this fact. He understood that kings need people, as much as people need kings, hence the Magna Carta. The collective has forgotten that, and as a result, we are slowly surrendering our birthright. Meekness and humility are not a manifestation of cowardice, Gandhi proved that, and he still points the way. Today, we need only grant those who would be king sufficient power as is needed to run the country, and it for us alone to determine what is sufficient; we were not paying attention, and they appropriated too much power, so now we must take it back.'

Mac raised his finger, and Father John nodded.

Mac said, 'What I find most upsetting, is not that opinion-makers come to believe in the lies and inventions they propagate, nor that they then stand up in public and insist on justifying their methods of control and repression, it is that we, the citizens of this country, whose rights and freedoms they are stealing, laud them for it. This stems from a failure to recognise the objective truth about being, from which flows our ancient rights, resulting in an inability to recognise the human dignity of everyone, regardless of their failings. The abandonment of the universal principles that underpin our rights mean that we cannot expect, or trust, governments, or the courts, to protect us. In fact, the way that our so-called democracy is heading, is more likely to result in our courts legalising every conceivable iniquity, since the only foundation upon which laws will be constructed is an ephemeral notion of equality, resulting in great harm to the individual, and the eventual destruction of our entire way of life. Truly, reason is sleeping. Claiming to protect the public, politicians have set about repressing rights and limiting freedom. Their aim is to create a culture of control, born out of fear, fear they have induced, this is a new culture, to which we will all have to submit, accepting the right of the government to control our behaviour, requiring us to see our very existence as a gift of the state. Governments since the French Revolution have been inventing dangers and threats out of expediency; however, they consistently fail to substantiate such claims, and the young are growing increasingly cynical.'

Father John smiled, and said, 'Mac is right, place your hope in the younger generation, all is not lost, I was walking through Preston a couple of weeks ago, when a group of about six young people walked towards me, they parted as they walked around me, and collectively said, "Good afternoon, Father", I was so surprised I barely managed to say bless you, by way of reply. I turned and watched them walking off, they were dressed in the uniform of the young, running shoes, jeans, and t-shirts proclaiming their preference for this or that musical combo. Save one, she had: *Their power comes from our obedience – disobey*, emblazoned on the back of her top, such understanding is a product of truth, and truth will always find a way, it can be gagged for a while, but never silenced forever. Sufficient is a good word, it means having enough, an adequate amount, but not more than is needed. It is a virtue we should all cultivate; it should be our watchword. By accepting it into our lives, we ensure that others get their share. I think I should explain Distributionism to you…'

Mac tapped on the table, and smiling at Father John, said, 'To get back to the point… I believe that my duty is to my family, my friends, my neighbours, and only then, to my country. If something threatens my family, and those in power do nothing to prevent it, or worse, encourage it, what am I supposed to do?'

Tony said, 'Defend them, of course.'

'That's right, protect them. We are not robots, or ants, even though the political class would prefer it if we were,' said Father John.

Mac said, 'So we must act to end this vile… hell I can't think of an appropriate word… since the institutions of the state will do nothing, then we must act.'

'All well and good, Mac. But it still amounts to nothing more than vigilantism, mob rule. Alright, it's not mob rule, you do not propose an unthinking, brutish…'

'Simon, all I am asking is that by using our training and experience, and sticking to the rules of evidence, we do our best to ensure that this is investigated thoroughly. I appeal for natural justice, are we supposed to turn our backs on those children, who right now are having unspeakable things done to them? Do you intend to ignore the murder, rape, infanticide, and sodomising of children, simply because it doesn't make you feel comfortable?'

'No, but...'

Mac interrupted, 'You feel uncomfortable, because, as a police officer, you are being asked to act outside of the normal rules of engagement, but who wrote those rules? Some of the very people we will be investigating. Simon, your concern, and I suspect Tony's, is for a justice that does not exist, it is as elusive as the notion of democracy. What makes something just? Is it Parliament? Is that it? The government defines this or that as just, and that makes it so? Government cannot legislate what is right and wrong, only what is legal. Is justice only a construct, or does it exist beyond society, does it not in fact have to exist before there can be a civil society? And what of our history, and the line of unjust laws passed by Parliament, repealed only when people rebelled and took the law into their own hands? Surely justice comes from something deeper, innate, it's a virtue, in a class of ideas that exist distinct from us, something acquired from outside of us? Do we live in a democracy, because our society demonstrates and upholds democratic principles, or is it because the political class tell us that it is so? Life, liberty, and the pursuit of happiness are ours by right. They are not the gift of governments, to be diluted, or removed at a whim. Governments will always seek the means to reduce those rights, to further their power and self-importance. You look doubtful? You have only to look at the powers that governments around the world gave themselves, following the attacks on the Twin Towers. Legislation really intended to exercise control over their respective populations; none are effective in preventing terrorist attacks, the very excuse given for the conferring of these extraordinary powers. They talk of rights and equality, as if these conditions are their gift to us, but their notion of liberty bears no relationship to our inalienable rights, and given that all men are created equal, they are messing with our birthright. It is not in their gift, to take from, or give these things to us. They twist notions of freedom and equality to fit an agenda, which they demand the right to impose on us. I think what appals me most, is that when they seek to dilute, or remove these freedoms, they demand our approval for doing so!'

Peter said, 'It's the same with the notion of justice, politicians apply a veneer of respectability, then demand that we accept, as a true proposition, that our country is just. However, their cloaking of the reality of justice is done to ensure that none of us sees the truth. Their assertions do not change the lie. Do we ignore natural justice, must we surrender our desire for truth to the functionaries of the state, can we not discern veracity for ourselves, are we unable to act, or think, without their approbation? Is something only true when it has been defined and approved by government? Open your eyes to what is going on. We live in a nation that daily dispenses justice in secret. Trials are held in camera up and down the country, they cannot be reported by the media, the individuals who are subject to these proceedings are not allowed to know who accuses them, or even what the accusation is, frequently they are excluded from the court to prevent them from hearing evidence, their court appointed defence lawyers are not allowed to question the validity of the accusations made. This slap in the face of the Magna Carta, has no place in a free society, and yet it is the law of the land, approved by Parliament. People are sent to prison in this country by a system sanctioned by Parliament, that denies them the most basic human freedom, the right to know who accuses them, what the accusation is, and the right to an open trial, to be judged by a jury of their peers. Is that justice, Simon?'

'No.'

'Is it in keeping with the often-vaunted freedoms and democratic principles of this country?'

'No.'

Mac said, 'And yet it is legal, it is law, passed and authenticated by Parliament. Our justice system must be the envy of most dictators. And you have qualms about what we are going to do? The problem is that you, along with many in this Realm, believe that for something to be just, it must be a product of our parliamentary system, but Parliament is inherently anti-democratic and partisan. Parliament has a long history of producing unjust and oppressive laws. The periods when fairness held sway followed revolt in the face of political tyranny. During the short periods that followed a revolt, democracy thrived, before the creeping political class acted, and smothered justice. Without a trace of irony, it is these periods of enforced parliamentary tranquillity that our politicians point to, as proof of democracy in action. So, Tony, should we meekly submit to the tyranny of politicians?'

'No.'

'Is our search for the truth going to result in an injustice, can only the Court lay claim to objectivity?'

'No, I guess not.'

'How many injustices, or failures of the system been inflicted upon us by our courts, not a year goes by without some establishment induced wrong being subject to enquiry, following investigation by ordinary people, people who themselves were failed by courts biased toward legalism, and prejudiced against justice? Should journalists set aside their investigative exposure of wrongdoing at the top of society, just because they are not part of the justice system? Should they be prohibited from examining political chicanery, just because they don't have a warrant card in their pocket, because their enquiries are not approved by the very people whose behaviour they are investigating? Do you consider a team of investigative journalists to be a gang of vigilantes?'

'No.'

'So, we stick to who, what, why, when, and where, then we ask how; we follow the evidence we uncover, which should lead us to the truth.'

Peter said, 'It's the next bit that has you worried. We are not a bunch of hillbilly shit-kickers, I'm guessing that none of us knows how to play a banjo, we are not a lynch-mob. We confront a great evil, one protected by the system, because some of those in the system have been corrupted by that evil. I am happy to dispense justice under these circumstances, and that justice will be far better than that administered by some parliamentary appointee in a wig.'

Simon said, 'Okay, but isn't it true, that only God can judge us?'

Peter said, 'That is true. Father John has on many occasions told me that it is for God alone to judge. All I'm going to do is put them in front of God... a little sooner than they anticipated or hoped.'

There was grim laughter around the table.

Simon said, 'Peter, you don't even believe in, God.'

'Yes, I do.'

Father John smiled and said, 'I want to say that in combating evil, we are doing God's work, but I know that to most of you that will sound slightly odd. I am convinced that we are doing the right thing, and for the right reasons. We are on the side of the angels, and if I am correct in that, then I have a feeling that you will not have to do anything that threatens your immortal souls.'

'In that case, how can we not see this through to the end, whatever it be?' said Simon.

'You have no choice,' said, Mac, 'You are a serving copper, a detective inspector for goodness' sake, you have a duty to investigate.'

'I know that, but it's out of my jurisdiction.'

Peter said, 'Just now you were horrified by the uncaring response of the West to the slave trade in the Third World, now you are doing the same. It's not my responsibility. Let someone else do it. It's too hard. It might harm my career…'

'Alright, I get it. But what then, after we have investigated, once we have the evidence, then what?'

Peter said, 'Then you stand aside and let us deal with it.'

'You can't mean…?'

'There is only one way we can win this, and only one way we can end it. If we decide to go after them, there are only two possible outcomes, they kill us, or we kill them. This is not a fucking game, there can be no pragmatic accommodations, and if you are not happy with that fact, then you're free to leave, just give us a little time before you report back to Cartwright, at least a month.'

'I'm in for the duration. I will do all I can to ensure success, even if it means…'

Mac, turned to Tony, 'What about you?'

'I'm not happy with the possibility of that outcome… but count me in.'

'Good, I know you have reservations, we know that the two of you are uncomfortable with this, we all are, I would be concerned if you weren't. We have to confront this evil, because if we don't, who will?'

Mac raised his cup of coffee and said, 'A toast. This far and no further.' They all raised their cups and repeated the toast.

Peter said, 'I've been thinking about this, and it seems to me that we have joined an ancient debate about the difference between morality and legality, and how to position justice. In this country, it is a discussion being chaired by irresolute opinion-makers whose speculations are being acted upon without any reference... without the advantage of being filtered by virtue, or morality, thereby ensuring that justice is excluded from any conclusion they arrive at... am I making sense?'

Father John, smiled. Peter said, 'Yeah, ok, I was listening. I paid attention. Happy?'

Father John said, 'Continue with your line of thought.'

Peter paused, then said, 'Adultery is not moral, it's harmful to both individuals and society, but it's legally permitted. Expressing a critical view of the European Union is illegal, but not morally wrong. Clearly, there can be instances where things are morally wrong, but legally acceptable, and vice-versa. So, what do we do, follow the diktat of the law, something written and imposed, generally without reference to the views of the public, by people who are in some cases, morally bankrupt, or our own consciences? Is it better to be legally right, or morally right? Some laws are clearly unjust, yet they remain legal, I think the way forward is clear, we follow the still-small-voice-within, we have no choice. Let's get it done.' All nodded in assent. Peter, continued, 'It will not be easy. It's going to be dangerous, and we are going to need help...'

Father John said, 'I urge you all to have faith. Christianity is not an opinion to which you accede, but a reality to which you capitulate. It is not our strength that protect us, but our weakness...'

'And a .50 calibre bullet,' laughed Peter.

'I didn't catch that?' said Father John.

'Nothing.'

Mac said, 'Pete's got a point, I am worried not only about where this will take us, but how we may have to respond. We know that at some point we will be opposed by force, we will confront violent, armed men, and we will have to kill to save ourselves, to save any children caught up in this cesspit. Knowing that this is a possibility, should we even entertain the idea of embarking on this investigation? It's hardly downing evil in an abundance of good, will we not be fighting fire with fire, and therefore in the wrong? We have a great deal to discuss; time we took a walk. We'll leave this old prelate to his books.'

Father John said, 'I want to hear what you decide... go on, leave me, what do I care.'

Peter, patted him on the back, 'We still love you.'

'Go, off with you, attend to your musings, you heathens.'

They walked off towards the woods, crossing the field Mac stopped and said, 'All this talk, you must be wondering... it is not an exercise in excusing, or justifying what we may have to do, I need you to fully understand the nature of the problem, and I hope that by talking it through we can find... look, I understand your concerns, and your reservations. You're serving police officers, the Office of Constable, which gives you a power of arrest, is enshrined in law, when you exercise your power, you do so with the full backing of the law, and that grants you legitimacy. You fear that going beyond that legitimacy, of not having that protection and support, the loss of... what is it that makes an action legitimate? Is it only man-made law that has legitimacy? What if the government passed an oppressive law, which the courts supported, does that make the imposition of that law licit?'

Mac paused and looked out across the farm to the hills

beyond, then said, 'What would you do? Let's assume that an extreme government, in order to obtain compliance, forced its citizens into acting in ways, which the majority despised and found odious, and did so by making the law its instrument. Such a law would be legal, and as a police officer you would be expected to enforce that law, but should you? How would you feel executing such a law, coercing your fellow citizens into compliance, having to implement morally bankrupt legislation? Would you?'

Simon said, 'No, under those circumstances I wouldn't obey.'

'You would be happy to break the law, to bend it, to act outside the law?'

'Yes, under those circumstances.'

'It is not easy, this morality stuff, but it must be understood, it's one of those areas of life that most never truly encounter, and is easily avoided, especially by those who subscribe to the idea that there is no absolute truth, for them there can be no right or wrong answer, just an answer, that is subordinate to individual flexibility, and circumstance, a subjective leaf in the wind. I guess for them, it is a case of whoever wins is right, but we don't have that luxury. If we cannot collectively decide that what we are doing is both morally right, and requires immediate action, then we must stop, and look for an alternative solution.'

Simon said, 'How do you answer the question?'

Mac laughed and said, 'That's easy, I'm a Catholic, I believe with every fibre of my being that there is such a thing as absolute truth. The Church teaches the need to respect the transcendent dignity of each person, which entails respect for their rights. These rights are prior to society, innate and God given, and must be recognised by all authority, in fact the Church teaches that the moral legitimacy of those seeking to govern is based upon that recognition. I not only can but must oppose any in authority who deny dignity to man. I know we have already talked about this, but where does this, or any government, get its authority to act, its legitimacy, if you like? Through the ballot-box, in theory this provides our governments with a mandate to create and enforce laws, since they have been elected, they have that right and a duty to do so, but as I hope I have shown, such legitimacy is tenuous at best, especially when a government receives less than fifty percent of the potential vote. We congratulate ourselves on our electoral process, smugly declaring it to be the best there is, I guess we base this on the fact that it is not the VIAB system.'

Simon said, 'VIAB system?'

Peter said, 'Vote-in-a-box, in many countries there are two boxes in the polling station, you put your vote for the President in one, or you go in the other.'

Mac said, 'We are governed by people who are busy creating political fire-escapes out of trivial notions of equality, and partisan ideas of justice, yet are happy to ignore the greatest injustice of all, the inequality between the Third World and the West. Further, they ignore, and at times deny the existence of an organised slave trade. They sit, happily holding forth on trivialities in the margins of our society, dreaming up ways to constrain, and micro-manage our lives, while millions are condemned to live an appalling existence, many dying for want of water, food, shelter, medicine, and justice, whilst others are killed by weapons supplied by our arms industry. These hypocrites, to whom you look for approval, are drafting laws and policies that condemn millions to slavery, poverty, and a life of degradation, all to feather their own nests, either directly, or indirectly, some leave office and within a remarkably short space of time emerge as millionaires, arrogantly demanding the right to pontificate on the world stage; how did they amass such wealth? I'm guessing that in a few cases their so-called foundations are simply a financial convenience for the charitable donations that they could not accept whilst in office, because they might be seen by the unenlightened as a bribe. Yet, it is hard not to notice that these charitable donations come from individuals and organisations who benefited from policies put in place by the now retired legislator. You believe that without their consent what we intend do will be devoid of legitimacy? They have rendered politics redundant. We have right on our side, we neither need, nor do we require their approval, we will investigate this case because it is the right thing to do.'

'I'm sorry Mac but I have to object, I don't agree with what you just said, I have met many men and women serving in parliament who are committed whole heartedly to representing everyone in their constituencies, they're not in parliament because of what they can get out of it personally, but out of a sense of duty.'

Mac said, 'You are quite right Simon. I stand corrected, I should have qualified my remarks. I did not intend to sully the reputation of all politicians, only those who are in it for themselves, those who place the interests of their party, its backers, and big business ahead of their own constituents. Unfortunately, that does mean that the good MPs, the ones you're talking about, those found on all sides of the political divide, who conscientiously represent their constituents, are usually marginalised, confined to the backbenches, where their influence is constrained and managed in the interests of their party. All to ensure that their ambitious colleagues, those who have politicised politics, the ones that I despise, whose ambition get people killed, and who set aside truth and justice to further their own ends, usually the acquisition of influence, power, and wealth, have a free run at the prize. If parliament was full of the ones of which you speak, we would live in a better country, and I doubt very much, that what we are now confronting, would have happened. The main problem is not solely the politicians, the vast majority enter politics out of a sense of duty, but that sense of duty is driven by an ego that is motivated by an arrogant assumption that they know what is good for society, and that they have the right to ensure it is adopted. In most cases, common sense and decency ensure that this aspiration is constrained, the real problem is found in the political system, which encourages ambition and greed, whether that be for power or money. This system teaches that if you want to get ahead in politics, then the interests of party, lobbyists, corporations, and financial backers, take precedence over constituents and the national interest, which those so enticed will often hide behind to keep secret their nefarious activities. We need to change the arrangement of polit-ics in this country; in truth, we are the main problem, for we elect these buggers, as individual voters we need to look past party politics, and look at the candidate's character, are they vir-tuous, honourable, and decent? Please accept my apology, I made my case too forcefully, and in doing so besmirched the reputation of a group of individuals who do not deserve it.'

Simon nodded, then said, 'Please don't take this the wrong way, Mac. I'm a little confused... you and Peter served in the Royal Marines, your time there was not spent counting loaves of bread, or piling up tins of beans, you saw combat, you killed... so why this discussion about law and morality, both channel behaviour, and act as regulators of conduct...'

Mac interrupted, 'Not law and morality, but legalism and natural-law, the driver being our conscience, informed by a mor-ality predicated upon the teachings of Christianity.'

'Okay, but what's with this obsession concerning the justific-ation of the use of lethal force? You were both trained to kill, and have put your training to the test, and not been found wanting. So why all the angst?'

Peter looked at Mac, shrugged his shoulders, and said, 'You explain it.'

Mac said, 'From the time we commenced our training, and for the following two years, we paraded every day, whether in camp or in the bush, and on every occasion, we were collectively asked the same question, "Why are you here?" The answer was, "To kill Russians, sir." I had never met a Russian, I had no views on Russia, and no particular feeling for Russians, but I was left in no doubt that my job was to kill them. Remember, this was at the height of the Cold War, and Russia was our enemy. I was young, not given much to introspection, so I didn't think about the implications of what I was saying. I became skilled at arms, accomplished in tracking, sniping, making and defusing improvised explosive devices, in boat-handling, and mountain climbing, I became a warrior. It was in my seventh year of service, when Pete, myself, and ten others were sent to a fly-blown sandpit, that was hot as Hades in the day, and colder than penguin shit at night. We were sent there to further the ambitions of the British Government, and to line the coffers of their friends in the oil industry. The Russians also sent a team to this camel-bordello, to frustrate the aims of our government, and to clear the field for their own objectives. The miscalculation made by both sides was the fact that the denizens of this piece of real estate were unhappy at the arrogant assumption of both governments, that they could just wobble in, dump a load of fat-cats to asset-strip, blow the shit out of things, and leave. The problem for us, was that they were well-armed, the result of several failed alliances, they had a modicum of training, sufficient for general defence, and they knew their terrain. Which is why we, and ten Russian special forces, engaged in an early embodiment of détente, and combined our numbers to defend ourselves, we holed up in an abandoned French Foreign Legion outpost, in the middle of land so barren the rocks wept. For two weeks we fought side-by-side, only when both governments realised that the body count made the place resemble the battle of Omdurman, did they order in air cover and two paraffin-parrots to evacuate all of us…'

Simon interrupted, 'Paraffin-Parrots?'

Peter said, 'Helicopters.'

Mac, sounding slightly exasperated, continued, 'Such was our skill at arms that we had no dead, and no wounded. When we returned to base, I got to thinking, and for the first time began to confront and question many of my assumptions, we were four months from the end of our enlistment. Pete and I had agreed, prior to our jaunt in the furnace, that we would re-enlist, make a career out of the Navy. I had my eyes opened, the foe had become my ally, I had discovered that we were no different, the same fears and concerns that tormented us, troubled them, they had become human beings, now they were my neighbour, not my enemy. I had a new adversary, those who politicise politics, and feel free to send men to kill, or be killed, just so that they, or their benefactors in the corporations, can line their own pockets. The ancient Greeks had the right idea, if you were top-dog and wanted to take the city to war, you and your sons had to be in the front phalanx, they didn't start too many wars. That was the beginning a chain of reflective evaluation that continues today, with age comes experience, with learning comes knowledge, hopefully, if the two are properly harmonised, wisdom will flourish. The callow youth, imbued with arrogant righteousness, who walked into that desert, no longer exists. I grew in understanding, in faith, and through a particular sodality, found a social conscience. I cannot bear arms imprudently, I must understand the implications, and do so in a manner that keeps God's Law, I have a duty to you and to myself, we cannot, regardless of our intentions, find ourselves in circumstances that see us as agents of evil.'

They walked on in silence, each deep in thought, they crossed the meadow and walked up to the old barn on the edge of the woods. Tony looked up at the wooden lintel above the door, carved into it, still faintly visible, was an inscription: *Non semper erit aestas*. 'What does it mean?'

Peter said, 'It's Latin, John said it translates as, *"It will not always be summer"*. Apparently, it was a common saying among the Romans; make hay while the sun shines, is another way of putting it.'

'Appropriate.'

Mac said, 'There are three choices left to us: firstly, do nothing, and pass the buck to Simon, and hope that no one looks our way. Second, we can bring what we know to the attention of the authorities, initially through, Cartwright. The likely outcome of both scenarios is that nothing will be done. We know that, because Cartwright sent Simon to dump it on us. The only way this gets dealt with, is off the books. We could take it to the press, in the hope that they would alert the public, ensuring that the authorities would have to respond, but it's a story that will be stillborn, and we will have placed ourselves in the spotlight, which is where we are going to be, whatever happens, because if we decide to kick it back to Cartwright, he will alert the other side, in order to prompt a reaction. Which brings us to the third option, we make the first move, we get proactive, get in first, and then we deal appropriately with whatever we find. It may be the only way to ensure our survival, because that's really what this comes down to. Me and Pete have decided that we are going to see this through to the end, for us it is unfinished business, it has been a weight hanging over us, and we need answers. We trust you, and we like you both, but you must understand that there is a good chance that we will not survive this, we may not live through it. We don't know who, or what we are up against, we will be blindly navigating uncharted waters; governments, their agencies and police forces, will oppose us, some because they're involved, others because they don't understand, and the rest because they do not care, they are merely protecting their fiefdom. We will not know who to trust, nor understand how groups, and individuals are connected, it's a nightmare. I have made arrangements for Teri and April, Anna and Katie, to go somewhere safe, a place I hope that is well out of the reach of those who will seek to harm them. You see this is not just about us, it threatens our families. And because of that, Tony, we cannot take you with us.'

Tony, began to object, but Mac cut him short. 'You have a wife, and family, it is not worth the risk. You can still help us, there is plenty of stuff needs doing, collating information for one, which is just as important as gathering it, more so, because by setting it some sort of order, you will help us understand the context and relevance of the intelligence. We will be moving away from here, we need to go under the radar, I will need you to keep an eye on this place, to see if we get any visitors…'

Tony interrupted, 'What if you don't come back?'

Peter said, 'Then deny you ever had more than a casual relationship with us, nothing more than that of a local bobby with one of his flock. Forget all you have seen and heard, if you want to live, if you want your family to live, never speak of this, or of us again…'

'But…'

Mac said, 'Never speak of what you know, not even to your wife, remain silent for the rest of your life, and pray they never suspect you.'

Peter said, 'At the slightest hint of trouble, if you get suspicious about someone in the area, come here at night, take the spare guns and ammo, leave the rest, they will expect to find certain things. Learn how to shoot, and hope you never have to.'

Mac said, 'Simon?'

'Oh, I've got no one, between relationships, so to speak. I have no family, and my social diary is not exactly full, and thanks to, Cartwright, I am as much a target as you, so I'm following you, wherever it leads.'

'Just so we are clear, this investigation is going to lead us into danger, there is a very good possibility we could be killed.' Mac looked at each of them, 'Fine, I hope you are all prepared. John told me something the other day, which is appropriate, he said, "We are required to live well, not indefinitely." Are you all committed to the path we are taking?'

Each answered in the affirmative. 'Good, then we are decided. All that is left, if you haven't already done so, is to write your will, and put your affairs in order,' said Mac, grimly.

Chapter Twenty-Two

The church appeared from behind a mound, an operagoer at a transport cafe, a self-conscious object of curiosity, quieted by prudence, settling uncomfortably into a landscape whose geography had been shaped by war and agriculture, a feeling of general unease pervaded its aspect, as it slowly attempted to merge with nature.

Wariness underlined the atmosphere inside the church. In common with many old places of worship there was a presence, a sense of continuity with the past, the silent reverberation of prayer down the ages, yet Peter felt a reticence, a not quite extending of the hand of welcome, of veneration tinged with unease.

He gave an involuntary shiver, and looked around, the interior of the church was small but well lit, it seemed to him that even the warmth of the sunlight streaming through the windows was begrudged.

He spent the next 20 minutes closely examining the interior, taking photographs as he had done outside, and making notes, setting down his observations and impressions. Having completed the task, he sat down on the front pew, and stared at the stark, unadorned altar, unbidden he found himself quietly saying the Lord's prayer.

When he finished, he sat in silence, waiting. He was roused from contemplation by the disrespectful thrusting open of the door. He turned around to face the back of the church, saying aloud, 'Bloody John.'

A voice from the other side of the sunbeams said, 'I'm sorry I didn't catch what you said, the door you see?'

Peter stood up and began walking back along the aisle, 'Nothing, it was nothing… you just startled me.'

'Sorry, apologies… you were praying?'

'No, no… I'm finished… I'm just going.' Peter, stammered in embarrassment.

'Please don't go on my account, I'm the unofficial sexton, well more self-appointed, David,' he extended his hand, and continued, 'I thought I would get in early and set things up for Evensong, I've a lot to do this afternoon, and can't be sure of getting back in time to prepare.'

Peter smiled, and said, 'Well, I'll be off; get out of your way.'

David said, 'I didn't see a car in the car park, most of our visitors drive here, we're a bit off the beaten track, you see, that's why I thought the church was empty, no car, you see? Didn't mean to intrude.'

'It's all right. Really, no harm done. I walked here, I'm on my way to Wyevale, I'm meeting the blacksmith there for lunch.'

'Lunch? It's already one o'clock, and you're three miles away from Wyevale. Let me run you over there, it's the least I can do for disturbing you.'

'That's kind of you, but I couldn't impose.'

'You're not imposing. Paul, has fixed a shovel for me, and I should have picked it up by now.'

'Well, if you're sure, thank you.'

'Wait here, I'll go and get the car, I only live down the road.'

Peter watched him walk away; alarm bells were ringing, as

soon as he had gone out of sight, Peter phoned Mac. Advising him of this development he stressed the need for caution, his instincts were telling him that something was wrong. Mac agreed with him, they quickly discussed tactics, and settled upon a simple background story hoping it would suffice.

Ten minutes later David drove into the car park, behind the wheel of a Morris Traveller.

'Nice car,' said Peter, sinking into the passenger seat, he turned and reached up to his left.

David said, 'No seat belts, too old, you see.'

'Of course.'

They sat in silence, while David manoeuvred the car out of the car park, and down the lane. 'What brings you to the black-smith in Wyevale?'

'Very long story, but I'll give you the short version. I'm a blacksmith up in Lancashire, and I came down for the sale at Belmore Manor. My pickup gave up the ghost couple of days ago, so I had to catch the train to Hereford, which is why I am walking today. Anyway, I successfully bid for all the contents of the old forge, including a wagon-wheel jig, which Paul has already moved to his new forge on the Wyevale Estate. I also bought a pickup-truck from the Manor, which Paul has hope-fully driven over fully loaded for me and is now awaiting my collection.'

David, looked across at Peter, and said, 'How are you going to get the wagon-wheel jig back to Lancashire, it's too big to load onto a pickup?'

'It is… a neighbouring farmer owns a flatbed lorry with a little crane on the back, and he has agreed to come down and collect it for me, he should be arriving sometime between two and three, depending on motorway traffic.'

There was a long pause, before David said, 'I'm surprised that

Paul didn't bid for it himself, since he's been using the wheel-jig, and most of the other stuff from the estate's forge for years?'

Peter replied, 'Paul and I go back many years, we met as apprentices. Paul alerted me to the sale. I asked him if there was anything he wanted, but he said his forge was full, and any case he's going to take on more restoration work, churches and cathedrals, and the like, there isn't much call for a wheel-jig in the restoration of churches.'

'I see, it all makes sense.'

Peter thought, *Fucker, I bet it does*. Then said, 'What of you, what brings you to this part of the world? Do I detect a York-shire accent?'

'You do. Howgill, like many I moved to London to work, and then five years ago relocated to this part of the world, my wife's family are local, and I have no one left in Yorkshire, but what about you, that's a Cockney accent isn't it, what took you to Lancashire?'

'Work, and like you, my other half is from there, but mainly work.'

David said, 'Nearly there, the forge is down a turning towards the end of this lane, just before it enters the village, but then you already know that.'

'Actually no. I've known Paul a long time, but the last time we met he was still at his old forge on Belmore Manor Estate.'

Peter watched as David collected his spade, then thanked him again for the lift. David's exit from the forge was delayed by Mac's arrival. David was forced to reverse back into the yard, to allow Mac to manoeuvre the flatbed lorry he had borrowed from Michael. Peter, noted that the arrival of the lorry, confirming yarn he had spun, appeared to brighten David's demeanour, he seemed less suspicious, his repeated good-byes were said with rather greater enthusiasm than before.

Paul watched him leave the yard, looked at Peter, and said, 'Queer one that, very odd, always wanting to know your business, I trust him as far as you can piss; he's definitely a wrong'un.'

Following introductions, Mac and Paul quickly loaded the lorry, while Peter acquainted himself with the new pickup, checked and secured the load. Peter's sister invited them both to stay for the evening meal, with regret they declined, and set off for Cumbria.

They followed Paul's directions, taking country lanes south, then east, and north, a route that brought them out the other side of Hereford City, and joined the main road to Worcester and the M5 motorway. Ten minutes into their journey Mac spotted David, sitting in his car, facing out of a track leading to a spinney, he was talking on a mobile phone.

Mac called Peter and informed him of his sighting of David. They drove without stopping all the way back to the farm. Peter dropped back from the lorry to ensure that no one was following them; between Worcester and Manchester this proved impossible, but beyond Manchester the traffic on the motorway thinned, and it got easier. Over Shap, they were the only vehicles on the motorway, they should have taken the turning for Keswick and the Southern Fells, but Mac thought it better to take the Penrith exit. It was after ten when they turned onto the farm track. They both agreed that the unloading of the vehicles could wait until the morning.

Father Peter presented them with a sausage salad and a couple of beers, 'Go alright, get what you wanted?'

Mac said, 'Well we collected all Pete's stuff, a motley assortment, and we have undoubtedly found the caretaker. He's a complete prat, but an observant one, potentially dangerous, in so much as he is the eyes and ears for someone. We appear to have passed the suspicion test, he thought we were what we claimed to be, but I'm not sure what Pete discovered?'

Peter looked up at Father John, his mouth full, he mumbled a reply, chewed then swallowed, took a sip of beer and said, 'I found out that when it comes to yomping, I am out of practice.' Mac and Father John laughed, Peter continued, 'The church is odd, it has an atmosphere.'

Father John said, 'Atmosphere?'

Peter said, 'Yeah… it was kind of weird. I was not comfortable while I was inside the church, I felt… a sense of foreboding, maybe I was looking too hard, expecting something, the anticipation of which resulted in my feeling as I did, perhaps… anticipating what I was hoping to find. But I thought about it on the drive home, and I am right, that place has an undercurrent of dread. The carvings are strange, take a look.'

He handed his camera to Mac, who flicked through the images before passing it on to Father John. Peter took advantage of the break and carried on eating.

Mac said, 'What do you reckon, some crusader came home from the wars with a bag of hashish which he shared with the stonemasons, and this is the result?'

Peter swallowed, then laughed, 'I've thought about those carvings, they're not satanic or sinister, just vernacular. Indigenous, possibly common to local stone-carvers, or maybe they belong to a style favoured by the masons brought in to build it? The church, if it has a part in this, is no more than a meeting place, it's easy to find, has a large car park, gets its fair share of tourists, so strangers won't raise any suspicions locally. Plus, it is a good place to have new members park and be vetted, before moving on to the main venue. Makes sense from a security point of view. I think we can disregard the church. But David, our gatekeeper, he's a whole different bag of trouble.'

Father John said, 'I'm concerned about the atmosphere, clearly you felt something, and it wasn't benign, can you expand on that before we move on?'

Peter thought for a moment, then said, 'Mm… it was peculiar, no doubt about it… peculiar, but not sinister or menacing. When I was a kid, we used to spend the summer holidays in darkest Sussex, with my grandfather, my mother's father. He was a vicar, and a widower, he lived in a large rectory next to his church.'

Father John said, 'You've never mentioned him before. A vicar, eh?'

'I didn't want you labouring under the illusion that you already had a foundation to build upon.'

Father John laughed, and said, 'Not much fear of that.'

Peter smiled, and continued, 'We would all go down, my father drove us in his van, he would stay for a week, then go back to London, leaving Mum, my sister, and me, in Sussex, he returned toward the end of the holidays, spent another week with us, then we would all go back to London. Sometimes we would join my grandfather at Christmas. I loved the holidays; my grandfather was great company and taught me so much. He had a favourite saying, "It is what it is, but it will become what you make of it." I've never forgotten… I still miss him.'

Peter paused, drank some beer, and continued, 'I spent every day of the holidays with my grandfather. We went on long walks, and at least once or twice a week we would visit other vicars and explore their churches. He used to say that if you wanted to know the history of a place, find the parish church, it's all there, provided you can interpret the signs and symbols. He also used to say that if you are troubled you should find a church, even if you don't believe, a church is a great place to go and think. He said that all churches have a sense of the Other, and if you sit silently, you will feel that connection. One thing he said stuck, "Respect and listen to the democracy of the dead, for theirs is the silent continuity of prayer that joins with eternity." Father John said, 'Your grandfather was a wise man.'

'He was… you would have liked him. He showed me what to look for, both inside and outside of a church, how to read the building and its ornamentation. I look back on those days with good memories. Sadly, when I was sixteen, he had a stroke and died.'

Father John crossed himself and said a short prayer for the dead.

Peter nodded his thanks, gathered his thoughts, and said, 'I had been in the Marines for about three years and was helping run a short course at Lympstone, when Paul drove down to see me. He seemed worried about something and clearly wanted to talk to me, at his suggestion we went for a walk. He had brought a book with him that listed walks in the area, all the walks had a pub at the beginning of the walk, with parking, and a pub around the halfway point where refreshment could be taken, very civilised. We picked one with a twelve-mile route, and set off, stopping for lunch after about seven miles, at the pub recommended in the book. Paul had his dog with him, so we sat at a table outside in the garden of the pub to eat lunch. Eventually, he got round to telling me why he wished to speak to me. He wanted to marry my sister and was seeking my approval. He had my father's blessing but was worried about how I would respond. I was taken aback, why would he worry about how I felt, he had my dad's permission after all.'

Mac and Father John exchanged knowing glances and smiled.

'I could see he was really worried, so I played up for a while. Sternly asking him about his intentions towards my sister, the usual things, I asked him loads of questions, and left him in no doubt about what would happen if he ever mistreated her. He was sweating, rarely have I seen someone so worried, to lighten the mood I told him he had my blessing and complete support, but only if I could be a bridesmaid, then congratulated him and ordered a double single malt for each of us. We were a mile down the road when the penny dropped and he laughed, "A Bridesmaid", I couldn't figure out why he was so concerned about how I would react to what was, after all, great news.'

Mac and Father John both laughed. Father John said, 'Really?'

'No… I'm not that bad.'

Mac said, 'Yes you are, then and now. I'm seriously worried about any boyfriends Katie brings home.'

'Not a problem, I'll castrate them.' Peter laughed, 'If I may continue? About a mile from the end of the walk, in the middle of nowhere, we encountered a very small church, centred in a large unkempt boneyard, encircled by tall trees. We decided to have a break and go in and explore. Paul was working on a wrought iron rood-screen and was hoping for some inspiration. His dog was reluctant to enter the gate, and point blank refused to go into the church, so Paul tied her up outside, and we went in. To this day I wish we hadn't. The church was completely devoid of ornamentation, none of the usual decorations, emblems, or carvings, nor anything that you would expect to find, there was no stained glass in the windows, just plain glass in leaded frames, yet it was dark, darker than it should have been. There was a malign presence, later when we discussed it, we both agreed we had seen a tall shadow pass in front of the altar, it was hostile and threatening, there was something evil in that church. I won't say that the atmosphere in the church at Colpuck was the same, it wasn't, but there was a reluctant hospitality, a hesitancy, such welcome as was forthcoming was begrudged. It was as if the church itself was fearful about what lay beyond its curtilage, as if it was preparing for battle... does that make sense?'

Father John said, 'Sadly, it does.'

Peter said, 'As for the house, the grounds are still guarded by an eight-foot-high chain-link fence, which is in good repair, of the house, there is nothing left, about two courses of brick, the fire gutted the lot, but someone is looking after the property. The grass is cut, the grounds are tidy, and there is a freshly painted steel door leading to the cellar. I had a good look around, that door to the cellar has not been opened since it was fitted. It's my guess that there are bodies buried in the grounds, and that is why they continue to guard the site. We had suspicions at the time, and I see no reason to think differently. Maybe we should consider starting there, could it be our way back into this mess?'

Mac said, 'No, I'm not sure that would be the right course of action. The group we uncovered, who used the house, have been dispersed, and as soon as we go digging the place up, assuming we can get local Plod interested, we signal our involvement, and we still have no idea who is behind this, we must figure out who we are dealing with, before we start sending up flares.'

Father John said, 'Pete, I agree with Mac, we need to know more, much more, at the very least we need to know who to go after. Tom's working hard to uncover something we can use, let's wait a little longer. The house is going nowhere, it's a hornet's nest we can stir at any time, but it is interesting to know that they still maintain and keep an eye on the place. It does rather confirm our earlier suspicions. You agree?'

Peter, his mouth full, said, 'Mm.'

Father John, threw his arms in the air, grabbed a bottle of beer, and said, 'Unbelievable, give him food and beer, and he could care less.'

They sat in silence, each deep in thought.

'What's wrong, Mac?'

'John, it's… I just can't see the way ahead… no, it's more than that, I don't like the direction we are going in, I am uncomfortable with what we may end up having to do… the implications… this investigation is developing a life of its own, it is going to take us to places we have never been before, and frankly, I don't want to go.'

Father John said, 'I agree, Mac. We must decide what we do next, how far we are willing to go, so let's talk it through. I don't mean right now, or in one go, but over the coming days, as we learn more. I need to develop my thoughts, to articulate my concerns, I also want to understand the implications of where we are going, and by the sound of it so do you. I'm happy that you are comfortable with the issues surrounding your moral legitimacy to act, but we need to discuss… between your concerns, my rants, and Peter's contrariness, I am sure answers will emerge, they may not be to our liking, but they will provide us with some idea of the direction we must take. But there is something more, there is something deeper troubling you.'

'There is, John. I'll get to it. Of more immediate concern is the fact that we need to put ourselves ahead of developments. Circumstance is dictating our actions, we have become dangerously reactionary, we must get proactive. We have to gain control, not just to prevent us being swept along by events, but also to protect ourselves, otherwise I fear we will be sucked into a maelstrom which none of us will survive.'

Chapter Twenty-Three

Mac, Peter, and Simon walked down from the stable block and joined Father John, Tony, and Tom who were seated at the long table under the wisteria. Tom, in order to bring Tony up to speed, had been going through some of the evidence uncovered in the earlier investigation.

Tony sat stunned, 'It's all true?'

'Every word,' said Tom.

'Dear Lord,' said Tony.

'Just so,' said Mac.

They all sat silently contemplating the task ahead, until Tony, addressing Mac, said, 'Changing the subject for a minute, what made you quit, why did you leave the police?'

'That's not an easy question to answer, I guess it goes back to why I became a copper. If you are one of those for whom the Job is nothing more than a career, an opportunity for advancement, whose only ambition is to climb up the ranks and get as far away from the streets as is possible, what we used to call a flour-grader, then you will never understand. Are you a flour-grader?'

'No, I joined because I wanted to be a police officer.'

'Can I take it, that like me, you joined because you felt called, for you the Job is a vocation, you wanted to make a difference?'

'Corny as it sounds, yes.'

Mac said, 'You can be taught some of the skills. How to develop better powers of observation, an understanding of language and human nature, which when honed by experience, can result in a reliable street copper. But mostly it's innate, the sixth sense of the hunter, the instinct that allows you to spot what is not there, to sense the presence of your quarry, being able to hear and understand the silence, these are gifts not given to many, those who feel the vocational tug usually have that gift. Having learned the trade, you apply your knowledge, skills, and experience, to one end, the maintenance of justice. That's what it is all about, that's what we mean by making a difference, creating a truly a just society, but for it to be meaningful, there must be real and ever-present justice. Justice cannot be something merely aspirational, it is never abstract. Justice maintains the balance and preserves the rule of law without which no society can function, and it ensures our freedom. I know that some see freedom as the fiefdom of politics, but that's not the case, the law stands a rampart against the tyranny that politics, if unchecked, would impose. Only a truly just society can make people free, and justice is ours by right, not something handed down by the beneficence of our political masters. The problem is that the law no longer fulfils that role, it has become tainted by politics, it is no longer free, nor fair. A country can be completely democratic, or like ours, play lip service to democracy, it matters not, because if we have a just society, one that feels and is fair, then people will have confidence, build lives, commit socially, invest economically, and our nation will be sustained. It is not politics that give us freedom, but an incorruptible, principled, and impartial legal system. Without justice there is no freedom, and true freedom as I see it, is being able to live your life harmed by none, whilst doing harm to none, with the law monitoring to restrain those who transgress, maintaining the

213

balance between rights and duties. However, for there to be real justice, it must be predicated on natural law and natural rights; it must be blind, completely impartial, and accessible, available equally to all, requiring parity in both access and application; without these conditions there is no justice, no freedom, and no rule of law. What replaces it looks like justice, but it is nothing more than the legalism of a despotic system. I know that at times justice can be strained, but it must never be broken. If natural law prevails, then a sense of fair play will be present, and faith in the law will endure. Justice is to the law, what democracy is to politics, it's a leveller.'

Tony, smiled weakly, 'I'm not with you?'

Mac, nodded and said, 'Do you think we live in a democracy?'

Tony said, 'Yes, of course we do.'

Peter said, 'How can that be true, since our electoral system permits a party to form a government when it is in receipt of less than half the votes available nationally? Our first-past-the-post method of electing politicians is woefully out of date. In theory we elect a local representative, who attends Parliament on our behalf, in truth, the individual we've elected represents the interests of a political party. So why, when our present system is so unfit for purpose, don't we have proportional representation? The present method can and does allow parties to form governments, and claim a mandate to govern, when they are in receipt of less than the combined votes cast for the other parties.'

Mac said, 'Why does Parliament refuse to reinstate the death penalty, when the majority want it brought back for murder? Our elected representatives have the effrontery to claim that their refusal to submit to the will of the majority is in the interests of democracy. When politicians claim to be voting by their conscience, what they mean is they are following an agenda set by a liberal cabal, a minority consensus that confounds choice. They claim that it would not be right to submit to the tyranny of the majority, which really means that they don't like what the majority are requesting, so they ignore their appeals, forcing upon the majority the absolutism of the minority. We don't live in a democracy, at best it is a benign dictatorship, and every four years or so we get to elect a new dictator.'

Tony said, 'I'm not sure that I can agree with you on that.'

'Really? The needs of the electorate are a long way down the political food-chain, well behind those of the special-interest groups, and the various lobbyists, the desires of multi-national corporations, their party, and the MP's own interests. Just as there is very little that is democratic about our political system, so there is nothing just about our courts. Our original case demonstrated to me that everything I was engaged in, and hoping to achieve, was pointless. I was engaged in a quest for something that no longer existed, political interference, and the demands of power have usurped justice. Justice is no longer blind, it is very partial, few have any meaningful access to justice, and it is no longer applied equally, but bent to the will of those with real power. I could not continue being a part of that, so I quit. Pragmatism and compromise, both favourites of the political class, are the two most dangerous positions for an individual, and a country to adopt, for together they destroy justice and eliminate freedom, which is why they are beloved of politicians. I quit because I realised that what I was doing was not only supporting a corrupt system, but it was also utterly pointless.'

Simon interrupted, and said, 'Apologies, Tony. Mac, it surprises me that you support capital-punishment?'

'I don't, and nor do most coppers I know. I would like to see the fulfilment of the promise made by politicians when it was repealed; that the ending of capital-punishment would mean life in prison for those convicted of murder, but I remain firmly against the idea of state sanctioned executions. As you know, we don't always get it right, witnesses can and do commit perjury, the forensic evidence can and does provide false or misleading results, and juries are prejudiced, it's a bit late to come up with new evidence when the accused is dead. Another important reason, which is rarely considered, is repentance. Not the, I'm sorry for me because I'm about to be hung regret, but genuine remorse, the result of years of reflection, that ends in contrition.'

Tony said, 'I agree with you, capital-punishment is barbaric, I would not like to think that I sent an innocent man to his death, because I made a mistake. As a country we have a right to punish, but that doesn't give us the right to act out of vengeance. However, I am confused, given your view of the court system, why conduct this investigation?'

'Partially, it is unfinished business, and partially, to get justice for the victims, but, mainly out of self-defence.'

'Well how, if the system is as skewed as you claim, do you think you will achieve justice? Do you not think that the outcome will be just the same?'

'No.'

'How can you be so sure?'

Peter interrupted, 'Because we will be ensuring that justice is done.'

Simon said, 'So it's vigilantism, that's your justice?'

Peter looked at Mac, smiled, then said, 'You sure he is on our side?'

Mac laughed, 'He says he is, and if he isn't, we'll send him back.'

Simon laughed and said, 'The hell you will, I'm in it to the end. I don't understand all you have said, but I do accept most of it, and like you, I am worried about where this case will lead us, I do know we are on the side of the angels, so I'm in all the way.'

Father John said, 'But, which angels?'

Mac looked at Peter, and said, 'So who's cherub, are you?'

Peter's reply was drowned out by laughter.

When the laughter subsided, Tom said, 'Who is, Matt?'

Simon and Tony said, in unison, 'Matt?'

Tom said, 'Mac told me before we sat down, to expect someone called, Matt?'

Peter said, 'A friend, a good friend, someone we are going to need.'

Tom said, 'Trustworthy, reliable, going to be able to keep things to himself…?'

Mac interrupted, 'I trust him with my life, I trust him with April's life.'

'Good enough. What's your connection?'

'We met way back, in another lifetime, when Pete and I were in the Marines. It was a Hereford job; we were assigned as back up. A simple extraction they said, nothing for us to do, a boat ride. We were to be inserted offshore from a sub, then travel up a river to a point ten miles inland and wait, to be there as back-up, if needed. A fall-back position in case the first RV was compromised, if something prevented the planned extraction by paraffin-parrot. I'm not sure what their mission was, we were only privy to the information pertaining to our role…'

'Yup, the usual JANFU.' Interrupted, Peter.

Tom said, 'JANFU?'

'Joint army-navy fuck up.'

Mac continued, 'We left the sub in two high-power inflatables, they dropped us in the mouth of the river about two in the morning, we rowed until daylight, completing the rest of the journey the following night, for obvious reasons we kept the engines inboard and the running lights off. We got to our designated location about a day before we were required and hunkered down.'

Peter interjected, 'Fucking typical, hurry up and wait, sitting on our arses, being eaten alive in a humid, tropical green labyrinth.'

Mac laughed, 'I forgot about that. Pete got bitten taking a piss, you can imagine where, anyway it swelled up, and not in a good way, it did look bad…'

'It went septic.' interrupted Peter.

'Only because you kept playing with it. I told you at the time, treat it and leave it alone.'

'Whatever, it took bloody weeks to heal, and it was fucking painful.'

'And womankind has been grateful ever since!'

'Bollocks.'

'Your anatomy is rather confused, a little higher up, perhaps?' Laughter drowned out Peter's response.

Mac said, 'Anyway, halfway through the next day we get a call, the intelligence was up to its usual crap standard, and everything's gone tits up. The lads from Hereford are being tracked by a hostile force of about twenty. The call was to go upriver to rendezvous with the SAS team halfway between their present location and our current position. We travelled another three miles upstream, hid the boats and made our way inland towards the gunfire. That was the first time we met, Matt. The next time was in the Bulls Head at Barnes; used to be a good jazz pub, but it's been a while since I was there.'

Simon said, 'How did you get out of there?'

'The Bulls Head? Barely standing.'

'No, the jungle.'

'The SAS team numbered six, which with our two guns making eight, was more than a match for the fifteen left when we arrived, quite a firefight ensued, and all but one was slotted, he had run off at the beginning of our… disputation. We let him watch us row upriver, before he ran off to tell his mates. We waited half an hour, fired up the outboards and got the hell downstream. By the time the bad guys reacted we were long gone, halfway back to the sea and an appointment with the sub.'

Tom said, 'You said, extraction, who did they bring out?'

'No idea, once it got hot, they cut his throat, and yomped out of there. They did bring out a leather briefcase, so I guess it wasn't a complete failure, but we'll never know. It's not like there's feedback, but that didn't matter, we played our part, and got our passengers out safe.'

'So, you never knew what it was about?'

Peter said, 'That's not how it works, we did our bit, and that's it; for us, completing our mission was the objective.'

Mac said, 'Pete and I had both joined the Met by the time we ran into Matt again. He looked us up, he figured he owed us, and we never disavowed him of that. He was working for a firm that do things for Five and Six, arm's length from the security services, a deniable distance, if you get my drift, officially unofficial. He will be a very useful ally. Tom, I'm looking to you to bring him up to speed on where we are, introduce him to the others on the team, and fill him in on anything else you think he should know.'

Tom nodded.

Mac said, 'We've been drinking buddies ever since the evening we met at the Bull's Head, we used to get together two or three time a year. So, he is in.'

'Sounds like he's going to be a useful addition.' said, Tom.

Father John said, 'I hope he's not a loose cannon Mac, or it could end badly.'

'Only for the bad guys,' laughed Peter, turning away from Father John's glare.

Mac said, 'He's not, John. The last thing any of us want is a pile of bodies. Matt is not another character like Mason. He's a consummate professional, this is a hunting party, and Matt's a great tracker.'

Tony, said, 'So, given your opinion of the justice system, even if we can track down those responsible, exactly how are we going to achieve the justice you want?'

Peter frowned, and said, 'We will achieve it by being judge, jury and executioner. Once we have all the facts, with clear evidence to satisfy all the usual conditions, we will pronounce on the guilt, or innocence of the accused, then, if guilty, act.'

'Isn't that vigilantism?'

Mac said, 'No, we are not a lynch mob, we are not going to surrender blindly to our emotions, we are going to coldly and dispassionately examine all the evidence, and if there is not enough, we will keep digging until we find it. We are experienced investigators, so we will sift the evidence until we have proved the case beyond all reasonable doubt, establishing the guilt, or innocence, of each suspect.'

Tony said, 'Then what, execute them? I thought you are against capital-punishment.'

Peter glared at him, saying, 'We've been through this, we can't put them in front of a court, can we? We will have to assess our options at the time, but most likely before we get to that point, we will have had to kill them. Once they know who we are and what we are about, they are going to come at us full bore. We are going to war.'

'You okay with this?' Simon looked at Father John.

'No, of course not. If there was another way… but the system…

it's their system, and it protects them. As Mac has pointed out, justice is now partial. These are evil men, infecting society with their diabolical poison. You do realise that we will never be able to tell anyone outside of this investigation what the truth is, even if we showed them all the evidence, they would still not believe us, they can't, it would require them to set aside their version of reality. In a relativistic world there is no place for truth, only ideology. There are things as they are, things as we perceive them to be, and things as we would like them to be, this is the tension we create between reality, appearance, and wishfulness, between what is true, what we tell ourselves is true, and what we would like to be true, which sets up a paradox. I do not know how we can convince the world of a truth it has already rejected. It is important to do your duty, but you must do so without losing your humanity. You cannot fight evil with evil… devotion to duty cannot override compassion, for to do so would lead to savagery, then you are lost. Things have gone too far, I know that there can be no turning back, these men will kill us, kill our families… I cannot condone what you must do, but I cannot condemn it. I cannot justify what you may have to do, I cannot… but God help me, I do understand… I understand,' Father John turned away, visibly upset.

Peter scowled at Simon, and said, 'The only question is, are you in?'

'Yes. I already told you, yes.'

'All the way, and I mean, all-the-way?'

'Yes.'

Mac, seeking to lighten the atmosphere, said, 'Time for beer, Pete fetch out a couple of those cases of San Miguel, John look in the pantry, crisps, pork scratchings, those Mexican things, then we'll have a story.'

About fifteen minutes later the table was laden with beer and snacks.

Mac said, 'This is the story of James. The moral of this tale is knowing when is enough is enough. James, a friend we met through Matt, who ran into him under strange circumstances in Algeria, which is another story, and one for Matt to tell you, if he ever trusts you. Anyway, about a year after the fall of communism. James, who could sell you a video of paint drying, and leave you convinced it was worthy of an Oscar, got real busy selling the good people of Russia the things they needed, and quite a few they didn't. He travelled to Russia, stayed there for six months and came back wealthy. He had a wife and two kids in Brighton, there was only one fly in the ointment, his wife, she's Polish. She liked the money he was earning but loathed that she and the children were living off Russian money, so she took it out on James, with lashings of tongue-pie. Tired of bleeding from the ears, his visits home grew shorter and less frequent, inevitably they separated, then divorced, but he continued working in Russia. On one occasion, he asked if Matt and I could meet him at Gatwick, he was returning home carrying over a million in US dollars.'

Mac drank some beer, ate some crisps, and continued, 'We both warned him about what he was doing, and raised concerns about who he was doing it with. At the time of his divorce, Matt told him that choosing money over family was just plain dumb. By then he had amassed enough money to last him a lifetime, he had about ten million stashed away, but it was still not enough. Another year went by before we heard from him again, he contacted us with an invitation to join him for a meal at a posh restaurant in Dorking, his treat. After, we went back to a flat he was renting in an old country house outside of Redhill, it was there that the reason for his invitation was made clear. James told us that he had money, a fortune, in various banks in Bermuda and the Cayman Islands, offshore accounts he continued to fill. He had left the locations of those accounts with a solicitor he trusted, together with his will containing instructions for the disposal of the money in the event of his death. He then gave each of us a sealed envelope, these contained all the passwords and access codes to his bank accounts, split up among the three envelopes. He asked Matt to be his executor, and he agreed. In the event of his death the solicitor would contact Matt, hand the will to him, together with the location of the bank accounts. Upon being contacted by Matt, Pete and I would then bring our envelopes, and assist Matt in carrying out James' wishes. We all agreed to do as he asked but urged him to think again about working in Russia, his ex-wife still hoped they could be reconciled, but he didn't want to hear, he had to make more money, enough was not enough. About four months after our meal together, James was in the Ural Mountain Region completing a deal for ten large tractors. The deal went south, the mayor, who was a bandit, stole the tractors, and kept the money that the farmers' cooperative had paid for them. James was locked up in the local jail, while the mayor decided how and when to kill him. Three days into this nightmare, a genial man in an Armani suit opens the cell door, freeing James. They step over the body of the mayor, who had been beheaded, leave the jail and cross the road to a cafe, which James notes, they have all to themselves. The man then explains that he is head of the Bratva, the Russian Mafia, that he has watched James with interest, he believes James to be an honest and honourable man, one with whom he can do business.'

'Honourable, and stupid,' said Peter.

Mac said, 'Stupid, maybe? Misguided, lost, blinded by greed… possibly. Unable to discern the difference between sufficient and too much… definitely. Anyway, this man, we'll call him Yuri, gets James to work for him. The money rolls in, James buys a luxury apartment in Moscow, a house in St Petersburg, collects a trophy Russian wife, and starts living the life of the uber-rich. We still see him, not as often, but he stays in touch. Five years go by, he is wealthy enough to own his own jet, a home in Barbados, and another in New York. He is sent to a small unpronounceable town near Novosibirsk, a simple deal, he is there to sell earth moving equipment to some locals, which they need to complete a project overseen by the mafia. The clients are happy with the deal, it's not their money, it's government funding that is paying for it, following the signing of the contract James takes them out for a meal to celebrate. They leave the restaurant late that evening and walk into crossfire. At that precise moment, two rival gangs bring their disputation to a conclusion in the street. The shoot-out leaves James, his clients and three other innocent by-standers dead. James died because of where he was, and he was there because he could not grasp the notion, that enough was enough. He wasn't stupid, he just didn't understand the concept of sufficient. And this failure placed him in harm's way. He did not see that in every case, regardless of circumstance, the cause of death is always life. He could not recognise the line, he did not know how, when, and where to stop, and knowing that is important... in this investigation we may have to recognise the same line and stop; if you think we are in danger of crossing it, shout out, and we can discuss our next move.'

Simon said, 'What about the envelopes?'

'I called Mac and Peter.'

They all turned round to see a slim man of athletic build, about five-foot ten-inches tall, with a genial face and shaven head, standing in the yard.

'Matt,' said Mac, rising to meet him, 'your most welcome, pull up a chair, grab a beer, you can finish the story. I thought you were arriving tomorrow?'

'I was, and I will,' laughed, Matt.

Sitting down, he took a beer and some pork scratchings, and said, 'I was going to arrive tomorrow, but I had nothing to do, so I thought, fuck it, I'll go and see those two bastards today.' He looked at the faces around the table, alighting on Father John's, he said, 'Sorry Padre, didn't see you there.'

Father John said, 'Bless you my son, you're the only one to apologise, I've known Pete too long to be upset by earthy language.'

Matt joined in the laughter and said, 'I'd better finish the story. I called these two, ff... gentlemen...'

Father John, nodded, and Matt continued, 'The solicitor had already been in touch, they came over with the envelopes, well, Mac did, Peter was out of the country, but Mac had retrieved Pete's envelope. After that it was all very straightforward. James was a financial wizard, he laid it all out, step by step. 'After the funeral, I went to Bermuda and the Cayman Islands and returned with three account books, one each in the name of his two children and his ex-wife. The wife in Russia had been taken care of, she got the properties in Moscow and St. Petersburg, and the contents of his Russian accounts, around one-hundred million pounds. His ex-wife and the kids shared six-hundred million, the house in Bermuda, and the penthouse in New York. They now live in the south of France, where she has relatives, they are financially secure, but they would rather have James, so learn when enough is enough. As my old sergeant used to say, there's a difference between scratching your arse and tearing it to pieces.'

Father John said, 'Elegantly put, Matt. Too many lose joy in the search for happiness, be content with what you have, the wise know that what they have is worth far more than the futile fulfilment of avarice.'

Mac said, 'Thank you, John. I'm sure we will all benefit from mulling over…' he stared hard at those around the table, suppressing the laughter he knew would come, 'your sage advice. This story may have a more direct bearing on our investigation, we may have another addition to the team.'

Matt said, 'About a month after the funeral I got a call from an old friend, Ivan, he's in the SPAZ… the Russian SAS. I'm not sure that is his real name, but I've always called him Ivan, it was the name Pete gave him when we first met, but that's a story for another day. Ivan contacted me on behalf of Yuri, who wanted to know if, James' ex-wife and kids were financially secure. He also wanted me to know that James' death was not the work of the mafia, and that they had executed all those involved. They had taken revenge for the death of their friend.'

'Their golden goose, more like,' said Father John.

'No Padre, James was their friend, they liked and respected him, somehow they felt that they owed me for the loss of my friend, for them it was a matter of honour.'

'Honour, among thieves?'

'Sometimes, yes. I have seen more honour among thieves than is found among the so-called great and the good, we have all encountered pillars of society who are less trustworthy than a cackle of hyenas.'

Peter said, 'Could that sense of debt be something we could call upon? If so, James' death may not prove entirely pointless.'

Mac said, 'I'm not sure we should get into bed with Yuri, it would take something for me to ask the Russian mafia for help.'

Sounding shocked, Tom said, 'But you're not ruling it out?'

'I am. Who does interest me is Matt's Russian friend, Ivan. He could be very useful. Matt, could you enlighten the others about Ivan's background?'

Matt said, 'When we first met, he was a Praporshchik, a Master Sergeant, in the Spetsgruppa A. Now he is a senior officer in the Vympel, the Spetsgruppa B. He hasn't been demoted A to B, it's a totally separate organisation, an elite unit that carry out operations on foreign soil, operatives must be able to speak two foreign languages fluently, luckily one of his is English. Our paths have crossed more than a few times, and there have been occasions when we have each rescued the other from... complicated situations. We exchange birthday and Christmas cards, and I was invited to attend the Christening of his youngest son, I didn't go, but it was nice to be asked.'

'Sounds to me like you know him well,' said Tom.

'Well enough, to know that we can trust him.'

Mac said, 'I guess we've reached that point, it's time to stop talking, and get it done.'

Peter said, 'If we can get Ivan on board, I'm thinking James' ill-advised career choices, may prove beneficial for us, his premature demise may in the end count for something.'

Mac said, 'If it comes to it, let's make our deaths count for something.'

'You're a cheerful little soul,' chuckled, Father John.

Beer, raucous laughter, and hair-raising tales, flowed throughout the rest of the evening.

Chapter Twenty-Four

Only in the evening did Tom emerge from the stables and his self-imposed exile, leaving his cell of seclusion to walk in the woods, muttering alarmingly to himself. Entombed in his own world, circumscribed by thought, his existence encompassed by deliberation and discovery, interpretation and methodical evidence-sifting; they left him to it, not wishing to break his reasoning, food was placed on a tray just inside the door, mostly it went uneaten.

Towards the end of the ninth day, he flung the door open and rushed over to where Mac and Peter were sitting, a remonstration of chickens scattering ahead and around him. Tom, spoke loudly and rapidly, startling Peter, 'One question, would you classify Mason as belonging to the Far-Right?'

'Yes, odd that you should ask...'

'Good... that's it.'

He ran back to the stables, panicking the already ruffled hens, who took off towards the fields.

Peter said, 'What the fuck was that about?'

Mac, staring at his rampaging flock said, 'I'm sure I don't know; it will be a week before those hens lay again.'

Peter said, 'It's time we spoke to Tom, he's getting a little edgy.'

Mac laughed, 'Edgy? He's got a kangaroo loose in the top-paddock; he's borderline strap-down resort, we better find out what's going on.'

They walked over to the stables, entered and found the room beyond the hall covered in notes. These were stuck to everything, at the far end of the room Liz's large paintings had been turned round and leaned against the wall, their backs, a mass of notes interconnected by different coloured woollen-yarn, a web of relationships.

'You've redecorated,' observed Mac.

'Yes… well…' Tom started distractedly looking through a pile of papers on the floor, 'you see… it's quite easy really… it was there all the time…'

'What was?' snapped Peter, 'What are you babbling about?'

'The answer… the answer as to who and why… the answer you need…' Tom trailed off and began to rummage through another pile of papers.

'Are you going to enlighten us?' said Peter, sarcasm dripping from each word, he glanced at, Mac, who smiled.

Tom looked at them, hurt registered in his face, until he caught Mac's smile.

'Pair of… sit… sit, and I'll show you what I have discovered.'

'Sit? Where the…'

Mac interrupted the approaching obscenity, and said to Peter, 'Fetch a couple of chairs from the kitchen.'

Tom looked about the room, smiled weakly and said, 'Yes… so many papers, your files, mine, and Simon's papers… plus, there was the stuff Robin sent, and the books and files you discovered at Mason's, then Vale's…'

Mac interrupted saying, 'I understand, it's okay, you had to sort through things, I'm not bothered by the mess.'

Tom waited until they were both seated, then said, 'When

you began your initial investigation, you thought that you had uncovered a paedophile ring, masquerading as a satanic sect. What you inadvertently stumbled on was part of a high-level, Europe-wide, satanic cult. One that requires its adherents to have sex with underage boys and girls, and even infants. The sect also demands that members take part in the ritual killing of the babies, their underage mothers, and of the boys shortly after the onset of puberty. Clearly, such directives are in place to ensure the absolute loyalty and obedience of adherents; whoever controls this cult has complete and uncontested authority over a large select group of powerful men and women. Judges; lawyers; journalists; captains of industry; politicians; civil servants; doctors; psychologists; lecturers; senior officers in the police and armed services; all individuals who operate the levers of power and who influence national parliaments, as well as those who mould public opinion, the list is a veritable who's who of a few of the most powerful people. The sex and the ritual killings, acts of indescribable depravity, bind this group together in a bond of evil, and ensure complete compliance, obedience, and secrecy. Not one of them dare risk exposure, so they are joined in a mutual entwining of corruption and wickedness. As Father John described in his original report to the Vatican, "… a wicked confederacy, a freemasonry of iniquity, a brotherhood of demonic degenerates pleasuring in the destruction of innocence". It is this blood-guilt that both binds them and gives them their power.'

Tom paused, and looked at Mac and Peter, the blood had drained from their faces.

Mac said, 'Please continue.'

Tom said, 'What your investigation uncovered overlapped into my enquiry, it helps to explain the import of barely pubescent girls and boys into this country, and the export of young children and babies from here to Germany, France and the Low-

Countries. The house you discovered in Herefordshire, what did you call it Mac? Ah yes, the harem, very apt. That building was also the location for some of the rituals, although most appear to have taken part in a large house near the Thames, somewhere upstream from Richmond. I have yet to establish its exact whereabouts, that will be a priority for us. It looks like there may be another twelve of these houses spread across Europe. These documents suggest that in total, there are thirteen such locations...' he trailed off, and began sorting through a pile of papers, 'it's here somewhere... don't worry, I'll find it.'

Tom walked over to a table by the window and began searching through the books and papers stacked on top, 'Here it is,' he stepped back, and from a chair next to the table he retrieved a black leather-bound notebook, 'I've been looking for, you,' he unwound the leather thong, as he walked back. 'This is interesting, and explains much, I found it among the papers you took from Mason. It was not authored by him; I must say the individual who wrote it has a good hand. The first half of the journal is in the form of a ceremonial rite, a handbook if you like, a guide to the conduct of an ancient ritual. In the preamble the anonymous author explains the origins of the rite, from the Babylonians, through the Egyptians, up to the present day. Essentially it is based upon a ritual dedicated to *Ahemait*, an Egyptian deity, known as the devourer-of-the-dead, or soul-eater. Down the years, each age has added to the ceremony, which culminates in the summoning of their god, in the hope that he, as a disciple of the Devil, will confer upon those present, his acolytes, some of his power, but largely the rite has remained unchanged since the sixteenth century. I checked with a friend at Oxford, a medievalist, I had to promise to lend it to him when we are finished with it, he confirmed that the ritual, as described in this journal, is authentic; of course, that does not imply that

231

it is anything more than merely superstitious nonsense. However, its adherents can, and do, point to its antiquity, and its continuity with the past, and in their warped universe that provenance counts for everything. The second half of the book is a diary of events going back twenty-seven years, every single meeting conducted in this country is listed, giving the initials of the group, the date, time, location, number of participants, how many children were involved, their sexes, and finally the number of babies, if any, present. I'm guessing, that since the totals underlined do not correspond to the number of children remaining at the conclusion of the rite, that this discrepancy indicates the number killed during the ritual, and therefore needing replacement. The book states that the boys will need to be slightly older than the girls, thirteen or fourteen, they are used and abused by the female members of the group, there are far fewer boys than girls, then women are only twenty percent of the membership; still, a figure much higher than I would have predicted. Eventually, the boys share the same fate as the girls; the lad is hung by his wrists from the ceiling, suspended inches from the floor, his legs held by two men, the woman who has been using him steps forward, seizes his genitals, and if he is lucky, with one cut removes the lot. The boy is then left to hang while he bleeds out, his blood is collected, but I cannot find any reference as to what they do with the blood, or the discarded genitals. The girls, mostly from Eastern Europe, the Far East, and Africa, are sent to one of the houses, there is reference made to a rota, so there is some form logistics applied to their dispersal. Once in the system, they are subject to sexual abuse and rape, during rituals presided over by a small group of invited adherents, until such time as they fall pregnant. The girls are looked after until they give birth. The cages you found in the basement of the house at Colpuck are typical of the conditions in which they are kept. Once they have given birth they are returned to the ritual-roster, to be impregnated again. The babies are removed at birth to be looked after by nannies in the nursery, from the photographs, I surmise this to be the other room in the basement you came across. Only at those rites attended by all the adherents of a particular group, are babies, who have been kept alive for the purpose, ritually slaughtered. The journal goes on to explain that the method of killing had been changed, it seems that the screams of the babies disturbed some of the more delicate souls attending the rite. One of the High Priests, a medic had travelled to the States to study a method devised by a doctor there, who carried out late-term abortions, he would induce labour in women who were up to seven months pregnant. Obviously, the infants were born alive, and viable, but since this procedure was an abortion not a birth, he had to find an effective and efficient means of dispatching these babies. He did so by sticking surgical scissors into the baby's neck and severing the spinal cord. The revised ritual now required two devotees, one to kill the child by severing its spinal cord, the other to cut open its chest and remove the heart. The tiny, still beating organ, is then shown to all present, before being burnt in offering with incense. This could be repeated up to seven times, at any one ritual. This precious repository of innocence was seen as...'

Tom, stopped speaking, tears ran down his cheeks, his face a mask of vengeful anger, he turned away, 'Sorry, give me a moment.'

Mac and Peter, sat stony-faced, silently confronting their own thoughts.

After a minute, Tom turned round to face them, and continued, 'The girls remain in service, falling repeatedly pregnant until they reach thirteen, or even fifteen, if they do not appear

233

too sexually mature, then they too are disposed of by way of ritual sacrifice. Having said that, lately they appear to have developed a lucrative trade in body parts. Some of the girls and boys are shipped to clinics in Turkey and India, to be harvested for transplants, hearts, lungs, livers, kidneys, eyes, and so on. It seems to generate quite an income, and a recent development has seen some babies spared ritual slaughter, trafficked instead to clinics, something to do with stem-cells and DNA, which I don't fully understand, but it appears just as lucrative as the trade in transplant organs.'

Peter said, 'Sorry to interrupt you Tom, but that doctor in the USA, is he still…?'

'No, I'm pleased to say my enquires have shown that the evil bastard was caught and convicted by the authorities in his home State, but not before he had murdered hundreds of infants… talking of America, there is a reference to a lodge in the US, interestingly it is the only time that word is used to describe cells in this organisation.'

Mac said, 'Is there a link, or a direct connection between the sect in America and here?'

'Not that I've found so far but give me time… this sister-organisation is discussed in a short paragraph, it seems to be an off-shoot, it looks like this septic infection has migrated. The writer of this journal makes several references to a second journal, which undoubtedly contains additional information, but it is not among the rest of Mason's papers.'

Peter said, 'If that fucker couldn't find it, then I doubt we ever will…'

Mac interrupted, 'Let's just concentrate on what we have, I don't want to be side-tracked by speculation. Stick to the facts, unless you can find a direct link, something that connects our case with an organisation in the States, forget it.'

Tom said, 'It would be worth investigating… if this plague has migrated across the Pond and is infecting our colonial cousins…'

Mac said, 'Agreed, but it would hardly be surprising if it has, given the number of years the US was involved in Germany, and given the sheer number of American troops and civilians stationed there; if you ever find a link, then at some point we can sit down and figure out who to tell, but for now, pencil it in for future investigation.'

'Okay, Mac.'

Peter said, 'It does make you wonder how far this thing spreads.'

Mac said, 'Yes it does, but for the present, we play the hand we've been dealt.'

Tom and Peter, in unison, said, 'Agreed.'

Mac said, 'The word lodge, is used, is there a link to the Freemasons?'

'No, in fact…' Tom paused and began to flick through the journal, 'well it's in here somewhere. There is a reference to Freemasonry, this sect is careful to avoid selecting members who are part of that organisation, who they see as a threat.'

'Rivals then?'

'No, the journal entry indicates that the writer perceives the moral constitution of Freemasonry as much of an existential threat to the cult, as he does the Catholic Church.'

Mac grimaced, and said, 'That's not a sentence I ever thought I would hear uttered.'

Tom laughed, then said, 'To continue, in Germany the girls are not passed around the group, but individually become the property of a particular adherent, the baby resulting from their union is then sacrificed, killed by its own father.'

'Judas Priest.'

Mac and Peter turned round, Simon and Tony, had been standing in the doorway for the last five minutes.

'That's what this is about?' said Tony.

'No, not quite,' said Tom.

Peter said, 'Grab a couple of chairs from the kitchen, you may as well join us to hear the rest.'

Simon and Tony returned, each carrying a chair.

Tom continued, 'Your earlier investigation managed to identify about eight well known individuals, a couple of politicians, a senior member of the armed forces, a couple of university lecturers, a surgeon, a psychologist, and a judge. From what I have discovered, they were about a third of the total number of that particular group, important and influential enough to get your enquiry stopped in its tracks. You had the metaphorical justice system door slammed in your faces, and you can guarantee that those responsible for doing so, number among those whose identities you failed to discover. You realised, that important though these people were and embarrassing though the case could be to the government, what you had uncovered was only the tip of the iceberg. It is at this point in the proceedings, following orders from on high, that the investigation was discontinued, and Mason appears, he had been dispatched to protect those whose names you had yet to discover, names you never unearthed, individuals who are clearly important and influential, people whose exposure could have collapsed the government, and let's be honest, had you been able to uncover what little we now know, it could have brought down the entire political edifice, here and in Europe. You both suspected Mason's direct involvement with the group, but by then your enquiry had been shut down, and an accommodation reached that ensured your safety in return for your silence, the two of you were then separated, not long after that Mac left the Force…'

'They can do that? I mean I know... well I've read about such things... they can stop a police investigation, just like that?' said Tony.

Mac said, 'It happens every day, someone influential is caught in a compromising situation, usually by members of a Vice Squad, then it is covered up, hushed up, someone further up the food-chain has to make that happen, so favours are owed, and corruption grows. It even happens here; I guarantee that your Force has seen its share. This case was closed, not because we solved it, we were far from doing that, but because an individual, or individuals, in a position of power required it. The corruption it generates is not for personal gain, but for influence, again not personal, but at force level. A bill is placed before Parliament, its passing could prove detrimental to policing, so calls are made, and various individuals, opposing their party's policy on the matter, defying the whip, vote as requested, and all because they have been caught in a compromising situation, and can be blackmailed. More usually, the bill is shaped at the committee stage, by compromised politicians, previously caught in flagrante delicto.'

Peter said, 'At the time it seemed to be just another case of power protecting power, we thought that it was a group of child-molesters who had developed a systematic method of ensuring they had a ready supply of victims, we were puzzled by their somewhat theatrical approach, but we didn't know anything about these rituals, and struggled to make connections beyond what we discovered. Their organisation appeared to be a one-off, and given that we had disrupted and dispersed them, we hoped they would be too scared to reform, and took that as the best result we could achieve under the circumstances. It seemed to us that whilst we were being forced to compromise, shutting them down was almost a result, and we thought that there were cases needing our attention that were far worse.'

'Worse than this, I doubt it, I feel sick.'

They watched Tony rush to the kitchen and winced as he retched into the bin.

Mac said, 'A good time for tea. Pete, can you get some organised? I'm going to find John and Matt; they need to hear this. Tell Tony to re-join us when he's finished and get him to wash out that bin.'

Twenty minutes later they reassembled. Tony thought that the tea and biscuits were a little incongruous given the nature of their deliberations.

Tom continued. 'I guess I should say something about this satanic sect, I don't yet know what they call themselves, the overarching organisation is based in Germany. Each sub-group calls itself by another name, usually something quite innocuous, your little group was called the Colpuck Lepidopterists, presenting themselves to the world as amateur butterfly enthusiasts. The church at Colpuck is a complete red herring, nothing more than a geographical marker, with the house being close by, it was a useful place to mention in letters or electronic communications, it was also a safe location to which new members could be invited and checked out, without revealing the actual whereabouts of their meeting place. What threw us were the seemingly pagan and satanic carvings that adorn the church, a coincidence, but utterly unconnected. Those carvings, and the church they adorn, have nothing to do with this matter, we can forget that line of enquiry, in fact most church historians are convinced that the symbolism is neither pagan nor satanic, more the result of a naive interpretation by a rural stonemason, some even suggest an influence from the Low-Countries. David, who claimed to be the church sexton, has nothing to do with the church, he's the gatekeeper and guardian of the nearby house, the one Mac called the harem. We will have to deal with him eventually, but for now he can wait.' Tom paused, 'Nice cuppa,' he smiled at Peter.

'Your most welcome,' said Peter, bowing his head.

Tom finished his tea, then continued. 'Now we come to the truly interesting bit, this story begins with the SS in Nazi Germany, namely the Ahnenerbe, a group set up by, Heinrich Himmler, to produce a history and an anthropology that fitted the Nazi ideal of race and Fatherland. Himmler, who had tenuous links with the Thule Society, used the philosophy of the Society as a platform upon which to build an esoteric cult, justified by his cherry-picking facts from the already slanted research of the Ahnenerbe, this, it would appear, resulted in a secret society, whose rituals it is claimed were written by Himmler, called the Vril Circle. The Vril may, or may not be a fiction, I cannot tell. There is a massive amount of bullshit written about the subject, but that's not important, all that matters, is that within Far-Right circles it is believed, is popular, and is seen as credible, which is crucial.'

'What has this history lesson got to do with our case?'

'Patience Peter, all roads lead to Rome, or in this case back to Berlin. First, I need to continue the history lesson.'

Mac and Matt's laughter was met by a glare from Peter.

'Thank you, ladies. If I may? At the end of the Second World War, it was alleged that an organisation called ODESSA, *Organisation der Ehemaligen SS-Angehörigen*, the Organisation of Former SS Members, was created to smuggle junior SS officers out of Germany, to prevent their prosecution, and given their relative youth, to allow them time to rebuild, and create a Fourth Reich. There were several successful networks that helped SS officers to escape from Germany at the end of the war, such as *Sechsgestirn*, the Constellation of Six… don't ask,'

Tom stopped Peter's question in its tracks, then continued,

'The SS set up an international network in the last days of the war under the control of, *Die Spinne*, or The Spider, a secret organisation established and led by a colonel in the Waffen-SS, these rat-lines created a web of interlinked escape routes allowing a large number of junior SS officers to escape capture, taking advantage of the confusion in Europe after the conflict ended. Millions had been displaced, vast numbers of people were moving around Europe, the agencies trying to accommodate the refugees couldn't distinguish good from bad, unable to verify the claims made by those presenting themselves for help, they simply assisted all who asked. It seems that ODESSA never actually existed, it appears to have been Nazi propaganda. Once the Cold War with Russia got going in earnest, NATO took a good look at those arrangements. Impressed by the efficiency of the networks and communications systems that were employed, NATO lumped them together under, for want of a better title, ODESSA, and adapted them to set up a clandestine, stay-behind, fifth-column operation, called Gladio. Its symbol is the short sword deployed by Rome's legions, the gladius, prophetically a double-edged sword, hence the name, Gladio. The purpose of Gladio was to carry out sabotage and assassination, in the event of a Soviet invasion of mainland Europe. Set up in nineteen-forty-seven by the CIA, with the connivance of MI6, its role was to stop, by means of intimidation and assassination, the spread of communism in Europe. Basically, in every country across Europe, there are secret armies, paramilitary groups, which given their linage, lean toward Nazism. These groups were funded and equipped by NATO, but controlled by the CIA. Most still exist, and it is alleged, continue to be paid for by the CIA, there is a suggestion that over the years they have made full use of the Vatican Bank to launder mafia drug money to fund the operation of these units. I will have to do some more research…'

'It all sounds a bit far-fetched… a bit conspiracy theory,' said Simon.

'I thought so too, so I asked a contact I know in NATO, he's in intelligence, and he confirmed everything, he also said that despite several national governments claiming that these units have been disbanded, they are still active. Both MI6 and the CIA, were, and are actively involved in the setting up and running of these clandestine units. Gladio units number among their upper echelon senior military, police and politicians. Units, designed to be a fifth column to fight the communists, were built upon existing networks, then brought and moulded together. They were staffed initially by ex SS and Nazi party members, hence the Nazi bias, a bias which has seen some of the more esoterically inclined members drawn to the pre-existing SS occult beliefs. The direct link to the SS left the Gladio family susceptible to a Nazi version of the occult. The Gladio are heirs of the SS. In Germany one unit, part of the Gehlen Organisation, the forerunner of the Bundesnachrichtend-Lenst, or the BJD, the Union of German Youth, was reported as having been disbanded in the early 1950's, but according to my friend in NATO, the group was still being referred to as active in documents he saw, dated as recently as last month.'

Tom paused, drank some tea, then said, 'Here in the UK, a Gladio funded group, Column 88, popped up in 1971, it was apparently disbanded in 1981. A neo-Nazi group, its members, weapons and communications were dispersed into smaller, self-contained units around the country, where they remain embedded to this day. Across Europe the story is the same, the larger groups have been split into smaller, stand-alone units, these new Gladio teams have line of communication direct to the CIA. Governments turn a blind eye to their existence, they are looking to the future, and see a use for these units in combatting the feared Islamic takeover of Europe. I have been unable to discover more about their present disposition. As an aside, since I am talking about Far-Right groups, did you know that the number 88 is neo-Nazi code? It represents the eighth letter of the alphabet, H, so 88 becomes HH, or Heil Hitler. Another symbol to look for is 4R, the four is at the top, and the R grows out of the leg of the four. He drew the symbol on the board.

$$4R$$

'It stands for the Fourth Reich. A couple of those signs to look for, that Father John bangs on about. Technically we should not call them right-wing, the Nazis are left-wing, the communists were not their opponents, but their rivals. The clue is in the name, National Socialism, but after the war, socialists, communists, and left-leaning intellectuals were concerned about the connection and began the successful process of rebranding Nazis as right, not left-wing. Ironic then that the cropped-haired knuckle-draggers are unwittingly promoting what they claim to hate, they are advocating an extreme left-wing template for the future.'

'Far-Right, Far-Left, as far as I can see it's all the same bullshit, dangerous evil bastards pursuing power, looking to control…'

Frowning, Tom interrupted, 'Thank you for your contribution, Peter. Most enlightening… if I may continue, how does all this connect to our case? Mason was involved with Column 88, he was also associated with one, Eric Powell, a senior officer in

MI6. This link turned up in the paperwork Mac recovered. The connection to Powell is clear, and according to Mason's notes, Powell is tied into a group in Germany, part of the Gladio family, but we don't know what they are called, or where they are located.'

'What about the remnants of Column 88?'

'No chance, Mac. They are too deep, not active enough to ripple the surface, and given the flak I took, heavily protected. I do not believe that they have anything to do with this sect, not all the Gladio network is involved in this satanic crap, from what I have discovered, only one Gladio group in each country is inculpated, hence the disparity between the thirteen satanic cells and the total number of Gladio units. It is confined to single unit from among the units based in each of the thirteen different countries. Each of these thirteen countries has one elite-Gladio unit, containing individuals drawn from among the most powerful and influential individuals in that country. They probably do not even know that they are a part of the Gladio network, or it could be they use the title as a cover. The former Warsaw Pact countries are, for obvious reasons, not included in the thirteen.'

Mac said, 'Will this come back on us, have you stirred things up?'

'No. Thanks to Simon's last visit with Cartwright, I was able to obtain the passwords and links to his computer, so I've hacked it, and in a way he will never discover.'

'What if someone suspects that it has been hacked, or assumes that is the case?'

'Then my routing the link through several countries will make it impossible to trace back to here, in any case I drove over to the next county and used the Constabulary's wi-fi network to access the web, I've been doing that since we started. So, if someone is that good, the trail will lead them to Lancashire's HQ.'

'Well done,' said Mac, 'I think we need to absorb what we have just heard. We'll all meet back here in the morning.' He got up and walked out of the stable block into the full glare of the low evening sun, the light felt purifying. Mac, sat down on the bench outside his workshop, his thoughts turbulent.

Chapter Twenty-Five

T he sun slowly pervaded the fields, a gentle breeze carried soft fragrances, bathed in warm sunlight he stretched, and turned onto his side, delighting in the tranquillity of it, his being suffused with peace, a languorous daydream distracted his wakefulness, he sensed there could be another life, and from this moment he would actively seek it, but for now he would allow warmth and serenity to enfold him; sleep summoned, and he surrendered.

Mac walked past, looked down at his troubled friend, and silently wished him peaceful dreams, then quietly walked away. It was flaming, too hot to work, too hot to walk, too hot to read, the incessant clamour of his thoughts harried him, and his mind refused to surrender to the indolent day. He walked off towards Liz's studio, and sat on the bench outside, random thoughts rampaging. Sadness entered his heart; he knew that the life they had dreamed of was fading into the space between thoughts. Teresa, as much as he loved her, and he did, was not Elizabeth. April was growing from a child into a young woman and would soon seek a life of her own. *What was it the old philosopher said? You can never step into the same river twice.*

Life with Peter as an ever-present companion, was never going to be the same. He thought of his friend, the violent youth who had grown into a valiant warrior, and wondered if he would achieve the next stage in life, that of a wise and tranquil old man, *Tranquil, Peter? Not a hope*, he laughed out loud, which dispelled some of the shadows that had begun to settle on him. First, they had to live through the trial that was coming.

The following morning Mac, Peter, Matt, Tom, and Simon sat down to go over their plan of action one last time. For the next few weeks, the farm would be the command centre. Tom would run things from the old stable block, assisted by Father John and Robin Masters. The intention being to follow up all enquires and leads on the fringe of the case, in the hope that new links would emerge; Simon and Matt, would use the opportunity to form a partnership.

An hour later Teresa and Anna loaded up the new Nissan Navara pickup, herded the two girls onto the back seats, and prepared to set off for Plymouth, where they would catch the ferry to Santander, there they would be met by Teresa's uncle, Aitor Agirre. Mac and Peter checked that the bags and cases were secure in the back, closed and locked the steel tonneau cover, before saying their goodbyes.

Matt climbed into the Land Rover, he was going to follow them as far as the ferry port, to make sure they boarded safely, and that they were not followed. There was a concern that those with a vested interest might try to kidnap them. Although Tom thought it highly unlikely that they were being watched, he agreed that adopting a cautious approach was sensible, and on the way back he arranged for Matt to call in on a contact in Bristol, to pick up some equipment they might need.

Mac finished hugging April, closed the door, and watched them drive off. He walked over to the Land Rover and said to Matt, 'Take no chances, if you feel there is a threat, eliminate it.'

'Relax, you know they're safe, no one knows what we are

doing, no one is looking at us, not yet anyway. Anything happens I will deal with it.'

'I know, I know, I'm…'

'Get your war-face on, when it kicks off it's going to get serious, and you need to hit the ground running. Get your fucking shit together, Mac.'

Mac smiled, and said, 'I hear you. Now you get going, O Wise-One.' Mac watched him leave; Matt caught up with the pickup as it topped the hill before leaving the farm.

Over the next three weeks, at Tom's behest, they checked facts, visited locations, and covertly observed certain individuals. Mostly low-level stuff, nobody who was surveillance conscious, people whose role in the scheme of things was little more than a link in the chain, mostly bit-part players. This information would form the background of any subsequent report Simon would submit to the Yard, nonetheless, low-key or not, the intelligence gathered proved invaluable.

It spotlighted the role of two individuals, one, a member of Parliament, who had not shown up until now, the other, Eric Powell, most of the information their enquires uncovered seemed to loop back to him. Tom felt that the MP could wait, he thought that Mason's links to Powell and MI6 was key, and that looking at Powell was their next move, he was the nearest that Mason had to a handler.

'How do we play this?' said Matt.

Peter said, 'Tricky, very tricky, given his seniority, and the fact that he's in Six, it's not going to be easy. Surveillance is out, he will have twenty-four-hour cover, and if we try to take him, they will come looking.'

Mac said, 'Up to now we have stayed below the radar, but Pete's right, given the level of protection he has, covert, overt and electronic, anything we do will set alarm-bells ringing, and it will not take them long to identify us.'

Simon said, 'But he works for MI6, and they only operate abroad, so it might take them sometime to discover what we are doing?'

Mac, Peter, and Matt snorted their derision.

Tom said, 'It will take them no more than an hour to place and locate us. So, what to do?'

Peter said, 'The first problem is his Close Protection Officer, he's like his fucking shadow.'

'Snatch them both, kill the CPO.' said Matt.

'No way,' said Mac, 'We don't touch the CPO, he's one of us, and most likely, he's ex your mob.'

'I'm with Mac on this,' said Tom, 'I know that we might have to… cancel a contract or two along the way, but not…'

Mac interrupted, setting aside the comprehensive report Tom had prepared on Mason, said, 'Follow me on this. We still have the secret-squirrel van we liberated from Mason, and it's full of all sorts of clever equipment designed by Five, it's their stuff. We know that Powell is dirty. What we have discovered is only going to be a small part of the mischief he's into, so…'

'If we use the kit to watch him,' said Tom, raising his hands in apology for interrupting Mac. 'His minders in Six will inform him that he's under surveillance, which will shake him, especially when the equipment being used is identified as belonging to Five. His own controllers will want to know why, and in the confusion of allegations and denials that will follow, there is a good chance he will panic, think he's been discovered, and jump-ship.'

'Spook a spook?' said Peter, 'How can we be sure that he has been playing away from home, we have no evidence to suggest that he is a double agent, and if he is, who is he working for? If your guess is right, and I suspect it may be, then we're in even deeper shit. We have no idea who's behind him, this could back-fire on us, badly.'

Mac said, 'It might do, but if we snatch him when he breaks cover, whoever his contacts are, will believe that Five or Six have him, and the security forces will think that whoever he was working for, has him; and we will stay off their radar a little longer. In any case he will have neither the time, nor the opportunity, to contact his friends, he will not dare risk it, not while he believes he is under surveillance. When he runs, we take him. The subsequent confusion will create the time we need to question him.'

'But what about your precious CPO?' said Matt.

Tom said, 'When Powell breaks cover it will be for a face-to-face meeting, or to seek the temporary sanctuary of his safe-house, or to leave the country. To set that up he will need to get clear of London, and to do that he will have to ditch his CPO, he will take care of the problem for us.'

'Okay, but questioning him may take quite a while, he's been trained, remember. The initial period of confusion will not last more than a couple of days at the most. What then?' said Simon.

Mac said, 'I've got an idea, and it involves, Ivan.'

'Fine and dandy, but what if he is not working for someone else, what if he doesn't run?' said Peter.

'Did you really just say fine and dandy?' said Matt laughing.

Mac fearing serious violence was about to break out, said, 'Then we have to set this up, so it never comes back to us. But he will run, even if he's clean, he will run, to create distance, to give himself time to find out who is behind the attempt to besmirch his reputation. He will want to know who set him up. The shadow world is one of ever-present betrayal and esurient ambition, when you get as high up the tree as he has, you have a safe-house and an escape plan in place, even if you are as white as the driven snow, and this bugger ain't.'

'Then we had better plan this down to the last detail.' said Tom.

'What now?' said Peter and Matt, in unison.

'Yup. Right now,' said Tom.

Mac said, 'We need to ensure that we anticipate every conceivable scenario, and have practical solutions in place, so that nothing takes us by surprise. Now let's get on with it.'

Chapter Twenty-Six

Five days later, they began what Tom called, Operation Trojan Horse. Matt parked the surveillance van close to Powell's MI6 supplied ground floor flat, in the Muswell Hill area of London. Switching on the equipment in the rear of the vehicle, he left to join Simon, who was parked in the Ford transit round the corner, Mac and Peter, were positioned on motorbikes nearby.

Tom had set up the remote surveillance equipment, the van was as it had been on the day they liberated it from Mason. He had removed a couple of the items he thought might prove useful, but it remained a standard MI5 observation vehicle. Using the remote access system, he waited until he received a signal from Simon that Matt was clear of the location, and he began the surveillance.

Matt, following Tom's instructions, had aimed lasers at the windows to assist with eavesdropping, Powell's computer was accessed via the domestic electrical grid, high speed state-of-the-art computers began downloading data from his laptop. The program, designed by some anorak in the bowels of Millbank, was impressive, Powell's domestic wi-fi was password protected, and all his emails were encrypted, protection that lasted for all of 20 seconds, the stream of data surprised even Tom, it would take weeks to go through it.

He had estimated that they had about forty minutes of uninterrupted data collection, he thought it would take that long for the cyber-geeks at Six to register the attack, confirm that it was being done by Five, for the round-robin of accusations and denials to reach a point, when someone senior would order the shutdown of the surveillance operation. Powell would then be informed of a possible threat, which he would correctly interpret, and if Mac was right, he would get out of there almost immediately.

Tom was wrong, it only took eighteen minutes, it took them another three minutes to locate the van, but by that time Tom had already broken the multi-routed network he had set up, he was certain that they had run a trace only as far as the twenty-fifth link in the chain, they were still safe, and under the radar.

Tom and Robin, had laid out a set of Ordinance Survey maps, covering the whole of England south of a line running from the Wash to the Bristol Channel, they waited. Peter and Mac were parked at either end of the street on motor bikes, Simon and Matt, in Mason's black Ford Transit van, had moved two streets away.

Twelve minutes later, Powell emerged with his CPO in tow, they got into a blue VW Golf and drove off towards the City, Powell was driving. He passed through the City of London, at Gardiners' Corner he drove east along Whitechapel, then Mile End, eventually joining the A12 towards Chelmsford.

Powell drove slowly and deliberately. Mac and Peter stayed well back, almost out of sight, but turning onto the A12 forced a change in tactics, Mac overtook the Golf and headed up the road to the Green Man roundabout, there he turned off, parked up, and waited in Holly Road.

Matt and Simon followed, keeping at least a mile behind, Peter maintained eyeball, Matt called in to say that Ivan had been in touch, and was also mobile, somewhere in Essex. Tom asked Matt for Ivan's mobile number, and then called him to suggest a possible location for him to head to, he was working on the assumption that Mac was right about Powell heading for the Norfolk coast.

At the Green Man roundabout, the Golf turned off into Holly Bush Hill, then turned right onto the A113. Opposite the entrance to Wanstead Hospital the car turned left and pulled up outside some houses, which were set back from the road. The Golf turned around facing the way it had come in, the passenger door opened, the CPO left the vehicle holding an envelope, and walked over to one of the houses.

Tom called over the radio, 'He's going to lose his CPO.'

Peter stopped a little further ahead, in Alexander Road. Mac doubled back and stopped at the junction with Holly Bush Hill, the Ford Transit turned into Sylvan Road, further down Hermon Hill from the hospital entrance, and parked up.

As the CPO put the envelope through the letter box, Powell accelerated away, he turned left and continued his original route along Hermon Hill, and into Chigwell Road, then he turned onto the North Circular Road, heading towards Waterworks Corner.

Tom radioed, 'He's going to ditch the Golf, and soon. I'm playing a hunch that you're right about Norfolk, Mac. Simon, at Waterworks Corner drop off, go back and head up the M11, get off at junction seven, and find somewhere to wait. I'll have Ivan meet you there.'

Simon said, 'Whatever you say, you're the boss.'

Mac radioed, 'Tom, you sure, junction seven is up at Harlow, that's a long way out?'

'Trust me, I'm good at playing hunches.'

The Golf, turned south at Waterworks Corner into Lea

Bridge Road, Mac and Peter followed at a distance, even at this hour traffic was heavy.

Mac radioed Peter, 'Tom's right, he's going to change vehicles, and I think I know where he is going. Mason used have a lock-up in Church Road, Leyton.'

Peter replied, 'The one close to that row of houses in the one-way system?'

'Yes, I think so. Drop back, return to Waterworks, find somewhere to wait, I'll follow him, he is going to head north again after the switch, he's headed for Norfolk. Mason had a safe house there, damned if I can remember exactly where it is, but that's where he's going. Tom, Mason mentioned it in one of his notebooks.'

Robin radioed, 'Mac, I'll find it.'

Mac watched as a small, off-white, Renault van, turned into Church Road, Powell was driving, he was wearing light blue overalls. Mac followed, the van retraced the route taken by the Golf, back to Waterworks Corner. Powell meandered north, in no apparent hurry, leaving and re-joining the motorway, about an hour later they went past junction seven on the M11.

Matt radioed, 'If we can take him in the next three-zero minutes, there's a safe-house we used to use, not too far from here, well its more of a hangar than a house, but it is out of the way on a disused private airfield.'

Mac replied, 'Not sure what we can do, until he stops?'

They left the M11, joined the A14, then looping round the top of Cambridge, took the A10 towards Ely. The other side of Stretham, just after two o'clock in the morning, Powell pulled into a lay-by, he got out of the van, and walked over to the hedge to relieve himself. So suddenly had he braked, and entered the lay-by, that Mac was forced to continue along the road.

Simon, Matt, and Ivan, who they had picked up earlier, drove into the lay-by at speed. Ivan was on Powell before he could react, by the time Mac and Peter joined them, Powell was trust up in the back of the Transit van.

'Good job,' said Mac.

Matt said, 'What about Powell's van?'

Peter said, 'Just leave it, it looks like the rest of the shit-heaps the retards drive round here, it's not going to be registered to anyone traceable, forget it.'

Mac said, 'Burn it. We can't risk prints, or DNA. Burn it but check it first. Simon, get going, Matt will direct you. Ivan, good to meet you, we'll talk later. Peter, torch it.'

Simon drove off, Mac followed, hanging back to wait for Peter to join him. They caught up with the Transit and followed as they drove onto an airfield near Newmarket. Inside the hangar, the Ford and the two bikes were parked facing towards the large, closed door.

Powell was tied to a chair in the middle of the hangar. He assumed an air of arrogant indifference, even contempt. He shouted, 'Who's he? Who's the Russian?'

Mac said, 'Ivan? He's *SPAZ*, and a friend, a member of the *Vympel*, a senior officer in the *Spetsgruppa B*.'

Ivan bowed gracefully to Mac and smiled at Powell.

Powell said, 'Who the hell are you? Do you know who I am. Do you realise how much shit you are in?'

'I'm the man whose wife you ordered killed.'

Powell looked momentarily confused, this information wrong-footed him, it was unanticipated, and the presence of the Russian frightened him.

'And yes, I do know who you are, I know all about you. Eric Powell, career MI6 Officer, we know everything there is to know about you.'

'If you know who I am, then you know you are in trouble,

people will be looking for me.'

'No, they won't, well not here anyway. We followed you from the time you left home. It's you who's in deep shit.'

Mac nodded at Matt, who stepped forward holding a club hammer.

'The threat of torture? How crude.'

'No. Not the threat... crude... true but effective.' Matt smashed both Powell's knees with a blow to each, Powell's scream died, as he lost consciousness with the second strike of the hammer. When he came round the fire and the arrogance had gone.

Mac spoke, his voice even, and cold, 'You have information we want. We need you to confirm what we already know, and I need you to understand what we will do to get it.'

'Why should I, you're going to kill me anyway?'

Peter said, 'It's up to you, there are many ways a man can die. Quickly... a bullet in the back of the head, or slowly, agonisingly, over a couple of weeks,' he nodded towards Mac, 'and he's an expert at it, I watched him take two weeks to kill someone, and every last moment of that man's life was a living, brain-screaming hell. You killed his wife, so what do you think he is going to do to you?'

Matt and Ivan exchanged glances, impressed by this new information.

Powell, tears in his eyes, looked at Mac, 'Your wife? I don't even know who she is, how could I be involved in her death?'

'Mason. Does that name ring any bells?'

'That's you? It was your fault; you broke Mason's stupid agreement when you started checking up on me.'

'No. Liz, my wife, was a freelance journalist, she was doing a piece on people who had recently moved from London to the country, all about lifestyle changes, the challenges of rural life, a load of nonsense. She approached your wife, because you had just moved from Chelsea to Herefordshire. None of us had heard of you, we knew nothing of your connection to Mason, but we know all about you and your activities now.'

'Kill me, see if I care, take two weeks, I've been trained. But know this, if you do, all of you and your families will be slaughtered.'

Mac looked at him and said, 'What… you're hoping Mason will turn up and rescue you?'

Peter said, 'Sorry old boy. Mason is dead. He is no more. He is an ex-agent. Mac cancelled his contract.'

Powell, stared at Mac.

Mac wanted him dead, he lusted for his death, to kill him, slowly, agonisingly, he wanted to get medieval on him, seriously fucking medieval. Mac's face betrayed that thought to Powell.

'You're going to kill me?' he sobbed.

'I want to. Fuck, how I want to, but I'm not. You are useful to us, we have questions we want answered now, and I have no doubt we will have more in the future. For you, staying alive is dependent on your continued usefulness. I am not going to kill you, I'm handing you over to Ivan, and I have no doubt he has other questions for you to answer…'

'You're going to hand me over to him, the enemy? I'm a patriot, you cannot betray your country?'

'Firstly, you are many things, but a patriot? I doubt that you even know what the word means, let alone what it really entails, that would require that you have a moral compass. This is not about Russia, or the Great Game, it's simply a bunch of coppers seeking the truth, looking for justice, nothing more, it's about righting a wrong, that's all. And to save you an argument, my country right or wrong, doesn't cut it. If my country requires the death of innocents and needs to support and cover up evil in order to survive, then it isn't worth it. My country must mean more than that, it has to stand for something higher, and I'm afraid that's a concept beyond your ken.' Matt stepped forward without the hammer, and squatted down in front of Powell, he placed his hands lightly on Powell's knees, almost tenderly. Powell winced in anticipation. Matt spoke gently, softly, 'Here's the nub of it, you can answer our questions, and we will check what you tell us against the information we already have, did we mention we have all Mason's diaries, notebooks and papers? When we are done here, Ivan will take you back to Russia, from time to time we may need to confirm something, and we will give Ivan a call, and he will pay you a visit, or you can decline our offer, and we will leave you to Mac and his tender ministrations. You will die slowly, it will be a painful, terrifying, and unspeakable couple of weeks, it's up to you. I don't give a flying fuck either way.'

Matt pushed himself back to his feet, using Powell's smashed knees to do so. Powell's primeval scream was brief, curtailed again by the sanctuary of unconsciousness.

Ten minutes later he came round, the others had disappeared, Mac was standing there holding a pair of long-nosed pliers.

His voice pleading, Powell said, 'Alright, there's no need for that, I'll tell you what you want to know.'

Two hours later Tom, who had been listening via a WhatsApp link, interjected, 'I think that's everything, hand him over to Sergei, tidy up, and while you make your way back to base, Robin and I will go through what we have. Well done everyone.'

'Sergei?' Matt looked at his Russian friend.

'How does Tom do it? Sergei Ulyanov, at your service,' he said, bowing.

'Nice to meet you Sergei,' said Mac, extending his hand, 'damned if I know, but Tom is a genius with a computer.'

Sergei embraced Matt, and said, 'Sorry old friend, I should have told you sooner, but I liked being called Ivan, and… well it kept my name out of things. In Russia it is sometimes better not to be noticed.'

Peter laughed, and said, 'Don't sweat it… Sergei. But your tergiversation is going to cost you a bottle of good vodka.'

Looking puzzled, Sergei said, 'Tergiversation, this is not a word I understand?'

Matt laughed and said, 'So comrade, the Zaslon school just outside Moscow didn't teach you everything? What Pete means is that your evasion, your failure to tell us your real name, is going to cost you a bottle of your best vodka… for each of us.'

They cleared up, Peter and Mac were going to head off back to the farm, Matt and Simon were going to take Sergei and Powell down to Blackwater, where Sergei had a boat and a crew waiting. Then, after they had abandoned and set fire to Mason's Transit, they were going catch a train back to London, and from there take the train to Preston, where Father John would be waiting. Powell was laying in the back of the Transit van, Mac walked over to him, as he did so, Peter handed Mac a skinner's knife. Mac leaned into the back of the van, pinned Powell's head, and sliced through his right eye, 'An eye for an eye. Get this piece of shit out of here.' He slammed the door shut, muting Powell's sobs, turned and shook Sergei's hand, 'Thanks for everything, I'll be in touch.'

Chapter Twenty-Seven

Three days later, at four in the afternoon, they assembled in the main room of the stable block. Tom quietened them down, 'I'm sorry it has taken so long, but I had to double check the information Powell gave us, and wait for Father John to get back from Rome, and then Tony was on early turn today, so this is the soonest we could all get together.' He pointed at Powell's photograph on the board behind him, 'as you know, Mr Eric Powell, late of…'

'Late of?' said Father John, glaring at Mac, 'You…'

Tom interrupted, 'Not what you think. He is very much alive and singing like a bird. He is in good… well reasonable health.'

Matt and Peter's laugh was cut short by Father John's frown.

Tom continued, 'Had you let me finish, I was going to say, late of MI6.'

Matt said, 'He will be in Russia by now, on his way to a private gulag run by Sergei and his mates. They have promised to keep him alive; they have a few questions of their own, but I am sure the Spetsnaz will be gentle. He is alive, but I can only guess at what kind of hell he finds himself in.'

Father John looked contrite, 'How long will they keep him there?'

'Until he dies, an old and broken man.' said Matt.

'Okay… I guess I should apologise…'

'No need, John,' said Mac, grateful that no one had mentioned Powell's injuries.

'May I continue?' said Tom.

There was a murmured affirmative response.

'Powell was Mason's handler, not that he exercised much control. Mason may have worked for MI5, but he was up to his neck with Powell in setting up and running Gladio units, here and abroad. It seems likely that Mason was connected to Column 88, years after it was split up and sub-divided, he was tasked with reorganising and improving the efficiency of the various cells. Mason's diaries and notes have provided us with the names and locations of each group, the names and addresses of every individual member, and a complete inventory of the logistics of each cell, their communications equipment, weapons, specialities and the role they are to play in the event of an invasion, or a coup.'

'A coup?' said Peter.

'Yes. It's shocking, an additional role has been recently added to every Gladio unit across Europe and the UK, should the real power in this country deem it necessary, each unit will join with the civilian police and the military to aid command and control, and help lock down the country. It's all here in a manual written, I guess, by some history-major at Langley. Ever wonder about all that senior officer training on Command and Control at the Police Staff College, training that went way beyond simple major incident management, well, read it and weep. Simon has agreed not to mention the manual in his report, we are going to need an ace up our sleeve after this is over, a guarantee that we get left alone. For the record, the only names Simon will include in his report will be those of the key players, Mason and Powell, and anyone else of importance we come across, the rest of you will be given noms de guerre. When this is over, and the report is completed, you will each be given a copy to read, only with your approval will it be sent to Cartwright. Powell was instrumental in setting up Gladio units in France and Germany, and he helped in the reforms that led to the creation of Column 88 in this country. But the unit we are most interested in, is based in Germany, it's called, Neu-Neu Volk, I'll call them NNV. Father John will throw some light on this group.'

Mac said, 'Sorry John, before you commence your bit… Tom, I am worried about our security, are we still off the radar, will NNV know we are coming? Pete and I had some bad experiences in Germany.'

Tom said, 'I think we are still alright. Powell had not contacted anyone, and we can't be certain that it was members of that group he was going to meet. It might have been a contact in this country, I will get Sergei to ask him. You intercepted him before he had gone to ground, so I don't think… but I can't be sure. Sergei has been feeding the rumour mill, both Five and Six think he was a double agent, and are, as we speak, engaged in a turf war. My sources tell me that Five have even claimed responsibility for the surveillance and are saying that they had their suspicions all along. It is my guess that they think Mason is behind it, their van was logged out in his name, and they still think he's alive, that secretive bastard was so twisted that even his employers know little or nothing of his activities, including how to find him. They are too busy squabbling and engaging one-upmanship, to notice us. As for NNV, they have no idea who, or what we are, let alone that we are coming. I am certain we are still off the grid.'

'I'm too not sure about that.' said Father John, 'My trip to Rome may have alerted them.'

'How so?' said Mac.

'To explain that I will have to go back to our original enquiry. About six weeks after I came to London to assist you with the case, you and Peter travelled to Osnabrück in Lower Saxony, to meet a woman, Mary. She had been working with children who had survived satanic abuse, and she was secretly being assisted by the local bishop, he had made the resources of the diocese available to her through a priest, Paulo Kramer. He and I go way back, he's now a senior Vatican exorcist. Mary thought it possible that everything that you and Peter had uncovered here in the UK, was somehow linked to the pattern of abuse she had catalogued, and that it was widespread throughout Europe; Belgium, at that time, being a particular hot spot. She suspected that there might be a link between the sect that you and Peter had stumbled upon, and other such groups across Europe, but the three of you were unable to find anything that confirmed the connection. Mary suggested that digging in Germany was most likely to unearth the connection. However, before you could start excavating, you were both arrested and locked up by the local Police Chief, and after a few days of questioning, which rendered the Germans nothing, they took you to the airport and put you on a plane back to the UK. Interestingly, no complaint was made by the German authorities, so no one at the Yard was any the wiser. What none of us knew at the time, was that a perfectly innocent visit to Peter's aunt in Wewelsburg village, triggered that response. You see Wewelsburg Castle was the bastion of Heinrich Himmler, the place is sacred to the cult he created, and that sense of the profanely sacred continues to this day. The area is the location of a predicted battle between East and West. The so-called, Battle at Birch Tree, will occur there, and according to the legend, the East will be defeated, apparently next to Peter's aunt's house. Wewelsburg is still a pilgrimage site for right-wing occultists, and that's why you were marched out of Germany, well flown out. They knew of your investigation, Mary was being watched, as was Father Kramer, so when you went to Wewelsburg you started some very big bells ringing. I went to Rome a few days ago to visit Paulo, to seek his advice, and to find out what information he had that might be of use to us. He was most helpful and gave me his file on Osnabrück. He mentioned *Neu-Neu Volk*, the file also contains a description of two regular visitors to the sect, I think you will agree they are good descriptions of Powell and Mason. Paulo explained that NNV have been around for quite some time, they pre-date the Gladio. NNV have their roots in the back-to-the-land movement that sprung up across Europe in the latter part of the nineteenth and early twentieth centuries. This movement came out of a general dissatisfaction with industrial society, in most countries it morphed into benign guilds. Here in England, it was the catalyst for movements championed, mainly, but not exclusively, by the Catholic Church, that led to Distributism, an utterly genial movement of beer-drinking, pipe-smoking, dreamers. The community they established in Gloucestershire was only wound up in the nineteen-nineties, due a lack of residents. In Germany it spawned a forbidding romanticism, that crystallised into a sinister chauvinism. Their version of the simple-life movement was driven by a malevolent undercurrent. It was this movement that Himmler adapted and warped, moulding its mythology into a creed that could support the philosophy of National Socialism. There has been much speculation about the cult that Himmler created at Wewelsburg Castle. Teutonic Knights, blood oaths, a round table, and esoteric rituals, it's hard to know what is true, fact and fiction were fused into legend by the Nazi's. The trouble is that most people are comfortable seeing the Second World War as a simple fight between good and evil, and in a sense, it was just that, a battle between the powers of darkness and light. Yet it was not that straightforward, nothing is ever that simple. This has allowed certain myths to flourish, to go unchallenged, even by academia…'

Mac, fearing a lengthy diatribe, coughed theatrically. Father John, stopped talking, paused and said, 'Ah yes…'

Tom, leapt to his feet saying, 'Tea break.'

Twenty minutes later, Father John continued. 'Whatever the source of the esoteric ideology of Himmler's SS, it resulted in great evil. They created, and encouraged, a savage ethnocentrism, predicated upon the rejection and hatred of every individual, philosophy, and culture, that was not Arian. This was inevitable, following their adoption of evil, and their total rejection of the Truth. They systematically smashed social constraints, which are there to curb depravity, and in doing so they set a terrible malevolence loose in the world, its power still reverberates today. An evil that has done its utmost to ensure that people would rather deny its presence, than admit that it exists, and to that end it has been supremely successful. Working by degree, through those hoodwinked by its lies, and enchanted by its promises, it has even managed to bring about the demise of the very language we use to describe it, disabling our ability to articulate the notion of evil…'

This time it was Peter and Matt, who together, interrupted with a cough.

'Ah, the grunts of the sceptic…'

'Or should that be septic?' interrupted Mac, looking at Peter. Everyone laughed.

'Enough,' said Father John sternly, 'the interesting question is why, after all that has happened, Hitler's death camps, Stalin's gulags in Russia, Mao's Laogai prison system in China, and Pol Pot's Killing Fields in Cambodia, nearly a quarter of a billion murdered, why are people still attracted to Communism and Nazism? Why do these evil systems continue attract adherents, why are they allowed to thrive in society? Why do people love evil, and revel in being wicked? It is not that they are simple-minded, do not dismiss the purveyors of evil as retarded or weak, that would be a serious mistake. Evil attracts many intel-lectuals; you will find that these sects contain judges; lawyers; psychologists; doctors; politicians; professors; lecturers; teachers; scientists; journalists; senior police and military officers; indus-trialists and bankers. I am convinced that it is the appeal of the esoteric, and the salivating lust for power it engenders, that pulls so many down. There is an odd, seemingly inconsequential, banality about evil, which masks its intent, and its inherent danger, rendering it opaque, making it difficult to acknowledge as malign, but its signature is always present, a quiet and determ-ined hatred of all that is Christian, coupled with evil's justifica-tion of privilege. It is a culture of death, and not of life, look at its affirmation of eugenics. Be aware of the threat this represents to your soul, none of us is immune. Paulo gave me the names of those at the head of *Neu-Neu Volk*, they are husband and wife, Walii and Fieke Seidel. A pair of sadistic, murderous Nazi fanat-ics, they like to be called, *Schäfer* and *Schäferin*, shepherd and shepherdess, why, I don't know? *Neu-Neu Volk* presents itself as a liberal extension of the *Volkisch* Movement, the back-to-the-land faction, promoting the simple life. But, in reality they are a neo-Nazi group, and a major player in this satanic network. Mason was often seen in their company, more frequently in the last eighteen months, but there is no intelligence that would explain why; we can speculate, given what we now know, but I think we should ask Powell. I suspect that he ordered Mason's visits to Germany, I'm certain that's our next line of enquiry.'

Peter said, 'Are you sure he went to Germany to meet with

these people, it's unlike him to place himself in the spotlight.'

'Paulo's file included photographs of him meeting and socialising with the pair of them, and other members of the group, and it is clear from the video footage that he was on intimate terms with most of them, and that they held him in high regard, and were slightly fearful of him, but given our dealings with him, understandable.'

'Photographs, video footage, are you a church or an agency?' said Matt.

Father John laughed, 'There have been times in our history when we have been more one than the other, we are a bit of both, but this intelligence was donated by someone in the BfV.'

Blank looks followed this statement. 'The Bundesamt für Verfassungsschutz, or the BfV, Germany's version of MI5, with more efficient paperwork,' said Matt.

Father John acknowledged Matt with a nod, and continued, 'Paulo thought that the information came from someone in Department-Two. They spend a lot of their time watching NNV, and other groups like the GUDFS,' more blank looks he looked at Matt, who shrugged, The German Union of Democratic Federal Socialists, don't ask me to pronounce the German title, this party is a coalition of all the small Nazi sympathising groups, and a couple of the larger, mainstream political parties, although they publicly deny even the existence of GUDFS, let alone that it plays an active role within their parties. The GUDFS act secretly behind the scenes, controlling a number, but not all, of the Gladio units across Germany. It is a large sophisticated political organisation, they claim to occupy the ground between Capitalism and Communism, the so-called Progressive Way. They are neo-Nazi's, with a huge militia at their disposal, and have undoubtedly placed sympathisers in positions of power and influence. For now, they seem to be marking time, but Paulo has reports that suggest a more sinister and subtle form of political change is underway, and coercion is part of the process. The German government view them as a threat to the stability and safety of the state, which is why part of their internal anti-terrorist unit watches them day and night, but such suspicions remain just that, suspicions.'

Mac said, 'Does Father Kramer, think that there is a direct link between the GUDFS and NNV?'

'He believes that there is, and that it is above and beyond the simple command and control that GUDFS exercise over all the Gladio units under their authority, but he had nothing he could offer to substantiate his suspicions. If Paulo believes it, then as far as I'm concerned there is a link, we just need to find it. He's going to go through all the evidence to try and identify each of the individuals photographed.'

Tom said, 'Thanks for that, and for these files. It looks like both Father Kramer, and the BfV suspect a direct link, but in the absence of anything substantial I think we should concentrate on NNV. Meantime, I'll send Sergei some questions to ask, Powell.'

Mac stood up and walked over to the board and started to pin up some of the photographs, 'Anything else, John?'

'Yes… sorry, I forgot what I was going to tell you. I said that I thought we had been discovered, well… it may be something and nothing, as I was leaving Paulo's office yesterday, I was stopped by Cardinal Guido Bertonus, who said, "We're watching you", his exact words, then he walked off.'

Mac said, 'Bertonus, who's he?'

'On face of it, no one special, he is a very liberal Cardinal, a German Jesuit, there have been almost continual rumours about his sexuality, and his carnality, but none of the allegations about his alleged proclivities have ever been proved. It is said that he's a member of the Entity, the Church's intelligence service. Paulo, thinks he's a member of the Octogonus.'

Peter smirked and said, 'What's an Octogonus?'

'It's… you don't need to show so much pleasure at my discomfort.'

Tom said, 'No one is enjoying your distress, we know that you spent many years working in the Vatican, and we respect you for it, but if it is a mystery to us Catholics, it must be a Byzantine enigma to those outside the Church,' he looked disapprovingly at Matt and Peter.

Father John said, 'I have spent most of my working life in the Vatican, interpreting Canon Law, writing reports on law enforcement, attending national and international conferences on policing, as both an observer and a participant; during my time there I was privy to examples of wrongdoing in the Curia, and in the wider Church, even conducting investigations. I will admit that I came across several scoundrels, and a few who were just plain evil, but considerably less than I met in ten years of service with the police, whilst I encountered the odd example of corruption within the force, most of what I came across involved local and national politicians. The vast majority of priests and prelates I worked with were decent, hardworking, pious individuals, who only wanted to serve their fellow man, to do good.'

'So why does it get such bad press, why has it got such an appalling public image? It gives the impression of being a very secretive organisation, one with only its best interests at heart, which results in the perception that the whole place is up to no good,' said Simon.

'Good question. I will admit that the history of the Catholic Church leaves an impression of an organisation lurching from saintliness to sinfulness, and back again, and some of its past is shameful. It is a flawed institution, it may have been instituted by the Divine, but it is run by humans, so it is inevitable that from time-to-time it will fail. I'm not excusing the immorality, corruption and sacrilegiousness, that has marked some periods of its existence. I include the present ignominy that stains Holy Church, the great harm done to innocents, by those pederastic bastards, some of whom still infect our beautiful institution. The degraded sexual behaviour of some of our bishops and priests is quite literally criminal, it shames us all, truly the smoke of Satan has entered the sanctuary, their crimes and sins… what we are doing will, I hope, destroy some of that evil.'

The frustration and rage in his voice stunned them, no one spoke while he drank some coffee, and tried to regain his composure.

'I don't say this to excuse the opprobrium of the Church, but you must look at it in context; the times when wickedness marched through the Church coincided with periods of great evil in the wider world, over the last two-thousand years most countries have far worse records of depravity and corruption. Remember, the Catholic Church is not a museum for saints, but a hospital for sinners. Whilst it encourages saintliness it cannot turn the corrupt and sinful into saints, only the Grace of God can do that, all the Church can do is encourage people to want to understand; its role is to guide people along the path that leads to Truth, and that is only possible if those in the Church live for others, not for themselves. It is inevitable that a few rogues and scoundrels will circumvent the barriers placed to keep them out, but most of them are betrayed by their actions, living only for themselves, refusing to serve others. Although the Church has a responsibility to those living at this moment, its main purpose is to prepare souls for the next life, it will always be slow to react to the concerns of the present. I would like that to change, the Church needs to become more aware, more reactive to events, an approach that does not require compromise, or the dilution of doctrine, merely a greater acceptance of its own human frailty… once again you have encouraged me to be side-tracked.'

This was answered by tender laughter.

'Where was I? Yes… the Octogonus. I am not sure that it exists, or even that it ever did, but the legend is of an organisa-tion made up of eight people, four from the laity, and four who are ordained priests. Usually a cardinal, a bishop, a monsignor, and a priest, three of the lay members are drawn from the Papal Knights, and unusually for a secret society started in the thir-teenth century, the fourth member has always been a woman, latterly, a nun. It is said that it's the political arm of the Entity, that the Octogonus makes alliances and deals the rest of the Church does not want to know about, if there is a fog of clandes-tinity obscuring an issue, it will be claimed by some that the Octogonus is behind it, think of this organisation as the Church's mouchard. If it does exist, and I doubt it, then it sups with the Devil. From the beginning of the fourteenth century there were rumours concerning its existence, and yet to this day there has never been a shred of proof, if it exists, then it is clearly an organisation that is highly effective at remaining secret, dis-creet beyond the bounds of possibility. There is no evidence, outside of the minds of conspiracy theorists, that it exists, or ever existed, but the speculation persists.'

'Yet you have heard of it, and are able to describe it to us, does that not prove that there is an element of truth in the rumours?' said Peter.

Father John said, 'For centuries people claimed that the earth was flat, entire libraries were written to justify and defend that position, but that didn't make it so, the Octogonus exists only in rumour and innuendo, nothing more. But, Bertonus is connected and protected, so he belongs to something, or someone. He could be a problem. I told Paulo of my encounter, he will keep an eye on him, he did say that Bertonus had a powerful patron outside the Church. Despite his obvious shortcomings, he is influential, and he's politically adroit, which makes him dangerous.'

'Who's his patron?' said Tom.

'Paulo, didn't know.'

Tom said, 'Thanks. We will have to keep an eye on your cardinal and his anonymous protector, in case they start to interfere with our investigation, but for now our next step is to discover as much as we can about NNV, and Mr. and Mrs. Seidel, before paying them a visit. Jump in when you have something to add,'

Tom began to write bullet points on a sheet of paper pinned to the wall.

They discussed the issues back and forth for the next hour.

Until Tom said, 'Glad that's sorted. Mac, next week you and Pete will have to go to Germany, we need to be on the ground; go as bikers and keep a low profile, and do nothing until I contact you. Matt, I need you to go to Russia and speak to Sergei, I will give you a list of questions we need answered, and I think we are going to need his help, also I will copy a set of our files for him, it might encourage him to see the urgency in getting Powell to tell us what he knows about NNV and the rest.'

'I'm pretty certain he will not want to meet me in Russia.'

'I leave the arrangements to you, but we must find out where NNV are based, before Mac and Peter leave for Germany. After you meet with Sergei, come back here and brief me, then you and Simon can travel to Germany to act as backup. Simon, you and I can work out the logistics later, before that, while Matt is busy drinking vodka with his old mate, you are going to have to tie up a few loose ends here, there are two people who need looking at in the Home Counties. I don't think they are that important, but when this is over you may want to haul them in, you never know what it might turn up, no harm in a little digging, and it helps square the circle.'

'Yeah, no problem, we wouldn't want to miss something, write me out an action and I will get right on it.'

'Great, well that's about it. Next week, Father John, Robin, and I will relocate everything to Mount Pleasant Monastery. Tony will keep an eye on things here and make us aware should we have any unwelcome visitors. Tony, I think that for now, that should be the extent of your involvement.'

Tony nodded, but his frustration and not being allowed to play a more active role was self-evident.

Tom continued, 'I understand that the neighbouring farmer is going to maintain the agricultural side of things, so I guess we are good to go. Just one other thing, money and passports. I have managed to acquire passports for each of you in false names, I have written a new identity for each of you, learn it well. Money, you are going to need a lot of cash, fortunately among the pile of cash Mac liberated from Mason's safe, was about forty-five-thousand Euro's, I've split it into four, take it and spend it wisely. Do not take anything that could connect you to your present life, no credit cards, mobile phones, photos, watches, rings or other jewellery, if you are wearing or carrying anything, place it one of those bags on the table, and hand it to me before you leave, and make sure you write your name legibly on the label, I don't want any arguments later. One last thing, communication, please do not ask me how, but I obtained these satellite phones, they are encrypted, work off any system, including military networks, foreign and domestic, and do not rack up charges, since they effectively hack into, and piggy-back on, the closest system, and can do so without being detected, they have a very long battery-life, and charge up quickly; and I want them back, in one piece if possible. Another trick they have, is being able to listen into calls being made on mobiles within a half-mile radius, so if you can see a suspect making a call, you will be able to listen in, it will also send a voice recording of the call together with details such as the caller and the recipient's numbers back to the base station, which we are going to set up, allowing any such calls to be logged and stored. Neat, eh? One other thing, the red switch on the top. Slide the cover to the left and depress the red button. Not now Peter… if you hold it down for five seconds it will transmit a distress call to all the radios sharing its encrypted frequency, together with your location, that information will be stored in any radios in receipt of the distress call. You then have another thirty seconds, within which you must depress the button again, you will have to hold it down for another five seconds, failure to do so will trigger the self-destruct mechanism, it will catch fire, turning it into a useless lump of plastic and metal.'

Pete said, 'Interesting, where did they come from?'

'I told you, don't ask. Just don't whip one out in front of anyone from, Langley.'

'Firearms?' said Matt.

'Yes, got that covered, I've got you each a Glock 40 MOS, a good man-stopper, and for those more subtle occasions, a Sig Sauer P938 9mm ultra-compact, with a suppressor. Each pistol has six fully loaded magazines, as well as the one in the chamber; should be enough, even for you cowboys. If there are any other weapons or bits of kit you require, let me know after the briefing. Simon, you had better let Cartwright know that you are going off grid for a while but be careful what you tell him.'

'Don't worry, I've learned to be cautious in all my dealings with him. I'm very careful about what I say, he's getting annoyed at the paucity of reports, and what he considers our lack of progress.'

Mac and Peter laughed their approval, Peter slapped him on the back, 'You'll do.'

Tom said, 'We all clear on what we are doing? Good, we will make the move to the monastery, and by the end of the week we should be up and running. Any questions? Mac? Pete? Simon? Matt? Great.'

Mac said, 'I need to say something. The kids who were the centre of our original investigation are dead... please don't think I'm wandering through a graveyard, they're... I want them to be at peace. They need, and I need closure, even so, I am troubled... what we are about to do, what we may get into... you are all risking your lives... I know we can't walk away from this, especially given the effort we've made, and with what we have learned, there are other children out there... we cannot turn our backs... how can we? We can't take this to authorities, who could we trust? We'd be dead by the time we put the phone down. We're boxed in, it's now a case of kill or be killed... what the hell did we do wrong? And taking to the media is pointless, look at how many journalists and editors are part of this mess. This story will never make it into print, nor will it ever be broadcast, as for the internet, only a few will read it before it's taken down at the behest of... even if it was widely read it would be dismissed as yet another conspiracy theory promulgated by some spotty, all-hormones-and-angst teenager. If we could get our story out there, if it was read and believed by many, what then? Paradoxically, things would be worse, if what we now know became public knowledge, it would pull down the whole structure, good and bad together. Then what? Total anarchy, revolution, followed by extremism, we cannot allow that, so we are on our own, we cannot walk away from this, I'm afraid we now own it. Let me be absolutely clear, this it is not about revenge, if that was all I wanted, well I got it. Three men were responsible for Elizabeth's death, Mason, Powell, and Vale. Two of whom were instrumental in stopping our original enquiry, Mason and Powell. Mason's dead. Powell? He's going to spend the rest of his life in a living hell, and Vale? I could have killed him, I had the chance, I stood behind him and put a gun to his head and knowing that is enough for me. He understands his life was not one of service to the Crown, but that of a dupe, Mason's stooge. He faces a constrained financial future, remains fearful of discovery, and is lonely and isolated, I killed his only friends, his dogs. What more could I have done to any of them? I think we've gone too far to pull out, and in any case, if you're right, John, they know who we are, so what we are engaged in takes on a degree of self-preservation. There is nowhere for us to go, save down this road, and I have been getting a strong feeling that this road was already chosen for us. If we don't accept this trial, this quest, no one else will, and this evil will continue unabated, but it sits heavy with me. What have I talked you into? For all my arguments about this being morally justified, it is still by definition extrajudicial, and there is a fair chance we will end up killing, and my conscience weighs heavy on me, the use of force to oppose evil is a difficult area for Christians. Are we not taught to turn the other cheek? But complete passivity in the face of great evil would very soon result in the total eradica- tion of all who are good and decent, what would that leave, dis- aster, destruction, and death?'

Father John said, 'There is always prayer…'

Matt interrupted, 'That's all very well Padre, but prayer, and what's your other thing… forgiveness? Nothing fills graves faster, we must act, if we don't do something…'

Father John said, 'You are right, prayer must be accompanied by charity, and charity requires action, but the challenge facing us, the question that Mac is concerned with, and I suspect troubling most of you, is what form that action should take.'

Simon stood up and said, 'I'm not a deep thinker, I prefer simple, easy solutions. We all know that once we take this enquiry to the next level there is a very good chance that we will encounter violent opposition. Given what we have unearthed over the last days and weeks, I am sure that none of us believe that it would be right to just walk away, we cannot step back from this, to do so would be negligent, we would be failing in our duty, it would be cowardly.'

'Well said,' interjected Tom.

Simon, nodded, and continued, 'The problem as I see it, concerns the degree of opposition we are likely to encounter, and the likelihood that this will involve the use of deadly force; how should we, under those circumstances, respond? Knowing that we will in all possibility be violently opposed, can we use deadly force, and anticipating that this will happen, should we go ahead? I mean, we would be deliberately placing ourselves in circumstances where, in all probability, we will have to respond by killing... so do we proceed?'

Peter said, 'Fuck me, you're a dark horse. That's the whole issue in a nutshell.'

Father John said, 'Thank you, Peter. Simon, you have described the issue quite succinctly. I will say this, you have the right to defend yourself, you have a duty to defend others, to protect the innocent. So, you train and prepare and master the art of war, but the emphasis is one of intent. You do all you can to avoid conflict, to avoid the use of violence, and you hope your preparedness acts as a deterrent, that those who seek to oppose you, upon seeing a well-armed, well-prepared force, will decide that discretion is the better part of valour. Christianity is a religion that advocates peace, we pray for peace, but accept that we should be prepared for war, ours is not a religion of non-resistance, for that would allow evil to prevail. It is sometimes necessary to use violence to prevent greater violence from conquering. In some circumstances, if we fail to oppose evil with violence, we permit evil to flourish, we acquiesce in the creation of an abomination.'

Simon said, 'What about pacifists, Christians who refuse to use violence under any circumstances?'

'Not all pacifists are Christian, I would think that there are as many, if not more, non-Christians who ascribe to that erroneous theory. As far as I can see, there are several problems with the arguments they put forward. By stating that they reject the use of violence under all circumstances, even to accepting the necessity of surrendering to tyranny, they allow evil to thrive. Further, if their nation was under threat of attack, or even invasion, they would be happy to allow both to occur unopposed, to surrender to whatever evil is forced upon them. More serious than that, they would happily leave the defence of their country, and therefore themselves, to others, some of whom will undoubtedly die doing their duty, which seems to me the worst kind of hypocritical righteousness, if not downright cowardice... I should not have said that I don't know that it is cowardice that motivates them, I cannot know what is in their heart.'

'True,' said Mac, 'but not being able to discern their intent is part of the problem for most of us. Many who espoused their non-violence as a matter of principle, still joined the military, where they were employed as stretcher bearers and medics, making them real heroes, but too many just stayed home hiding behind a convenient conscience, to me, they are cowards.'

Father John nodded and continued, 'In the case of Christian

pacifists it all stems from a false reading of the Bible. The fifth commandment is wrongly translated as, thou shalt not kill, it should read, thou shalt not murder. They also ignore those passages where Jesus instructs his disciples to buy a sword, even if they have to sell their cloak to do so, Jesus told Peter to sheath his sword, note he did not tell him to get rid of it. I could go on…'

'Yeah, we know,' laughed Peter.

Mac glared at Peter.

Father John frowned, and continued, 'We must hate evil, but we are required to love the evil-doer. You may kill out of self-defence, or to protect the innocent, what is important is your intent when doing so, you cannot, and must, not kill out of hatred for your attacker, only out of the desire to protect yourself and others from evil. If you are motivated by hatred, you are in the wrong. It all comes down to intent. Whatever action you take must be tempered by proportionality. You must not use a disproportionate force against an aggressor, the violence you employ must be proportional to the harm that is being threatened. You must not use more force than is necessary to achieve the elimination of the threat of harm. If fighting and killing prove necessary, and cannot be avoided, then it is to be undertaken only in response to aggression, and not for revenge, nor can you kill someone who is no longer a threat. You must limit the violence, such that when you have won the killing stops, to avoid the risk of what is defensive becoming offensive, of good becoming evil. This is not merely semantic; it is about your souls. Your intention always must be to use force only to protect the lives of the innocent and that of yourself, and then only to use as much force as is necessary. These are the arguments applied to justify the use of deadly force, and it is by adhering strictly to such narrow margins that you can be absolved, I fear for all of you, and I must admit I do not feel comfortable in the use of deadly force to bring about good.'

Mac nodded, and said, 'Have I the right to ask all of you to join me? If we're caught, we will be branded as terrorists, tried in secret, and locked away until we are dead, no one will ever know. So why continue? To right a great wrong, to combat evil, assuming we are successful, it will only stop for a short time, before the diabolical finds a way to begin again, so is it worth it? That's what really troubles me, you are risking your lives, and for what? I asked the same question before I left the police. Is what I am doing worth it? Great evil is being perpetrated by so-called pillars of society against the innocent, an entire political system is being corrupted and perverted, placing terrible power into the hands of a few faceless individuals who operate the system of government, and all under the gaze of an indifferent and passive public, since they don't care, why should we?'

Tom said, 'We have all thought the same, but the truth is this task has been given us, it's what we do, it's what we're good at, and right now there is no one else to do it. Look at the skills, knowledge, and experience, in this room. If we can't get the job done, then no one can. We're doing this because we can, because we want to, because it makes our lives worth something, because it needs to be done, because it is the right and only thing to do. We have been called, all that is left is for each of us to accept or decline this mission. We are not alone in this, we have Sergei, and the not inconsiderable services of his team, and we have some in the Vatican. They have our backs, so don't sweat it, we are all big boys, we know the risks, we understand how it could all end. Someone has to make a stand, and today that's us. Why us? Simple, because we're here.'

Matt stood up, 'Enough talking. Let's get it done.' Peter, Tony, Simon, and Tom looked at Mac, and nodded their heads in agreement.

Tom looked across the room, 'Father John?'

Father John had knelt down, crossed himself, and began to pray out loud, slightly embarrassed, they all knelt, and silently followed his prayers for the protection of the innocent, for them and their families, for success in the investigation, and for God's blessing on all of them. He then said the Lord's Prayer out loud, which, to his amazement, they all joined in.

Father John stood up, he handed each of them a laminated card, saying, 'Keep this with you at all times, read it when things get tough.

'May God bless you and keep you, may he make his light to shine upon you, and be gracious to you. May the Lord show you his face and bring you peace.'

They all said, 'Amen.' Tom, Robin, and Mac crossed themselves.

Peter, read the words on the card out loud: 'Hodie mihi, cras tibi. Today it's me; tomorrow, you.'

He nodded his approval and placed the card in his wallet.

Father John, explained, 'If we don't help each other today, then tomorrow we fight alone. I hoped that it would inspire you and help to show you the way.'

'It will, Father. Thank you.'

Chapter Twenty-Eight

Four days later Matt returned from his meeting in Finland with Sergei. He had answers to some of their questions, including an approximate location of the NNV base; now they could begin. They trooped out of the stable block, milled around the courtyard saying their goodbyes. Matt, realising that Mac and Father John were still inside, said to Peter, 'The padre, is he talking Mac out of this? He's a... I mean...'

'No, he isn't. Father John is uncomfortable with this, with what we may have to do, it sits heavy, he's worried about our souls, even your pagan one, but he won't stop it.'

'You sure? I not that comfortable having a God-botherer around.'

Peter laughing said, 'Why? You afraid it's catching; you think Christianity is an infectious disease?' Mac is Catholic, his faith has always mattered to him.'

Matt said, 'Yeah, I know, I only found that out a few weeks ago. And Sergei's one, not a Catholic, but the other lot, Russian, you know?'

'Orthodox,' said Peter.

'That's it.'

Peter looked pained, and said, 'Bloody hell, Sergei as well?'

'Yeah. He told me in Finland, said he was happy we had a

priest with us...' Matt stopped speaking, he'd picked up on Peter's sarcasm.

Peter said, 'Mac's been a Catholic since he was born, you've known him all these years, and it never made a difference, why should it now?'

'I know, but... well at least you're not one.'

'Not quite, but I'm nearly there.'

'Christ.'

'Exactly; it's a start, as Father John says.'

Laughing, they both made their way across the yard toward the vehicles.

Father John said, 'Mac, you seem troubled?'

'I am, John.'

Father John, paused, uncertain of how to proceed, then said, 'I have tried to find a way for you to understand how you must act in the face of the evil you will confront. Christians cannot confine their faith and beliefs to just their private lives, setting them aside when dealing with the world, to do so would place us at the mercy of the faithless, we must be in the world, but not of it. Trust in the Lord, allow him to lead you, He may take you to places you would rather not go, but trust in His Love, permit His Grace to work in you. I know it's not easy, the Cross is an overturning of values, and it can seem to those, whose hearts are not open to love, utterly repellent. You know that we must do good and avoid evil, but we are allowed, in circumstances of extreme danger to protect ourselves and others, in fact we have a duty to do so, but any force we use can only be justified if it is an act to prevent a greater evil...'

'Sorry to interrupt you, John. But I'm worried, Simon articulated the problem earlier, we are knowingly walking into danger, deliberately placing ourselves in harm's way, going where we know there will be violent confrontation; confrontation we may have to initiate, caused by our being there, we will undoubtedly find ourselves in circumstances where we have to fire first...'

'I do understand where you are coming from, I see the problem. Catholic teaching allows the opposition by force, of those who seek through criminal means to seize control of society. You may confront such evil, but not with revenge in your heart. Only with the intention of saving and protecting the innocent, and then only using such force as is necessary to achieve the right outcome. Let me read this to you, it's from Pope John Paul's encyclical letter, Evangelium Vitae, here he discusses the tension between respect for human life, and obedience to the 5th commandment, he summarises the issue perfectly...'

Father John paused, smiled and set aside his notebook, 'As you would expect, St Thomas Aquinas also had much to say on this subject, and there are many Papal encyclicals, and the Catechism of the Church, that I could quote to you, but I am not sure at this stage a lengthy diatribe on the Just War Theory will help.'

He paused, then said, 'A young electrician on a film set was sent on an errand, as he was about to leave the studio, he spotted one of the stars of the film, the comedian and actor, W.C. Fields, flicking through a copy of the Bible. The young man approached and said, "Mr. Fields, I didn't know that you believed." W.C. Fields looked up and said, "I don't, I'm just looking for loopholes".

Mac, smiled.

Father John continued, 'I guess that's what you are looking for, but there are none. Clearly, you cannot walk away from evil and permit the innocent to suffer, but you cannot heal evil with evil, two wrongs can never make a right, better to drown evil in an abundance of good...'

'So, what do I do? If I do nothing, it's tantamount to giving my blessing. Yet if I act on what we now know I will inevitably run into violent men, and it is more than likely I will have to kill them.'

Father John pondered for a minute, then said, 'Mac, none of this is easy. Yes, you may have to confront armed and dangerous individuals, you can challenge them, and if necessary, use force against them, even lethal force, but only in defence of the innocent, of others, and of course yourself, and then only as an act of defence, not revenge, it comes down to intent on your part. Think carefully about what constitutes self-defence, you can under some circumstances anticipate their response and act accordingly, but try at all costs to avoid instances of confrontation, in other words don't go looking for it... I know, in one sense that is what you are about to do, but is saving innocents an act of aggression, especially if their lives are in danger?' Are you your brother's keeper? Yes. If you see someone suffering, and do nothing to save them, then you are guilty of their suffering, doing nothing makes you guilty. You must act, even if ultimately, the action you take proves inadequate, you are duty bound to try to save them.'

Mac said, 'But, we are taught not to do evil, even to people who deserve it.'

Father John nodded in agreement, then said, 'It is never right to do evil in the hope that good may come of it, good intentions, and even good consequences are not sufficient, for that way of thinking leads to ethical relativism, which will result in the removal of any moral reference point, making the acknowledgement of truth impossible, rendering all your actions culpable.'

Mac sighed, and said, 'Then we have no choice but to act, and then with restraint, that's your answer?'

'Mac, all I am sure of is that we are all our brother's keeper, and what we do matters, and it matters for all time, so we must act. But under no circumstances may your actions be motivated by revenge, whatever the provocation.'

'John, I will do whatever it takes to confront this evil, to solve our original investigation, and destroy this corruption, and then I will come and discuss it with you, and if it proves necessary, you can tell me how far I am from salvation. Perhaps by then you will have figured out how we can change the world.'

Father John said, 'I cannot change the world, it is just too large an undertaking, I believe that I must start with those things God places before me. I can change myself, and in doing so, by example, change the behaviour of friends and family. If I can manage that, then together we can influence the community we live in, and since the world is made up of countless communities, if our community influences others...'

'So, you can change the world?' laughed, Mac.

'I'm not really making much sense... we can't change the world, only ourselves, but small steps taken with humility, powered by our weakness... if enough of us change, and commit to it, then since the world is made up of individuals, then yes, I guess the world will change, but only if it is wrought by gentle example. I am reminded of a line from Each and All, a poem by Emerson: "Nor knowest thou what argument, thy life to thy neighbour's creed hath lent..."

Father John paused, looked at Mac, then continued, 'The powerful, who demand that humanity genuflect and acknowledge their dominance, have set their heretical desires loose, they are chasing down something they will never catch, faith. It is beyond their capacity to understand, and impossible for them to acquire, so they react by proscribing it, for they know that individuals forced to live without faith lose their dignity and humanity, becoming nothing more than exploitable drudges who can be made to serve the plutocracy. The elite, who by renouncing faith, repudiate God in order to convince themselves that conscience is nought but a primitive impediment to their sordid inclinations... things must change, these people must be opposed, but, if that change is to last, it can never be imposed. If we use strength and might to accomplish our aim, we will fail. Force is always met by an equal resistance. Strength is weakness, weakness is strength, and in that paradox, we find the answer.'

Mac said, 'I'm not sure I can agree with you. I know where you are coming from and understand the teaching you are drawing upon... but my experience is telling me that the evil hostility awaiting us will have to be withstood by an equal measure of force.'

'Mac, you must see that the wealth of the meek and humble is their faith, their unwavering belief in God. It is wealth beyond the grasp of nihilists, who out of a malicious resentment seek to outlaw it, and so reduce everything to the void that occupies their hearts, which is why they deny dignity and justice to others. We have a duty to stand up to them, to deny them their ambition. You must remain steadfast in faith, do not envy them, pity them, pray for them, and forgive them. If you are successful, what you do will remain hidden, unknown to the world, yet it will change many lives, accept that what you undertake in life may remain unfinished, may come to nothing, will gain you no worldly accolades, but do it anyway, do it with love, and in hope. I am happier today than I was. I have been praying for guidance, praying for all of you, and last night, in the middle of prayer it came to me, and with it, great peace. I slept well, better than I have in quite a while.'

Father John fell silent, he seemed to be searching for the right words. After a long pause, Mac laughed, and said, 'Okay... what is it?'

'Simple really, evil consumes evil, trust your instincts, trust yourself, trust in the Lord, remain faithful, and at all times do what your conscience tells you. I know all will be well. Our opponents' weakness is in their strength. Our strength is in our weakness. They will be undone by pride; we will win through humility.'

Mac smiled and said, 'I'm not sure that applies to us... there's not much humility, or weakness evident in the team we've put together... but I can assure you that we will do our best to oppose and defeat this evil'

Mac knelt in front of Father John, who heard his confession.

Twenty minutes later Mac joined the team in the yard, they laughed, embraced, and wished each other luck. 'See you in Germany,' said Matt. Looking at Simon, he said, 'Come on, we're wasting daylight.' He nodded to Tony, and he and Simon climbed into a Citroen van to keep their appointment with the ferry.

Tom ran out of the stable block shouting, 'Stop them.'

Mac banged on the side of the van as it began to move off, Matt braked, stuck his head out of the driver's window, and said, 'What?'

They all trooped back into the stable block.

Tom said, 'Sorry about this, I thought you should all know, I've just received a message from an old friend who used to be in the CIA, he said that he had heard we are investigating Gladio units...'

Peter interrupted, 'If the CIA are involved, then this... we should not be found playing on their pitch...'

Tom said, 'I agree, I was ready to pull the plug on this investigation, but I have received another message... they want to meet.'

Mac said, 'How in the hell do the CIA know about our investigation?' He looked around the room, 'Who has been discussing our business outside of this group?'

Silence.

'Simon, what exactly have you been feeding Cartwright?'

'Nothing, only what you and Tom have seen and approved.'

'So how the fuck have we ended up on their radar?'

Again silence.

Simon interrupted, 'It could have been me... I have been sending those enquires you didn't want Cartwright to know about through a trusted colleague, a friend. I guess they could have intercepted our calls.'

Mac said, 'Then we need to meet your friend, and I mean right away. Who is he?'

'His name is Francis Overton, everyone calls him Frank, he's a detective sergeant. I've known him for seven years, I was instrumental in his recent promotion, I trust him completely.'

Peter said, 'Well I don't... set up a meet.'

Two days later, at about one in the afternoon, Mac, Peter, and Matt entered the saloon bar of the Windmill Pub on Clapham Common, in South London, Peter and Mac sat at a table to the left, just inside the door, while Matt ordered three Young's Ramrod and Specials.

Fifteen minutes later a man entered, he was five-feet-ten-inches tall, with short black hair, light-black complexion, aged about thirty-eight, the European features of his face and pale-blue eyes giving away his mixed-race parentage, he fitted the description Simon had given of Frank. He went up to the bar and ordered two pints of Young's London Special, his accent South London meets New York, not enough to be described as mid-Atlantic, but enough to disguise his origin, he took the two pints of beer and walked to the rear of the bar, setting them down on a small table. He was wearing black trainers, black chinos, a black t-shirt, and a tan coloured sports jacket, which he removed, folded, and placed on a bench, and sat down next to it, his back was to the door, but he was facing a large mirror on the rear wall.

Five minutes later, Simon arrived, he squinted as he looked around the bar, adjusting his eyes to the gloom after the bright daylight outside. Frank raised his right arm, Simon said, 'Have you got them in?'

'Of course, I got you a pint of London.'

Simon sat down opposite him, and drank deep from his pint glass, and said, 'Sorry.'

Frank said, 'What?'

Peter, Matt, and Mac, taking their beers with them walked over to Simon and Frank, and sat down.

Mac said, 'Do you know who we are?'

Frank said, 'Yes.'

Peter said, 'Then you know why we are here?'

'Yes, my boss at Langley has requested a meet, and you want to know how he knew about you and your investigation, you want to know how the information leaked.'

Matt said, 'Boss in the CIA. Well, I guess that answers everything.' He glared at Simon.

Frank said, 'Don't blame him, he had no idea, no one does, so my telling you is to show our good faith. Let's finish these beers and take a walk.'

Mac said, 'Drink up.'

Having emptied their glasses Mac got to his feet and said, 'Okay pal, this way.'

The others stood up, and with Peter leading the way, they walked down into the cellar.

Mac said, 'We know the licensee, and this is much better,

cooler, private, and nobody around pointing direction mikes at us, and if you're wired, well it won't work down here.'

Frank said, 'I'm not wired, knowing you I'd have to be stupid, so what now?'

Mac said, 'You have partially answered our question concerning how the good people at Langley know all about us, but I would like to hear the whole story, how does a South London detective sergeant come to be working for the CIA?'

Peter said, 'Simon feels betrayed… don't you,' he glared at Simon and continued, 'if you really do count him as a friend, he deserves to be enlightened, and we also have a yearning to know the truth.'

'No problem, I have been cleared to tell you everything. I was born here, my mum is English, my dad is from New York, at the time my parents met, Dad was an aeronautical engineer with the US air force, based at Lakenheath, and Mum was a nurse at Brandon hospital. After his service in the military was over, Dad got a job with Boeing at Plant 42, in Antelope Valley, not far from LA. Mum got a post as a theatre sister. They are both retired now, and live near Dad's family, in upstate New York. I was ten when we moved to the States, after I finished college, I joined the Rangers, and became an army sniper. I was nine months into my second tour in Afghanistan when I was approached by a CIA operative. I had another two years of service ahead of me and did not fancy spending them chewing sand in Iraq or Afghanistan, so when they offered an alternative, I took it. I spent the next two years travelling the world, visiting interesting places, and killing people. Time was up, but rather than retiring it was suggested that I continue in their service…'

Matt interrupted, 'You're a sleeper?'

'No, I'm still active, during the first tour I travelled the world on my British passport, I have dual-nationality, and they always flew me on British Airways, which is how I met my wife, she was an air-steward. The bosses at Langley suggested that we settle in England, my wife is from Sussex, we live in Dorking, not far from her parents. She runs an agency for relief aircrew and stewards, the CIA pay my wages through her company.'

Matt said, 'You're not a spook, so if you are still active what do they use you for?'

Frank said, 'Five months ago, the Iranian military attaché…'

'That was you,' Matt said, clearly impressed, 'nice kill, mate. Made it look like a street robbery gone wrong, gutted him, spectacularly messy, sent out a clear message.'

'High praise coming from you, Matt.'

Mac said, 'So you really do know who we are, why does your boss want to meet us?'

'That I don't know… genuinely… I have no idea. But you can trust him, he is one of the good guys.'

Mac said, "Alright, I'll agree to a meet. He comes to the farm, alone, and I mean alone. Got it?'

'Not a problem, when?'

'Tomorrow afternoon, three o'clock.'

'That's a little soon, he's still in the US.'

Peter said, 'Then he better catch a fucking plane this evening.'

Mac said, 'No need, he's already here, quite possibly outside.'

Frank smiled but said nothing.

Mac said, 'Tomorrow then, but Simon stays with you until it is over,' he dismissed both their protestations, 'Simon, you will be Frank's shadow until tomorrow evening. I don't want anyone tempted to put his particular skills to use,' Mac drew back his coat to reveal a holstered pistol. 'Agree to this or…'

'Okay, it's not a problem, I guess we have some catching up to do.'

Peter said, 'Anything happens to Simon, I'll kill your entire family, and make you watch while I do it.'

'A little dramatic, but I got it. Nothing will happen to Simon, he really is a friend, and my lot only want to talk.'

Mac said, 'Tomorrow then.'

They all left the cellar and returned to the bar, Frank made to leave, Peter grabbed his arm, 'Not so fast, it's your round.'

Frank laughed, and said, 'Coppers and beer.' Mac said, 'We'll trust you to carry on getting info for Simon, but we don't trust your paymasters. Stay in touch, you hear anything you think we need to know, then get it to us a minute before you hear it.'

Frank said, 'Will do.' Clearly upset he looked at Peter and said, 'You didn't have to threaten me, I know what you're capable of doing. Simon is my friend, and I place friendship beyond all else.'

Simon said, 'Glad to hear it.'

Mac took Simon to one side, and said, 'Bring Frank up to speed on our investigation, all of it, but no mention of Sergei and his pals. Giving him an idea of what it is we are dealing with, may make his assistance more forthcoming.'

An hour passed while they drank and swapped war stories, and while Simon and Frank remained to carry on drinking, Mac, Peter, and Matt took their leave, and left to catch a train north.

The following afternoon, at exactly three o'clock, a red Jaguar saloon parked by the barn, a fifty-year-old white male, around five-foot-nine inches tall, slim, with crew-cut grey hair, wearing a suit in a check-pattern, popular among a certain type of American civil servant, left the vehicle and walked over to Mac.

'Mr Mackenzie, I presume?'

'At your service.'

'Andrew Donovan,' he offered Mac his hand.

Saying nothing, Mac led the way to the house, they sat in the kitchen.

Father John said, 'Tea, or coffee?'

Andrew said, 'Tea please… don't look so surprised. I was posted to London for twelve years… in one capacity or another.'

Mac said, 'Well Andrew… is that your real name?'

'It is today.'

Mac smiled, 'Okay, Andrew. I guess that's as close to honest as this is going to get, so why your interest in our activities, and why this sit-down?'

Andrew said, 'I note that Father John is present, where is the rest of your team?'

'Out hunting, but they can hear every word we are saying.'

Andrew said, 'I came alone, as you requested, and I am unarmed.' He stood up, removed his jacket, turn around slowly, and pulled up each of his trouser legs, to show he had no weapons.

Mac stared at him, and Andrew said, 'It's in the glove compartment of my car, and yes, I am usually armed, and to save you a question, my team are enjoying the delights of Cockermouth, but they can also hear what we are saying.'

'Cockermouth, that's over forty minutes from here, very trusting of you?'

Andrew said, 'Knowing what I do about each of you. I am as safe here as I would be in my embassy. I am not your enemy, I give you my word, I am here to assist you.'

Mac said, 'Your word? My father served with distinction in the war, he used to say, "You can trust a Russian. If he gives you his word, it is for life, but a Yank, his word lasts until he is out of sight, and not even that far if he gets a better offer." Your word?'

Andrew winced as Mac was speaking, then forcibly said, 'We really are on your side, you can assist us, and we can help you. I am not going to ask for the details of your investigation, we know enough to surmise that we have a mutual interest in… have you heard the word Gladio before?'

Mac said, 'Yes.'

'It has recently come to our attention that these… hypothetical units… you understand me?' Mac nodded. 'It seems that some are not in our employ, even though we… would that be a correct assessment?'

Mac replied, 'It would. We have an interest in thirteen of these units, and one in particular, it's based in Germany, I would be obliged if you didn't run interference.'

'We have no intention of doing so, do you know who has hijacked them, why they have gone rogue, is the Russians?'

Mac said, 'Not the Russians, they have nothing to do with this, it is far worse than you can imagine, I'm guessing you do not know what they are up to, at least I hope you don't.'

Mac then told Andrew everything, leaving out the names and the roles played by Mason, Vale, and Powell, he made no mention of any Russian assistance.

Andrew, visibly shaken by what Mac told him, said, 'If you agree to share what you discover, channel it through Frank, we will continue to provide you with information.'

Mac said, 'We run the investigation our way, without any interference?'

'Yes, but we want to know everything you are doing…'

'No, only after, trust has to be earned, and you came to us.'

'Okay, agreed. I admit, I am wholly appalled at what you have told me. We had no idea, if you get even a suspicion of who is behind this I want to know, I will deal with them.'

Mac said, 'If we need to, can we utilise Frank's special skills?'

'That would depend, but I can foresee circumstances where it might be appropriate. About Frank, he is a very useful and loyal asset, we would be seriously unhappy if his association with us was exposed… very unhappy, do you get my drift.'

Mac said, 'I do, and you need have no concerns in that direction, you exposed him as an act of good faith, we will not break your trust, his secret, your secret, is safe.'

Andrew said, 'I am glad to hear that, but expected nothing less from you, we really do know all about you. The successful operation you completed in Georgia, you have both my respect, and my gratitude.'

Mac looked shocked, Andrew said, 'I told you; we know your history. I would ask that you allow us to assist in identifying those units who have left the reservation. I suspect that this could end in a conflagration of epic proportions, it's our wildfire to douse.'

Mac nodded his agreement, and said, 'Then we are done, you agree no interference, and to provide us with any necessary intel, and to cover our backs. Obviously, we will not expect any assistance if it compromises your organisation, and we all understand deniability.'

'Good, then we are in agreement.'

Mac said, 'However, if we find that in anyway your agency is involved in this matter, or has been complicit, then all bets are off.'

Andrew said, 'I would expect the name of the individual involved, so that I could deal with them, regardless of their position, or sphere of influence. I mean it… truthfully, I am unable to take in all of this… it's beyond belief. I cut the communication link just before you told me about the nature of your investigation, and what these units are doing. I want that name, even if it is someone from the Agency.'

He paused, looked at both Father John and Mac, then said, 'I'm not a Catholic, but I am a committed Evangelical Christian, both my wife and I are active members of our church, my faith matters to me, more than anything. Trust me when I say I need to know, and I will act upon it.'

Father John said, 'Bless you, we will inform you if we find that someone from the CIA has been or is involved in this sordid affair. I am certain that your agency is not involved, this is something else entirely, your malign influence is no part of this…'

'Our malign… do you know the extent of Vatican involvement with the Gladio network?'

'Sadly, I do.'

Mac said, 'Play nice children… Andrew, your troops will be on their way, if you wish to avoid a firefight, and your own demise, I suggest you re-establish communication, and settle their nerves.'

'Yes, of course.' Andrew switched his device back on, and quickly made contact, 'They were on the way, but have stood down.'

They drank tea, ate some of Father John's carrot cake, and discussed various innocuous matters. After fifteen minutes Andrew said, 'I think that will be all, I better be getting back.'

They shook hands, and Mac and Father John watched as he returned to his car and drove off. Mac spoke, 'He's left, but all of you stay in situ for an hour or so. I will tool-up and go on a roving patrol around the property.'

Peter laughing, said, 'Well he's a Yank, and he's out of sight.'

Mac spoke, 'True, so keep your eyes and ears open.'

Mac returned to the kitchen to collect his Wilson Combat Recon Tactical WC-10 .338 rifle.

Father John said, 'Did your father really say that about the Americans?'

Mac said, 'He did. During the war he fought alongside Russian special troops as liaison and to assist with their task of disrupting German supply lines and communications, then for two years after the war, he worked with the American military in Germany. I understand what he meant, but my experience of Yanks is somewhat different from his, I have served alongside many, and found them to be true warriors, honourable and good people. As you know, my mother is Irish, virtually all her family lives in the States. I have never encountered anything akin to that which my father experienced in the period after the war. Both my family in America, and the other Americans I've met, have all been men of their word. The Americans my father met after the war was over, were all on the make, doing their best to loot the country, acting like conquerors. The good ones had either been killed, or returned home, none of those he met had seen combat, most were sons of senators or captains of industry, who had a "good war" driving desks in Washington, the only wounds they received were paper cuts. Truth is, I don't imagine there is any difference between your average American, average Brit, or an average Russian, we are all just people, with the same hopes, dreams, and fears, it's politics that gets in the way of our common humanity. But, saying what I said to him served a purpose, it wrong footed him, he became defensive, let the mask slip, and showed his real character. He's a true patriot, someone we can trust.'

'Yes, he is, but insulting his country…'

'What about… "your malign influence is no part of this". That hurt more, did you see his face?'

'Go play soldier, I'll get on with preparing our evening meal.

Chapter Twenty-Nine

Tom said, 'Have we heard from Mac?'

'Not yet,' said Robin, 'But Simon has been in touch. He and Matt are in one of Sergei's safe houses, over the border in the Czech Republic, not too far from where Mac and Peter are located, and fairly close to the location of the Seidel's base. That's if Sergei's information and your calculations are correct.'

'I'm as certain as I can be, but I'm worried that I wasn't able to give them an exact location. I hope that Matt, Simon, and Sergei are within striking distance of Mac and Pete. Too many things can go wrong.'

Robin, smiled and shook his head, 'Simon, said that Sergei has a helicopter on standby, if they need to get to Mac and Pete, they can be with them within half an hour.'

'Good, keep monitoring the radio. I'll not relax until I know this is over.'

Two hours later Peter made contact, Robin and Tom, listened to his report. 'We rode from Calais to Strasbourg, then to Stuttgart, and from there to Augsburg, across to Regensburg, and down to Lusen. Three days of hard riding, my arse will take a month to recover. Sergei had his people rent a cabin for us, just outside Lusen, it's comfortable, and it's not much of a ride from Rachel, which is an interesting place. We spent the day there, walking and doing touristy things, in case there were any curious people watching. Tomorrow we will take the adventure trail through the Watzlik-Hain area; pretty tough walking, if Tom is right, it should bring us close to the location of the house. Mac wants to know, everything alright your end?'

'Yes, fine,' said Robin, 'have you made contact with Simon and Matt?'

'We have, and we have arranged a rendezvous, the whole team will be joining us… got to go, diners ready. Out.'

'Diners ready?' Tom and Robin, turned to see Father John entering the room, holding a couple of large maps, 'Doesn't he think of anything but his stomach?'

Robin said, 'Are those the maps of the area around the adventure trail, Father?'

'Yes, they cover the area of forest twenty miles either side of the trail. They're the best I could find.'

Tom said, 'John, I'm sure they'll do. Right, let's see where they are?'

Father John, opened them out, laying them flat on the table in the middle of the room, all three examined them, plotting the locations of the two teams, the routes they would be taking, and Tom's best guess for the location of the Seidel's new base.

'That's a lot of walking,' said Robin. 'Sergei's party might have a three-day hike ahead of them.'

'Two and a bit, they're all fit, but Mac and Peter will not get to the area where I calculate the Seidel's base is located, much before evening the day after tomorrow,' said Tom.

Father John said, 'Well, there is nothing much for us to do here but wait. We had better take turns in monitoring the radio, I'm happy to do the night shift.'

Tom said, 'The plan was, that we would leave them too it, maintain radio silence, until it is over, but now I'm not sure that was such a good idea…'

Robin said, 'Tom, you can't superintend everything. They're all big boys and can look after themselves.'

'I know, but…'

Father John said, 'Go, get some sleep, you're no good to anyone if you're too tired. Both of you leave, I've got this. Robin, relieve me around six in the morning… no, make that a quarter to six, I want to attend Prime. Now go.' Father John ushered them out.

Chapter Thirty

Mac set a good pace, by ten on the morning of the second day with the sun dominating a cloudless sky and the thin air of the mountains allowing no respite, it was a relief when the trail suddenly dipped into the trees and there was a brief reprieve from the swelter.

'Hold up,' said Peter, 'I've got to catch my breath… the air, and this heat…'

'No problem, it's time for a brew,' said Mac, who was just as uncomfortable, but determined not to show it, although the relief in his voice betrayed him, causing Peter to laugh.

They moved off the path and into the wood. Finding a shady hollow, they set up a Kelly kettle and boiled some water for a pot of tea.

Peter said, 'How much further?'

'About nine miles, but it will get easier, in another mile we reach a plateau, we should arrive in the area that Tom suggested around three. But it is only a rough location for the house, and there's a lot of big trees, this is one large forest. Where's the satellite when you need it?'

'We could ask our new mates in the CIA?'

'No! Do you want to start a war? Imagine if they turn up, and so do Sergei and his band of merry men?'

'Then just get us to where we need to be. I trust Tom's judgement. For our part, we'll need to find somewhere off the track to bivouac, preferably at the back of some high ground overlooking the area of forest Tom suggested. Anything suitable on the map?'

'A couple of likely spots.'

'Mac, I'm confident if we wait for night, the house will stand out... old-school.'

'I hope you're right, but I'm not that confident, if they are professionals, then they will be using blackouts and following a dark-regime.'

'Maybe, but I still think we will find it easier at night. If not, we still have all tomorrow to go exploring, the others will not be joining us until the day after.'

Mac laughed, 'Sounds like a plan... drink up, we've still got some miles ahead of us yet.'

They made it, as Mac predicted, around three in the afternoon, it took another hour to find a suitable piece of high ground that faced the right direction from which to watch the forest below.

Peter said, 'Never thought I would be doing this again, night-obs, and cold rations.'

'No, nor me. Just so long as it's not a night of whinging.'

'Whinging?'

'Aye, whinging.'

'I never whinge.'

'The hell you don't.'

Peter, sulked for the next hour, scanning the forest below. He didn't want to admit it, but Mac was right, you could park a town in that forest, and never see it. He orientated the map, selecting, then taking bearings of features to assist in navigation come morning.

As dusk fell his labours were interrupted by Mac, 'Sorted?'

'I was reading,' he waved a National Park booklet he had picked up at the tourist information centre in Lusen, 'there are bears, lynx, wolves, and aggressive wild boar in these forests.'

'Then you better not fall asleep on watch.'

'Fall asleep?'

'Do I have to remind you?'

'One time, one fucking time…'

'Whinging.'

'Fuck off.'

Both laughed, each exhilarated that the adventure was about to begin. Mac dug out their rations for the night.

At exactly eleven in the evening a light flashed through the trees, 'I've got a bearing,' said Peter, 'what do you think, a car? A torch?'

'Not a torch, too bright, and the wrong shape; and not a car, it wasn't bright enough, again the wrong shape, and it wasn't moving.'

'What then?'

'A door opening?' Mac voice betrayed his doubts.

Peter said, 'Could be.'

There was another brief flash of light from the same location. 'Pulsar! It's a door opening and closing,' laughing, Peter continued, 'bloody Tom, he's on the money again.'

'I hope so, it'll be light around five, then we'll go down and take a look.'

There were no other lights in the forest during the night, Mac took first watch, Peter relieved him around three, and spent a tormented couple of hours reacting to the sounds of the forest, he woke Mac at five.

'Didn't get eaten by a wolf then?'

'Bollocks.'

They packed up, and re-joined the trail, taking it to the valley floor, then turned left onto a deer path, following the compass bearing they made their way through the trees, after a mile this path crossed a logging road, there they stopped. Peter crossed to the other side of the road, they faced each other, then turned in opposite directions, and each walked fifty metres down the road, now a hundred metres apart, they crossed to the other side of the road and walked back towards each other, slowly examining the dusty surface.

'Well?'

'Vehicle traffic, mostly four-wheel drive, no pedestrian traffic, this could be it,' said Peter, 'we could follow the road in the direction of the light we saw.'

'Agreed… but I think we should backtrack to the animal trail we just passed, it seemed to go in the right direction, this logging road is too exposed, and I don't want to be caught in the open.'

They walked back along the path they had just taken, then took another game trail, it was about thirty yards inside the treeline, paralleling the logging road. Half a mile further on, Peter spotted him, atop a high seat, its ladder leaning against a tree a couple of feet back from the edge of the road, it would have afforded an alert sentry a good view in both directions, but this one was fast asleep. Mac nodded at Peter, and they moved off, deeper into the forest, circumnavigating the guard.

'I guess we are in the right place,' whispered Peter.

'He could be a hunter, waiting for a shot at one your aggressive wild boar? He's using a high seat, which they favour in these parts,' said Mac.

'Nope,' smiled Peter, 'it's not hunting season, and that was no hunting rifle on his lap.'

'Agreed. Just testing, to see if you are awake.'

'Fu—' Peter was interrupted by a voice from the road, the

man was speaking in German, he was laughing, the man on the high-seat responded, banter in any language. 'Changing the guard?'

Mac said, 'I guess so. Let's move while they're distracted. We'll get ahead... over there.'

He pointed to a small rise in the forest about one-hundred yards away, seventy feet from the logging road, 'We'll follow, and see where sleeping beauty goes.'

Peter nodded his agreement, and they moved silently off towards the mound. After much banter the young guard made his way along the road, Mac and Peter followed, keeping him on their right and just ahead of them.

After half a mile the guard turned off the road onto a track to his left. Mac realised that this would bring him within feet of where they were, they sank down behind a recently felled behemoth of the forest.

He stopped a few feet from them, the other side of the fallen tree, Mac and Peter held their breath, Peter eased the Sig Sauer out of its holster. The sentry sighed contentedly as he broke wind, then resumed his commute.

Peter whispered, 'More tea, vicar?'

Mac suppressed a snigger. They waited until he was out of sight, then followed. Mac and Peter moved, constantly swapping the lead, following at a distance, keeping about one-hundred-and-fifty-feet away from the track, and far enough behind to maintain eyeball, their progress helped by the old game track that meandered through in the trees, roughly paralleling the dirt road the night-guard was purposely trudging.

They crested a small rise and stopped. Ahead was a large traditional wooden house in the middle of a stockaded clearing. Mac pointed just ahead of them, to a narrow newly worn path, recently walked by someone in combat boots. Peter nodded, they both looked back into the trees, looking for the right spot. Peter tapped Mac on the shoulder, and moved silently off, stepping over the narrow path. He led them deeper into the forest, and up a small rise. Peter stopped by an overgrown tangle of windblown trees. Mac checked it over, and gave a thumbs-up sign, they both moved round behind the pile of trees.

While Peter removed a gillie suit from his rucksack, Mac probed the fallen tree trunks for ants and snakes, finding none he donned his gillie suit. Using twigs, mosses and ferns, they dressed each other's suits, satisfied with the camouflage, they took up positions, and waited. The location gave then a good view of the back, and one side of the house, and almost all the compound.

About once every half hour, throughout the day, a patrolling guard passed along the narrow path, pausing to look around and catch his breath on the rise he had just crested, while waiting for the other sentry, who was walking the same path around the compound in the opposite direction, to join and then pass by him, these encounters were always accompanied by banter and the exchange of cigarettes. The guards were young, bored, and clearly not military.

Mac and Peter took turns in keeping watch, taking an hour about, they established that there were two guards on a roving patrol, four more in the compound, who interchanged with them every hour, and there was at least one in the high seat back down the roadway, and surmised that there could be another one further out along the road in the other direction.

Assuming that there were as many off duty as on, they agreed that there could be up to thirty-three, if they were running a three-shift-system, one on days, one on nights, and one off, Mac felt that was unlikely, he thought that they might not number more than twenty-two, and likely less if fewer guards patrolled at night. There was no sign of the Seidel's, but the presence of armed guards confirmed Tom's theory. Mac broke radio silence to inform Tom, and then Sergei.

Night fell, and Peter resentfully ate his cold rations. Mac pointed out that no wildlife had approached, indicating that the disturbance in this location was recent, since the animals had yet to become accustomed to the disruption. For him this was the final piece of confirmation he needed. Peter agreed.

Around eleven at night the back door of the house opened and closed in quick succession, as the night watch relieved their colleagues, for three minutes it was a lighthouse in the forest.

'Bloody amateurs.' whinged, Peter.

Around four in the morning, Mac woke Peter, 'I'm going to make the rendezvous with Matt and Simon, keep your head down.'

'Yes, mother.'

Mac moved slowly off, walking further back into the forest, the gillie suit made progress slow, after he had passed the sentry in the high seat, who was fast asleep, Mac stopped and removed his camouflage.

At nine in the morning, he reached the previously agreed meeting place, secreting himself in the trees, he waited. About an hour later, the arrival of two men took him by surprise, they silently and quickly checked the clearing, Matt, Simon, and Sergei joined them, one of the men turned round and pointed in Mac's direction.

Mac stood up, 'Impressive,' he bowed at the Russian, who grinned in response.

Sergei embraced Mac, 'Good to see you. Peter?'

'He's keeping watch.'

Simon said, 'You're sure this is the place?'

'Certain as I can be, still no sign of the Seidel's. This is the place, unless we have stumbled on something else, but that's unlikely, Tom is usually right, and I cannot imagine that NNV would tolerate anyone else in the same location, nor would they choose a site with neighbours.'

Matt said, 'How far?'

'About two hours, some of it is hard going.'

'Then we had better have a brew, eat, and get ready,' said Matt.

Sergei spoke to his men, two more entered the clearing from the treeline, about twenty feet from where Mac had secreted himself earlier.

Mac looked over at Sergei, who laughed. An hour later, fed, watered and primed, they set off. Mac kept a good pace, and around two in the afternoon they arrived at a point about a hundred yards from Peter.

Sergei's four men paired up and moved off in different directions. Donning their gillie suits, Mac, Sergei, Simon, and Matt, moved slowly down to Peter's position. Simon had great difficulty in moving whilst wearing the gillie suit, but to the relief of all, managed to do so quietly.

Peter said, 'What took you so long?'

'We stopped off for a beer,' said Matt.

'Funny.'

Mac said, 'Any activity?'

'Yeah, our friends the Seidel's arrived about mid-morning, that's their car, the far side of the compound, you can just see the bonnet sticking out. There, to the right of the house.'

'Got it. Anything else to report?'

'Yup, but you're not going to like it. About half-an-hour ago a minibus drove in, and five girls, all aged about ten were led into the back of the house, the minibus is just to the left of the car.'

'Shit, that complicates things.'

'Mac, we cannot leave them in there,' said Sergei, 'you know what will happen to them… we have to get them out.'

'I know, but we don't have enough intel. The house, the guards, the layout, routines. You know the drill.'

Peter said, 'Fuck that, just do it. They're not military, we can take…'

'That's as maybe, but they've got guns,' said Mac, 'But you're right, we have to get those kids out of there.'

They retreated into their own thoughts for a while, until Sergei said, 'My men will deal with the guards outside the compound, which leaves about four inside the fence, once my men re-join us we go in and take out those four, which leaves between eleven and twelve if Mac is right, and I think he is, once in the house, this could be over in minutes, Simon stays here as overwatch, to make sure we are not surprised by any late arrivals. What do you think?'

Matt said, 'I like it.'

Peter said, 'It could work, especially if we could get it done by eleven, when the guards come out for their nightshift, that would get rid of a load more. Which just gives us those inside the house to deal with. What does that leave, maybe no more than a handful if they are running two shifts? It's a risk, but worth taking, at the very least it reduces the odds.'

Mac thought it over, 'Okay. Simon, when this is over, I'll call you and give you the number of children we have, then you contact John, he will have to warn Mary that they are on their way. If this goes south, and we don't make it, bunk out while it's still dark, head back to Sergei's mates. Duck and run.'

'Will do.'

Chapter Thirty-One

Around ten-fifty in the evening the four Russians returned and confirmed that all the outer guards were dead. Matt joined Sergei, everyone split into pairs, Mac took out his knife and silently indicated to all of them that he wanted noiseless killing, he looked into the eyes of each of them, satisfied that they understood, they grimly approached the compound from different directions.

Ten-fifty-five, and it was all over, they had infiltrated the stockade, and had taken out the sentries, Sergei's men had donned their jackets and hats and were now patrolling the yard. Matt and Sergei, Peter and Mac, took up positions either side of the rear door of the house.

Four minutes later the rear door opened, and the night-watch spilled out into the yard, milling around, smoking, talking, laughing, calling out to their mates. Mac and Peter grabbed one each, taking his victim from behind, Mac placed his left hand over the guard's mouth clamping it shut, his fingers gripping the right cheek, he bent the head back toward him and twisted it to the left, at the same time, using the knife in his right hand he severed the windpipe, pulling the body back and to the ground, he cut the carotid artery.

Three minutes later the four Russians, Mac, Peter, Matt, and

Sergei entered the house by the rear door, and split up. After eight minutes they re-grouped in the hallway, Matt and Sergei had the Seidel's in handcuffs. Sergei conferred with his men, and confirmed that the house was clear, he sent a pair of them to double check, the other two were tasked with finding any paperwork that might be of assistance.

Mac said, 'Do you speak English?'

Neither replied.

Matt stepped forward, lifted Wallii Seidel to his feet, then stepped to one side, while Peter kicked him hard between the legs. He screamed, Matt let him drop, and Seidel fell to the floor sobbing.

'Do you speak English?' Mac repeated his question.

'You know we do,' said Fieke Seidel.

'Good. Where are the children?'

'Fuck you and fuck them. Soon they will be dead, there is only enough air until the morning.'

'I will not ask you again. Where are the children?'

Fieke Seidel spat at Mac, 'You will get nothing...'

Her last words were cut short by a bullet fired by Matt, point-blank into her brain. He looked at Wallii Seidel, who knelt, stunned, staring at the fountain of blood spraying from the skull of the still twitching body of his wife.

'Where are the children?' Matt pulled out his knife, 'I'm going to begin by cutting bits off you, starting with your balls, now where are the children?'

Seidel sobbed out his response, ten minutes later Peter and Matt returned with eight terrified little girls, aged between seven and eleven.

Mac said, 'Eight?'

'The other three must have already been here...' Peter was interrupted by the return of two of Sergei's men, they had two guards in handcuffs.

Sergei said, 'They found them cowering in the cellar.'

Mac said, 'Keep them alive for now, they may prove useful.'

Sergei relayed Mac's instructions to his men, the children appeared to be following his words, one little girl sobbed in Russian, pleading for water.

'Russian? They're Russian children,' Sergei and his men moved towards Seidel. Mac stepped between them, fearful of what was coming, 'Not in front of the kids. Sergei, detail two of your men to take them to Mary, she will be waiting for them at the church in Passau, but feed them first they look half-starved, and give them a drink. Have your guys check out the minibus in the compound. I'll give Simon a call, he can contact, John.'

'Okay, Mac.' Sergei stepped over Seidel, his trailing boot accidentally colliding with Seidel's testicles. Seidel collapsed to the floor, sobbing.

Sergei looked at Matt, and said, 'How did you know which of them was the weakest?'

'He was cowed when we took him, she was defiant, she clearly wore the trousers. What is it they say about terrorists? Shoot the women first, they're the deadliest. He's a coward, he's pussy-whipped, have him interrogated by a couple of your female officers and he'll tell us all we need to know.'

Sergei went off to make arrangements for the transportation of the children, while Mac contacted Simon.

Mac said, 'Pete, you and Matt take two of the Russians. Go and pick up the bodies of the guards, I noticed a couple of quad bikes with trailers out in the yard, I would use them. The place you found the kids, is it well hidden?'

'Yes. If he hadn't told us where to look, we would never have found it.'

'Air-tight, apparently?'

Peter nodded.

'Good dump all the bodies, and the weapons in there, then lock it up. We are going to leave this building like the Marie Celeste, I want it locked from the inside, and when we leave the compound, I want the gate barred and locked, that should give them something to ponder.'

Sergei said, 'What about them?' he indicated the two guards.

'Take them and Seidel with you, I want you to keep them alive in Russia, I'm quite sure after all they have seen they will be talkative, and there is much we still need to know.'

'Okay, I'll guarantee his survival, but I cannot promise that the two guards will make it. The children... my men want...'

Mac nodded, 'Seidel, then.'

They saw the children off, then set about their tasks, by ten in the morning they reached the rendezvous point. Having said their goodbyes, Simon, Matt, Sergei and his men, took the path back to the Czech Republic, taking Seidel and the terrified guards with them. Mac and Peter took the trail back towards their cabin.

They stopped for lunch, Mac rang and briefed Tom on the events of the last twenty-four-hours. Tom was able to confirm the safe arrival of the children, and that they were in the capable hands of Mary. The two Russians had agreed to remain with Mary, to ensure that there would be no interference, until the children had been taken back to Russia.

Mac said that he and Peter were going to take some time out, and that they did not anticipate being back at the cabin for another three days, when hopefully Sergei would have more information for them, and the next step could be calculated. Tom thought it an excellent idea.

Chapter Thirty-Two

In the event it took Mac and Peter four days to get back to the cabin. They made a few detours, as suggested in Peter's booklet, they were not disappointed, both remarked upon the rugged beauty, the solitude, and the sheer grandeur of the scenery. The second night on the trail they bivouacked on a ridge overlooking a wide, forested valley, as dusk fell, they watched a bear with a cub, which given its size, was probably born that Spring, move slowly up the slope the other side of the valley. Night was dark and clear, under starlight, Mac and Peter talked of the future, and of their hopes.

Mac said, 'What do you make of Terri and Anna's plans for the farm?'

'I'm impressed, they've both thought it through. Their research is meticulous, they've put together a comprehensive plan.'

'I agree. I'm taken aback by the degree of flexibility they've built in.'

Peter said, 'I think it will work, we can make it work, but it is going to take a serious effort by all of us. Still, they seem to be under no illusion about how much hard graft it will take.'

Mac nodded, 'I've made some notes, just a few ideas to tweak the plan, but I also think there is something missing… polytunnels.'

Polytunnels?'

'The farm is just too far north for many crops to grow outside of a protected environment. I always meant to buy one, but never got around to it, polytunnels will allow us to grow tomatoes, cucumbers, aubergines, sweet and chilli peppers, and we could give one over entirely to growing salad vegetables.'

'How many are you thinking of?'

'Four, and they will need to be large. It will mean giving up a part of the lower pasture to accommodate them, but it will be worth it.'

'How much are we talking about?'

'Not sure, the tunnels and the other bits and bobs we'll need, around thirty, or forty… fifty grand max, but there is slack in the budget. With the polytunnels in place we can grow vegetables other than those that we know will thrive in our latitude. It will extend the growing season and increase the range of different produce we can sell, the more varieties of fruit and veg we offer to the public, the more likely we are to build a sustainable customer base.'

Peter said, 'You swallow a fucking farm manual?' Quickly gauging Mac's response, he raised his hand and continued. 'Calm down, I'm joking. I'm with you all the way, it makes sense and sounds like a good addition to the plan, we'll put it to Anna and Teri when this is over.'

'Soon, I hope. My main fear is that whoever is behind all this, has organised things in silos. Seidel may not be able to tell us much, he may not know who the next link in the chain is, and if he does, how many more links will there be?'

'Well, whatever he knows, we will hear soon enough, I can't see Sergei and Matt taking too long to extract it.'

'No, nor I.'

'Mac, these plans for the farm have got me fired up, and like

316

you, I just want this over and done with, we've got a life to build. Truthfully, I won't be too unhappy if we run into a brick wall.'

Mac nodded, and said, 'Unfortunately, we have got to see this through to the bitter end, if we don't cut the head off this particular snake, it will come back and bite us. I just hope we are still under the radar.'

They both lay back, lost in their thoughts, looking at a sky crowded with stars. Mac said, 'How can anyone contemplate this, and deny the existence of, God?'

Peter said, 'You asked me that question thirty-one years ago, in that desert to the left of Wherethefuckarewestan; my answer has changed... but I'm not ready to talk about it just yet.'

Mac smiled, turned over and surrendered to sleep.

Chapter Thirty-Three

They reached the cabin late afternoon on the fourth day, as they climbed the steps to the veranda, Peter turned to Mac, and said, 'When this is over, we should all take a holiday.'

Mac nodded his agreement.

Showered and rested, Peter volunteered to cook diner, Mac made the short walk to buy beer. Twenty minutes later he returned, the door was slightly ajar, he could hear low murmuring from within. Mac put the pack of beers down on the steps, cursed himself for not bringing a gun with him, he took out the radio, slid the plastic cover to the left, and pushed the red button down, he counted to six and released it.

Mac pushed the door open slowly, saying, 'That smells nice, Pete. What is it?'

Peter was sitting at the table facing him, his hands palms up on the tabletop, his eyes moved left to right.

'Welcome, Mr. Mackenzie.'

Mac turned to his left, the butt of a shotgun struck him on his right shoulder blade, forcing him to stumble forward, the radio shot out of his right hand hit the table leg and clattered to the floor.

'Sit.'

Mac, sat at the table, opposite Peter. 'Hands on the table,

palms up.' Mac looked at Peter, there was a small cut above his left eye, Peter glanced at the radio on the floor, then back to Mac, who smiled. The radio burst into flames and was soon reduced to a molten lump. 'Sorry about your phone, still you will not be needing it. May I introduce myself, Marco Carpovilla.' He sat down at the table, 'I have been looking forward to meeting you.'

Two large very muscular men moved to stand either side of Mac and Peter.

'Never heard of you,' said Peter.

This earned him a punch to the side of his head. Carpovilla waved his henchman away. 'I do apologise, he dislikes it when people show me disrespect.'

Mac looked at both men, and thought, *Muscle nothing more, and not the sharpest tools in the box at that.* Concerned by the look he gave them, they reached under their jackets and produced handguns. Mac said, 'Like my friend, I have never heard of you, so I have no idea why you would want to meet us?'

Carpovilla smiled, and leaned forward, 'For a number of reasons, more recently for events that took place in a remote house in the forest, not too far from here. You gentlemen have cost me dearly, because of you I have lost some good staff, and these days people like that are hard to find.'

'Terribly sorry,' said Peter ducking, when the blow didn't come, he said to Mac, 'They don't do irony.'

Mac laughed, 'I'm guessing their repertoire is limited.'

'It is,' said Carpovilla smiling, 'limited, but effective, both have the ruthlessness of their fellow Serbians.'

'So, what do you want?'

'Your demise.'

'Well get on with it, unless you're planning on boring us to death,' said Peter, who received another blow to the head for his troubles.

Peter leapt to his feet, 'Pal, you've got the personality of a stunned haddock, put the gun down, and we'll see if I can knock some character into you?'

'Sit down... I said, sit down.' Carpovilla looked at Peter, then at Mac, the other bodyguard was standing behind Mac, his gun cocked and aimed at Mac's head. Peter shrugged and sat down.

Carpovilla said, 'All in good time, Mr. Armstrong. All in good time. There are things I need to know, for example how much you know about me and my organisation?'

Mac said, 'I assume if we don't cooperate you will have the information beaten out of us?'

'Pointless, I know all about you, you've both been trained, you will take a severe beating, and then feed me lies, making me believe it is true, no?'

Mac, shrugged.

'If I have to, I will use drugs.'

Mac said, 'Pete?'

'I'm too old for this shit, what the fuck, tell him what he wants to know.'

'What do you want to know?'

Carpovilla said, 'To begin with, why have you attacked my organisation?'

'Because your underlings, Alan Mason, and Eric Powell... I see you recognise the names, in carrying out your instructions to protect your... organisation, killed my wife.'

'Your wife?'

'Yes, my wife, which is why we are here.'

'Your wife?' Carpovilla seemed confused, 'Mason and Powell I know of course, but your wife, I knew nothing of their concern for her. I had no interest in her...'

'I'm quite sure that is true, Mason and Powell are secretive bastards, which is why you recruited them, but employing them was a dumb move if it is your intention to micro-manage, their kind people have a habit of going off at a tangent.'

'I will be having words with them.'

'Soon, I hope,' laughed Peter.

'Ah… I see. More of my staff.'

'Yup.'

'And you followed a trail that led you here?'

'We did, we came looking for the Seidel's.'

'And you found them. Where's Wallii?'

Peter and Mac, laughed.

Mac said, 'Dead, in the forest somewhere. It was dark.'

'Right… along with my Praetorians, I take it that the two we are missing are somewhere in the woods?'

'Aye.'

'Just the two of you?'

'Aye.'

'Impressive. The children?'

'Safe.'

'Ah yes, that's where you have been… the church, but which one? I know all about Father Roberts and his friend Mary, I know all there is to know about your interfering priest.'

A look passed between Mac and Peter, concerning Sergei, Matt, and Simon.

Misinterpreting it, Carpovilla said, 'I will find your meddlesome priest, and I will have his head.'

Mac said, 'So you're the big cheese, you're behind all this?'

'I am. There will be time enough to discuss this matter, but later, in a place and time of my choosing.'

Mac and Peter were injected, both drifted into unconsciousness.

Chapter Thirty-Four

When Mac came round, he was alone in a dark room. He staggered to his feet, his head ached, the darkness made it impossible to focus, causing his balance to undulate. He reached out and floundered forward until he touched a wall, he slowly walked clockwise around the room, it was little more than a cupboard.

Dizzy and feeling nauseous, he sat down, with his back to the wall opposite the door, and waited. He drifted in and out of consciousness, he was unsure how long he had been there, but he was hungry and thirsty.

The door opened, the two thugs entered and dragged him into the hallway, he sat blinking in the light, trying to focus, then threw up. He staggered to his feet, expecting a punch he tensed.

The larger of the two Serbians, laughed and indicated that Mac should follow him along the corridor, the other followed behind.

He was led down the corridor into a large bright room. He was shown to an armchair and invited to sit, he lost consciousness again. Mac oozed back to consciousness, his mind swimming, struggling to focus, his head ached, and he had to fight to resist the desire to vomit. He looked at Carpovilla, and unable to hide his contempt said, 'What now?'

Carpovilla smiled but said nothing. He reminded Mac of an oily lounge-lizard he had arrested, back in his days on the Vice Unit. Another parasite, who preyed on weak men, and vulnerable women. Mac tried to recall the man's name, but his brain was struggling to relinquish its enthusiasm for the haven of insensibility. A slap in the face from the large thug brought him back to the present. Carpovilla straightened his tie, brushed imaginary fluff from the sleeves of his Savile Row suit, he walked over to where Mac was seated, bound hand and foot in an armchair.

He indicated, with a gentle movement of his right hand, and the smaller Serbian brought over a chair. Carpovilla took it, planted it in front of Mac, and sat down.

'You have cost me dearly. I will have to find another couple to replace the Seidel's, and that will not be easy, they had very… special skills.'

His two henchmen laughed. Carpovilla raised his hand for silence, 'You also killed two of my best people, one of whom I will find it impossible to replace.'

Mac, smiled.

'You are wondering, no doubt, what I am going to do with you, and your friend? Yes, Peter. He's fine, well he's still alive.' Carpovilla frowned and looked at the larger Serbian, who looked away, the smaller one's snigger was cut short by an equally withering stare. 'I am afraid that my men get carried away, they do love their work. You will be joining Peter presently, and then we are all taking a little trip. One-way for both of you I am afraid, but then you've already guessed that. I'm sure you have questions?'

He nodded at the smaller Serbian, who untied Mac, and pulled him to his feet. Mac stood rubbing his wrists. Carpovilla, indicated a pair of armchairs in the corner of the room, 'If you please.'

Mac followed him over and sat down. They both stared at each other, neither speaking, the tension was broken by the arrival of a young oriental woman carrying a tray of drinks, which she set down on the table in front of them. Mac noted the terror in her eyes.

'Single malt, a double, no ice, correct?'

Mac nodded, took the drink, sipped it, and bowed his head in approval.

'Forty-eight-years-old, I bought the distillery last year,' Both men continued to look at each other, whilst appreciating the distiller's art.

Mac said, 'Why?'

'Why buy a distillery?'

'Why the children, the satanic sects, the Nazi bullshit?'

'Power, pure and simple. I don't believe in fairy stories, religion is for the weak-minded, only the foolish subscribe to such primitive beliefs.' He sipped his whisky then continued, 'I have no time for your Christian god, nor for the meekness your religion promulgates through its implausible claims.'

He took another sip of whisky, leaned forward toward Mac and said, 'I know that you have an insight into my organisation, and have some understanding of the way it functions, and the part played by those I exploit. Useful idiots all of them, they run around naked, sodomising each other, fornicating with children, which I ensure is digitally captured. Once I have them on camera engaging in their sordid, bestial acts, they are mine. Once in, there is no going back. I give them wealth, status, and a little power, and in return, they do my bidding.'

'But what about the girls, the babies…?'

'What of them? Collateral damage, nothing more, sacrificed

to the Project. They died for the greater good, anyway they are worthless, just scum from lesser-races.' Carpovilla laughed as he spoke the words, lesser-races.

Mac put his glass down, his face set, he snarled, 'You sick twisted bastard.'

The change in his demeanour, and the tone of his voice alarmed Carpovilla, who started to rise from his seat, his two bodyguards rushed over, guns drawn, but Mac settled into his armchair, picked up his glass, crossed his legs, and staring at Carpovilla, smiled and sipped his whisky.

Carpovilla waved them away, 'I'm sick and twisted? Look around you, Western civilisation is falling apart. The others are out-breeding you, they will in a very few years take over, it's simple demographics, do the maths. Those morons in the liberal elite are handing your countries to them on a plate. Your race is polluted, your countries despoiled, your women degraded, your culture defiled, such impurity must be eradicated. The lesser-races have dishonoured your heritage, you, and all those like you, have done nothing, save to look on without comprehension, blinded by hope and your great weakness, a belief in the goodness of your fellow man. I will purge Europe of all that ails her, and I am going to use the Marxists and their left-leaning fellow-travellers to achieve my goal. Once your politicians had honour, once they had faith, now they are weaklings, kowtowing to their great god, equality. Selling your birthright to accommodate the desires of sodomites and foreigners. Ironic then, that I should use sodomites and foreigners to achieve my goal, the creation of a New Europe, a Greater Europe.'

'I think we've heard that shite before, and it ended badly.'

'That is true. But then there were obstacles in the way of the truth, barriers that prevented understanding, not all the white races wanted to hear the message, you British still had an empire, and the arrogant certainty of your imperialism created a twisted sense of nationalism, which, coupled with a misunderstanding of the ambitions of other nations, obstructed the truth of Arian power. Now, with open borders across Europe, and a growing sense of the supranationalism of the EU, there is a lack of imperialism, of the petty rivalry of nations. The white races of Europe are ready, they are one, and long to hear, and want to follow. They desire a cleansing of their communities, to rid them of all that enrages, they are ready to take back everything that was stolen from them, to correct the insult, to restore Western culture. Take your own country, thanks to the new equality and human rights laws...'

'Legislation and concepts imposed and required by Europe, at your behest, it would appear...'

'True, but it cannot be traced back to me, no one knows who I am, or what I have done. No, those fools in the European Parliament will be held responsible. Ironic, given its total lack of real power. You should know, I didn't corrupt the existing system, it was wide open to subordination. I found many unscrupulous politicians already deeply mired in corruption; they were easy to blackmail into submission. Unfortunately, too many of a conservative bent share your deluded belief in the Sky-Pixie, they still refuse to assist with my project. The reaction of some among the Socialists was my biggest surprise, most of them came to the European Parliament following long service in their own national legislatures, men and women with unimpeachable reputations, and yet more than a few of them, when exposed to the truth, that they had no power to change or shape anything, succumbed to temptation, and plunged their snouts deep into the unfettered, unsupervised, trough of emoluments. The allowances and kickbacks they could extract from the projects they authored or supported, turned most into slavering capitalists, amassing Croesan amounts of money. Thus, the group I had feared would prove the most resistant, surrendered to their own impiety with unseemly haste. Perhaps a lifetime of compromise and failure permitted their pragmatism paramountcy over their principles.'

Mac hung his head.

'I see that the truth of what I am saying has touched a nerve, there may be hope for you yet. But back to what I was saying, in your country and across Europe, people are sick of politicians, and the courts who allow foreign terrorists, murderers, and rapists to avoid deportation, only to release them early from prison to rape and murder again. I know you agree with me, I can see it in your eyes. Take your country as an example, what kind of system allows the State to take children from parents by conducting trials in secret, denying parents and children their rights, denying them the right to know what it is they are accused off, and who it is that accuses them. Yet that same system grants rights, and protection, to terrorists, even giving them a small fortune in funding to defend themselves, guaranteeing them a public platform for their murderous views.'

'Legislation, you put in place?'

'No, I cannot take the credit for that, it was completely down to your own parliament and judiciary. People are angry and confused, they are ready. They are mine, and for this I must thank the political class, their self-indulgent belief in their own elitism, their right to rule, their conviction that only they are entitled to say what is acceptable and what is not, blinded them, they forgot that they are servants of the people, and not the other way around. An oversight for which I will reward them.' Carpovilla, laughed long and loud.

Mac said, 'Bread and circuses?'

'Yes... essentially nothing changes. But you are quite wrong, people are ready for this, they want... just one huge atrocity is all it will take, a massive attack that will outrage the world, hitting every European capital on the same day at the same time, a mass-assault, with mass-casualties, tens-of-thousands, all planned, facilitated, and funded by me... it will make Europe mine for the taking. I will implicate...'

'Not the poor bloody Jews, again?'

'No, that would be too obvious, and pointless, thanks to Hitler and Stalin, they are no longer the problem in Europe they once were. Now Israel, well that's a different matter entirely... a conversation for another time, perhaps? What was I saying... oh yes, I shall expose the politicians, their greed and lust will be there for all to see, and the liberal intellectuals will have a light shone on their incomprehensible support of Islam. I will demonstrate how those on the Left, and the Muslims, are responsible for... my beautiful outrage. I will show the world the complicity of those on the Left and their bedfellows in the liberal elites of Europe. I will demonstrate their collusion in the destruction of Western culture and civilisation, in their total betrayal of the values and beliefs that once protected society from the nihilism they promote, and how all this allowed the massacre to take place...'

Mac said, 'And what of those who played no part, even opposed those...'

'Sadly, there are many politicians who are honest and prin- cipled, if a little misguided, who will also be blackened, their reputations tarnished by the others, whose corruption and greed will be made very public. No matter, just a bit more collateral damage. I will imprison them all, good and bad alike, the blood of their victims will demand no less, eventually I will execute them, but initially I will use them to further my own aims. I will deport those Muslims who have not had the sense to leave, and then the rest of the lesser-races. There will be no death camps this time round... well not initially. And all this made possible by the political class of Europe believing themselves to be a special breed, above society and beyond reproach. Their arrogance and failure to look no further than the next soundbite, the next headline, and the next inducement, renders them culpable. They wilfully refused to hear what the populace was saying, failed to respond to their fears, dismissing them as under-educated racists. The resentment they have created, allied with a general lack of faith in politics and politicians, has established the fertile ground that allows me to consummate my dream. Eugenics will be the foundation upon which the Project will be advanced. I will build the New Europe... you disagree?'

'It will not... it cannot happen again; people are not stupid...'

'Yes, they are. They will only see and hear what I want them to see and hear. And once I have convinced them of what it is they want and need, I will give it to them. Simply by demonising the enemy within, by manufacturing and manipulating popular disgust and anger, the Project will be driven forward. It was that easy in nineteen-thirty-three, it will be even easier now, I have written a new version of the *Gesetz zur Behebung der Not von Volk und Reich*... the Enabling Act. I have ensured that this will lock into legislation I have already created, giving me total power, I will stand behind a newly formed European Senate, and carry out the political and moral cleansing of our public life. Remember people do not vote for high principles, they vote out of self-interest, mobilise that and even those who never bother voting, will engage with the process. I have been busy, creating a European government, where power is not in the parliament, but elsewhere. Those imbeciles who work for me, believe that the Europe they are building will be a Marxist elysian. Through my placemen I now dictate how Europe works, I draft and shape the laws to be passed by its parliament, laws designed to create a Europe that will enshrine the doctrines and philosophy of the Third Reich. It has proved unbelievably easy, no one seems to notice how much the policies of the European Union reflect the ambitions of the Third Reich, and it is upon this that I am creating a glorious New Project, a Fourth Reich.'

Mac protested, 'Europe's past is Christian, its values, art, architecture, music, faith, are all Christian, you cannot hope to replace a great civilisation with the retarded drivel that dripped from the lips of a pestilent lunatic.'

Carpovilla leapt to his feet, 'You and your kind cannot understand, you are blinkered by your blind faith in a feeble deity, a god who will not wield power. That is why I have begun the process of dismantling all that Christendom stood for. Slowly at first, marginalising it, mocking it through the power of the media, disrupting it, my functionaries destroying it from within. I have passed laws to ensure that its weak hierarchy are forced to make compromises, one after another, until it has surrendered all its principles, and stands for nothing, a hollow shell, devoid of dogma, lacking leadership, its credo crushed. Even now your leaders seek a place where the Church can co-exist with the secular world, they have capitulated in the face of the dominant anything-goes righteous-liberalism that is dividing society.'

Mac said, 'A liberalisation of attitudes you would appear to be responsible for?'

'No, not quite. Again, I only took advantage of what was already in place. The clerical betrayal you allude to was not of my making, but it has proved useful. I admit I have taken full advantage, placing my own people inside the Church, corrupting many, some are in senior positions, all to maintain the new and useful direction the Church is taking. I discovered a Church full of individuals who, for various reasons, were busy throwing out anything that smacked of tradition, and insisting that consensus be reformed. Their real love is not faith, but power, and it is in the political arena that they are able to demonstrate their new-found credentials. They crave the approbation of the liberal-media, and the atheistic-elite, they love being in the spotlight. It is this that drives them, not any notion of faith, or truth, or saving souls, that side of the Church embarrasses them. They are driven by a credo of social-justice and eco-politics, they have no need of the old dogma, it is far too rigid, they follow the ever-changing fashions of the world, tradition is just not flexible enough, and defending it would render them persona non grata in the eyes of those whose approbation they lust for...'

Mac interrupting, said, 'So you think that you can destroy the Church from within, and society from without? You really believe that the faithful, abandoned and misled by their priests, who are too busy courting worldly popularity and pursuing worldly pleasures, will just convert to your new-world-order and abandon God, or stand by and watch their communities being deconstructed, twisted into a parody of faith?'

'Yes, pretty much that is what will happen, is happening; scandal and indifference are eroding the faithful, as you call them. The rump that remains will be nothing more than a small group of insignificant adherents, traditionalists who will be dismissed as superstitious lunatics. I will ensure they are pitied, tolerated in my magnanimity, left as an example of anachronistic superstition, but know this, when they die out, so does Catholicism, and with it all trace of Christianity. As for the other faiths, since I will have driven from your lands all non-Arians, and any foolish enough stay will be enslaved, their creeds will constitute no threat. Then I will destroy the family, it is a stronghold against which even Communism could not prevail, those I control have already begun the process. Unlike the Communists, who made the mistake of replacing the old religions with the cult of the State, I will resurrect the mythology of the Nazis, stirring tales of courtly knights, great quests, and Arian superiority, these will become the foundation of a new religion, one wholly in tune with the glorious Project. I have already identified senior individuals in the Vatican who will assist us in this endeavour...'

'Cardinal Guido Bertonus, being one of them...'

'You are better informed than I imagined, Mr. Mackenzie. Yes, he and the others will become the new priesthood, we even have Catholic university professors and lecturers, working on the development of a new theology and philosophy, one that places man, not your god at the centre, one that will serve the Project. For their services, their reward will be in the here and now, not later, when they are dead. You fools believe that after you're dead there is a life to come, a reward in heaven? For that alone you deserve to die, such pathetic hopefulness has no place in the world of men. It makes weaklings and cowards of you. This life is all there is, this is all a man gets, his life is worthless if it is not wholly committed to the unquestioning service of his country, and its ruler. The value of a man, is in his heroic devotion to his country and his leader, he will be judged on his willingness to sacrifice all to that end.'

Mac said, 'You forget who you are talking to, I know that you also believe in an afterlife, you really are quite deluded, but you're no fool, I'll grant you that, you have achieved much,' he raised his glass to Carpovilla, and took a sip of whisky, 'Europe is legislatively beginning to resemble Nazi Germany, and like Hitler, you have sought to exercise power secretly, manipulating behind the scenes, subverting democracy, using place-men, but like that other madman, you have forgotten...'

'I am not mad, I have looked carefully at what is happening in Europe, and the only way out of this present suicidal plunge into the abyss of collective cultural destruction, is the restoration of the vision of the Third Reich. I have only made use of the system that was in place, I have channelled the corruption already endemic in political organisations, and if my activities have remained hidden, it is only because the structure in place was designed to hide the truth from a gullible public. I did not build this edifice, I only used what was already there, I found an institution that gives the appearance of democracy and the illusion of choice, and yet remains unquestionably dictatorial; how fortuitous for me. I have forgotten nothing, I have read, and learned from the mistakes made by the Führer, he was betrayed by fools, his ideas perverted by self-serving gluttons. I will not make the same mistake. You see I control…'

Mac interrupted him, 'Enough of this shite! If this cosy fireside chat is supposed to bring me round to your point of view, you insult me. Take me to, Peter.'

'As you wish, but I am disappointed, I could use men like you and Peter. I can raise you high, give you wealth, power and position. You could help shape the New Europe, and in doing so change the world, you could take your place in history. Then, you really would live forever. But you are a cripple, emotionally tied to your pathetic belief in your so-called creator. For an intelligent man, you are remarkably weak, mentally retarded by superstition. Take him to his friend.'

The Serbians walked over, Mac stood up, finished his glass of whisky, placed it slowly on the table in front of him, and smiled as a look of fear crossed Carpovilla's face. Mac then began to walk towards the door, he shrugged off their attempts to hold his arms, 'Leave him, he'll give you no trouble. Sleep well. Tonight, will be your last, spend it in prayer, maybe your god will save you.' Carpovilla laughed mockingly.

Mac turned back towards Carpovilla and said, 'Wait... just one question.'

Carpovilla waved his henchmen away, 'Go on. I think I know what you want to ask.'

Mac said, 'How did you know where to find us? How do you know so much about us?'

Carpovilla stood up, poured himself another glass of whisky, and walked over to stand in front of Mac. 'You were betrayed.'

'Who?'

'Cartwright.'

'Bastard.'

'An interesting, ambitious, and greedy man, just the sort I am looking for, there is a place at my table for such as Cartwright. Unlike you, he harbours none of the delusions from which you suffer, Mr. Mackenzie. His gift to me, in order to obtain a seat at my table, was you and all your little friends. Last week he attended one of my soirées. I now have him on camera satiating his loathsome lust with a twelve-year-old from Mali. He handed me everything he had on each of you. Carpovilla tapped a computer disc to the side of his head, 'It's all in here, he gave me...'

'Clearly not everything, you didn't know about the connection between Mason, and my wife's death.'

'That is true. There are several blanks, which I have yet to fill in. I will be having words with him. Thanks to him, I know where you sent your lovely daughter, maybe she would like to attend one of my evening get-togethers?'

Mac, snarling, his eyes blazing, started towards Carpovilla. A blow to the back of his head brought him to his knees, he was dragged off backwards towards the door. Carpovilla raised his hand. Mac was dropped to the floor, kneeling he looked back at Carpovilla who said, 'I have no intention of doing any such thing to your daughter, I'm not a savage. You think I am a Nazi, or some sort of barbarian… well it's not your fault, it is an impression I deliberately gave you, one I like to give. It makes things… simpler, easier to understand. It is true that the organisation I have created is structured along the lines of the Nazi system of governance, it closely follows its ethics and goals, but then it would. Hitler's vision, the movement he created, was inspired, I'm sure your meddlesome priest could explain that to you. Institutions like mine require order and structure, they also need a goal, and someone to obey and believe in, and why not the Nazi model of governance? Its beliefs and philosophy are easily accessible and so appealing to the masses? I am not a Nazi, but it is an idea with history, and it is simple to comprehend. I serve a powerful master, who is a corrupter and despoiler, and Hitler was his true disciple. I care nothing for humanity, nor any of your pathetic causes. What I seek is the destruction of all that stands in the way of…'

Mac made the sign of the cross, and in Latin, said, '*Vade retro Satana, numquam suade mihi vana.*'

Carpovilla screamed, 'Get him out of here.' The two henchmen hauled him to a room on the floor below, unlocked the door and pushed him in. The room was dim, light struggled through gaps in the locked shutters on the window. Mac waited for his eyes to adjust to the gloom, there was a bed, with a blanket to his left, and another, to his right, a bucket in the corner, which he guessed served as a toilet.

A low groan, that communicated pain and anguish, came from the bed to his right. Mac moved towards it, cautiously he raised the blanket.

'Peter?'

He looked at his friend, who was curled up in the foetal position, he turned him gently. Mac struggled to repress the desire to vomit. Peter's face was unrecognisable, his jaw was broken, his nose smashed flat, both eyes swollen shut, he was bleeding from his nose and mouth, but worse than that, there was blood and clear fluid running from his ears. His skull was fractured. Mac gently lifted the blanket, Peter was naked, there was no part of his body that was not bruised, he had been whipped, and his feet smashed. He had been doubly incontinent. Mac let the blanket down carefully, got to his feet and went over to the door. He banged on the door, shouting, 'Get a doctor, we need a doctor.'

His request was answered by sniggers from the other side of the door, and by schoolboy taunting. Mac realised that there would be no help for Peter. He listened as the two henchmen walked away; he heard the door at the end of the corridor slam shut and turned back to Peter.

Sitting next to his friend he gently held his hand. Peter, coughed and spat blood, 'I waited for you to come, I would not... the pain...'

'Save your strength, Pete. Rest...'

'I'll rest soon enough.' He spat more blood, his voice barely a whisper, his breathing shallow and rasping, 'Mac, promise me... Anna and Katie... promise me.'

'You don't need to ask, you know I will... Pete, save your strength, we will get out of this...'

'You must survive... I won't... take care of them... Mac, I'm sorry. Pray for me.' Mac watched as the light left his eyes, and Peter died.

Mac cried for his friend, and he prayed for him, and for Anna, and for Katie who had lost a father she had only just come to know. He demanded of God, vengeance. Then he prayed for forgiveness, for desiring so terrible a retribution, before sleep engulfed him.

Chapter Thirty-Five

They woke him early in the morning, dragged him from the room, tearing him from the body of his friend. Guns drawn, fearful of his vengeance, they threw him into the back of a van, feet and hands tied, blindfolded, driven to an airfield, and bundled onto an aircraft; when they landed, Mac tried to gauge where they were.

Excluding the crew, there were at least four others on board, yet throughout the flight he had heard nothing, so he concluded that the plane was a large jet, and the flight took hours not minutes, so he was not in Germany: the edge of Europe, Serbia, or further east? He wanted to focus on escape, but one thought kept intruding, why was he was still alive?

From the plane he was lifted and put into a van, then driven some distance, before the vehicle stopped. The doors opened, Mac, was thrown out onto the ground. His legs and hands were still bound, and the blindfold was still in place. he tried to work out his surroundings, the ground was stony, but warm to the touch, the air dusty, hot, and dry, there was no bird song; too little to go on. He realised that his captors were someway off, he could hear them talking, but they were barely audible. Mac began trying to remove the hood but stopped as soon as he heard footsteps coming toward him. The ropes binding his legs together were cut, and he was pulled roughly to his feet. his hands were freed, the hood and blindfold removed, he stood unsteady on his feet, blinking in the sunlight, rubbing his wrists, while he tried to take in his surroundings.

Carpovilla joined him, 'This is the end of the journey for you, my friend. Truly, I'm sorry it must end this way. I apologise for what happened to Peter, that was savage. If it is any consolation I admire you, men of principle, especially in the face of death, are a rarity. The Project could have made good use of a warrior like you. I consider your death to be a waste.'

Mac ignoring Carpovilla, looked around, 'Where are we?'

'At the bottom of an old stone quarry, it was decommissioned last year. It is owned by one of my Spanish subsidiaries… yes, we are in Spain, Northern Spain to be exact.'

Mac hung his head, 'No!'

'I am sure you thought that they would be safe here, out of sight, but nowhere is safe. The Project is everywhere, there can be no escape. No one can be allowed to stand in the way of progress, Europe must move from Christian retardation into atheistic evolution, we cannot be held back by mere superstition, and fecklessness. I will build a United States of Europe, the Project will last for a thousand years. Your bones, and those of your family and friends, will be the foundation upon which my vision will be realised. Did you really think you could stop me?'

He looked at Mac, but Mac's face betrayed no emotion, his eyes were cold, he set his feet and relaxed his arms.

'Don't do it, you'll be dead before you reach me, and then you will miss the execution of your family and your friends, unfortunately I have yet to dispose of your pestilent priest, but it is only a matter of time.'

Carpovilla checked his watch, looked over at his henchmen, who shrugged, 'News of his capture is overdue, I will incarcerate him for a few years, I intend his death to be a spectacle. First, prolonged and agonising torture that will see him publicly deny his god, and second, we will, quite literally, throw him to the lions.'

The quarry was filled by the sound of vehicles decelerating, two vehicles, a white van, and Anna's pickup, began to descend the roadway cut into the side of the quarry, Mac watched as both vehicles zig-zagged down one-hundred feet to the base of the quarry.

Carpovilla continued, 'There are eight men scattered around the quarry, all marksmen, and in those vehicles, four more, you don't have a chance. But if you need an incentive to obey, I'll let you shoot them. You can dispatch your family and your friends. A single bullet to the head, fired by you, or you can watch while my men pleasure themselves on your women and children, before mutilating them, then killing them slowly. It's up to you?'

Laughing, he walked off towards the end of the roadway, to wait for the vehicles. The white van pulled up next to him, the driver, who was wearing a balaclava remained in the vehicle. The passenger got out, walked around to the rear, and unlocked the doors of the van. The suddenness of what happened next stunned, Mac.

The bodies of four men were thrown from the back of the van, at the same time shots rang out, in less than a heartbeat all Carpovilla's men were dead.

The driver's door of the van opened, and Sergei got out removing his balaclava. Ignoring Carpovilla, who had been thrown to the ground, and was being stripped of his clothing, Sergei walked up to, Mac.

'Good to see you,' he looked around, 'Pete?'

'He didn't make it.'

'I'm sorry.'

They embraced. Mac stepped back and said, 'April, Teri…?'

'They're safe.'

'Thank God. How did you…?'

'Long story, I'll fill you in you later, we still have some work to do here. You can thank Matt and Simon, they managed to evade his men, and Matt got word to me. I rang Tom, and he, the priest, and the big man, escaped to Scotland. My men and I took care of the ones in Germany, that's how I knew to come here.'

'What about, Matt and Simon?'

'They're good. Carpovilla, activated one of the British Gladio units, six of them turned up looking for Tom and the others. Matt and Simon, and a team of special forces sent by your friends in the CIA,' Sergei, snorted his derision, 'waited at the monastery for Carpovilla's thugs to arrive. The CIA have disposed of the bodies, Matt, Simon, and someone called, Frank, are clearing up, so far, they have a warehouse full of files, weapons and medical supplies. I came here with the rest of my men, I'm sorry, but those we interrogated didn't know where you and Peter had been taken, but they were willing to tell us about this place, and that fool's plans for Teri, Anna, and the girls… I came straight here.'

'I'm glad you did. I'm so grateful they're safe.'

'We made these idiots think that Anna and Teri were somewhere other than with Aitor, instead they found us. Mind you, if they had gone there, I'm not sure the outcome would have been any different, do you know how many armed men he has, did you know that he is a member of ETA?'

'Yes. Aitor is Cupula *Militor for Euskadi Ta Askatasuna*, he's old school, ETA, that's why I sent them here, I knew he could protect them.'

'These guns, the money, it's all going to Aitor. You don't mind, do you?'

Mac didn't answer, a flatbed truck had pulled up, driven by a Basque he recognised, one of Aitor's inner circle. Mac nodded at him and was acknowledged by a smile. On the back of the truck was a large rectangular metal water tank.

Sergei threw Mac the keys to Anna's pickup, 'Go. I'll catch up with you when we've finished here. Aitor said to tell you they are at the Cherry House, he said you would know where that is.'

'I do… have you got a problem with the CIA contacting us?'

'Do they know about our involvement?'

'Of course not, and they will not learn of it from me.'

Sergei paused, then said, 'I'm not surprised, the Gladio units are within their purview, and it must have hurt to find they have been financing… so no, no problem.'

'Good, I'll see you later.'

'Or you could wait for a few more minutes, and watch, Raphael, create his masterpiece.'

Sergei indicated the Russian who was supervising the lifting of the water tank from the truck. Upon hearing his name, he turned and bowed to Mac.

'Masterpiece?'

'Raphael's, great-grandmother was a young bride when the Germans invaded Russia, she and her infant son, Raphael's grandfather, were sent to hide in the woods when an SS unit came to the village. From her hiding place she watched for five hours, while the SS tortured, mutilated, then killed her husband and brothers, all the men and boys in the village were slaughtered. Before turning their attention to the village women and girls. His great-grandmother watched them rape and mutilate all of them, but they did not kill them, they wanted them to be a warning to others who might defy the mighty SS. When his grandfather reached manhood, his mother made him swear a blood-oath, to kill any Nazi's he encountered, to avenge the dead. His father swore the same oath, when Raphael became a man, his father made him, and his brothers take the same oath. Today he is happy. Today he fulfils that obligation. Today he is killing Nazi's, the souls of his family will be at peace. He has been working on this all night.'

Mac said, 'I'll stay.'

He watched as the water tank was unloaded. The bodies of Carpovilla's men were being stripped, weapons, cash, watches and jewellery were placed in a large box in the rear of the van. The bodies of the men, and the ashes, from their burn clothing and identity papers, were thrown into a pit the other side of the quarry. Four men began fixing explosives to the rock face above the pit. Two more were preparing to blow a dam above the rock face the far side of the quarry, to flood the quarry when everyone had left.

The water tank was upended, Carpovilla was led naked and struggling over to it. Raphael stepped forward and punched him hard, low down, on the left side of his ribs. Carpovilla collapsed, the wind knocked out of him. The two men who had brought him over, hauled him to his feet.

Raphael tied ropes to Carpovilla's ankles and wrists, he was then pushed into the tank, turned round to face back out, and the ropes on his writs were fastened to rings welded to each corner of the top of the inside of the tank. These were pulled tight, so that his feet left the ground, leaving him suspended, the ropes on his ankles were tied to rings welded to the bottom corners.

The effect was to leave Carpovilla securely suspended, facing out of the tank, spread-eagled in mid-air, yet well within the confines of the tank.

Mac flicked through Carpovilla's clothes, he took a set of keys, an electronic key fob, a small leather diary, and seven computer files, he picked up the case containing Carpovilla's laptop, and re-joined Sergei.

Carpovilla stared at them both, hatred blazed in his eyes, his face and demeanour defiant.

Sergei said, 'I guess we will have to wait for the Fourth Reich, Comrade?'

Carpovilla spat at him.

Speaking with cold fury, Mac said, 'Every file, every photograph, every video, all the information you have carefully collected over the years, everything that helped you to build your empire, I am going to take and use to destroy the abomination you created, I am going to tear down every last vestige of your dream. No one will know what you have done, or who you are, it will be as if you never existed. Everyone in your septic organisation will receive an envelope. Posted from... somewhere in Europe. It will contain a copy of the evidence of whatever sordid foulness they have engaged in, and a letter informing them of your untimely demise, requiring them to disappear immediately, or have their dirty little secrets exposed. The Fourth Reich, the Project, the Progressive Way, the New Europe, whatever the fuck you call it, ends right here and right now. Your filth, the evil you unleashed, all that ends here and now.'

Sergei looked at Mac, and said, 'The world is sinking into a cesspit of corruption and obscenity, and he's only one example...'

Mac said, 'I agree, right now I wouldn't blame God if He hit the reset button, but I am praying he won't.'

Raphael said something in Russian to Sergei and smiled at Mac. Sergei said, 'We need to stand back.' They stepped back, and off to one side.

Raphael turned and spoke to the man next to him, who

343

walked off towards the truck, he removed a small canvas bag with long straps, from the cab, and returned, handing it to, Raphael, who produced a Stanley knife from his jacket pocket, and proceeded to inflict small, shallow cuts all over Carpovilla's arms, legs, torso and face, these small nicks began to weep blood.

He stepped back to admire his work, satisfied he put the Stanley knife back in his pocket. He then placed the canvas bag on Carpovilla's chest, while another man held it in position, Raphael tied the straps tightly round the back of Carpovilla's neck, and waist.

Satisfied that it was firmly secured, he reached forward and pulled off a strip of tape, revealing a small hole. Mac shrugged, and looked at Sergei, who said, 'Soldier ants. I wonder how much air there is, it's a big tank, forty minutes, an hour?'

Mac failing to disguise the distaste in his voice said, 'Creative. In the dark, face down on top of the bodies of his men, buried under tons of rocks, ants eating him alive, with about an hour of air. Nice!'

The tank was pushed over, onto the open side, muffling Carpovilla's cries. The men around it worked quickly, chains were attached to the tank, these were fastened to the bucket of a large excavator, the water tank was lifted six foot off the ground, with Carpovilla suspended underneath, but still within the tank. Mac watched as the digger drove off slowly towards the pit.

Sergei said, 'We call Raphael, Little Philosopher, he trained to be an Orthodox priest, but left the seminary before the end of his last semester, joined us several years later, he's a good soldier.'

Raphael had stopped grinning, he hadn't understood what Mac had said, but had accurately interpreted Mac's revulsion. He turned and signalled, the digger stopped, leaving the tank, and its occupant swinging gently. He spoke to Sergei, who translated. 'He wants to know... I want to know... what's wrong, do you disapprove? You want to kill him, is that it?'

Mac said, 'Yes, I do. That bastard is the reason my wife was murdered, he killed my best friend, and tried to kill me and destroy all I hold dear, for that alone he should be ripped to pieces. He also brought Europe to the brink, threatening both our nations, another reason he should die. But this... it's... he deserves to die, but... look it's up to you, do what you want.'

He turned and began to walk away, stopped and walked back to them. 'I understand where Raphael is coming from, but this... you must see, it's profoundly immoral... it reduces us to Carpovilla's level. It makes us no better than him and his aco- lytes. He is in effect, drawing us into committing evil, corrupt- ing us, bending us to his malevolence, just as we win, we lose.'

Sergei said, 'Are we not taught that evil consumes itself? Isn't that what this is, has he not brought this on himself.'

'No... we are responsible for what we do, for our own actions, if we kill him like this, then we are no better than him. Rest assured; this iniquity will be on us. This is about choosing between good and evil; we can still take the right road, surely, we are better than this, aren't we?'

Sergei translated for Raphael and the others, Mac stood looking at Carpovilla, while the two Russians conversed.

'Raphael asks, what do we do? Is it a bullet in the head, or are you suggesting we let him live? He feels unsettled, what he dreamed last night as revenge, as payback for the iniquities visited upon his family, and his ancestral village, now seems...' Sergei, spoke briefly to Raphael, then translating said, 'As bad as the evil wrought by the SS.'

'Sergei, I feel the same. Shooting Carpovilla's men was justi- fied, but this... it's ghastly, grisly even, not that it's anything more than he deserves, but I just think... if all we have been through, all we have risked... if Liz's life, Peter's life... if any of it is going to have any meaning, then... no, not this. We're better than he is, and that's really what this is all about. I think you should take him back to Russia, let Raphael be his jailer, lock him up with Powell and Seidel. I'm guessing that there's much he could tell you about Europe and the way it works...'

Sergei interrupted, translating Mac's words to Raphael, and the other Russians. He said, 'My men and I have discussed this at length, we can't take him back to Russia, how long do you think we could keep him, a month, six, a year maybe? This man has money. He's a trillionaire, with the power that brings, and he has the corrupting influence that comes from knowing such sordid secrets. He has followers and sympathisers, even in Russia we have Nazis. He will be out, free, and all this will have been for nothing. Peter, your wife, they will have died for nothing, and his evil will continue, and eventually, all our lives will be forfeit.'

Raphael spoke to Mac, Sergei translated, 'He agrees with you, this is not a good thing, it's what that bastard deserves, but for us, this is not good.'

Mac said, 'Fuck... of course you're right.' He stood looking about the quarry, conflicting emotions fought for his attention, coalescing in one thought, that of April dying in this place, at the hands of those men. Visions of the abominations that would have been visited upon her and Teri, before the blessed release of death, filled his mind, and rage etched his face.

He looked at Raphael, nodded, and walked towards him. Raphael smiled and held out a gun. Mac took it, walked over to the upturned cistern, he stood looking at the ground, Carpovilla stopped his crying, looked at Mac, sneered and said, 'I win, whatever you do I win. I am...' Mac silenced him with a punch to the ribs, he used the butt of the pistol to render him unconscious, then walked back to Raphael, returned the gun to him, and walked off towards Anna's car, after about five paces he stopped, turned and said to Sergei, 'No... take him back to Russia. Keep him alive and under wraps. I will go through the stuff on these discs and identify all those involved. Like I said, we'll send each one a letter containing proof of their degeneracy, informing them of the need to leave their present employment, that we will be watching them, that they cannot meet with anyone from the organisation, nor participate in public life or politics ever again. Granted, there is a risk that some may try to locate him, but if we, before they're aware of his abduction, empty his bank accounts, with no money and no influence, and fear of what may befall them, most will slink away hoping for a quiet life, fearful of what may happen. There is terrible power in these discs, and in the astronomic sums of money in his bank accounts, and all that now belongs to us. What is more, none of them know who we are, fear of the unknown is a powerful force, it will ensure compliance. I'm quite sure you can deal with the few foolish enough to try and locate him, and I am certain that Raphael will be happy to assist in retrieving any additional information we require. No one will come looking for Carpovilla, nor will they try to find out who has him, they will all duck, run, and hide. As for punishment, keep him in solitary confinement for the rest of his life, his loss of freedom, of power, and the failure to achieve his ambitions, these will be his torment; perhaps in his solitude he may even find the road to redemption. More importantly, we will not have corrupted ourselves.'

Sergei translated what Mac had said, then conferred at length with his men, while Mac paced up and down, ignoring the cries of pain now coming from Carpovilla. Sergei said, 'We are agreed, Raphael says he will kill him before he allows him to be rescued. I agree with you it is unlikely that anyone in his organisation would attempt a rescue, even if they knew where to look, so we will keep him safe, he will grow old, die alone and unremembered. For now, there are a number of questions we have for him, I think we can keep Carpovilla entertained, so that Raphael can feel he has honoured his vow, if not in deed, at least in spirit. One thing though, there is a risk that we may be tempted, for we now have what he had, the power that comes with money, and information.'

Mac paused, he felt a wave of guilty relief that Carpovilla was not to be savagely executed, this altered the trajectory of all the events that had led to this point in time, and he could at last see the path they must take. He acknowledged their agreement with a nod, then said, 'True, but that power will be divided, I will have the information, and you will have the money, and as you know power is only dangerous if those who wield it do so for personal gain. I'm willing to bet that you and your men will do nothing but good with the money, and you know that I will never use the power that comes from knowing what is on these discs. I have faith in you, all of you. You're good men.'

Sergei finished translating Mac's words, then after some of his men spoke, he said, 'And we trust you, Mac. We have all agreed.'

Mac walked over to Carpovilla, who was regaining consciousness and said, 'I know who you serve, I know that you do not fear death, because you believe that after death you will receive a great reward. In that you are right, you will receive your just reward, but it will not be what you have been promised, nor what you hoped for, you have failed, and your master does not forgive. Death will not be your fate today, nor in the immediate future, unless it be by your own hand, and since you know the terrible fate that awaits you, for now you will be determined to live.'

Mac paused, smiled, then said, 'How are you at riddles? This one is called, appropriately, heaven and hell… you have a choice between two identical doors, with an identical guard at each. One door leads to heaven, and one door leads to hell. You can ask one guard one question, and then make your choice on which door to pass through. One of the guards always tells the truth, and one of them always lies. So, what question do you ask?'

Carpovilla looked absolutely bewildered and said nothing. Mac said, 'Don't worry, you will have plenty of time to think about the answer. You will occupy a small windowless cell, with just the distant sounds of a world in which you will never again walk, to remind you of your failure. A life devoid of pleasure, money, power, influence, your beloved designer clothes, and fine dining; your food will be plain, but healthy, we want you to live for a long time, but it will be the same dish served with every meal, you will shit and piss in a bucket that you empty yourself once a day; whilst we will grant you access to books, there will be no music, no radio, no television, and no talking, save when your interrogators visit. Starved of conversation and human contact, you will tell them all they need to know, just to keep them with you, just to speak to another human being. Your future is going to be a nightmare, but death… no, that's too good for you. Now and again, I will visit… Peter's death is a debt you will pay, a piece at a time. In two years, I will ask you for your answer to the riddle, if you fail to answer correctly, I will punish you. Then I will give you another riddle, and so on… I'll send a written copy, it's probably a bit too much to remember right now.'

Mac re-joined Raphael, Sergei had been translating Mac's words, now he translated Raphael's, 'Hardcore, Mac. I agree, this is a better outcome, we can turn that which is bad into good. And that bastard will have the chance to consider what he has done, to know the evil he has brought into the world and what he has become. You are right, maybe he will understand and want to seek absolution, if he does, then we can forgive him, and perhaps ourselves, and in that, for us, there is mercy, hope, and maybe a chance of deliverance.'

Raphael moved and stood directly in front of Mac, looked into his eyes, and said, 'I have seen the burden you carry; no one gets out of this life unbroken, many think that if you can do some good along the way, then maybe in the next life you can repair the broken pieces. But that is not how it works, the life of Man is not simply the balance between good accomplished and evil done, it is not the sum of good deeds, with bad deeds subtracted, leaving a total in the ledger. No, we are each responsible for the other, and it is how we exercise that obligation that counts. Today, thanks to you, we have discharged our duty towards others, and avoided falling into the abyss. Some never find themselves in this life, but if you experience enough pain and failure, then somewhere down the road you will discover yourself, and it is only then, seared and improved by that burden, you can begin atonement.'

Mac's eyes filled with tears, Raphael's words humbled him, he walked forward and embraced him saying, 'Dóminus vobíscum.'

Raphael smiled, and said, 'Et cum spíritu tuo.'

Mac bowed towards the other Russians, and said to Sergei, 'I'm going to head off. Will I see you later?'

Sergei smiled and said, 'Yes. We'll finish up here, if I can get this bunch of philosophers back to Earth, I'll come and find you. We have much still to do. Mac... Anna, Katie... I do not envy you that task.'

Mac smiled grimly, turned and walked off towards the

pickup. Carpovilla's screams as they pulled the ants off him, echoed around the quarry. Under his breath, Mac said, 'God forgive me... I'm far from nowhere.'

THE END